"A few pages into *Outriders* and I forg.. ... .
world. Jay nails the mindset and the dynamics of a special operations
unit. Keenly written with authentic characters, *Outriders* was one of
the best sci-fi books I've read in a long time."

Kevin Maurer, author of Hunter Killer *and* No Easy Day

"Outriders is a gripping, elegant, high-tech romp. Posey writes like
he's some kind of gol-durned sci-fi Tom Clancy. Characters come
to full-fledged life with an ease that astonishes, and this plot has a
constant credibility that makes believing it a simple pleasure. Here's
hoping this guy hurries up and writes another one."

Jason VandenBerghe, Creative Director, Ubisoft

"Spoiler alert: the main character dies on page one. And then things
get very interesting. Posey's *Outriders* is thrilling, action-packed
science fiction that grabs and doesn't let go!"

Jason M Hough, New York Times bestselling author of the
Dire Earth Cycle

"Gritty action-packed drama so hi-res and real you'll believe you got
something in your eye."

Matt Forbeck, author of Amortals *and* Dangerous Games

"*Three* feels like the result of tossing *Mad Max, Neuromancer* and
Metal Gear Solid into a blender. If you don't find that combination
appealing, then I do not understand you as a human being."

Anthony Burch, writer for Borderlands 2

"*Three* is a great start into a new series. The post-apocalyptic world
that Jay Posey created in *Three* is brilliantly constructed, it's just
chock-full of the cool stuff, futuristic gadgets (guns and the like),
augmented people and not forgetting the Weir."

The Book Plank

BY THE SAME AUTHOR

JAY POSEY

OUTRIDERS

ANGRY
ROBOT

ANGRY ROBOT
An imprint of Watkins Media Ltd

Lace Market House,
54-56 High Pavement,
Nottingham,
NG1 1HW
UK

angryrobotbooks.com
twitter.com/angryrobotbooks
You've been selected

An Angry Robot paperback original 2016
1

A catalogue record for this book is available from the British Library.

ISBN 978 0 85766 450 1
EBook ISBN 978 0 85766 452 5

Set in Meridien and Fenton by Epub Services.
Printed and bound in the UK by 4edge Limited.

For Max, and for Pop

ONE

Captain Lincoln Suh had three minutes to live.

Two minutes, fifty-seven seconds to be exact. He wasn't supposed to know that, but he did because in the double-paned glass separating him from the observation room, he could just make out the ghostly numbers, reversed in reflection. Numbers, ticking down.

In other situations, he might have prided himself on having noticed the detail. But given what he knew about the people in control at the moment, he doubted that reflection was an accident or a mere oversight. *They* knew the kinds of people they brought into this room... the kinds of people who were used to noticing the little things. People like Lincoln, who had been trained to notice them, were *expected* to notice them. There wasn't much else he could clearly make out in that elevated observation room: shadows, blinking lights. But he could see that timer, counting down the last seconds of his life.

He himself was in a sterile beige room, along with two white-coated technicians. Only one of them, the woman, seemed to be doing anything useful. The other one was a beefy-looking fellow with hands too rough and eyes too sun-squinted to be a true egghead. He held a clipboard and moved from machine to machine, playing as though he were running through a checklist. He wasn't a very good actor. Conveniently, all the machines he was moving between happened to keep him between Lincoln and the single door. Which seemed unnecessary, since they'd strapped Lincoln's ankles, thighs, wrists, chest, and head all down to some sort of cross between a gurney and an inclined operating table. He'd thought it all excessive when they had first hooked him in, but now that his adrenaline was pumping, he wondered if it was enough. He tested the straps, just to check. They creaked a bit under the strain, and though they didn't stretch or give him any extra room, he felt some play in the strap around his right wrist. Maybe enough to get his hand free.

Two minutes, eighteen seconds.

Lincoln couldn't stop his mind from soaking up all the details, from formulating plans even though he knew he wasn't going to escape. They'd strapped him to the table, but he'd noticed when they brought him in that the table wasn't secured to the floor. There was an intravenous tube feeding fluid into his left forearm. If he thrashed enough, he might be able to tip the table. The big guy by the door would have to get involved. Get the right hand free, IV tube around the big guy's neck... How long before the security team crashed in? Thirty seconds maybe. Call it twenty.

No. He wasn't going to escape. Lincoln would have shaken his head at himself if he'd been able to do so; the strap around his forehead prevented him from turning his head at all. He'd spent so many years finding his way out of tough spots, it was impossible to turn it off even when he wanted to. He took a steadying breath and reminded himself that this was what he'd signed up for. More or less.

He glanced over at the lady technician, the *real* tech, and looked out of the corner of his eye to try to get some sense of what was about to happen to him. Well... he knew what the *result* was going to be. It was the process he was worried about.

She had her back to Lincoln while she worked some touchscreen. He couldn't catch enough of a glimpse to make sense of anything, and when she stepped away, the screen blanked out. The technicians had obviously been instructed to remain silent throughout the procedure, and even though she'd probably done this so many times for it to become routine, it seemed like maybe the woman coped with the whole situation by avoiding even eye contact with her patients. She moved amongst the various displays and terminals, checking settings, making adjustments; even when she had to interact with something near him, never once did her eyes stray to Lincoln. Her face was a blank slate; focused, running through her mental checklist. Lincoln knew the state well. He was the same way before every mission.

He glanced back up at the observation room.

One minute, ten.

His breathing had gone shallow again. And he realized his hands were balled into fists so tight it was making his knuckles hurt. There wasn't much else he could control at that point, but he didn't want to die like a man in fear. He had made his choice. He wanted to face it like the man he was; a warrior, resolute and strong. He inhaled, long and steady for five seconds. Held for five seconds. Let it out for another five. Held empty for five. Repeated the process. These were his final breaths. He'd do it under his own control, on his own schedule, not panting it away in a panic.

Thirty-three seconds.

The female tech moved over and stood beside Lincoln, checked the straps, made a final adjustment to the intravenous tube in his arm. As her rubber-gloved hand touched his forearm, her eyes flicked up to his. It was only a split second, but Lincoln saw not the cold, clinical evaluation he expected. Instead a warm sadness reflected there, belied by the otherwise flat expression on her face. A moment before she withdrew, she rested her fingertips on his shoulder for a bare second, a show of support and comfort, undoubtedly against regulations. A kind gesture of reassurance, reminding him that he wasn't alone in those final moments.

She pulled away and nodded to the white-coated grunt by the door.

Nine seconds.

It was true, Lincoln discovered, what they said about your whole life flashing before your eyes. But it wasn't the way he had always imagined. The flashes weren't sequential, they didn't come packaged in a nice, neat recap of all the important moments and happy highlights of a life well lived. It was more like waking up in the middle of the night in a cold-sweat panic, all the scattered thoughts hitting you from every angle at once and ricocheting off one another before there was any chance to grab hold of one of them. A firehose flood of acute images and raw emotion and dreams unfulfilled.

A click, a beep, a sudden whirring sound from somewhere behind Lincoln's head. He inhaled sharply as he fell through the bottom of the world.

Darkness descended, accompanied by a faint rushing noise, like a distant waterfall. Then, silence.

And so it was on a sunny spring Wednesday morning that Lincoln Suh, Captain, United States Army, breathed his last and died.

"Candidate One Seven Echo," a voice called in the darkness. An angel, come to guide his spirit to its final place of rest. Her voice was warm and stirred his heart. "Candidate One Seven Echo," she said again. Candidate One Seven Echo. It wasn't his name, but they'd called him that so often over the past fourteen weeks that he responded to it instinctively as if it was the name his own mother had given him. It took conscious effort to command his eyelids to open. The lights were low, and it took a moment for his eyes to remember how to focus. When they did, Captain Lincoln Suh realized he recognized the face staring down at him. Not an angel: the lady technician.

"You're done, candidate," she said.

"I died," Lincoln said. The tech nodded. "And now I'm back." The tech nodded again. Lincoln shrugged. "I don't see what all the fuss is about." She let slip a subdued smile and the way it brightened up the room, Lincoln thought she might be an angel after all. Half, maybe.

"Any numbness in your hands or feet?" she asked. "Metallic taste in your mouth? Ringing in your ears?"

Lincoln took a quick physical inventory, and then shook his head. "No ma'am, everything feels right as rain. Did you do something to me while I was out? Besides kill me, I mean."

"Any of those symptoms can indicate incomplete resynchronization with your nervous system. If you notice any of those, particularly with sudden onset, you'll need to report it immediately."

"What about out-of-body experiences?" Lincoln asked. The technician made a face but otherwise ignored the comment. She started towards the door while she finished the last of her obviously routine speech.

"We'll keep you under observation for half an hour or so and if your vitals remain steady, someone from cadre will come to escort you back to your facility. If you experience any of the symptoms I mentioned, have any unusual sensations that concern you, or any difficulty recalling previously strong memories, press the button on your right."

Lincoln glanced to his right and saw a beige rectangular box with a chunky red button on it. The whole thing seemed about fifty years older than everything else in the room with him. And it was only then that he realized he was in a different room than the one he'd died in. That struck him as the kind of thing he should have noticed pretty much the instant he'd come to.

"Any questions?" the tech asked.

"Sure," Lincoln said. "What do I do while I wait?"

She opened the door part way. "I recommend you rest, candidate."

"Uh oh," he said. "Ma'am?... I might have to press this button after all."

The tech stood at the door, eyebrows raised.

"Problem?"

"I press it if I have any memory issues?"

"Yes?"

"Well, ma'am, I can't remember the last time I got thirty whole minutes to myself to rest."

"You've been dead for an hour, sir," she answered. "So technically they gave you *ninety*." She flashed her quick smile then slipped out and pulled the door closed behind her.

Lincoln chuckled and laid his head back. Dead for an hour. And thirty minutes to recover. Based on everything else he'd been through for the Selection course so far, that seemed about right. He worked his jaw, flexed his fingers, wiggled his toes. He was still dressed in his T-shirt and pants. Even had his boots on. He didn't *feel* any different. Certainly not like his entire consciousness had been taken out and stored on a system for sixty minutes while his body went cold, even though that's exactly what had just happened.

The Process.

That's what his instructors had called it. Cadre Sahil had said it was *almost* the final test in Selection, and was the worst because it was the only one you couldn't prepare for. You either had it or you didn't. He hadn't specified what that *it* was, exactly, but Lincoln had the feeling that was just part of cadre's game. Cadre Sahil had just casually dropped that little nugget and then changed the subject, knowing full well that the candidates' minds would latch on to it and run wild imagining the worst possibilities.

Getting through Selection was mostly a mental game, and cadre loved to play it. It could seem almost like torture at times, but it was a mercy, really. If cadre could get in your head and make you quit, that spared you a lot of unnecessary pain and suffering in the short term, and saved a lot of other good lives in the long term. As rough as training could be, Lincoln knew from experience that "training cold" was never as cold as "real-world ops cold," and the highest-risk exercises were only about half as risky as the real deal. If training could break you, then the real world would destroy you, and in the small, special units that Lincoln served in, one person coming apart on mission was likely to take a bunch of friends down with him. Better to weed those folks out early, help them find a better fit.

It wasn't a failure, not really. This was the third special operations unit that Lincoln had volunteered for, and he'd been accepted on both of his previous attempts. He knew from experience that he wasn't fundamentally *better* than any of those candidates that had bowed out of Selection along the way, either this time or any of the times before. He wasn't even sure that he *wanted* it more than any of those other men and women. Lincoln just wasn't very good at quitting, and he'd served enough to know that his body was a lot more resilient than it would ever admit. And nobody had been able to kill him yet.

Well. Except the one time. The Process he'd just gone through was a thoroughly controlled affair, but for all intents and purposes he'd volunteered to let his country kill him and then bring him back to life. Death-proofing, somebody had called it. Seemed about right. Once you'd experienced the sensation and come back from it, the theory went, it made it easier to ignore the survival instinct-driven fear and just focus on getting the job done. Funny, they'd told him something similar about drowning when he'd gone through the underwater operations training course and they'd sent him twenty feet down with his arms and legs bound. It's not the water that kills you, it's the panic that robs you of your ability to clearly define the problem and find the solution. Ignore the fact that your lungs are filling up with liquid, and those extra seconds just might be what you need to get back home. Probably not a perfect analogy where literal death was concerned, but after everything he'd just been through it was the best his brain could do.

Lincoln didn't try to understand all the ins and outs of the procedure, but he knew the basics. Brain on backup. Some team of two hundred-pound heads had figured out how to map an entire consciousness, keep it in storage, and then reintegrate it back with the body. Theoretically, if Lincoln's body suffered catastrophic damage, it was possible to offload his... what? Soul, he guessed, until the doctors could get all his pieces put back together. Once he was all Frankensteined up, *zrooop* they put his soul back in, and the army got to count one less KIA. Theoretically.

People had a lot of theories.

Zrooop. That's the noise Lincoln imagined the Process made when his consciousness got stuffed back into its original organic housing. He didn't know why. It just seemed like a *zrooop* kind of procedure to him.

Apparently it was mindnumbingly expensive to run the program, which was one reason that not everyone in uniform rated the treatment. The other reason was that the whole thing was about forty different kinds of Ultra Secret. He'd had to sign about a thousand pages' worth of waivers and releases before he'd been allowed just to try to *qualify* for Selection. After qualification, he'd signed a whole truckload more. By that point, he'd pretty much given up reading them, so he wasn't even sure whether or not his own body was technically his property, or that of the US Government. He couldn't recall all the particulars, but he was pretty sure if he ever mentioned even the *acronym* of the codename of the facility where the Process had been developed, his existence would be formally and utterly erased. And given what he'd seen in his time amongst these people, he had very little doubt that getting erased was way worse than death.

Still. He'd done it. He'd volunteered, managed to stay in the Selection program long enough to reach the critical moment, and then when the time came, he'd given his life for his country. And they'd been kind enough to give it back.

Lincoln closed his eyes and tried not to think about it too much. Nineteen minutes later a man opened the door and walked into the room, and then knocked after he'd already let himself in. Lincoln looked up to find one of his instructors, Cadre Sahil, staring back at him. Early, of course. And of course it had to be Cadre Sahil. Lincoln still hadn't been able to figure out if he'd done something to make the man hate him, or if the instructor just thrived on the suffering of others, but no one had driven him harder or been more vocal about his disappointing performance than Cadre Sahil.

"Hey OneSev," Cadre Sahil said, swallowing the last syllable as he always did. "You ready to roll?"

"Don't know," Lincoln said, sitting up. "The nice doctor said I got thirty minutes."

"That's regular people time. You ain't regular people, are ya?"

"No, cadre."

"That's right."

Lincoln waited a couple of seconds to see if his instructor was going to say anything else. Cadre Sahil's expression didn't change, and he didn't seem likely to continue any further conversation.

"Well all right then," Lincoln said.

Cadre Sahil dipped his head in a half nod. Lincoln swung his legs over the edge of the bed and eased himself to his feet, taking it slow just to be safe. Every muscle was sore and fatigued, but that was normal these days. As far as he could tell, he was as fit as he ever was. He walked over and stood in front of Cadre Sahil. Practically towered over him. Lincoln was just a hair under six feet tall with his boots on, if he stood up as straight as he could; Cadre Sahil was maybe five-foot four. But by Lincoln's estimate, Cadre Sahil was about twice as wide in the chest and arms, and ten times harder than steel.

"Let's roll," Lincoln said. Cadre Sahil stepped to one side and gestured for Lincoln to head out. The corridor was empty, lit only slightly more than the room had been, and just as beige. It was like they'd built the whole place to blend into itself. Easier to be forgotten that way, maybe. Cadre Sahil followed him out and then overtook him to lead the way; he didn't seem to have any problem knowing which corridors to take. He always walked with a forward lean, chin down, long strides, like he was headed to break up a fight. Or maybe to start one. In the past fourteen weeks, Lincoln couldn't remember having ever seen anyone, regardless of age, rank, or size, who hadn't gotten out of the way when Cadre Sahil was coming through. They walked in silence for a couple of minutes, until Lincoln broke it.

"So what's next on the agenda, cadre?" Lincoln asked, as they walked out of the medical wing, or wherever it was they were.

"You know I can't tell you that," the instructor replied.

"Can't hurt to ask."

Cadre Sahil grunted his version of a chuckle. "Thought you woulda figured out by now *that* ain't true."

They continued down another corridor, this one a darker shade of beige. Lincoln might even dare to call it *mocha*.

"Couple folks gonna ask you a couple questions," the instructor added without looking at him. "Then we'll see what we see."

A minute later, Cadre Sahil took a right turn down another plain-looking hall, with six plain-looking doors. Scratch that. Five plain-looking doors. One had what looked like the remnants of a piece of red tape stuck on it. Lincoln smiled to himself at that; it seemed somehow appropriate that the only bit of decoration he'd seen in the military hospital was red tape.

They ended up at the last door at the end of the hall. One of the plain ones.

"This is it," Cadre Sahil said. He stopped and turned to face Lincoln. For a moment, the instructor stood there working his jaw, like he was about to say something. But he just shook his head to himself.

"Well," Lincoln said. "Thanks for the escort, cadre. I appreciate you not making me do any pushups along the way."

"Still got time," Cadre Sahil said, and one corner of his mouth pulled down into his version of a smile. But then he stepped back from the door and gestured for Lincoln to pass through.

"You're not coming in?" Lincoln asked. Cadre Sahil shook his head. And something in the man's usually unreadable eyes betrayed the gravity of the moment. This really was *it*. The final stage of Selection. Lincoln's heart rate kicked up a few beats per minute. "Well," he said. "All right." Cadre Sahil gave a quick nod; part good luck, part goodbye.

Lincoln returned the gesture, took a deep breath, and reached to open the door.

"Hey," Cadre Sahil said. Lincoln glanced back at him. "You done good, OneSev. Whatever happens from here out, it don't mean nothin' about the kinda man you are. That's settled business. Ain't many alive could do what you done. Don't let 'em take that from you." He paused, and then a moment later, added, with some significance, "I'd serve under you in a heartbeat."

Lincoln didn't know what else to do in the face of such a rare and shocking show of emotion from the man, so he just nodded and offered his hand for a shake. Cadre Sahil flicked his eyes down at Lincoln's outstretched hand, and then cracked a thin smile.

"Next time I see you, I'm gonna have to salute," he said.

"We'll both know it's just for show, cadre," Lincoln said.

"Nah," Cadre Sahil said, taking crushing hold of Lincoln's offered hand. "You're one of the good ones, no doubt."

"Be well," Lincoln said.

"Yeah."

The two men lingered one final moment, and in that wordless moment, some steel passed from instructor to student, a sensation Lincoln had experienced only once before when he'd earned his first special operations tab. Then Lincoln turned and walked through the door to face down whatever fresh, final hell awaited.

TWO

The man codenamed Vector curled the pinkie of his left hand into his upper palm, applied gentle pressure to the implanted dermal pad hidden there to open a channel to his handler.

"Cisko, this is Vector," he whispered, his words barely more than an exhale. Even after all these years and more than a few attempted explanations, he still didn't know exactly how it worked; however, long experience had taught him that the nearly microscopic network tattooed on his larynx would transmit the words with crystal clarity, no matter how quietly he spoke.

He held still, keeping the two men across the courtyard in his peripheral, waited six seconds for the response. The bare hint of a click sounded in his ear, subtle confirmation that encryption had been established now on both ends of the conversation.

"Cisko copies, Vector," a woman answered. Not *the* woman, but someone close to her. "I have you secure."

The signal in his ear chirped once. "Vector confirms secure."

"Go ahead."

"Target is on site."

"You have positive visual?"

"That's affirmative. Looking at him right now."

"Opportunity?" she asked.

Vector restrained the reflexive impulse to flick his eyes at the two men he'd identified as security officers.

"Security's light. Cover's good. Best chance we've had yet. I'd like to take it."

"Your team is in place?"

"Of course."

"Stand by."

"Vector, standing by," he said, and then relaxed his hand, releasing the pad. The two men across the courtyard moved to a table under the awning and sat down in low wicker chairs. One of them was heavyset, sweaty, sloppily dressed in cheap knock-off clothes patterned after the most expensive brands. Fairly typical low-rent thug pretending to be a respectable, important thug. The other man was almost the exact opposite: small-framed, quiet in his movements, easy to overlook. He was the dangerous one. And also Vector's true target. For the moment, the Target was intent on whatever he was viewing on his holoscreen, temporarily oblivious to his surroundings. Surprisingly out of character, given what Vector knew about the man, but it was better for Vector that way. Better for the job, anyway.

Vector. He shook his head at the codename, sipped his room-temperature, weak coffee. Tomorrow he would be someone else. Warble, maybe, or something even more ridiculous. He was pretty sure the Woman picked names for him that she knew he would hate having to say over comms. Her way of reminding him who he worked for, or more likely of gently mocking who he *used* to work for. For all her intensity, she did have a playful side that she wasn't afraid to let out once in a while. She had many names of her own, though he didn't know if any of them were real. He and his team had just taken to calling her "the Woman" so they all knew who they were talking about.

He leaned back in his chair, scratched his belly, scoped out the immediate area for the thousandth time. Half a dry pastry

sat on the chipped plate in front of him next to his cup of
terrible coffee. Twenty-two days he'd been here in Elliston
now. Martian days, anyway. Vector couldn't remember the
exact conversion to Earth time offhand. Not quite the same,
but close enough that he didn't mind the difference too much.
Not after three weeks. Three weeks of integrating himself
into the community; getting the lay of the land, establishing
a routine, becoming part of the background. Three weeks of
terrible coffee and dry pastries on chipped plates.

That wasn't precisely true. He didn't come here every day.
But he'd started visiting the restaurant attached to the hotel
every couple of days almost as soon as he arrived. Laying the
groundwork. Not enough to become a regular, never at quite
the same time each visit. But consistent enough to blend into
the scenery. The packet had indicated this was one of the
Target's favored spots for meeting his various contacts. Vector
just hoped he'd get the green light before anyone else showed
up. This wasn't the kind of thing he liked to do outnumbered.
Not any more outnumbered than he already was, anyway.

The seconds ticked by as he waited for a response from
the Woman. He surveyed the surroundings once more, trying
not to let the delay get to him. If he didn't look up, it didn't
take much effort to imagine himself in any number of cities
back home on Earth. Or, back where he used to call home,
at any rate. The architecture was familiar, if not exactly
culturally distinct. Some mixture of Cuban and Mexican,
maybe, translated across roughly two hundred and twenty-
five million kilometers of open space. The hotel was squat;
the outdoor seating for its restaurant was a square, walled
courtyard with two exits to the busy streets that hemmed it
in. *Outdoor.* The word didn't mean quite the same thing here.
It was a comfortable spot, sure, as long as you didn't mind
living in a bubble.

Down here, looking up, the vast membrane that kept
the artificial atmosphere and temperature stable and the

dust storms out was nearly transparent. Nearly. There was a silvery sheen to the sky that was obvious to Vector's Terran eyes, like a thin skin of oil on the surface of a pond. From a couple of thousand meters up, it looked like a planetary blister. From orbit, the collection of settlements clustered together made it appear that Mars had developed some horrendously disfiguring skin disease. But the Martians seemed pretty pleased with it. All the estimates back home said it'd be another fifty years at least until they could take their chances with a completely unshielded settlement. Then again, back home they'd been underestimating the rate of Martian progress since Day One.

Vector could still remember sitting at the dinner table as a kid, listening to his parents talk about *those colonists* and wondering why they always sounded a little angry when they said it. It'd taken barely two generations to go from *our brave brothers and sisters* to *those colonists*. And these days, it was getting harder and harder to think of them as colonists at all. Mostly they were just Martians.

The general consensus had been that the great Martian Experiment would draw the nations of Earth together. And like most predictions by the people who should know best, that consensus had been dead wrong. While Earth was busy squabbling with itself, the colonies on Mars just kept plugging along, expanding, crystallizing. Making the world their home. And anyone who had studied history even casually shouldn't have been surprised at the course things took. The colonists' ties to Earth weakened, their Martian identity strengthened, and before anyone knew it, Earth had a whole new group of people to squabble with.

Not that the Martians had the peace and harmony thing all figured out either, though; a fact Vector was here to exploit. As far as he could tell, no matter how far out into space humanity got, it would never be far enough to escape its own nature.

"Vector, Cisko," the voice finally spoke in his ear, as loud as if she'd been standing beside him instead of thirty thousand kilometers above. "You're a go."

"Copy that, Vector is go." He set his coffee on the table and leaned back in his chair, stretching. Casually, slowly, he swept his eyes around the courtyard, careful not to let them rest on the Target's security detail. They were locals, but he could tell by the way they held themselves, and from their level of focus, that they weren't amateurs. The two of them were standing at opposite corners of the courtyard, each stationed by an entry point. Not bad for controlling the courtyard, but, in Vector's opinion, that put them too far from the man they were supposed to be protecting. If he'd been running the detail, he would have had a third guard tasked solely with close protection. They probably had overwatch positioned somewhere in the surrounding buildings, keeping an eye on the general flow of the area, but that wasn't going to help them. Vector and his team had already successfully infiltrated the target zone. Of course, it was easy for Vector to spot all the flaws in the protection plan, seeing it as he was through the eyes of the attacker. It was always easier for the party who got to choose the time, place, and method.

The Target was still busy reviewing his viz, looking over whatever information the cheap Thug had shared with him. Or maybe digesting the morning's intelligence brief that his analysts had compiled for him while he slept. Vector couldn't help but wonder how shocked those same analysts would be a few minutes from now.

He cracked a knuckle and in the same motion switched channels on his comms. He picked his coffee back up and mimed drinking it while he spoke again.

"Kev, we're a go. You in place?"

"Roger that," Kev answered. "Say when."

"Hey, Kid," Vector said. "You got me?"

"Yeah, I gotcha," his long-time partner replied.

"What's your angle?"

"Clear line to the big guy by the door," she answered. "Heat signature's good on the other fella, but I'd have to shoot through to get him."

"Okay. Take the big guy. I'll get the other."

"You sure?"

"Yep."

"Roger. On you."

Vector replaced the coffee on the table in front of him, and rested his hands on his lap. This was the tricky part. As soon as he moved, he'd draw attention. Every space had its rhythm. It was his job to match it, to blend with it. Too fast, and security would perk up. Too slow, and they'd keep watching him until he'd left the zone. He allowed himself a few settling breaths.

"Doc," Kid said a few moments later, "you got a spotter."

"Yeah?" Vector answered.

"Just above you. Fourth floor, about the middle of the building."

"Shooter?" Even with a couple of decades of practice, Vector had to restrain himself from glancing that direction.

"Can't tell for sure. Better assume so."

"Can you take him and the big guy?"

"Depends on the order. Whatcha think?"

"I think I'd like you to take whichever one's most likely to kill me first."

A pause, while Kid thought it over. One of the reasons Vector liked her. She never hurried with answers.

"Spotter then," Kid said finally.

"Be sure."

"I am."

"All right. Let's do it," Vector said. He scratched his belly in an absentminded sort of way, let his fingertips brush the grip of the pistol he had tucked close against his ribs. It wasn't a complicated plan. Walk over, kill the bad guys, leave. But for all his years of experience, no matter how simple, Vector had never once seen things go exactly according to plan.

Go time. He laid his napkin on the table, brushed the crumbs from his lap. Kept his eyes away from his Target and the security team. Slow breath. Vector stood.

And as he was rising to his feet, he felt a hitch in his gut. Some warning instinct firing off that he'd learned long ago to trust. But he was in motion now, he couldn't stop or slow or change direction. He'd have to figure it out on the fly. He paused and drained the last of his terrible coffee, buying himself a few moments to scan the environment. In that cursory sweep, he saw the Thug was standing now, a few paces closer to the thin security officer. Bad timing; Vector and the man had just happened to start moving at nearly the same moment. Any security worth half its rate would take that as a potential concern. And if either of the two men were preparing to leave, that was problematic. Security was always a little tighter, a little more aware in transitions. He would have preferred to act while the guards were settled, when they'd gotten comfortable in the space and thus, hopefully, complacent.

There was still time to scrub the op. He could just walk out. Wait until another day. But no. The Woman's timetable could absorb a few delays. She was too smart, too experienced to think anything would work out exactly according to her predictions. But she did have a timetable nonetheless. He needed to wrap this job, and get on to the next.

Vector changed the plan on the move.

"Kid, scratch that, scratch that. Take the shoot-through first."

"You sure?"

"Roger, shoot-through, then spotter," he said as he placed his empty cup on the table and started towards the exit guarded by the big guy. "On my action."

"Shoot-through, then spotter, copy. On you."

Vector kept his pace steady, casual. Just another morning. All part of the routine.

Twelve feet from the big security guy by the door, Vector made eye contact with the man, gave him a nod then looked away. A brief acknowledgment; I see you, you see me, nothing to be concerned about.

Six feet away, Vector glanced back over his shoulder as if he'd maybe forgotten something at his table, angled his body away from the security officer.

"Kev," he whispered, "Come on around."

"Copy, on the way."

Three feet. When Vector turned back, the gun was in his hand, the grip pressed tight against his ribs as an index. Held that way, he didn't have to look at the gun to know where it was aimed. At least not at this range. He angled the pistol low. The big security guard's face changed, hands flared up in reaction. Too late. The suppressed pistol coughed twice, sending rounds through the man's pelvic girdle, folding him into Vector.

"Help!" Vector cried, catching hold of the guard. The man struggled weakly, and Vector fired a third round point-blank into his solar plexus as he lowered him to the ground. "Help! This man needs help!"

Vector crouched over the man, his pistol still held close to his body, swiveled on his heel and did his best to look helpless. The crowd sat frozen, unsure of what had happened, or what was happening. One man was caught halfway between sitting and standing as if he knew he should do something, without having any idea what that would be.

"Gun! He's got a gun!" another man shouted. Everyone looked, Vector included, and he saw the man pointing frantically at the thin security guard who was now moving towards the Thug. Vector fought back the urge to bring his own weapon up. Kid would handle it. After three steps, a puff of concrete burped off the exterior wall, and the security guard fell headlong into a table.

That's when the screaming started. The panic. The remaining patrons scrambled and clambered over one another in every direction, some towards the exits, others just *away*. To them, everything was happening too fast for comprehension, some lightning strike of utterly random and unpredictable violence, taking the lives of anyone who happened to be in its path. Only someone familiar with Vector's line of work would have noticed the precision, the fluidity, the careful unfolding of each step in its proper time and place. Vector left the big security guard and moved through the crowd towards the Target.

In the churning chaos, no one was looking four stories up, where Vector was certain the spotter was having just as bad a day as his two ground-level security companions. The Thug was by a table thirty feet away, in a partial crouch, with his hands splayed out to either side like he was trying to keep his balance. He was paralyzed by indecision, with his head turned such that he presented a perfect side profile to Vector. Only one person in the zone was paying any attention to Vector at all. *That* person was staring right at him.

The Target.

He too was standing now, but he was absolutely still, untouched by the confusion swirling around him. His body was tense and coiled, out of sync with the blank expression Vector saw on the man's face. Recognition of what was happening, refusal to accept it. Powerlessness to stop it. He raised a hand, part shield, part supplication for mercy. Neither had any effect.

Vector fired two rounds in quick succession, *pat pat,* into the center of mass, and the small man grunted and winced with the impacts. To Vector's surprise, the man didn't cry out; he just seemed to deflate as he sank to the ground, with a strange and sad look in his eyes.

The Thug looked at Vector with horror, fell backwards in

his haste to scramble away. He rolled to his side and writhed
in an awkward attempt to simultaneously regain his feet and
crawl away, all the while keeping his terrified eyes locked on
Vector's. Vector put a single round through the man's head,
and then another three rounds, haphazard, into his body as
he flopped back and lay still. Couldn't make it look *too* good.

Having handled the Thug, Vector calmly closed the
remaining distance to the Target with an even pace. On his
way out he passed by the man, who was now lying on his
side breathing the ragged last breaths of a man as good as
dead. Vector didn't slow as he fired a final round through
the Target's neck and continued with the same stride to the
eastern exit of the courtyard. That shot hadn't been strictly
necessary; the first two would have done the job. But it made
the hit messier, and that was a carefully calculated component
of the op.

He fired the remaining rounds from the stubby pistol into
the walls and floor, and then dropped the empty weapon just
before he exited the courtyard, leaving it behind. The Woman
had insisted on that particular point too. He hadn't asked
why. Vector had learned well enough that she always had
her reasons, and they were almost always good ones. And
anyway, there was nothing on it that could be traced back to
him, or to his team, or to anyone off-planet for that matter.

As he stepped out onto the street, the first shockwaves were
just spilling out into the general populace. A few patrons had
fled the courtyard in that direction, screaming. Several other
citizens were standing around on the sidewalks, trying to get
a read on what exactly was happening. No one took notice
of the white vehicle that pulled to a stop and opened its door
just as Vector emerged. Nor should they. It was identical to
the thousand other autopiloted vehicles of various colors that
moved around the streets at every hour of the day or night.
He slid into the seat and closed the door. Kev was sitting in
a forward-facing seat, a tablet in his lap and a mess of cables

dangling out of the forward dash.

Before the door was fully sealed, the vehicle was already pulling smoothly away from the curb, under Kev's illegally manual control. He kept it reined in, enough to look natural for the usual AI-managed behavior. But it was always reassuring to know he could punch it if he had to. Kev fiddled with the pad, kicked off an algorithm that would gradually transition the vehicle's white exterior to grey and from grey to some other equally forgettable color. The process was slow enough that casual observers wouldn't notice and the most perceptive ones might only think how interesting it was how different the light could be from street to Martian street.

It was a ten-minute drive to the drop off and then a twenty-minute walk to the shipyard where Vector's not-strictly-legal off-world transport was waiting for him. He had a couple of days of hard work ahead of him, crewing the hauler to pay his fare, which wasn't particularly appealing after three weeks of surveillance and planning. But it was all part of the plan. And it kept some truth in his cover; he'd claimed some local legal troubles to the ship's first mate, all a misunderstanding, best if he disappeared for a while. That story and three hundred *brin* had been enough to earn a spot on *Cortesia 3* as a loader, which meant a lot of manual work, not much sleep, and even less time for chit chat.

"We good?" Kev asked after a couple of minutes of careful driving.

"We're good," Vector answered. "You get the place buttoned up?"

"Clean as it can be without burning it to the ground."

Vector nodded and then leaned his head back and closed his eyes. The adrenaline was burning off now, and the weight of the whole planet settled on him. They rode in silence for a few more minutes, during which time Vector's mind replayed the entire takedown in pristine detail. Just over thirty seconds from tip to tail. And every second of it earned a review as he analyzed what he'd done and what he should have done. Good call to take the big guard first. But he could have acted sooner, gone with the original plan and been closer to the exit when he'd completed the task, rather than having to walk through the entire crowd to get there. More exposure than necessary. He was lucky there hadn't been any heroes in the crowd. Though there almost never were. Almost.

"You all right, Doc?" Kev asked, interrupting Vector's mental playback.

"Yeah," he said glancing at his friend and then rubbing his eyes with the palms of his hands. "Just beat."

"I hear ya. How long's your trip back?"

"Three days to link up, Lord willing and the creek don't rise."

Kev nodded. "Should be showing up about the same time as you then. She going to give us a couple of days off?"

"I wouldn't bet a beer on it."

"Yeah."

Kev wheeled the vehicle smoothly up to the drop off. "This is you," he said.

"Yep. Thanks Kev."

"Always, brother."

"Safe travels."

"See you soon."

The two men shook hands and then Vector hopped out. He didn't look back as Kev disappeared back into the flowing traffic. Kev had handled the hotel and surrounding area's surveillance feeds, which meant any viz of the crime would have to be collected from any eyewitnesses who had the presence of mind to record the event. Worst case scenario figured about fifty minutes for Elliston Police to get all the details sorted out and start distributing descriptions. Vector always cut the worst case estimates in half, which meant he needed to make a twenty-minute walk in about fifteen, without looking like he was trying to run away from something.

He set off toward the shipyard. Seventeen minutes later, as he was lining up to board the *Cortesia 3*, he checked in one last time.

"All right, Kid, I'm clear," Vector said.

"Copy that, Doc," Kid answered. "EPD showed up about twenty minutes ago. I'll sit tight for a couple of hours, see how it shakes out."

"You good on exfil?"

"Yeah, flight's out in two days."

"Keep your head down, Kiddo."

"Roger that. Catch you top-side."

"See you there."

Vector waved to *Cortesia 3*'s first mate and got a stony-faced single nod in response. Three days of hard labor. Three days of penance. And after that, a new name.

Vector boarded the ship, one job completed and another no doubt eagerly awaiting his return.

THREE

The room Lincoln entered had a single chair with its back to the door, placed in front of a long table with seats for five. On either side of the table stood directional lights on tall stands. Those lights were off, but they were angled towards the lone chair. The intent there was pretty obvious; anybody sitting in that chair with those lights in his face wouldn't be able to see anything else beyond. There was a second door in the back wall. No windows, nothing on the walls. A small glossy black sphere in the ceiling caught Lincoln's eye. Camera. Someone was watching him. Probably several someones. He hesitated by the door, uncertain of what he was expected to do. He had a pretty good guess which chair was for him, but he wasn't all that anxious to take it just yet.

"Candidate One Seven Echo," a voice said over a crackly speaker. "Please be seated."

Lincoln walked confidently across the room and sat down at one of the chairs behind the table.

"In the other chair, candidate," the voice said, clearly not amused. Lincoln smiled to himself. Everything about Selection was a mental game. Funny how they didn't seem to like it when he played too. For a moment he thought about sliding over to the chair next to him, still behind the table, but he dismissed the idea. He'd had his little moment of fun.

When he sat down in the lone chair, just as he'd anticipated, the overhead lights went off and the bright directional lights flared, bathing him in strong white light. The lights were angled so they weren't beaming directly into his eyes, but there was no way he could see anything else going on behind them. And apparently there wasn't anything else he was expected to do, other than sit. So he sat there. Waiting.

And waiting.

It was almost impossible to keep track of time sitting in that bubble of light surrounded by a sea of darkness. Another part of the game, undoubtedly. Anything they could do to rattle him, or put him on edge. Anything that might make his cracks easier to see. Lincoln folded his hands in his lap and closed his eyes, focused on his breathing. Steady in, steady out. Everything else was beyond his control anyway, so he just let it do whatever it was going to do.

Some time later he heard the rattle of a door open from somewhere behind the lights. Quick footsteps clacked across the faux-tile floor. Four or five people by the sound of it. Five made sense with the number of chairs behind the table, but Lincoln wouldn't put it past these people to manipulate even that little detail. Putting out more chairs than they actually needed, or maybe fewer. That was one of the things he'd picked up early on in Selection; they made it such a point to mess with your expectations and assumptions that eventually you came to expect that everything was a trick. Being comfortable with the uncertainty was probably one of the reasons that Lincoln had made it this far.

Chairs scraped, uniforms rustled. His interrogators made themselves comfortable. Lincoln didn't open his eyes. Not yet.

"Candidate One Seven Echo," a voice said. Stern, clipped, feminine with a hard edge. The same one that had issued instructions over the speaker before. Lincoln didn't respond immediately. Just kept his eyes closed, and finished two more full cycles of breathing. They'd kept him waiting, and he'd been patient. They could wait a little longer.

"Candidate One Seven Echo," the voice said again, louder with the fuller weight of authority behind it.

"I'm listening, ma'am," Lincoln said. But he still didn't open his eyes. He *was* listening, intently in fact, picking out whatever little details he could with his ears, knowing his eyes wouldn't show him anything new. Two people were whispering at the right end of the table. The woman who'd spoken was at the other end, in either the first or second seat. Someone in the center of the table was hurriedly sketching designs on the table with a fingertip; most likely reviewing Lincoln's file on a holoscreen only the user could see.

"Very well," the woman said. "We're going to ask you a number of questions, candidate. It is important that you answer them to the fullest possible extent, with the utmost honesty. Many of these answers we already know. Any deception on your part will be grounds for immediate release from Selection. Do you understand?"

"On *my* part," Lincoln said.

"Pardon me?" she said.

"Any deception on *my* part, you said," he answered. "Kind of leaves the door open for you there, doesn't it?"

There was a pause, and though he couldn't hear it, Lincoln liked to imagine at least one of the people on the other side of the table cracking a smile. Someone on the left cleared his throat. So that made five of them after all. Or, at least five.

"Do you understand?" the woman repeated.

"Very well, yes, ma'am."

"Good, candidate," the woman said. "We will begin."

Lincoln opened his eyes.

"Candidate One Seven Echo," said a man on the right side of the table. "What's the most impressive thing on your service record?"

Lincoln took a breath before he answered.

"Depends on who's looking at it, sir."

"In your opinion."

"In my opinion, the most impressive thing about my service record is the many fine men and women I've been allowed to serve alongside, sir."

"That's very diplomatic of you, candidate, but you're not getting graded on humility here."

"Utmost honesty, sir. Your rules, not mine."

A second voice broke in; a man on the far left. That put the woman in the second chair from the left, then.

"Atmospheric and suborbital jump rated; fair number of successful zero-G operations; operational combat profiling and combat tracking; Ranger and Pathfinder quals; high marks for intelligence; and communications certs. Decent linguistics. A few medals to show off. That sound like you?"

"That sounds like just about anybody in my line of work, sir."

"I miss anything important?"

"No mention of my wit and charm?" Lincoln said.

"There's nothing listed in the record," the man replied.

"Ah. Strange," Lincoln said.

"An officer with this kind of record and this many years in the service, seems like you'd rank a little higher."

"My greatest weakness, undoubtedly, sir."

"How's that?"

"Too much time in the mud, not enough polishing the brass," said Lincoln, with a smile.

The man didn't sound amused. "You feel you've been unfairly overlooked for promotion?"

"I'm not a particularly smart man, sir. I mostly go where I'm pointed. I'm certain if my betters thought I was fit to serve in a higher capacity, they would have elevated me appropriately with all due speed and urgency."

"I should note," the woman broke in, "there *is* a mention in your official record about a tendency towards sarcasm."

"My second greatest weakness, ma'am," Lincoln said. "Undoubtedly."

"Any issues with subordination?" the woman asked.

"None," Lincoln said. He flashed a smile. "At least for my part."

"How many doors are on this hall, candidate?" one of the men asked.

An oddball question. But the image came to mind easily enough.

"Five plain ones," Lincoln said. "And one with a little extra character."

"Mm," the woman responded. And then followed with, "Tell me about Royal Warden."

The two words instantly robbed Lincoln of any sense of control he thought he had in the situation. Apparently they were done with the pleasantries and were now going straight for the throat. He did his best to maintain his steady breathing, but he couldn't escape the sudden rush of heat to his face. Unwelcome memories threatened his calm.

"I'm sure you have all the details already, ma'am," he said.

"I'd like your perspective, candidate." She said it with such coolness, as if she was asking his opinion of the particular shade of beige they'd chosen for those walls.

Lincoln took another settling breath and swallowed. Gathered himself. "Royal Warden was the single greatest personal failure of my life, ma'am."

"In what way?" she pressed.

"Sixteen of the finest souls I've ever known, lost. On my orders, by my direction."

"Please elaborate," she said.

So this was how it was going to be. Lincoln thought he'd prepared himself for just about anything. For some reason he hadn't considered that they might rake him over the coals again for a decade-old operation, especially not in such clinical terms. But the only way through it was forward. He adopted a professional attitude, reporting on past events and trying to ignore the role he played; his shield against the memories.

"While serving in an advisory capacity to the Honduran National Defense Force..." he said, then paused to clear the tightness out of his throat. "I received intelligence of an arms shipment moving towards my area of responsibility. Our analysis determined the shipment was intended to equip elements that were actively working to further destabilize the region. Having operated in the area for several months, I was aware of extensive tunnel networks in use by those elements. The concern was raised that if the shipment was allowed to reach the network, the arms would be impossible to locate until they were being used against our allies. After consulting with local informants and senior enlisted, I dispatched a force comprised of ten Honduran National Defense Force troopers supported by six United American Federation soldiers under my command to intercept and capture the shipment in transit."

Boone, Shepherd, Ryoko, Jimenez, Harrison, Singh. Their faces and voices flashed through his mind. Smiles, inside jokes, names on tombstones.

"You mention local informants and senior enlisted," the woman said. "What course of action did your superior officers advise?"

"I did not receive counsel from higher command until after the operation was underway, ma'am," Lincoln answered.

"Because?"

Lincoln knew he was stepping out onto a tightrope. He spoke his next words with deliberate care. "Because I dispatched the force before my superior officers had time to analyze our report and provide direction."

"You launched an operation on your own," she said.

"I responded to an immediate threat to my area of responsibility," Lincoln said. "Ma'am."

The man on the left piled on. "Your detachment was

supposed to be serving in an *advisory* role during this time, is that correct?"

"That is correct, sir."

"But six of your soldiers accompanied the Honduran-led force outside the unit's designated area?"

Lincoln knew what the man was looking for him to say, but he wasn't going to take the bait.

"Correct, sir," he said. And then added, "On my orders."

His decision. He would own it. Lincoln waited patiently, content to let his hidden interrogators drive the conversation.

"And what was the outcome?" the woman asked.

"The force successfully intercepted the shipment," Lincoln continued, resuming the report. He paused again, letting a ripple of emotion pass through him. "While the team was securing the shipment, an improvised explosive device in the vehicle detonated, instantly killing four troopers and two of my soldiers. When the remaining force moved to render aid, they received fire from a previously undetected aerial support element. All sixteen members of the force were killed in action. Given the loss of life, I consider Royal Warden to be the single greatest personal failure of my life. Ma'am."

"Did you ever determine the cause for the detonation of the vehicle?"

"Not personally," Lincoln answered.

"You read the reports," she said.

"I did."

"Stepping back from the personal loss," she continued. "Your team did prevent the flow of weapons into the area. The overall mission objective was accomplished. And subsequent analysis of the shipment's contents and the engagement provided incontrovertible proof that the Sino-Russian Confederacy was operating in the area."

"There's no greater failure than losing a soldier under your command, ma'am." Lincoln said. "I lost sixteen. And none of the rest of that brought any of them back."

"The initial order," she said, "to intercept the shipment. Would you give it again?"

"Knowing what I do now? No, ma'am, I would not."

"Knowing what you did then, candidate," she clarified. "Did you make a mistake?"

"I ordered sixteen warriors to their deaths, ma'am."

"Given what you knew at the time," she said, and there was a directness in her words that commanded his attention; a clipped precision, looking for a specific answer. "Was it the wrong decision?"

Lincoln had wrestled with that question for years. Probably would for the rest of his life. But not because he didn't know the answer. Because he didn't like it.

"No, ma'am," he answered. "It was the right decision. Given what I knew at the time."

There was a half-breath's worth of silence before the man on the left bit in again.

"And after your force suffered its casualties, what action did you take?" he asked, and the tone in his voice suggested he didn't much approve of the answer he already knew.

"I'm sure that's recorded, sir," Lincoln said.

"Again," the man said, "we're looking for your perspective."

"Several of the remaining UAF advisors scrambled to get a reaction force together and went to get our people back."

"Who led them, candidate?" the man asked.

"The ranking officer," Lincoln answered.

"Which was…?"

"At the time, it was me, sir."

"You left your command post."

"Yes sir, I did."

"In a moment of crisis."

"Yes sir."

"Did you notify your superiors?" he continued.

"I did."

"Did they direct you to pursue a particular course of action?"

"They recommended one, yes, sir."

"And?"

"As the ranking officer in the immediate area of operation, I felt I had a clearer understanding of a fluid situation that required a timely response."

"You chose not to follow an order, then."

"A recommendation," Lincoln said.

A pause. "That was not the commanding officer's recollection," the man said.

Lincoln shrugged. "I thought we were talking about *my* perspective here, sir."

"And I thought you said you didn't have any issues with subordination," the woman responded. Lincoln may have imagined it, but he thought he could hear the barest hint of a smile in her words.

"For my part," Lincoln said. "Ma'am."

"Candidate," said the man on the far left, "when you chose to lead the reaction force, at what probability did you estimate additional hostile activity in the area?"

"One hundred percent, sir."

"Seems high," another woman said, further to the right. Her voice was higher pitched and softer around the edges of her words, like she'd said something encouraging.

"Seems accurate, ma'am," Lincoln responded. "Given the outcome." The scene flashed through Lincoln's mind, familiar from too-frequent mental rehearsal. The approach on the rutted road. Immediate incoming fire. The hard impact of a round punching his collar bone. They'd given him a little ribbon for that.

"You responded emotionally," the man in the middle said. "Let your desire for vengeance override protocol."

"My people were down in the field, sir."

"And your solution was to put more lives at risk, including your own, the ranking officer," the man said; his tone was neutral, offering neither commendation nor accusation.

Lincoln started to respond, but stopped himself. If they wanted an answer, they could ask a question. He didn't feel the need to explain himself to a bunch of people who didn't even have the courage to show their faces in an interrogation.

"Candidate?" the man on the far left said. The guy that had it out for him.

"Sir," Lincoln answered.

"No answer to that?"

"What was the question, sir?"

"Did you or did you not needlessly put additional lives at risk?"

"No sir, I did not."

When the man responded, he sounded surprised. "You're saying you did *not* put additional lives at risk?"

"I did not do so *needlessly*, sir."

"Your intercepting force was already dead," the man continued. "Were you unaware of that fact?"

"No, sir."

"Then what did you hope to accomplish, other than reckless vengeance?"

Lincoln took a breath, steadied himself.

"Did you ever serve in the field, sir?" he asked. There was a heavy pause.

"That's not relevant, candidate."

"That's what I thought," Lincoln said. The man made a noise somewhere between a grunt and a cough, but there came a sound of a quick motion that silenced him. Someone laying a hand on his shoulder or arm, perhaps.

There was a moment of silence, three, maybe five seconds at most.

"You majored in history," the man on the far right said, changing the subject. "Why is that, do you think?"

The question was jarring; it seemed so out of place, like the man hadn't been listening to anything they'd just been discussing. The old crazy uncle at Thanksgiving, opening the door to his own little world. It gave Lincoln cognitive whiplash.

"I beg your pardon?" said Lincoln.

"At university, why did you choose to study history, candidate?" the man asked, enunciating his words.

Lincoln blinked while his brain ground its gears to change direction.

"Well, sir," he said. "I figured if I was going to go to war, I'd better get some idea of what I was in for."

The man grunted.

And as wild as those first few grueling minutes proved to be, they were just a taste of the hours that followed. Lincoln didn't actually know how long he was in that room, answering questions about every single aspect of his life. He quickly discovered there was no way for him to predict what they might ask next, no way to prepare; one moment they'd be discussing happy childhood memories and the next, the most brutally horrific moments of his years of service. And they covered everything. How they knew so much about him was beyond Lincoln. Details about his parents, his sisters, his schooling, about childhood memories that he couldn't be sure even *he* remembered accurately. If he'd been able to think clearly, it might have been frightening. Instead he just felt numb. Drained. Having to answer for what felt like every single decision he'd ever made in his life, and some he hadn't even been able to choose for himself. It was no wonder Cadre Sahil had sent him in with such concern.

He was in the middle of answering a question about one of his first days in basic training when the woman in charge cut him off mid-sentence.

"Very good, candidate," she said. "You're dismissed."

Lincoln sat stunned, mouth still open with an unfinished word. He clamped it shut and then licked his lips.

"You may exit the way you came in," she added.

It took a moment for the meaning of the words to filter through the mental fog. When it finally did, Lincoln nodded and got to his feet. In standing, he felt something he'd never experienced before. A strange combination of disassociation from himself with a painfully intimate sense of exposure. All his secrets laid bare, as viewed through the lens of a neutral observer. Something like feeling embarrassed for someone else's public humiliation.

His body automatically found its way to the door, without any conscious direction. Of everything he'd been through during Selection, somehow this had been the worst. And he wasn't even sure he was feeling its full effects yet. He'd been through psych evaluations with his own people before, and one interrogation from someone else's people. This... whatever this had been, was something on a completely different level. More like Judgment Day.

Death, then judgment. Seemed about right.

When he exited the room, there was a young woman waiting for him. First lieutenant, last name of Kennedy.

"This way, sir," the lieutenant said. Lincoln followed in a haze. It took about thirty seconds for him to realize she'd called him *sir*. Not *candidate*. He wasn't sure if that was a good sign or a terrible one.

The lieutenant led him to a narrow office, motioned him in, and then closed the door behind him without entering herself. An intense woman sat behind a too-small desk in the middle of the room, staring at him like he was grossly late for an appointment. The name plate on the desk read "Lt. Col. Coralie R. Martel".

"Candidate One Seven Echo?" she asked, as soon as the door was closed.

"Yes, ma'am," he said, saluting. She stood and returned the gesture as if she was swatting a fly away.

"Captain," she said, "the unit would like thank you for your time and commitment. You've shown yourself exceptional amongst the truly elite, and that's an accomplishment you can and should be proud of. You've been designated non-select and at this time your service in the unit will not be required..."

Lieutenant Colonel Martel said a whole lot more after that, but it all sounded like static to Lincoln. Even when she stopped talking, he stood stunned.

"I'm sorry," he said after a too-long pause. "...what?"

"You've been designated non-select, captain."

He blinked at the words. "... I didn't make it?"

"It's nothing to be ashamed of, Captain Suh. Less than one percent of candidates are placed, and when you've made it this far into Selection it usually comes down to variables well outside of your control. Your previous areas of operation, your language proficiencies. They're looking for a very particular fit."

There was no way there had been enough time to make the final decision. He'd barely finished his last evaluation. Or had they decided while he was still sitting in that room, answering for his whole life? Had the decision been made even before that?

"A transition officer will be contacting you shortly," Martel continued, "to help walk you through your next steps. For now, Lieutenant Kennedy will lead you back out. You can return to Housing to pick up your belongings."

Lincoln stood staring at the woman, mind struggling to process what was happening.

"That's all, captain. You're dismissed."

She sat back down at her desk and turned her attention to the embedded display. Lincoln's mind swirled with a million questions, and he struggled to find the right starting point. While he was in the process of trying to pick one, somehow he ended up leaving the room and being escorted out of the building.

He found himself standing on the front steps of the facility, blinking at the afternoon sun. Men and women in uniform streamed across the courtyard in front of him on business of their own. A Wednesday. For everyone else, just another Wednesday.

For Lincoln… what? Death, judgment, found wanting.

Hell.

Everything seemed too bright, too loud, too fast. For fourteen weeks, he'd endured with only one goal. A goal he knew he'd reach, as long as he just kept enduring. And now here he was, out of the race, an inch short of the finish line. Out on "variables well outside" of his control. No one had mentioned anything about that before.

"Captain Suh," a voice said from his right. It'd been so long since anyone had called him that, he didn't even think to respond at first. "Captain Suh?"

Lincoln turned his head to find Lieutenant Kennedy standing a few feet away, looking at him with expectancy.

"Yeah?" he said.

"Sir, we have a vehicle waiting for you, if you'd like to come with me."

"Oh? I had not been informed of that courtesy."

"Yes, sir," she said.

"Is this usual treatment for the castoffs?" he asked.

"I wouldn't know about that, sir," she said.

Lincoln grunted. He was tired. Tired right down through the middle of his bones. But it wasn't that far of a walk back to the housing facility, and he didn't love the idea of being carted around like some invalid, just because he hadn't made the cut.

"Well, if it's all the same to you, Lieutenant Kennedy, I think I'd prefer the walk."

"Due respect, sir," she answered, "it's not the same."

He looked her straight in the eye, and she held his gaze. She had some steel in her, for a junior officer. After a moment, she stepped closer and leaned forward.

"Five minutes of your time, sir. Ten at most."

Unusual behavior to say the least.

"I'm not much for conversation just now, ma'am."

"How are you for listening?" she said.

That didn't have much appeal either. Maybe she had some weird thing for guys who'd just had their hopes and dreams destroyed. Lincoln was just about to blow her off, but something in his gut checked him. She was too professional, too focused. And it wasn't like he had much of anywhere else to go today, or to do. He gestured for her to lead the way. She nodded and swiveled around, leading him towards a nearby avenue. He followed along after her, watching her move. She was all sharp angles and precision; a projection of confidence and certain intent. Wherever she'd come from, it was obvious to Lincoln that Lieutenant Kennedy wasn't a typical first lieutenant.

She led him to a plain white vehicle that was parked right along the thoroughfare. It was one of the smaller four-seat affairs with darkly tinted windows, and it hummed to life as they approached.

"You're not planning to do anything untoward to me, are you, lieutenant?"

Kennedy stopped at the side of the car and turned back.

"Not me," she said with a smile.

The door slid open. When Lincoln saw who was sitting inside staring back at him, he physically flinched and immediately hated himself for it. He'd reacted that way because the man sitting in the car was a legend in the special operations community. It just so happened that the man in the vehicle also bore heavy scarring, his bald head and face mottled with scar tissue that stretched down his neck into the collar of his impeccable uniform. The disfigurement wasn't why Lincoln had flinched, but he knew it would be the man's first impression of him.

"Captain Suh," the man said. "I'm Colonel Mateus Almeida."

"I know who you are, sir," Lincoln said, snapping a salute.

Colonel Almeida returned the gesture with easy grace and an undisguised prosthetic hand.

"Got a bit of a reputation, do I?" he said.

"A bit, yes sir."

Almeida gave him a broken grin. "Only the worst parts are true."

"I doubt that very much, sir."

"Well," he said, "I hear the worst parts are also the best parts."

Lincoln smiled. "That may be. What can I do for you, sir?"

"You can get in my car so I don't have to sit here staring up at you."

Lincoln nodded and slid into the rear-facing seat. The door slid closed, and Kennedy walked away as if she'd had nothing to do with any of it.

"Alberton, 109," Almeida said. The vehicle pulled away from the curb, headed to an address on the other side of the base. The opposite direction from Housing, where all of Lincoln's gear was. "Don't worry, captain, I won't make you stare at me for long."

Lincoln wanted to apologize, or to explain himself to the man, but he couldn't find the words. He just said, "It's an honor to be sitting here with you, sir."

Lincoln was no stranger to the physical realities of combat and trauma. He'd seen plenty of both. Colonel Almeida's injuries had clearly been severe; he'd lost an eye, an arm, and most of his face to a white-flamed fireball with a shrapnel heart. But the colonel's career in the field had ended at least a decade prior, probably closer to two. There'd been more than enough time for reconstructive surgery to have patched him up so perfectly that no one would ever have known he'd even seen combat. The fact that he didn't even have a simple synthetic dermal covering for his prosthetic made it clear that his appearance was a conscious choice.

The colonel furrowed his brow. "And here I thought you were a straight-shooter, no-nonsense type."

"I do try, sir."

"Well try harder, son. My face is a wreck. You know it. I know it. If you're going to come work for me, it's better to get it out of the way now so I don't have to listen to you trying to talk around it all the time."

"I'm sorry?" Lincoln said. Almeida had him completely wrong-footed.

"I look more like a Martian terrain feature than a man, eh? What do you think? Gimme the truth, boy. Always the truth with me."

Lincoln didn't know what the colonel wanted from him, and his mouth formed the words without ever checking with his mind.

"I've seen worse, sir."

The colonel chuckled at that. "Close enough! Though if that's actually true, I feel sorry for the poor kid that got blown up worse than me."

"Oh, he wasn't blown up, sir," Lincoln said, and he finally risked a smile. "Just ugly."

Almeida grinned at that. "Then I feel sorry for his mama."

"Colonel, I have to ask your forgiveness sir. I guess I'm a little behind. You mentioned something about me working for you?"

"I did."

"This is the first I'm hearing about it."

"I've a got a new command, captain. Working in the 301st Information Support Brigade. I'm heading up the 519th Applied Intelligence Group."

"Congratulations, sir," Lincoln said. "I'm afraid I'm uh… I'm not familiar with the unit."

"Really?" Almeida said with mock surprise. "But we have patches and everything." He gave it a moment and a crack of a smile before continuing. "On paper, the 519th is a support group, but it is in reality a special mission unit. It was officially formed only in the past few months, but we've been operating for oh, I dunno, about three years now. You work in the right circles. Ever hear mention of Grey Aegis?"

Lincoln shook his head.

"Victor Dawn?"

"No sir."

"Element Five?"

"Oh," Lincoln said. "Those guys."

Almeida dipped his head. "Those guys."

"Not great with names, are they?"

The colonel shrugged. "I had to change it so often, I never really put a lot of thought into it."

"That's great, sir, but I'm not sure why you'd want to talk with me. I'm not an analyst. Intel's never been my main department."

"The 519th isn't a traditional intelligence apparatus."

"Sure," Lincoln said. "They're *applied* intelligence."

"That's right."

Lincoln shook his head. "I don't know what that means."

"We can kill a man from orbit without spilling the cup of coffee on the table in front of him. But all the precision in the world doesn't matter if we don't know what cafe he's sitting in," Almeida said. "The one lesson from the McLaren Incident that everyone *should* have learned, is that we can't keep our people off the front lines and expect to stay ahead of the curve. Information is only part of the problem; usually we have too much of it. We can see just about everything, but ninety-eight percent of the time we can't tell what we're looking at. Not until after the fact. That's what happened with McLaren. Had all the pieces, didn't know how to put them together until the bad guys showed us.

"I need people with field experience, people who are familiar with violence and the what-comes-before. People with the instincts to recognize the pre-incident indicators, and who can do something about it. I need people to tell me what we're looking at, before it happens.

"Ultimately, we're problem solvers, captain. Quiet ones. Intelligence collection's part of the game, but we maintain the capacity for direct action operations as well. And that's about all I'm going to tell you. Until you come work for me."

Lincoln smiled at the use of the word *until*. "For the 519th."

"That's right."

"Which I know nothing about."

Almeida nodded.

"Not giving me a lot to go on, sir."

"Get used to it. The ability to operate on incomplete information is a requirement, captain," the colonel said. "I expect my people to be comfortable living in that reality. You'll be making a lot of high-stakes decisions on partial data, some of it likely false. You'll have to act decisively, and you'll have to make the best of the consequences, come what may. But..." Here he held up a hand and ticked off the points as he mentioned them. "Some highlights of the job: pay's not great; most sergeants will have command of more people than you; you'll be in the Information Support Brigade, which makes you sound like the biggest weenie on the planet. Oh, *and*, if you do the job right, a bunch of other people will always get the credit. It's pretty much a career-killer."

Lincoln blinked at the job description. A moment later, he added "... and the downside?"

"Responsibility."

"How much?"

"A world's weight, at least. I need a team leader. Someone I can put in the field and trust do the right thing without a lot of handholding. We move fast. The nature of our work requires it. I need someone who isn't afraid to figure things out on the fly." The colonel leaned forward. "Someone who isn't afraid to act on a clearer understanding of fluid situations that require timely responses."

Almeida let the phrase hang in the air, an echo of the very words Lincoln had used earlier that day. Had Almeida been in that room? Or did he have people reporting to him? Either option had uncomfortable implications.

"I'm honored that you'd consider me, sir," Lincoln said. "But I'm sure there are a lot of other individuals out there better suited for that than me."

Almeida shrugged as he sat back and cleared his throat. "It's currently a list of one, captain."

"That *is* flattering, sir, but I would expect someone of your caliber to have a, uh…" Lincoln paused, searching for the most diplomatic word he could think of, "… more robust set of options available."

The colonel rumbled with a chest-deep chuckle. "Yeah, OK, so there might be a few other folks in line. But you're at the top. And first. I haven't offered this opportunity to anyone else yet, cross my heart."

Lincoln looked down at his own hands, clasped in his lap. Most of his career had been in more traditional special operations forces, and while he'd certainly done his best in every one of them, he'd never considered himself to be a superstar or a stud. He could have easily rattled off the names of fifteen men and women who'd be better suited to lead a Special Mission Unit, as far as he was concerned.

"And what makes you think I'm the right one for the job?" Lincoln asked.

"I don't think. I know. And I know because it's my business to know," Almeida said.

"Can you be a little more specific?"

The colonel scratched his nose with his prosthesis, a gesture that would have looked completely natural if not for the gunmetal grey surface of the hand. "I've been at this a long time, captain. If you hang around the halls long enough, you hear names picking up buzz. Rock stars in a community of superheroes."

Lincoln's eyebrows went up at that. He'd never gotten the impression that anyone knew who he was outside his immediate circle of peers.

"And," Almeida said, "I've never once heard anyone talking about you."

Lincoln let out a single, involuntary bark of a laugh. "Easy, colonel, you keep talking so nice, I might start getting uppity."

"Well, you've never been in the spotlight, never been singled out by the brass for exceptional contribution. Seems you've even been passed over for promotion at least once, maybe more. And yet, somehow, when I ask around, every team member you've ever worked with puts you in the list of folks they'd call in a heartbeat if they needed to get something done. There's a pattern to your career, captain. The reason you don't pop up on anyone's radar is because not many people know how to measure what you do. You make the people around you better. That's what I need most. A leader who gets things done and doesn't need a lot of attention or pats on the back for doing it.

"Bottom line, I believe in you, Captain Suh." Those were powerful words coming from such a man, particularly after Lincoln's recent failing. "But we can't wait for you. I'm looking for men and women who can seize the initiative. I thought that was you. If I was wrong, no harm done. Better to find that out now." The colonel brushed some lint off his pant leg with the back of his prosthetic hand and then continued. "But I can tell you this. The unit you just volunteered for? Wherever *they're* going, you'll be there first. In some cases, to prepare the way for them. In more cases, to keep us from having to send them at all."

"The unit I just failed out of."

"You didn't fail."

"'Non-select'. Same thing."

"No, you did *not* fail, son," Almeida said, "I had you selected."

Lincoln looked back at the colonel. "You did what now?"

"*I* selected you."

"You selected me... out of Selection?"

"Cheaper than setting up my own program. Budgets, you know."

A knot of emotion coiled and then bloomed in Lincoln's chest; relief, bewilderment, anger. He hadn't failed after all. And yet, the outcome remained the same. He ran his hand over his mouth, stroked his chin. When he spoke, he tried to keep his tone neutral and wasn't completely successful.

"I just spent fourteen weeks slogging through that course so you could pluck me out at the last second…? What if I say no?"

"Then you get out of here and by the time you walk back to Housing, a very apologetic second lieutenant will be there to explain about the unfortunate clerical error that led to your premature dismissal. And no one will have any recollection of us ever having this conversation. But you're not going to say no, are you?"

"All due respect, sir, I died and then got resurrected a couple of hours ago," Lincoln said. "And that was the *easiest* part of my day. Easiest part of my last three months. I don't know that I'm in the right frame of mind to make any career decisions just now."

"I already told you, son. There's no career in this. Just a job that needs doing, with precious few people qualified to do it. You might not be sure of yourself, but I am. You're the right one for the job. But I'm only going to ask you once."

Lincoln glanced out the window again. He was used to doing things a little outside of normal. He sought it out. It's why he'd been attracted to special operations in the first place. Some people thought it was a high-risk occupation; Lincoln had come to consider it one of *precisely calculated* risk. Every man and woman he'd served alongside in the teams had been willing to risk it all, but the ones who had excelled had developed a habit of leaving absolutely nothing to chance.

But this was so far from normal it wasn't even on the same planetary map. Forget all the things he didn't know about

the 519th. He'd heard the stories of Colonel Almeida, but he
didn't really know the man.

The vehicle slowed and drew up alongside the curb in front
of a low building that was nondescript even by base standards.

"I'm getting out here," Almeida said. "You can stay if you
want, take the car back to Housing, try your luck with the
unit. No hard feelings." The colonel shifted himself to the seat
next to the door and rested a hand on it, preparing to open it.
"Or," he added, "you can come with me right now and do the
thing you were made for."

He paused long enough to let the weight of the moment
settle, and then without another word he opened the door
and stepped out into the bright sun. He remained at the
vehicle's side just long enough to don his cap and straighten
his immaculate uniform. Then the door closed behind him
and Colonel Almeida walked towards the building with a
sharp stride. No hesitation, no looking back.

Lincoln sat in the vehicle, strongly tempted to take the bait;
to swallow the hook he knew was there and just see where
it took him. But there wasn't enough for him to go on. He'd
dreamed about joining the unit for years. And now, on the
cusp of realizing that dream, or at least finding out for certain
whether he had what it took, this man he didn't know was
trying to entice him into throwing it all away, just to solve the
mystery. There was no calculation to it. Lincoln didn't have
any data to calculate. It was all risk. All chance.

It was crazy, is what it was. Lincoln glanced out the tinted
window at the shadow world beyond. It certainly looked like
the normal world was still out there, doing its thing. Was any
of this actually happening?

The car chirped twice, signaling its availability for a new
address. A few words, and Lincoln would be on his way
back to Housing, and the very apologetic second lieutenant.
A few words, and this would all fade into a weird memory,
something in time he could probably convince himself was

just a fever dream brought on by the trauma of his very difficult Wednesday. Just a few words.

And before he'd consciously made the decision, Lincoln found himself opening the door and stepping out of the car.

"Colonel Almeida, sir," he called. Almeida didn't miss a step. He swiveled right around and marched back over to Lincoln at the exact same pace.

"Captain?" he said when he reached Lincoln.

All risk. All chance.

"Sir," Lincoln said. "Where do I sign?"

Almeida flashed his broken smile.

"We don't like to leave a lot of records lying around," Almeida answered. He extended his prosthetic hand. Lincoln clasped the cool metal in his own, firm grip, shook it. When he drew back his hand, there was a weighty coin in his palm. A challenge coin. A long-standing military tradition. On it was a simple design; an angular shield with a sword laid on top. Or, on second look, maybe the shield was a coffin. Along the top in scrollwork it read "519th Applied Intelligence Group", with the nickname of the unit underneath. The bottom edge of the coin read simply "No Grave Too Deep", which sounded just vaguely ominous enough to seem like a bunch of weenies trying to sound like tough guys.

"Captain Suh," Almeida said. "Welcome to the Outriders."

FOUR

Piper swept two slender fingers across the panel to her left, switched the view from Sol-side to the Deep. Another deft motion and the view expanded to fill the entire station wall in front of her. It was just a constructed image of course, not a real actual window into outer space. When she'd first seen pictures of people working a hop, she'd thought they had real honest-to-goodness windows, big old panes of glass separating the watchers from the vacuum. Then she'd learned about what a grain of sand moving at velocity could do to the outer hull of a ship and she came to appreciate why no one had ever once made a hop with a real honest-to-goodness window. It was still a little disappointing.

Most of the watchers preferred to look back from the station, back towards the sun. Back towards home. Not Piper. The stars had always called to her, always been her destiny. She'd spent her formative years staring up at them from her family's little patch of dirt in the eastern lowlands of Peru; when she turned seventeen, she signed up to see how close to them she could get. It'd been almost nine years since and even though her current assignment was the furthest out she'd ever been, it didn't feel nearly far enough. She hoped that by the time she was her parents' age, people would finally take space travel seriously and really find a way to get out there amongst the stars. For some reason, her great-grandparents' generation had celebrated just for getting off Earth, and her grandparents' generation seemed to think colonizing Mars had made them a space-faring race. To Piper, that was like moving to the house next door and patting yourself on the back for being well traveled.

Still, she was off to a good start. Right now she was sitting about sixty-five million miles from Earth, and, as far as she was concerned, maybe infinity miles from home. She really ought to call her parents, she thought with mild guilt. But talking with them always had a way of pulling her mind back Earthward, to oppressive humidity and too much rain, and to promises broken and hearts too often betrayed. Here, sitting in front of the crystal-clear projection where the perfect image made it seem like the hull of the hop had been sheared cleanly away, she could almost believe space was embracing her, inviting her further out, promising only hope, and discovery, and joy. She loved her parents. She did. She'd get in touch with them soon. Maybe not today, but soon.

Piper cleared her head with a shake and settled in to work. The console in front of her glowed softly with subdued blue lines, gentle traces in the darkness of Hari's preferred display configuration, the colleague she'd just replaced. Piper glided fingertips over the surface, waking it and calling up the sensor suite. The console recognized her prints on contact and instantly reconfigured the layout of the screens to her liking. A message appeared in the main interface.

Hello Piper.

"Hey, Gus," she said. Her coworkers argued both with her and amongst themselves as to whether Piper was a technophobe or just old-fashioned for disabling the voice features on the console, but they all agreed it was a strange choice. Neither side was right, of course. She was just an introvert and always got more than her fill of chat down on deck. The bubble was her one place of solace on the whole

station, and she didn't see any reason to clutter it up with
unnecessary chatter. Gus was the perfect gentleman, only
speaking when spoken to, and then only in text.

Piper ran through her checkpad of diagnostics, making sure
all the sensor systems were in shape and tracking. Technically
it wasn't necessary; it was part of end-of-shift protocol to
ensure the next watcher had everything they needed. Hari
had reported all systems green before handing the station
over to her, but Piper always double-checked. It's not that she
didn't trust her coworkers. She just knew how routine too
often led to complacency, and the fact that nothing had ever
been out of order in the four years she'd been on station made
it all the more likely that everyone else had just gotten used
to assuming things were working fine. She wasn't confident
that everyone was keeping a close eye out. And Piper always
kept a close eye out.

Satisfied, she settled back into the mesh chair, situated
herself for a long shift. Someone had adjusted the armrests.
Again. Piper loved that chair. She'd spent hours searching
out its most-guarded mechanical secrets, learned the ways
of every knob, switch, lever, and slider. Weeks of testing and
experimenting had unlocked a comfort she'd believed, like
sunrises and ocean waves, she'd lost forever. The adjustment
was only moderately annoying, though. There generally
wasn't much else for her to do anyway.

The hop she was assigned to was officially designated
Veryn-Hakakuri Station YN-773; VH was a minor corp in the
grand scheme of things, and YN-773 was pretty out of the
way even for them. It wasn't along any of the main trade
routes. She'd only seen three big cruisers since she'd taken
the job out here. Smaller craft docked more frequently, but
never for long. Just to get tooled up, or to re-sync the latest
bounce report on their way to whichever station was their
final destination. Piper liked the little hop, though. It was the
first one she'd been on that was synced up with Mars's orbit

instead of Earth's, and even though they maintained a Terran day-night schedule and the orbit didn't actually make any difference in her day-to-day routine, it still felt more exotic, somehow. And there was some kind of executive suite down on the lowest level that was off limits to all the techs and corporate peons like her, and that at least gave everyone something to talk about.

It still struck Piper as funny that the station had a down. Technically the station's top-most section was supposed to be aligned along the same axis as Earth's magnetic northern pole, but that didn't really make any sense either when you thought about it, because it's not like ground folk went around with all their heads northward. And it all seemed a little sad to her too, the amount of effort everyone put into trying to make life in space just like life on one of the planets. Such a waste, to get so far out and then to refuse to embrace all the promise the Deep offered. Like going to the beach for the first time and spending the whole day inside.

Maybe Piper had never really been meant to live on-planet. She had some affection for Earth, and a mild loyalty to the United American Federation, but she credited that more to her place of birth than anything else. Many of her hopmates spent endless hours talking about the politics between planets, making predictions about what the latest treaty or interplanetary report would mean, arguing about whose fault it would be if a war ever started, and who would win. But to Piper that was exactly the kind of thing that was holding the entire human race back. Her forebears had moved to a neighboring planet, but nothing had really changed. They were all still doing the same things they'd always done.

For Piper, it was a disappointment to see people so concerned with such petty nonsense. There was so much more out there, so much waiting to be discovered, and yet everyone was still obsessed with deciding which patch of dirt belonged to whom. Terran dirt, Lunar dirt, Martian dirt – it was still just dirt, and there was a whole universe full of it.

The strained relationship between Earth and Mars had about as much impact on YN-773 as any of the millions of disputes that took place on either planet's surface every single day. It was all too distant to matter, the station too remote to feel any noticeable effect. And yet it was still a constant source of chatter. The fact that her coworkers relished the meaningless debates probably played into Piper's decision to volunteer for so many shifts on watch. Though, if she was being fair, she had to admit there usually wasn't a whole lot else for them to do. It just all seemed like a waste of energy and brainpower to her.

Of course, there had been a bit of excitement of late, at least as far as the hop was concerned. A hauler, called *Destiny's Undertow*, was limping its way towards YN-773 and had been for a couple of weeks, supposedly all the way from the belt. According to the ship's captain, they'd been hoping for a gravity sling off Mars to help them get all the way back to Earth, but took damage from a collision and missed the window. Somehow that put them far enough out of the way of anything that 773 was the closest hop that could provide service, and so they were slowly trundling their way towards the station.

The story didn't completely add up. Unless the captain was really bad at math, there was no way 773 was the best choice for anyone trying to sling Mars. Of course everyone on 773 had their own theories about what had really happened. The most elaborate involved pirates and an attempted hijacking. The most mundane were that the captain was trying to save money and ran his ship too long without good maintenance. The most likely, at least in Piper's mind, was that they'd been hauling something they shouldn't have been and whatever deal they thought they were going to make didn't go so well. People didn't just show up at 773 for convenience. It was too far out of the way from... well, everything.

Still, business was business and any business that showed up at 773 was probably good for everyone. No one thought much about the out-of-the-way stations until they were low on juice and drifting, then everyone prayed for one. *Destiny's Undertow* was finally close enough that a couple of tugs had gone out to meet her and were bringing her in. Piper pinched one of the sensor windows to compress it and then expanded a new window from exterior cameras to check out the progress. The tugs were already flaring thrusters in their slowing protocol, which meant they were maybe a half hour out from starting the docking procedure. Maybe when it got closer to time, she'd flip her main view around to watch the ship come in. Maybe.

For the time being, Piper was content to let her gaze fall out into the soft and endless expanse of the Deep. A few minutes later, out in the nothingness, motion caught her eye. Reflexively her gaze snapped to it, but when she looked, she saw nothing out of the ordinary. Just the pinprick lights of stars so distant they might no longer exist. It struck her then, oddly; the idea that some of those pale, cold lights might be ghosts of things long dead. And while she was staring out into the emptiness pondering what such an ending would look like, and whether she'd ever get to see such a spectacle, one of the stars winked out. Vanished.

No. As she continued to look, a shadow shifted across the void; a blackness against the deep charcoal of the Deep.

Something *was* out there.

Piper sat up in her chair and swept her fingers over the console, waking it from standby. With a few deft strokes, she brought up the short and medium-range sensors. It took a moment for her to orient herself to where her current viewpoint was on the top-down display, and a few moments afterward to confirm what she knew ought to be... namely, there was nothing there. But when she looked up at her giant window, she couldn't stop seeing it. It looked like a hole in space.

She thumbed a virtual slider and opened comms to Gennady, her supervisor. He answered on the fourth tone, which probably meant he'd been out cold.

"Yeah, Pip," he said, and then cleared his throat. "What's up kid?"

"Hey, chief, sorry to wake you, but I think something's busted up here."

"Annoying busted, or can't-wait-till-morning busted?"

"The can't-wait kind."

Gennady let out a heavy exhale that was about a fifty-fifty mix between resigned sigh and gearing up for the effort to hoist himself out of bed. "All right. Be up in a couple."

"Thanks, chief."

"Yep."

Piper spent the next few minutes staring intently out into the void, torn between hoping she really had spotted something and hadn't awoken her supervisor for nothing, and hoping she was wrong. And just when she'd about convinced herself that she'd imagined it all, the star that had winked out reappeared for half a heartbeat. Piper shivered. Things weren't supposed to surprise you out on a hop. Not when a stray chunk of comet could tear a hole through your life support and send your friends spiraling out to a horrible death. Sometimes in the break room they'd argue about whether you'd freeze to death before your lungs got sucked out through your mouth. Fortunately, no one had settled that one yet for sure.

The door slid open behind her, and Piper swiveled her chair around to see a groggy Gennady stumble in. He'd taken the time to throw on a T-shirt and some pants, but his zipper was down.

"What's bothering you, Pip?" He still had a bit of a Russian accent. On other hops Piper had worked on, that would have been a source of friction since most of the Veryn-Hakakuri crews were strictly United American Federation. But out on 773, no one really held original nationality against anyone else. All the unpleasantness was too remote for any of them to really worry about, and the further out you got, the more ridiculous it all seemed anyway.

"I think there's something out there, chief."

"Yeah? What's the sensors got?"

"Well, that's kind of the thing. They aren't showing anything."

Gennady's eyebrows crumpled together like a crushed beer can. "Then why do you think there's something?"

"I saw it."

He crossed the tiny room in three steps and bent over her to look at the display. "Where?"

Piper pointed out the details on the console as she talked. "I'm showing Cam 61 through 64, composite. So that's here, looking out that way. But see? Nothing out of the ordinary."

"Yeah, so how'd you see something then?" Gennady said, scanning the console and checking its various readouts. "You mean like it showed up on one of these and then went away?"

"No, chief, with my eyes. Look." She pointed at the wall-sized projection. Gennady looked up at it like it was the first time he'd noticed it.

"What, out there?"

"Yeah. There was a star, and it went out. Something got between it and us."

Gennady stood up straight, let out another heavy sigh, and ran his hand over his face. "Please tell me you didn't get me out of bed because a star went dark."

"There's something there, chief. I can see it, just barely. Look, right there," Piper said, and she leaned forward over the console and touched the projection. "Doesn't that look like a dark patch to you?"

"It's space, Pip! The whole thing's one big dark patch!"

"Well why wouldn't that... thing, whatever it is, show up on the sensors?"

"I dunno, maybe 'cause it's five light years away? Maybe it's some dust cloud moving through? If the sensors aren't showing it, it's because it ain't a problem. I got early shift tomorrow, Pip."

He was just turning around to leave again when the hole in space suddenly glinted, light reflecting off a rough edge for the span of a blink.

Gennady looked at the projection, and then at Piper.

"You see that?" he asked.

"Yes. Did you?"

"I dunno."

He checked the sensors again, fiddled with the settings.

"Is that a ship?" he said, more to himself than to Piper. She answered anyway.

"I don't think so. It looks more like a rock, chief."

"Don't say that."

"I'm just saying."

"Well don't."

Gennady patted her shoulder three times with the back of his hand, and she slid sideways out of the chair to let him take over. He plopped down and started opening a whole new set of windows, some that Piper had never seen before.

"*Straussveeja*, Gennady," the console said in Gennady's native Russian.

"Hi Gus," he said. "Any trouble lately?"

"*Nyet.*"

Gennady grunted and focused in on the console display, reading a long, streaming block of characters Piper couldn't interpret. There was a good reason everyone called him chief. After a couple of silent minutes working the console, Gennady finally looked up at the projection again, squinting at the spot Piper had pointed out. A few more stars had disappeared.

"You ran diags when you came in?" he asked.

"Yeah."

"Everything green?"

"Yeah."

"Well…" Gennady said as he scrolled through data, "there's

nothing on the charts, so at least it's not a rock."

"Just because it's not on the charts doesn't mean it's not a rock. Could be the charts are wrong."

"It's the latest, crossindexed from Earth, Luna, and Mars. Maybe one of them would miss it, but not all three. Maybe it's a dead ship."

Gennady opened another window on the console and had a quick verbal exchange with Gus in Russian that Piper couldn't follow. A few moments later, his expression darkened.

"OK, so yeah, something's definitely not right," he said. He pointed at a data field on the display that read NULL. "That's all right, if there's nothing there." He moved his finger to a jagged line, which Piper took to be some representation of sensor data. "But that form's a little too regular for my liking."

"What do you mean?"

"I mean it looks manufactured to me."

"That doesn't help, chief."

Without looking at it, Gennady traced over the line with irritated haste. "No random spikes or dots. No outliers. No stuff that looks out of place. *That* doesn't look random, it looks like someone *wanted* it to look random. *Manufactured*."

That opened more questions than it answered, but the way he'd said it had been enough to frighten Piper into silence. Gennady was former Russian Navy. It was a rare occasion that he ever mentioned anything about that past life, but whenever he did, his voice took on a particular tone and his vowels got a little sharper. Just like when he said that form looked *manufactured*. He obviously meant more by it than she understood, but she understood enough. Bad things. Piper had a thousand more questions; fortunately she had sense enough not to ask any of them while Gennady was staring at the display with such intensity.

After a couple of minutes of strained silence, Gennady's brow suddenly smoothed, his face relaxed. But not in any kind of relief. Some thought, dawning on him.

"That hauler," he said, looking at her. "We did a sync with it?"

"I think so, yeah," Piper answered. "Came in on Annie's shift, though. I could check."

"Anybody talked to the captain?"

"Sure, a few times."

He looked back at the console, said something in Russian to Gus, and then started working some figures again. "Anybody confirm he's actually on that ship?"

Piper didn't understand the question.

"Where else would he be?"

Gennady shook his head.

"What is it, chief?"

"You checked the pod lately?"

"Every shift," Piper said. "Why?"

"I want you to get in it."

She blinked at him. He might as well have said it in Russian.

"Get in the pod," he repeated, still not looking at her. He was too focused on the data streams flooding his console. "Now."

"Why? What's going on?"

"I don't know, Pip, but I got a bad feeling. I think that hauler slipped us something."

Piper looked at the console, then at the projection. She raised her hands from her sides and then dropped them again, feeling lost and momentarily useless.

"I'm about to do something here," Gennady said. Finally, he looked up at her. "And I'm not sure what's going to happen when I do it. So I don't want you standing here."

"You're scaring me, chief."

"It's because I'm a little scared myself, kid." He stared at her for a few moments, long enough for her to see he wasn't lying. She'd never seen his eyes like that before. "Look, just hop in and button up. For me. I'd feel better if you were sitting in there. If I'm wrong, no harm done."

"I'm more worried about if you're right," Piper said.

"Get in the pod, Piper. Please."

Piper couldn't remember Gennady ever saying *please* to her. She nodded and moved to the hatch that led to the emergency lifepod. It was a small affair, just a two-man pod, intended for the usually single inhabitant of the bubble. Someone at Veryn-Hakakuri probably thought they were being extra cautious by putting a two-man pod up here. All the big ones were below. Piper typed in a code and both the inner and outer hatches eased open. She glanced back at Gennady; he was hunched over the console, fingers flying, muttering in Russian to Gus, who was chattering right back. If he noticed her looking at him, he didn't make any sign of it.

With a deep breath, Piper turned back and ducked down through the hatch. It was slightly shorter than a normal doorway, but the connecting corridor was only a few steps long so she didn't have to hunch over long. The pod was pretty straightforward. A couple of crash couches with harnesses, nav rig, full sensor suite. Supplies were locked in a rugged case. Efficient, but not without some thought for at least a little comfort. Whoever had designed it seemed to understand that people might have to sit in there for a couple of weeks before anyone found them. Piper tried not think too much about that as she slipped inside and punched the code to close the hatches. She sat down on one of the crash couches, but she didn't strap in. That was a little more than she could handle.

She'd never actually used a lifepod before, except for the basic training scenario everyone had to go through before getting assigned to a hop, and that one had been back on-planet. There was something eerie about the real thing; knowing that she was hanging out in space, just a few button presses away from being cut loose. To her surprise, space didn't seem quite so inviting at that particular moment.

It was only a minute or two before Piper couldn't handle the silence anymore. She picked at her fingernails, thought about opening the hatches again so she could at least hear Gennady working, but decided against it for fear of interfering with whatever the "something" was he was planning to do. Finally, she decided to power up the pod's sensor suite and see if she could get a different perspective on whatever was going on. She scooted over to the console and ran through the activation protocol. Pale blue patterns arced to life as the sensors cycled online. The console bleeped once with a cheery tone.

And then promptly went dark.

Everything went dark.

A moment later, the pod vibrated with a dull, metallic thunder. Piper shot up from the crash couch, punched at the panel by the hatch. Too late. She went lightheaded and fell back into the couch. A few seconds later she started falling the wrong direction, up from the floor towards what used to be a wall.

The pod was tumbling out of the station's gravity aura.

Gennady had cut her loose.

Piper snatched the strap of a harness on one of the crash couches, scrambled to pull herself into it. She hadn't been in zero-G since her emergency training course almost ten years before. It took her almost a full minute to get her body under control. While she was still fastening the buckles, the pod's power spun up again as if nothing unusual had happened a few minutes before; sensors came online, the nav rig initialized, internal gravity stabilized. Piper immediately went to work on the nearest console, running a sensor sweep and bringing a projection up on the pod wall.

"Show me the station," she said, "YN-773, one-one-hundredth scale."

"Certainly," the console replied, "YN-773, one-one-hundredth scale."

The image appeared, crystal clear like there was nothing between her and the station but empty space. And from top to bottom, YN-773 was dark. Completely, totally, dark. She'd never seen it like that before. As her mind tried to process what she was seeing, a silver-thread halo appeared around the hole in space.

From the silhouette she could tell now that it *was* a rock, moving at incredible speed. An enormous one, maybe as much as twenty percent of the size of the station.

Piper's mouth dropped open, but nothing came out. No sound. Not even a breath. The rock smashed into the center column of YN-773 and too many things happened at once for Piper to comprehend. The station twisted, compressed, expanded, and folded all at the same time, a physical impossibility made manifest by the force and shockwave of the asteroid tumbling and tearing its way through the structure. A flash of light and then the rock, too, flew apart in a billion fragments, a planet-killing shotgun blast of minerals that disintegrated the station from the middle outward. If she hadn't known better, Piper would have thought it looked like a detonation.

A rippling distortion emanated from the point of impact, a powerful wave of debris. It hadn't fully registered with her that what she was seeing was real when the edge of the ripple reached the pod. The force hit with such violence that the tumbling of the pod outmatched its internal gravity; in one moment the straps of the harness cut into her shoulders, the next, she was crushed back into the crash couch. Sensations came too fast to process; a stab of pain through her hand, bursts of white light, shrieks of wrenching metal. Warning sirens screamed feeble and futile cries amidst the chaos as the pod's subsystems sputtered and failed.

Piper had no concept of how long it took for that initial blast to pass through the tiny vessel. Seconds maybe, or minutes. At some point she simply became aware that she could hear herself breathing; panting, really. The pod was lit in dusky hues. Most of its interior lights were out or sputtering weakly. Without any input from its single occupant, the lifepod automatically attempted to stabilize and did so with a broken, staccato rhythm. Its thrusters fired sporadically, jerking the pod first in one direction, then back in the other as its damaged navigational systems overcompensated. After a minute or two, the pod managed to reduce its tumble to a mere slow roll around a single axis.

The constructed image on the wall was patchworked with black squares or strange colors, unsurprising indications that the pod's sensors and optical array had suffered substantial damage. In the sections that persisted, however, the shattered remains of YN-773 were crystal clear. Piper covered her mouth with both hands. The devastation was complete, and incomprehensible in scale. Veryn-Hakakuri Station YN-773, her home for the past four years, was now nothing more than a field of debris, spiraling and expanding out into the nothingness of the deep.

"Scan for lifepods," Piper said weakly. The console chirped and futzed out a broken static reply. Piper couldn't make out the words, but it didn't matter. She could see for herself. No beacons showed on any of the displays, no telltale strobes flashed in her visualization on the pod wall. Even the hauler was gone. Piper was alone.

A chill poured down on her, a waterfall of dread mingled with trembling despair; numbness overtook her mind, froze her thoughts. The paralysis crept down into her chest, gripped her lungs. From somewhere outside herself, as if she'd become a detached observer, Piper realized that she was going into shock. She'd have to do something about that. If she could only remember what.

She didn't have time to. A dark silhouette spun across her view, and Piper barely had time for the shape to register before the impact came; just time enough for a final thought to flit through her mind... She should have called her parents.

The pod juddered with savage intensity and the force whipped Piper violently into blackness.

FIVE

Lincoln dropped his ruck on the floor of the entryway and took his hat off. After all the hassle he'd gone through just getting into the fenced-off, checkpoint-controlled section of base, he'd been expecting that someone would be there to greet him. There wasn't. As far as he could tell, he was the only one in the facility at all. Lieutenant Kennedy had been pretty thorough with the instructions on getting *to* the 519th's main planning facility: keep your credentials handy, be prepared for at least one security check, and if anyone asks, you're a *technician* for the Information Support Brigade. She'd been surprisingly light on details about what to do once he actually *arrived*.

The small entryway was relatively bare; cheap tile floor, cinder block walls painted a pale yellow that may have been some shade of off-white in its prime. Not exactly the slick, high-tech secret hideout for an elite Special Mission Unit that Lincoln had imagined. In fact, his first impression was that the place was kind of a dump.

He took a deep, slow breath. Sure enough, the air was mildly stale, with a faintly damp smell that lingered just below the strongly antiseptic pine scent of the cleaning solution the army had been using... well, probably since the day of its founding. It smelled pure military. It smelled like home.

The entry led to a short corridor with doors on either side. A woman stuck her head out of one of the rooms; dark hair, dark eyes. Mid-thirties, maybe. Serious. She didn't say anything, but her chin dropped and her eyebrows went up, and Lincoln got the distinct feeling that he needed to explain himself and quickly.

"I'm Captain Lincoln Suh," he said. "Lieutenant Kennedy sent me over?" He made it a question, even though he didn't mean to. Something about the look in the woman's eyes drew it out that way.

She stared at him for a moment longer than was comfortable, and then disappeared back into her room without a word. Lincoln stood there in the entry waiting for some further development. He was just reaching for his pad to make sure he had the right building when the woman reappeared, walking towards him and wiping her hands on her pants.

"Sir," she said with a quick salute. Lincoln returned it. "Mind if I check your creds?"

"Not at all," Lincoln said. He reached under his left sleeve and swiped a fingertip across the dermal pad on his forearm and then used a quick series of hand gestures to call up the necessary details and transmit them to the woman. Her eyes went unfocused briefly as she reviewed them on the holographic display only she could see. A moment later she nodded and extended her hand.

"Sergeant Wright," she said. Lincoln shook her hand. Her grip was strong, but Lincoln could tell it could get a lot stronger. "Probably want to wash up after that. I was in the middle of cleaning my weapon systems."

"Good to meet you, sergeant," he said. "And a little elbow grease never hurt anyone."

"Never an enlisted, anyway," she said without missing a beat.

"Truth is," Lincoln said, leaning forward slightly with a

quick wink, "it's good for my nails."

Sergeant Wright's expression didn't change at all, not even in that polite way people sometimes used at least to acknowledge that you'd made a joke. She was dressed in her standard issue pants and a tan T-shirt, but there were no markings or insignia anywhere on her person. She had a hard look, though; sharp eyes, an aura of intensity that spoke of many years of service. And Lincoln knew from the way she held herself that she was undoubtedly a combat vet.

"You're not *just* a sergeant though, certainly," Lincoln continued. "EC-7?"

"Eight, actually, sir."

"First Sergeant Wright, then?"

"Master sergeant, sir. But yeah. We're not real big on the formalities around here though."

"Sounds like my kind of place," Lincoln said with a smile.

"Well don't get too comfortable just yet," Wright said. She let it hang for a moment without elaboration. It wasn't rude, but she was clearly establishing boundaries. A moment later, she simply said, "You can walk with me, I'll give you a quick look around."

"Yes, ma'am," Lincoln said, and then nudged his gear with his foot. "What do I do about this?"

She turned and started back down the hall, talking to him over her shoulder as she went. "You can leave it. It won't wander, and we don't get a lot of visitors through here."

Lincoln followed along behind Master Sergeant Wright with light steps, tried to keep a respectful distance. He didn't know anything about Wright yet, but he had no doubt that she'd been one of the colonel's original team members. It showed in the way she carried herself, in the professional way she treated him that extended only as far as military etiquette required. This was by far her team more than his, no matter what the ranks said. Nothing he'd done before mattered now. He'd been the new guy enough times, the officer getting added in to well-knit teams, to know how it worked. He'd be starting over, again, proving himself, again. But for the first time in years, Lincoln found he couldn't quite feel certain that he'd be able to do it here.

"So," she said, holding her arms out to either side. "This is the place."

There wasn't much to distinguish those first front rooms from most of the other facilities Lincoln had been assigned to over his career. A little smaller, maybe. As they passed the room Wright had initially stuck her head out of, he saw a wide table laden with hardware, arranged in tidy piles and neat rows. From the quick scan, he recognized parts to at least four separate weapons platforms, though they were all stripped down to their barest components. Tools, cleaning solvent, and bottles of gun oil lined one long edge of the table. A single chair sat at a crooked angle.

"Looks like a pretty thorough cleaning," Lincoln said, nodding back towards the room after they'd passed it.

"I like to be sure," Wright replied. She paused at a T-intersection where the front hall transitioned to the rest of the building, and pointed to the left. "Business," she said, then pointed to the right, "Everything else. You been down to the shop to get fitted yet?"

"Uh, no," Lincoln said. "I didn't know I was supposed to."

"You *are* armor-rated, though?"

"Yeah, just been a while since I had to run it live. And I never did get to run the big assault stuff."

She nodded. "All right," she said, and then shook her head slightly. "You really are hot off the press, huh?"

"Yes, ma'am. Colonel Almeida plucked me out of the fire yesterday, Kennedy threw me in the pan this morning."

"Didn't brief you much?"

Lincoln shook his head. "I'm a little behind on my reading." Lieutenant Kennedy had prepped a data package for his review; a couple of weeks' worth of study on the Group's role and responsibilities, doctrine, and methodologies. She'd only handed it off about twenty minutes before sending him to the team's facility.

"I'll let you meet the team, then we'll see if we can get you squared away with all the big ticket items."

Wright tipped her head and led Lincoln away from the "business" wing, towards the "everything else".

"Back there's where we do most of our briefings, draw up plans, all the boring stuff," she said as she walked. "Down this way's where we spend most of our time though. We operate on big boy rules around here, sir. Unless of course you plan on changing that."

She glanced back at him briefly, just long enough for him to shake his head, but not long enough for her to see the response. She continued, "Keep yourself and your kit mission ready at all times, and don't wander off too far. We have to be able to go from zero to a hundred and twenty in about five seconds. I assume if you needed somebody watching over you all the time telling you what to do, you wouldn't be here."

"I'll try to keep up," Lincoln said. "Or at least not get in the way."

Wright gave him a cursory tour of the nonessential places: kitchen, lockers, crash rooms for grabbing a couple of hours of sleep when the team was on call. Nothing fancy, and all the rooms felt like they were three-quarters the size they were meant to be, but the layout and amenities confirmed what Lincoln had already suspected. Everything was set up to keep the team close at hand, and to minimize the need for wandering over to other facilities.

"You at least get your housing sorted out yet?" Wright asked.

"Lieutenant Kennedy's working on it," Lincoln said. "Haven't had a lot of time to check it out for myself yet."

"Might want to get used to that," she said. She took him to the far end of the hall and paused at the door. "Apart from the range and the kill house, this is probably where we spend most of our time." She opened the door and revealed the largest room Lincoln had yet seen. The gym.

Like everything else he'd seen so far, there wasn't a lot of fluff. The room was spartan in its furnishing; bare walls, bare lights hanging from the ceiling, a lot of weights. The only real standout feature was the large mat that dominated the far side of the room, on which two individuals were apparently in the process of trying to murder one another with their bare hands.

"Should we do something about that?" Lincoln asked, gesturing at the two.

"Nah, not yet," Wright answered, and she motioned towards a man who was in the middle of benchpressing what appeared to be about a hundred and fifty kilos.

"That's Sergeant Mike Pence," Wright said. "Probably the nicest guy you'll ever meet who can kill you from two klicks out."

Even though the guy was lying down, Lincoln could tell he was tall; six three, maybe six four. He was obviously fit, but had a rangy look, like he'd originally been a couple of inches shorter and had gotten stretched out. Certainly he didn't look massive enough to be pushing the stack of weights he had loaded on either side of the bar. But the weight was going up and down nevertheless. Wright stood patiently by the door. After six more reps, the last one of which Lincoln wasn't sure Sergeant Pence was going to complete, the man finished his set, re-racked the bar, and then lay with his hands over his face, breathing deep. Wright took a few steps towards him.

"Hey, Pence," Wright called. And then again, booming, "Pence!"

Sergeant Pence reacted to the second call, glanced over at them and then removed a bud from his ear. Music blared out of the headphone; sharp, dark, angry tones. He tilted his head back.

"Mas'sarnt?" he said, slurring Master Sergeant Wright's rank into a single syllable. "What's the news?"

"Mom sent us a care package," she said. Pence rolled up off the bench and walked over. As he approached, he flicked his gaze at Lincoln for a brief moment, looked at Lincoln's eyes, down to his feet, back to his eyes, and then back at Wright. He didn't seem particularly impressed.

"Yeah? Anything good?"

Wright tilted her head Lincoln's direction. "New brains, gifted to us from on high."

"Oh," Pence said. He saluted with a lazy fluidity. "Sir." Lincoln returned the salute and then extended his hand.

"Lincoln Suh," he said.

"Mike," Pence replied. "You the new shot-caller?" He had a bare hint of rural twang to his vowels, but Lincoln couldn't place it.

"I don't know about that," Lincoln replied. "Colonel Almeida told me a bunch of pretty stories to get me here. That's about as far as we've figured things out."

"Yeah, sounds about right," he said.

"You're throwing up some pretty hefty stacks over there, sergeant."

Mike glanced over his shoulder at the barbell, sagging under the load. "Well, you know what they say. If you can't be smart, you better be strong." He flashed a smile, and then said to Wright, "You're not gonna make me watch him, are ya, mas'sarnt?"

"Nah," Wright replied. "I'd never ask you to do two things at once, Mikey."

"It's called focus, hon," he said, flashing a grin. "You going to interrupt the grudge match over there?"

Wright glanced over at the mat. "I'll give it a couple."

The three of them walked over together to watch the tangle of fury on the mat. Both the men were wearing padded gloves, but that was the only protection Lincoln could see.

One of the combatants was lean-muscled and dark-skinned, wearing a sleeveless compression shirt; his bare arms were covered from wrist to shoulder in tattoos. The other was harder to see, since he was underneath the first guy. The two were clinched in a tight knot; the tattooed fellow was astride the other man's torso, but his head was caught in a hold that kept it pinned to the other's shoulder. That didn't stop him from trying to land punishing blows from whatever constantly shifting angle he could find.

For a minute or so, Wright, Pence, and Lincoln just stood by, watching. The guy on the bottom managed to intercept most of the strikes with his upper arms and shoulders, but after one particularly frenetic exchange, a blow snuck in with a meaty *thwack* and caught him on the cheekbone.

"Oop," Pence said. "That'll do it." He said it with a neutral tone. Lincoln couldn't tell whether he meant it was time to step in, or what. A moment later, he understood.

There was no way to tell exactly what the guy on the bottom did, but he whipped his arms down and in, and in the next second it looked for all the world like gravity had just briefly reversed for the man on top of him. He flew upwards, two, maybe three feet in the air, spinning off to one side. The big guy was up on his feet before the first one had hit the ground, and looked like he was about to absolutely demolish the other.

"Sergeant Nakarmi!" Wright called out, and the big man froze. When he turned around, Lincoln was astonished.

"Cadre," Lincoln said. Sergeant Nakarmi stood up a little straighter, gave his half smile. Sergeant Sahil Nakarmi. Cadre Sahil.

"Hey OneSev," Sahil said, snapping off a crisp salute. "It's just sergeant to you now. Told ya I'd be saluting you the next time I saw you."

"For show," Lincoln said, returning the gesture and feeling awkward about it. Sahil had just spent fourteen weeks telling

Lincoln when to jump and how high. Lincoln didn't see how he was ever going to be able to give the man an order. "What are you doing here?"

Sahil touched his cheekbone. "Gettin' beat up by a girl, sir."

His opponent regained his feet, and Lincoln saw now, sure enough, he was a she. She was broad-shouldered and tall, maybe six inches taller than Sahil, which put her around five feet nine or so. Her hair was cropped short and her eyes were fierce brown flecked with gold, and they hadn't yet lost their fire from the battle. Still breathing hard, she backhanded Sahil's arm as she drew up next to him.

"I told you not to go easy," she said.

"Not sure which part of that was easy," he answered.

"Yeah, well, I thought I was doing all right until you threw me like a child."

"Hey now, that ain't fair," Sahil said, "I ain't never thrown a child in my life." The woman made a face at him and then finally turned to address Wright.

"Master Sergeant," she said by way of greeting. "Who's this pretty kitty?"

"The new boss, Thump," Wright answered. "If you ask nice, I'll let you pet him."

A brief wave of surprise swept over the woman's features before her face went professional an instant later. She popped to attention with a textbook salute.

"Sergeant First Class Avery Coleman, sir," she said.

"At ease, sergeant," Lincoln said, and then he glanced at Wright. "I thought we weren't real big on formalities around here."

"*We* aren't," Wright said without looking at him. She wasn't hostile about it, but she didn't leave any doubt whether she considered Lincoln part of that *we*, either.

Coleman relaxed into a more casual stance, and looked him up and down once.

"Huh," she said. "I thought your feet would be bigger."

Lincoln glanced down to look at his feet, puzzled. As he was looking back up, just before he asked what she was talking about, he made the connection and chuckled.

"Sergeant, if I were six feet taller and laid down lengthwise, I still wouldn't be able to fill Colonel Almeida's shoes. I'm not even going to try."

She gave a flash of a tight smile in response.

"And you," Lincoln said, looking at Sahil. "I don't think I'm going to be able to call you anything other than cadre, Sergeant Nakarmi."

"You'll work it out," Sahil answered.

"Did the colonel pull you out of Selection too?"

Sahil shook his head. "No sir, I been an Outrider for a while. Almost as long as this one," he said, gesturing at Wright.

Lincoln put it together. "So, probably not an accident you just happened to end up in the instructor corps when I was in there, then."

Sahil gave a little smile. "Mom takes recruiting pretty serious."

"Mom?" Lincoln asked. Wright had said something about Mom sending a care package earlier, but he'd thought she was just joking around.

"Yeah," Pence said. "That's what we all call the old man. Colonel Almeida. He loves it."

"I assume there's a story," Lincoln said.

"More'n a few," Sahil answered.

"If you ask the colonel," Coleman added, "he'll tell you it's because of his initials. Mateus Almeida. M.A., Ma, Mom."

"Sounds like a pretty tame way to earn a nickname for the army," Lincoln said. "Almost implausibly so."

Pence chuckled. "*Almost.*"

"All right, enough meet and greet," Wright said. "The captain needs to get by the shop to get suited."

"Oh," Lincoln said. "Is the rest of the team out on assignment?"

"The rest?" Wright asked. "Buddy, you're looking at the whole crew right here."

"It's just you four?"

"Just us four," she said. "And you to tag along, I guess."

"We've got support staff, of course," Coleman said. "But we have to share it with a couple of other units."

"It's more they have to share with us," Sahil added.

"Yeah, but I'm not sure *they* know that," Coleman replied.

"Well," Lincoln said. "The colonel wasn't kidding about a small team."

"Numbers like this don't typically rate someone of your caliber, huh?" Coleman said, deadpan. Lincoln couldn't tell if it was a joke or a challenge.

"Oh I'm sure you rate way better than me," Lincoln said. "The colonel probably figured on me mostly being smart enough to stay out of the way."

Coleman at least smiled at that.

"Hey, don't sweat it, captain," Pence said. "He pretty much expects each one of us to do the job of five, so I figure that makes us at least a platoon."

Wright held up a finger and dropped her gaze, and the rest of her team went instantly still. She swiped a finger across the dermal pad on her forearm.

"This is Wright," she said, communicating with someone absent. A moment later she added, "Yes sir, I'm on my way."

She closed the channel and addressed the people in the room with her. "Mom needs me at the PFAC. Captain Suh still needs to hit the shop and the lab."

"I'll take him around," Pence volunteered. "What's up?"

"Didn't say," Wright answered. "Probably ought to get your boots shined up, though."

"Roger that," Coleman said, and from the sudden shift in mood, Lincoln figured that meant an operations order was probably on its way. But surely they wouldn't deploy him so soon. Would they? Then again, given how he ended up here in the first place, he couldn't say it was out of the realm of possibility.

"Excuse me, captain," Wright said with a nonchalant salute. "I'm sure you'll be hearing from the colonel soon."

"Sure thing," Lincoln said. "Thank you, sergeant."

Wright nodded once and then turned and strode out of the gym.

"Same deal for us, cap'n," Sahil said. He tipped his head towards the door where Wright had just exited. "If she's movin' like that, we probably got work comin' down the pipe. We need to get squared away."

"Absolutely, cadre... sergeant," Lincoln said. "Take care of whatever you need to. Don't let me hold you up."

"Prolly easier if you just call me Sahil, sir."

"*That'd* probably be easier if you'd quit calling me sir, sergeant."

"Yessir," Sahil said to Lincoln with a smile, and then looked over at Pence. "We'll catch up with ya in a bit?"

"Yep," Pence answered.

"Sir," Coleman said, giving another textbook salute.

"Sergeant," Lincoln answered, returning the gesture. Coleman and Sahil returned to the mat to gather their belongings.

"Come on with me, captain," Pence said. "We'll see if we can get you set up before we roll out."

"You think we're going out?"

"I think we probably are," Pence nodded as he led Lincoln out of the gym. "Maybe not immediately. But I'd guess things are moving that way. I honestly don't know if Mom will let *you* out of the cage so soon, though. But let's not give him any reason to keep you back, yeah?"

"All right," Lincoln said.

Sergeant Pence led him out of the back of the facility. The 519th's building sat on the rear quadrant of the restricted area, so Lincoln had already passed by a good number of the other buildings when he'd ridden in. Even so, walking through the sprawl gave him a different sense of just how big the fenced-in area was. It was its own campus, a base within a base.

"Don't let the master sergeant hurt your feelings, sir," Pence said, as they walked. "She's like that with everybody."

"How's that?"

"You know, the sort of you-don't-belong icy vibe thing."

"Oh, it's no problem, sergeant," Lincoln said.

"You can call me Mike."

"Okay, Mike. I know how it is when a new guy shows up. It always changes the team dynamic."

"Yeah. Well she'll warm up to you eventually," Mike said. And then a moment later added, "Probably."

Lincoln smiled at that. "I get the impression she's the mama bear."

"Ehn, I dunno about that," said Mike. He glanced over at Lincoln. "Bears are a lot more approachable." Then he motioned towards a wide, arching grey building that looked more like a warehouse than anything else. "We're headed right there."

Mike led the way, buzzed in at the main door, and then held it open for Lincoln. A young corporal sat behind a low desk in the shallow entryway. Lincoln got the impression that everyone was supposed to check in with the corporal, but Mike just waved and walked past, and the corporal gave a nod like it was business as usual. Pence went through another door which led to a short hallway. When the door closed behind them, he stopped.

"Hopefully Kennedy's already given the fellas a heads up. This isn't the sort of thing you want to spring on an armorer unannounced."

"I don't even know what exactly I'm here to get, Mike."

"Oh," Mike said, with genuine surprise. "Sorry, I assumed you'd been briefed and all."

"Everything's been moving pretty fast."

"Yeah, wow, I guess so. Well, you're in for a real treat then. Maybe I won't spoil the surprise just yet. But man, it's probably a pretty safe bet that the paperwork hasn't come through." He glanced down the hall towards one of the doors, and then back at Lincoln. "No doubt you could get things moving if you pull rank in here, but these people you want as your friends. You want them thinking of you lovingly every time they touch any piece of your kit, with stars in their eyes, yeah?"

"These are our supply guys?"

Mike nodded. "Custom shop, though. Everything we get our hands on comes through these people first, and I don't think they've ever let so much as a tin cup out of this building without some sort of modification. And even the cup would probably get grip work and some polish."

They moved down the hall to a room. The door was open, but Mike knocked on the doorframe anyway.

"Hey, chief, you in?"

"Yeah," a voice boomed from inside. "That you, One-time?"

"You know it."

There was a sigh, a creak, and the shuffle of someone standing, and a moment later a stout man with carpenter's hands appeared. "Ain't ruined enough of my days yet?"

Mike feigned shock and hurt. "I can't just drop by to say hi?"

"You *could*, but you only ever show up when you need somethin'," the chief said.

"Well today's your lucky day, chief. I don't need a thing."

The chief didn't buy it. "Yeah?"

"My buddy here, on the other hand…" Mike said, tilting his head towards Lincoln.

"Yeah," the chief said, shaking his head. He sized Lincoln up.

"He needs a workup. Expedited, big time."

"Oh?" the chief said. "First I'm hearing about it. You got a req?"

"I'm sure Kennedy sent one over."

"Sure enough to show it to me?"

Mike smiled. The chief nodded and looked suddenly weary.

"But you don't have to wait for one," Mike said. "Not for me, right?"

The chief sighed with the weight of a man who got asked to move at least one mountain every single day. "You're killin' me, Pence."

"I know, chief. But you love me for it. Who else keeps you on your toes around here?"

"You gonna give up one of yours?"

"If I have to, yeah. I'm not yanking your chain here. We've probably got an hour before the order comes in. You don't want my newest team leader to go out there in one of those hand-me-down e-suits do you? Mom would have you busted back to boot for it."

The chief looked over at Lincoln. "Newest *technician*, huh?"

Lincoln nodded and extended his hand. "Lincoln Suh."

"Chief Guiterrez," the chief said. He shook Lincoln's hand and left little doubt that he could crush it like an egg if he wanted to. "Normally I'd tell you to get in line, but if you gotta be in charge of this joker, your day's already a lot worse than mine."

"I appreciate it, chief," Lincoln said.

"Yeah, well come on back, and we'll see what we've got laying around," Guiterrez answered, and pushed his way past Mike and headed further down the hall. "I can't release anything to you until that req comes through, but I can probably get a jumpstart on it. Not promising anything, though."

Mike nudged Lincoln and leaned close. "Chief's an under-promise, over-deliver kind of guy."

Guiterrez led the two deeper into the structure. Exiting the hall, they walked into what looked like an aircraft hangar; expansive floor, no wall, high ceiling. A number of workstations spread throughout the space, and, at every station, someone was working on some piece of gear.

"I don't think I've ever seen this much hardware in one place before," Lincoln said.

"All this is just the standard stuff," Mike said. "All the cool toys are in the back."

The trio continued through the open space to another door, where Guiterrez paused to let the system verify his clearance. The door clicked and slid open, revealing a smaller workshop. It was bright and clean, with well-organized steel racks throughout. If it hadn't been for all the tools and instruments neatly lining the walls, Lincoln would have been more likely to guess it was a sterile lab than a machinist's shop. A man and a woman were huddled over their own workbenches. The woman looked up when the three entered, got a nod from the chief and went back to her work. The man was too intent on the rifle on his bench to take any notice of the visitors.

The back of the room was dominated by a massive black container of some heavy metal, like a giant vault. Large double doors stood guard in the center.

Guiterrez motioned to a low steel platform in the back corner of the room while he headed towards the vault.

"Take off your jacket and go on and hop up there," he said to Lincoln. Lincoln did as he was told, and stepped up onto the round stand. Guiterrez swung open one of the vault doors and disappeared inside. After a couple of minutes, Lincoln started to wonder if the chief was planning on coming out again. Mike, who was leaning back on a nearby table, seemed to read his mind and held up a hand in a reassuring gesture. When Guiterrez did return, he was carrying an armful of... well, they looked like prosthetic arms. Forearms, really, complete with hands, as if he'd just lopped a few off at the elbow. They were all a dull, gunmetal grey. The chief dumped them unceremoniously in a pile on a table near Lincoln and then moved to a console by the platform.

"Hold your arms out to the side, feet shoulder-width apart," Guiterrez directed. "Like you're gettin' a pat down."

Lincoln complied.

"Right, hold still," the chief said. He fiddled with something on the console, which chirped once, then again a second or two later. "'Kay you can hop down."

"That's it?" Lincoln asked.

"That's it," Guiterrez said, already moving back to the table where he'd piled the arms. He spread them out, evaluated a couple, set three aside, and then walked over and held a pair of them out to Lincoln. He lifted one up, a right-handed one. "I think this here is about right, but try 'em both."

Lincoln didn't see what the chief did exactly, but the metallic arm whirred quietly and folded open lengthwise, down the center of the underside of the forearm while the hand portion remained intact, like a glove. A moment before it had looked like a single solid piece, and for the first time Lincoln realized he was looking not at a prosthetic arm, but at a component of armor. He'd never seen anything like it before, so sleek and natural it easily could have passed for flesh with the right paint job. The interior was smooth and padded with some kind of material Lincoln didn't recognize. The chief held the gauntlet steady while Lincoln slipped his arm into it. Once his hand was secure in the glove, Chief Guiterrez reactivated it and the forearm section closed around Lincoln's arm with the same quiet whir and click. As before, once the gauntlet was closed, it looked to Lincoln's eyes like a single, unbroken piece of armor, with no crack or seam.

"How's that feel?" Guiterrez asked. He was busy poking and prodding, checking the fit at Lincoln's elbow, tweaking values at the console, like some combination of tailor and mechanic. "Any play around the arm?"

Lincoln rotated his arm, rolled his wrist, wiggled and flexed his fingers. Every motion felt natural, unrestrained.

"It feels good, chief," he said.

"How's contact with your fingertips?" the Chief asked, and then said, "Do this." He held up his hand and touched each fingertip to his thumb in succession, pointer to pinky and back again. Lincoln mimicked the gesture and felt each touch with surprising sensitivity. The sensations were muted by the armor, certainly, but he didn't feel nearly as clumsy as he would have imagined. With a little practice, Lincoln thought he might actually be able to play his violin in these things.

"That's incredible," he said. The chief grunted and opened the other gauntlet he was holding. He helped Lincoln put it on his left arm.

"It'll feel a little numb until we get it synced up," Guiterrez said. "How about that one?"

The second gauntlet closed around Lincoln's left arm, and he tested that one with a similar series of movements. He opened and clenched both fists a few times, pressed the fingertips of both hands together.

"Yeah, it's good," Lincoln said. "They both feel great." Guiterrez shook his head, like Lincoln had given the wrong answer.

"No, no, no," the chief said, waving a hand. "They shouldn't *both* feel great. One's a better fit. Tell me which."

Pence chimed in, "'Good enough' ain't good enough for chief. The man's an artist."

Guiterrez ignored the comment, just stood there watching Lincoln intently. Lincoln gave it another shot, trying to focus intently on the sensations in his hands and wrist. Sure enough, when he really paid attention he could feel just a tiny bit of play around his left wrist, a slight delay in response when he rotated his hand back and forth slowly. He mirrored the motion with his right arm, but couldn't recreate the same sensation.

"The right one's better," he said. "Feels like a little gap around my left wrist, maybe."

"I figured," Guiterrez said, nodding as he reached out and removed the gauntlets. "You got skinny wrists."

He took the gauntlets back to the table with the other and then returned to the console. After a couple of minutes of tapping, a deep droning sound came from within the vault.

"Here comes the fun part," Mike said, flashing a smile at Lincoln.

A moment later, a large metal crate emerged from the vault and automatically navigated over to the chief on its multiwheeled base. The crate was about eight feet tall and maybe four feet wide and deep. It trundled to a halt in front of Guiterrez.

"That's not one of mine, is it?" Mike asked as the chief went to open the crate.

"Nah, I'd have to chop one of yours up and stitch it all back together," Guiterrez said. "This is one of Colonel Almeida's old ones."

Mike whistled and looked over at Lincoln. "Talk about filling big shoes. You're jumping right in, my man."

Lincoln was about to comment, but his words stopped short when the front of the crate swung open and revealed its contents. A full suit of powered armor. But like none he'd ever seen before. Typically, armor was bulky and ponderous, all angles and thick plating like heavy construction machinery. Even the scout configurations he'd trained in before seemed to have been patterned after light armored vehicles. The one that hung before him now was more like a racing motorcycle. Sleek, elegant. But powerful, like a lion at rest.

"In case you were wondering why our quarters are so ugly," Mike said, "it's because that right there is where we spend all our budget."

"What is it?" Lincoln asked, lamely. For the first time, Guiterrez smiled.

"That's fifth-gen recon armor," the chief said. Army Special Forces had a few suits of third-gen, which is what Lincoln had gotten most of his training with. He hadn't even known there was a fourth generation. The Marines were still mostly running first-generation assault suits.

"*Recon*, you understand," Guiterrez added. "You try assaulting any hills or storming any buildings in one of my babies, and I won't patch a single hole until you're out of the unit."

"Come on, chief," Mike said. "Who would ever be dumb or desperate enough to deploy a bunch of technicians into something like that?"

Guiterrez gave Pence a look that said he knew precisely who would be that dumb or desperate. Mike just smiled. The chief pressed a button inside the crate, and the rack that the armor was on extended. He waved Lincoln over.

"This one's gonna need a lot of work," he said, "but lemme check the fit and make sure it's at least a place to start."

Lincoln moved to the crate and spent the next half hour or so suiting up, with the chief's help. The armor was so well and intuitively designed he felt confident that, under normal circumstances, he could have donned the full suit in under ten minutes. Maybe five, with practice. But under the chief's watchful eye, everything took three times as long; always there were questions asked, adjustments made, notes taken. In every way, it felt like getting measured for a finely tailored suit. Lincoln learned quickly enough to find *something* that didn't feel quite right about the most recently added piece, because Guiterrez wouldn't believe him otherwise. The toes pinched a little, or the waist felt loose, or there was a catch in the shoulder joint.

But in reality, Lincoln was astonished at how natural it all felt. He hadn't operated extensively in armor, but he remembered well enough the weight of movement in it, the slight resistance it added to every motion, the small but perceptible disconnect between man and machine. But this... even wearing a suit that had been custom tailored for someone else, movement was effortless.

The final component to try was the helmet which, like the other sections, seemed to be all of one piece. Before the chief handed it to Lincoln, he activated something from the console and the grey metal faceplate separated in the middle, its halves sliding into housings hidden on either side, revealing a clear visor underneath. Guiterrez tapped the visor.

"This here's only rated for small arms, so in the field you keep buttoned up at all times," he said. "I'm just popping it for you now so you can see, until we get synced up with your net."

"Understood," Lincoln said. He slipped the helmet on with ease, and fitted it into the neck piece. The base of the helmet automatically compressed slightly, connecting with the suit and muting the outside world as the hermetic seal completed. For a few seconds, Lincoln could hear nothing but his own breathing. A soothing hum passed through the helmet, and the barrier between Lincoln and the outside world all but vanished. Once again, he was amazed at the suit and the sense of presence he maintained with the environment. Even with all the very expensive components that went into armor, his previous experiences with it had always left him feeling isolated from his surroundings. Many of his former teammates had complained that the helmets interfered too much with situational awareness and some of them had even gone so far as to operate without their helmets whenever the mission environment allowed. But in the fifth-generation gear, Lincoln could even hear subtle clicks and taps of the man working on the rifle at the bench across the room.

Lincoln nodded, then shook his head, and felt the helmet shift and slide with the movement. It was the first piece that felt too big.

"It's too big," Lincoln said.

"Looks like it's too big," Guiterrez said, a moment later. "Figures. Colonel's got a melon head."

"Mine's on the small side," Lincoln said. "Goes with the skinny wrists."

Guiterrez didn't respond, but Mike gestured at Lincoln.

"He's talking to you, chief," Mike said.

Guiterrez glanced at Mike, and then back at Lincoln. He held up a finger, fiddled with something on his console, and then said "Say again?"

"I just said I have a small head," Lincoln said, and this time he heard his voice both inside the helmet and in the room, with a thinner, processed timbre. He'd forgotten that they wouldn't be able to hear him through the helmet.

"It's all right, I got your measurements, I'll find somethin' that works," the chief said. "I'm gonna bring her online so you can check the layout." He tapped out a series of commands on his console, and a subdued heads-up display appeared on the interior of Lincoln's visor. "Everything's gonna feel a little sluggish until we get her set up on your wetwork, eye-tracking included, but take her for a walk around the room and see what you think."

"All right," Lincoln said. He took a slow tour of the workshop, putting the suit through a full complement of movements; side-stepping, walking backwards, moving in a crouch. He even got down on his belly and did a few pushups. The other man in the room continued to studiously ignore everything else that was going on, but the woman turned around on her stool and watched with a bemused expression as he put the suit through its paces. Lincoln went to the workshop entrance, then turned back and raised his hands into the position he used when miming a weapon at his shoulder.

"Uh oh," Mike said. "I think he's about to kill us all."

"Not all," Lincoln said, and he moved through the workshop at half speed, as though clearing it of hostiles in slow motion. This part his body did automatically, years of real-world experience driving the sequence; Mike was the first target, then Guiterrez, then the man with his back to the door. When Lincoln swiveled around to the woman, he swung his hands down in a smooth arc, careful not to point his imaginary weapon at her. He finished scanning the room, and then swept back around the other direction to re-evaluate the scene. As he brought his "weapon" down again to avoid endangering the woman, she smiled at him. And as soon he'd passed her by, she mimed drawing a pistol from under her stool and fired.

"Gotcha," she said, and then she turned back to her work.

Mike laughed. "No offense, but you oughta know better, sir."

Lincoln shrugged. "*Somebody* had to be the precious cargo. I probably should have saved the chief though, huh?"

"Sure seems like I'd deserve it," Guiterrez said. "But it's more than I'd expect. How's it feel?"

Lincoln walked back over to the part of the workshop they'd been using as a staging area. "I see what you mean about feeling sluggish," he said, mostly to appease the chief. "It's not much, but it's there. But yeah, for being straight off the shelf, I'd say it's feeling pretty good. I'm looking forward to running it after you work your magic."

"How long you reckon that'll be, chief?" Mike asked.

Guiterrez puffed out his cheeks, and shook his head.

"All the tailoring, need to flush the colonel's protocols, pull in your historicals, do a full refresh and restore... I'd say four days, maybe."

"Make it two and I'll love you forever," said Mike.

"That sounds like a threat, sergeant," Guiterrez replied as he reached up to help Lincoln remove his helmet. "You're not the only one who needs work done, you know. But I'll see what I can do, if it keeps me from havin' to see you every day."

Lincoln nodded, "I appreciate it, chief. Thanks for looking after us."

Guiterrez dismissed the comment with a wave of his hand, dropped the helmet off at an empty workbench, and returned to help Lincoln remove the rest of the suit. As he did, he rattled through the various features Lincoln could look forward to enjoying once the hardware was actually his in an unbroken stream.

"So, fifth gen has all your usual stuff you get with any suit, just better. The optics package is really nice, got a lot of the kinks worked out since third. Still composites from all detectable spectra, but the new visor does a whole lot better of a job translating it into something readable. Not all those crazy color schemes like the old ones. Reactive camo's basically the same as old suits. Runs a little lighter, maybe, so not quite as much of a draw on your power. Still can't run it all the time, though, so you got to be smart about using it when you need it and not when you don't. Maybe we'll get that figured out by sixth. Zero-G maneuvering thrusters, those haven't changed since second-gen, except for some streamlining. Operates the same though, same input, same output, so you shouldn't need much practice to get the hang of it. It's not nearly like the jump between first and second," he chuckled and shook his head. "Had a lot of hotshots busting their arms and heads with that, thinking they knew how to fly and then finding out pretty quick they didn't know everything. Anyway, commo's improved quite a bit, sensor suite's better. All in all, I'm pretty proud of this little bit of work."

"That all sounds great, chief," Lincoln said when the man finally took a breath. "Can't wait to run it live."

"Just don't run it into the ground," Guiterrez answered. "One of these things costs more than even one of *you*."

He put curious emphasis on the word, but didn't add anything more. The chief was quite a bit less meticulous taking the parts off than he had been putting them on; it only took about five minutes to get Lincoln out. As Lincoln was removing his last boot, Mike stood up straighter and sidled his way towards the door.

"Thanks a bunch, chief," he said. "I gotta get this guy over to the lab, so we'll leave you to it."

"Gettin' the full workup today, huh?" the chief said, slinging the boots in the pile and grabbing the helmet.

"Yeah," Lincoln answered. "They threw me in the deep end, and I guess I'm pulling a lot of people in after me. Sorry to swoop in here and–"

"Get on out of here," the chief said, interrupting. He was already at his workbench, hooking the suit's helmet up to some device. "Both of ya. I'm up to my eyebrows in it already without you two hanging around to give me advice."

"Roger that," said Mike. "See ya soon, chief."

"Thanks, chief," Lincoln said, and received a grunt in reply.

Pence led the way out, back through the main shop floor.

"Chief said four days," Mike said, as they walked. "Probably means you'll have it by midnight."

"I've used some pretty high-speed gear in the past," said Lincoln, "but... brother, I think I might be in love."

Mike chuckled. "Guess we better not leave you alone with it, huh?"

"I can restrain myself, sergeant. It's just hard to believe that it's going to be mine."

"Oh it's not *yours*, captain, make no mistake about that. Every one of those suits belongs to the chief, and he'll remind you every chance he gets," Mike said, as they exited the building and headed towards another facility that Lincoln assumed was the lab. "Though the lab rats probably take issue with that particular perspective."

"Yeah? What's their claim?"

"You know, with the Process and all," Mike said. Lincoln shook his head. Mike's eyebrows went up again, with the look that said Lincoln was in for another surprise.

"I maybe signed up a little too fast," Lincoln said.

"Yeah..." Mike said. "You signed a whole bunch of documents, though, right? Got death-proofed and everything?"

"Yeah, but that was for uh... back when I was applying for a different unit. Does that count?"

"A *different* unit?" said Mike, confused. "There's only one other army unit I know of that gets to..."

Sergeant Pence trailed off, and looked at Lincoln with a new light in his eyes. But Lincoln shook his head.

"I was non-select," he said. He knew better than to let even a hint of the rumor get started that he'd made the unit.

"Oh," Pence said. "Still though, you qualified. That's pretty impressive... Wait, is that where Sahil's been this whole time?"

Lincoln nodded. "You didn't know?"

Mike shook his head. "Knew he was on assignment as a trainer. Nobody said where, though." Lincoln was surprised that a team that small wouldn't know every detail about everyone else. But he was also a little relieved to learn he apparently wasn't the only one in the place that didn't seem to be getting the full story. "Doesn't happen a lot," Mike added, "but it does happen. Thumper gets called off to parts unknown more than the rest of us."

"Thumper?"

"Yeah, Avery. Sergeant Coleman. Our tech."

"Gotcha," Lincoln said. "But the Process... it's the same sort of deal, right, like death-proofing? Eggheads keeping your consciousness on ice while they patch your body back up?"

"Uh... mostly, yeah, something like that," Mike said, but his expression was strange. "Look, uh... somebody a lot smarter than me probably ought to be the one to talk you through all of this, but I figure the labcoats are gonna think you already know all about it. And you know how they are. They act like it's the most natural thing in the world. All about the science of it, no clue about the human side. Anyway. This place isn't nearly as fun as the shop, so keep your business face on. And feel free to pull rank any time you think it'll help."

Mike led him into the facility, and if the welcome at the shop had been all familiar warmth, the response in the lab was the exact opposite. Two security officers stood just inside the entrance, and they immediately closed in and blocked any further progress into the building. Even after an exchange of credentials and a thorough scan, the guards didn't seem entirely convinced that either Mike or Lincoln should be there.

By the time they'd walked through the two sets of controlled-access double doors, there was already a young man waiting for them in the hallway. Lincoln was disappointed to see the man wasn't actually wearing a labcoat.

"This way," the man said, and he walked briskly down the corridor, obviously expecting them to follow.

The man led them to a small office, and he took a seat behind a desk, brought up a screen on the embedded display. There were two chairs in front of the desk, but Mike remained standing, so Lincoln followed his lead. On the desk was a name plate reading Major Thomas Blackwell. The guy behind the desk seemed awfully young to be a major. And Lincoln wasn't even going to be able to pull rank.

"Which one of you is Lincoln Suh?" the presumed Major Blackwell asked, looking up at them. Lincoln and Mike exchanged a glance, and Mike suppressed a smile.

"I am, sir," Lincoln said with all possible professionalism.

"Right, OK," Blackwell said. He punched up some data on the display. "Authorization already came through…" He paused and looked at Mike, then back at Lincoln. "Do you have any privacy concerns with this gentleman being in here?"

"No, sir," Lincoln said.

Major Blackwell looked back at his display and continued.

"All the background's done, we have your files in order, and the numbers from the tolerance test all look solid. We just need your final consent for replica transfer in case of catastrophic death. Obviously there are some special legal concerns we have to be clear about. You know how lawyers are."

The phrase "catastrophic death" sounded both patently absurd and vaguely horrifying. Blackwell sent a document over to Lincoln's pad; Lincoln activated it, skimmed through the complex language. He'd already signed over so much of himself, he didn't feel the need to give it a close read.

"Replica transfer?" Lincoln said, as he signed the document and sent it back to Blackwell's terminal. "That's the official term?"

"Yes, of course," Blackwell said impatiently.

"Doc, I don't think my man here's been through the full briefing yet," Mike said cautiously.

"*Major*," Blackwell corrected, and then added to Lincoln, "You've gone through the Dire Medical Intervention Familiarization Course, though, yes?"

"Uh," Lincoln said. "That one doesn't sound familiar, sir."

"You should have gone through the Dire Medical Intervention Familiarization Course," Blackwell said. "Before we get to this stage, everyone's supposed to go through the Dire Medical Intervention Familiarization Course."

Mike apparently couldn't help himself. "I'm sorry, sir," he said, "I didn't catch the name of that course."

"The Dire Medi..." Blackwell answered, clearly agitated. He caught himself and made a face when he realized Mike was giving him a hard time, and then looked down at his display. "According to this, engineering started on your first replica weeks ago. It's already done. They're working on your second now. You really should have been through the Di... through the course before now."

This time when the doctor said *replica*, Lincoln felt a tingling sensation at the base of his skull, as if he was about to hear some very bad news.

"I'm sorry," Lincoln said. "What do you mean by replica, exactly?"

"Your auxiliary," Blackwell said. "Your personal reserve." And when Lincoln just continued to stare at him, he added with a more condescending tone. "Your backup body?"

Lincoln mind twisted as something he'd never imagined became sudden reality.

"You mean... what," he said. "Like... like a clone?"

"No!" said Blackwell, way too defensively, and Mike made a face like he'd meant to warn Lincoln not to use that word. "No, a *replica*! They are called *replicas*. They aren't *clones*."

Lincoln stepped closer to the desk and lowered himself into one of the chairs. Blackwell sighed heavily.

"Replica," the major said, regaining his composure. "The official term is replica. They aren't clones because they've never been alive, and could never be alive. It's just a body, until you inhabit it. And only *you – only* you – can inhabit your own. Nano keeps the physiology as current as possible and... well, they explain all of this in the Dire Medical Intervention Familiarization course."

Lincoln didn't have a response. His brain didn't want to process what he was hearing. And for the first time, Blackwell actually showed some measure of concern.

"Look," he said, standing. "I'll give you a couple of minutes." He waved a hand at Mike. "Maybe you can uh...." He waved his hand at Mike again. And then he walked out of the office and closed the door behind him.

Mike sat down next to Lincoln. They were silent for a few moments.

"Sorry, brother," Mike said finally. "I should have warned you not to say 'clone'."

"What," Lincoln said weakly, "and spoil the surprise?"

He ran a hand over his face. His mouth was dry, and he felt slightly faint.

"So," Mike said. "Yeah. The Process. So, in some cases, they can just patch you up. In most cases. Then it's like, you know, it's like you've just been asleep for a while or whatever. Like what you went through with death-proofing. But sometimes they don't just patch you up. Sometimes they can't. Damage is too severe, or sometimes something happens, and you can't get the body back. So we've all got a couple of backups."

"They've got... replicas of me? In storage?"

"Yeah. You can go see 'em if you want, but I wouldn't recommend it. It's pretty creepy."

"How do they do it?"

"Man, I got no idea. I never wanted ask too many questions. It's all your own DNA, of course. But outside of that..." Mike shrugged.

Lincoln shook his head. He tried to picture what it would be like, but the only image that sprang to mind came from a dream he'd had on a few occasions of attending his own funeral. That wasn't exactly comforting. The memory of the dream triggered another thought, and Lincoln fished around in his pocket, drew out the challenge coin that Almeida had given him, read the words again.

No Grave Too Deep.

He gave a humorless chuckle.

"I thought this was about there not being able a hole deep enough to bury a secret that you guys couldn't find it."

"Means that too," Mike said. "Works on levels, man. Levels."

Lincoln took a deep breath, held it a few seconds, and then let it all out in one strong exhale.

"Thing is," Mike added, "it doesn't always work. Labcoats will all tell you the failure rate is low, but you know... they're not the ones rolling the dice. And none of it..." He trailed off for a moment, looking for the words. "... It doesn't change what it's like to lose one of your own. Not as much as you might think. So don't go getting reckless. Nobody wants any of us to actually have to use these things. Not ever."

Lincoln nodded. There were still so many questions, but before he could ask any of them, he received a connection request through his internal channel. Colonel Almeida.

"One sec," he said. "Colonel's buzzing me." He tapped the dermal pad on his arm to open the line. "Captain Suh here."

"Captain," Almeida said through the channel. "I need you back at the PFAC."

"Yes, sir," Lincoln said. "We're at the lab now."

"Are you done?"

"Not sure, actually, sir."

"Well wrap it up and get over here. I need to bring you up to speed on a couple of things before we brief the team."

"Can you give me a preview?" Lincoln asked.

"Negative. Situation's developing. Be here now."

"Understood, I'm on my way."

Lincoln closed the channel.

"Sounds serious," Mike said.

"Yeah," Lincoln said, standing up. "Guess we better find the major."

He opened the door and Mike followed him out. Blackwell was standing in the corridor.

"I just got called in by my CO," Lincoln said. "You need anything else from me?"

"Technically, no," Blackwell said. "But you really should take that course."

"Yeah," Lincoln said. "I'll get right on that."

"Thanks, Doc," Mike said, flashing his smile. Blackwell scowled. Lincoln led the way down the hall and back outside.

Once they were out of the facility, Mike said, "If you want to talk through more of the details or whatever, maybe the colonel or Lieutenant Kennedy can give you a better briefing. But we should hustle back to the PFAC. Mom doesn't much like waiting."

"Yeah, I'm sure that's true," Lincoln said. He just managed

to stop himself from adding, *and that's about the only thing I'm sure of.*

They walked the rest of the way back in silence, and Lincoln's mind tumbled over itself as he tried to assimilate his new reality, to find a place for it to fit amongst the familiar pre-mission emotions. From the way Almeida had spoken to him, he knew work was coming, serious work that required his full focus and attention. And the more he turned his thoughts to the mission ahead, whatever it was, the less important seemed any of what he'd just learned at the lab. Maybe he was just rationalizing. He couldn't quite forget the idea of his replica, of course, but he was starting to convince himself that it was something he could think about later. Maybe even safely ignore. It was, after all, a contingency he planned never to need.

Still.

He shook his head as they neared the planning facility. Colonel Almeida had told him he would be making high-stakes decisions on partial data, and that he'd have to make the best of the consequences. When Lincoln had made his snap decision to join the Outriders, he hadn't quite realized just how much those consequences were already upon him.

SIX

Lincoln found Colonel Almeida in his office on the "business" side of the 519th's planning facility. With him was a grim-faced young woman in uniform, and the two of them were huddled over a display set in the colonel's desk. Lincoln knocked on the door frame.

"Captain Suh," Almeida said, glancing at him briefly and then motioning him into the office with a sharp gesture.

"Sir," Lincoln said.

"This is Lieutenant Davis," said the colonel, "from the 23rd Military Intelligence Brigade. Stephanie, this is my new team leader, Lincoln Suh."

"Good to meet to you, sir," Davis said.

"Lieutenant," Lincoln answered. "Stephanie Davis? You aren't by any chance related to Colonel Tim Davis, are you?"

"Tim's my dad, yes sir," she said cautiously, with a puzzled expression. "You know him?"

"A bit," Lincoln said. "He pulled my team out of some nasty business a few years back. A lot of mountains, a lot of gunfire. I seem to remember him having a picture of his little girl up front with him."

Davis gave a subdued smile, and nodded. "You've got a good memory for faces, then."

"Goes with the job," Lincoln said. "Your dad's an amazing

pilot. He's an even better man. Is he still with the 920th?"

"No sir, he retired last year."

"If you two are done..." Almeida said, all business. The intensity of his expression made him seem like a different man than the one Lincoln had ridden with the day before.

"Yes, sir," Lincoln said.

"Lieutenant, give us a minute," the colonel said.

"Yes, sir," Davis said. She slipped out into the hall and closed the door behind her.

"Davis and I are going to brief the team here in a minute," the colonel continued, once she was gone. "Normally, I'd want you up front running the show, but things are moving too fast right now. We've got to get rolling. Don't take this as any indication of my faith in you. I have every confidence in your abilities to lead my kids."

"Understood, sir," Lincoln said.

"I knew when I recruited you that I was throwing you into the fire," Almeida said. "I just didn't expect it to be quite so soon, or to be burning this hot. I was hoping to give you a couple of weeks to run with the team, to get to know them and how they operate. I'm afraid you're going to have to do all of that live."

"Are we deploying?"

"We're on standby. Decision hasn't been made officially yet, but I'd expect it soon."

Lincoln felt his gut twist with a strange mix of emotion; the familiar exhilaration that always came with a mission, tinged with an unusual note of anxiety. He tried to tell himself he'd done this all before, but he didn't really believe it. What had he gotten himself into?

"I don't make mistakes, captain," Almeida said, as if reading his mind. "You'll find your way."

"I'll do my best, colonel," Lincoln answered.

"I'm counting on it," said Almeida, nodding. "You can head on over to the briefing room, and send the lieutenant back in.

She and I will be there in just a few minutes. If anybody asks, tell them we've got a worthy one."

"Yes sir," Lincoln said. He saluted and left the office. Lieutenant Davis was waiting just outside. "The colonel said you can go back in," he said to her. She nodded and started back in.

"Lieutenant," he said, and she paused in the doorway. "Give your dad my best, if you would."

"Of course," Davis replied. She lingered a moment longer, and then nodded and disappeared into the colonel's office.

Lincoln drew a deep breath to settle himself, and walked the long corridors to the PFAC's briefing room.

When he reached it, Wright and Pence were already there; the master sergeant sat at the middle table in a seat at the far end, while Sergeant Pence sat on top of the table at the back of the room, feet dangling. The briefing room was smaller than Lincoln was used to, which was saying something. He couldn't remember ever having been in a briefing room that felt spacious. But this one had an especially close-in feel that made him instinctively tuck his elbows and round his shoulders, like he was walking too-narrow aisles of some fine-china boutique. There were three rows of tables, each a gentle arc bent towards the front of the room where a single podium sat off-center. Six chairs sat behind each table, but Lincoln figured if they ever had to fit eighteen people in there, he'd want to be really good buddies with his neighbors beforehand.

"Hey, boss," Pence said. "What's the word?"

Lincoln shook his head. "Don't know exactly yet. The colonel's still putting the final touches on the packet, and he was pretty light on details. He should be here in a minute." He lingered by the door for a moment. "You guys got usual seats?"

"Nah," Pence answered. "Just don't sit on the front row,

else mas'sarnt will pelt you with spitballs the whole time."

Wright's stern expression didn't change, and Lincoln didn't feel quite so bad that he hadn't gotten a smile out of her before. He took a seat at the near end of the middle row, taking Pence's suggestion without crowding Wright's space.

"Far be it from me to ignore the advice of senior enlisted," he said to Wright, and then smiled as he sat down.

As he was taking his seat, Sergeant Coleman walked in, followed by Sahil. Sahil moved to the back row, punched Lincoln in the shoulder with the back of his hand as he passed by. Coleman sat down in the first seat on the front row and then swiveled around to face Lincoln.

"Captain," she said. "I think you're sitting on the wrong side of the podium there, bud."

"I'm still too fresh off the farm," Lincoln said. "Colonel Almeida's going to run this one himself."

"Oh," Coleman said nodding. "He give you any previews?"

"He just said if you guys asked, to tell you it was a 'worthy one'."

"Uh oh," Mike said from behind him. Lincoln glanced over his shoulder.

"I'm guessing that means more to you than it does to me," he said.

"Well, yeah," Mike replied. "He's always griping about us getting sent out for work regular people could do. Just means he thinks this one's actually worth our time. Which means we're about to walk into a *reeeeal* goat rodeo."

"I'll give you three-to-one it's another NID bag," Coleman said.

"Three-to-one for or against?" Pence asked. She made a face at him, like it was a waste of breath to answer.

At that moment, Almeida strode in and everyone stood. The colonel went straight to the podium without even looking at the team. Davis trailed behind him uncertainly, a grave look on her face. She risked a glance at Lincoln and his crew, and then quickly returned her eyes to the floor in front of her. Coleman and Sahil looked at each other. Pence didn't return to his perch on the table, but instead slid into a seat next to Wright. From the general reaction of the others, Lincoln picked up that this already wasn't business as usual. The colonel tapped a few strokes on the podium's panel, dimming the lights and activating the projector.

"We're spinning up, kids," he said. "We've got a lot to cover and not a lot of time, so I'm just going to let the lieutenant here jump right to it. This is Lieutenant Davis, one of the top analysts over with the 23rd. Not how we usually do things, I know, but I'd rather you hear this straight from the source. She's going to run you through the highlights."

Almeida backed off to one corner of the room, and the lieutenant stepped up to the podium. She took a settling breath before she started.

"Afternoon, everyone."

After a moment, she brought an image up on the projector, showing a three-dimensional image of a man Lincoln didn't recognize.

"This is Henry Sann," Lieutenant Davis said. "Henry was the senior-most field officer for the NID's MARSCENT division." Pence let out a little grunt at that, undoubtedly impressed with the implied credentials Mr Sann must have possessed to be so high up the chain in the National Intelligence Directorate's Central Martian operations. That put him smack in the middle of the NID's most active area on Mars. The burden of responsibility he bore gave Lincoln a headache just thinking about it.

"Nine days ago, he was shot and killed in a cafe in Elliston, while meeting with a source," Davis said.

"*Nine* days ago?" Coleman said, incredulously. "How's this the first time we're hearing anything about it?"

Davis glanced at Almeida, who nodded. She looked back at Coleman.

"Because he was undeclared, sergeant," she answered. That gave everyone in the room pause. Working for the Directorate on foreign turf, even on friendly ground, made Henry Sann a spy. But being *undeclared* meant he was essentially operating on his own; he wasn't afforded any of the protections that usually came along with official cover. In the normal spy game, if he'd been detected or had his cover blown, the host nation would have quietly packaged him up and sent him home with a stern warning and maybe some diplomatic rumblings. Undeclared, though, meant being treated as a domestic if caught; prison, at best, and usually much, much worse.

"Someone blow his cover?" Mike asked. "One of our Eastern friends' agencies maybe?"

Davis shook her head. "Not that we've been able to pick up on. NID's notorious about keeping tabs on their undecs, and pulling them out at the first hint of trouble. Often unnecessarily. We've lost a lot of good sources because of their..." She paused, looking for the diplomatic option. "... *sensitivity* to risk."

"And we know the Directorate didn't burn him themselves," Lincoln said. A moment of tense silence followed. Out of the corner of his eye, Lincoln saw Wright glance over at the colonel with her eyebrows raised. It wasn't exactly good etiquette to raise the possibility, but Lincoln was never one to let politeness get in the way of understanding a situation completely.

"That's not how they operate," Davis said.

"You're *certain*," Lincoln said, pressing the issue. Because he knew all too well that, rare as it might have been, NID did in fact handle compromised officers and agents exactly that way. They just typically relied on other parties to do the actual work for them.

"As certain as anyone can be in this business, captain," Davis answered finally. "And then there's this..."

She cycled the projector to another image, this one an apparent debris field in open space. Some destroyed satellite, Lincoln guessed, or maybe a small shuttle. "Thirty-six hours ago, the civilian station Veryn-Hakakuri YN-773 suffered a catastrophic collision with an unidentified space body. The image you see here is what's left."

The young lieutenant paused a moment, either to let that sink in, or because she was wrestling through the emotions of the news. Even the smallest stations were vast structures; *catastrophic collision* must have been an understatement almost to the point of absurdity. Lincoln looked at the image with new perspective, felt his mind twist with the shift in scale. With the new information, his brain reorganized the debris, picked out different details; the section he'd thought might have been remnants of a shuttle cockpit must have been fifty times the size. An observation deck, or hydroponic capsule maybe.

"Search and rescue crews are still a few hours out," she added, almost as an afterthought, "but based on scans coming back from our whiskers... our current assessment is that there were no survivors." WISCR drones could travel much faster than any crewed ship and so the earliest reports on just about any event almost always came from them. No survivors. How many souls did it take to keep a hop up and running? A thousand? Two thousand?

"They have several hundred kilometers of open space to cover, though. So maybe..." Davis trailed off. Like any technology, WISCRs weren't perfect, but if they weren't picking up *any* signs of survivors, there wasn't much hope that search-and-rescue would have any more luck when they arrived.

"What kind of 'unidentified space body' could wipe a whole station?" Pence asked with a reserved tone.

"Whiskers are showing a lot mineral fragments in the debris field," Davis answered. "It'll be a while before forensics can determine anything for certain, but our working theory for now is an untracked asteroid."

"That doesn't make any sense," Coleman said. "Their sensor array would have picked that up a long way off, whether it was showing on official tracking reports or not. They would have had plenty of warning to nudge the station out of the way."

Davis nodded. "You're right, sergeant. They *should* have had warning. And for more than just the obvious reasons. YN-773 was the station's external designation, but its official one was LOCKSTEP. It was one of our primary SIGINT assets, shared between NID and Army intelligence."

"It was a spy rig?" Sahil said.

Davis nodded again. "LOCKSTEP was synced to Martian orbit and responsible for a substantial percentage of our signals intelligence."

"How substantial?" Lincoln asked.

"Losing it doesn't blind us completely," said Davis. "But it's certainly a strong poke in the eye. Most of what we know about MARSCENT had LOCKSTEP's fingerprints on it in one way or another. If they didn't do initial collection, they were usually the ones to cross-index sources, and to follow up and corroborate new reports. Some of NID's best people were on that rig." She hesitated a bare moment before she added, "It was also an undeclared asset."

"Mars didn't know we had military operations there," Lincoln said, clarifying.

"That's correct, captain," Davis said.

"So it was illegal," Master Sergeant Wright added.

"That's not true," Davis said. "Technically. The Directorate ran the station and maintained a fully civilian staff on board for its entire operation. Military activity was compartmentalized, off-station, at a declared site."

"So just because it wasn't staffed by official military personnel," Coleman said, "that makes it all right as far as interplanetary law's concerned?"

Davis pressed her lips together before she answered, "It's a grey area."

"Convenient," Wright said.

"I'm not sure we want to start looking too closely at the ethics and legalities of our particular duties, master sergeant."

"Maybe if your folks managed *yours* a little better, we wouldn't have to be so worried about mine, *lieutenant*."

"Settle down, Amira," Almeida said, from his corner. "Let's not pick on our guest. She's got enough on her plate already."

"Sir," Wright said.

"And, lieutenant," he said, leveling his gaze at her, "I don't mind you sticking up for yourself in here, but I would advise you to monitor the tone you take with my kids."

"Yes, sir," Davis said, and then shook her head. "Sorry, sir. And… I apologize, sergeant. I've been burning a lot of hours lately."

Wright brushed the moment aside with a nod and a subdued gesture of her hand. Davis reset herself, and continued. "As Sergeant Coleman pointed out, LOCKSTEP should have had ample warning of any kind of threat, particularly one of that nature. But as you can see from the outcome, for some reason that wasn't the case."

Lincoln was already putting the pieces together. "So maybe it was an accident, and maybe it was an attack. You think someone threw a rock at your station to show they knew you were there?"

"Could be," the lieutenant said. "But LOCKSTEP was undeclared for good reason. Whether this was a purposeful attack or a freak accident, we can't go around broadcasting the loss."

"You can imagine the diplomatic snafu this has already caused," Colonel Almeida added. "We've had multiple offers of support from several of the Martian administrations and a number of private organizations, and our people have had to decline them all. It's closer to them than it is to us, so I don't have to tell you how that looks."

"And Henry Sann's death," Wright said. "Not a coincidence."

"*Possibly* not," Davis said. "That's the trouble. There's no obvious connection between the two, no common threads apart from NID. But the timing is certainly... concerning."

"What about the hit?" Lincoln asked. "Any signatures you recognize?"

"I've got full packets waiting for you with all the details," Davis said. "I'd rather have you take a look and see what you come up with on your own."

"We're going into ISOFAC, kids," the colonel said, referring to the team's isolation facility, where they would hole up all together, cut off from the outside world until their mission package had been greenlit or scrubbed. "I can give you four hours to get your affairs in order. Then it's go time. We have a lot of very important people turning the screws to get answers on this."

"How much are we going to be bumping into NID?" Lincoln asked. "Are they running the show?"

"We'll have a liaison for you to coordinate with," Almeida answered. "A Mr Self. You can tell how concerned the Directorate is, because Mr Self is one of their seniormost guys. So senior, no one's authorized or willing to tell me anything about him. But apart from him, for now, NID is forbidden to act on any of this. That's why they're bringing us in. We can't say for certain whether either of these events were intentional, direct attacks against our nation. And if NID or any of our friends down the hall start buzzing around too much, we risk tipping off the wrong people that we've been hit. Both Henry and LOCKSTEP were undeclared for a reason. We can't operate as if these were attacks, and we most certainly can't pretend they weren't. Henry's murder would have been concerning no matter what. LOCKSTEP's destruction is a blow on its own. But the two of them together look an awful lot like the first shots of a war we don't want to have."

"*Possibly*," Davis reiterated. "Or they're two completely unrelated events that just happen to have horrible ramifications. That's what we need you to determine."

"I don't see it, sir," said Coleman. "Central Martian Authority can barely keep its member states from poking holes in each other's bubbles. I know we're not on the friendliest of terms, but why would anyone up there pick a fight with us?"

"Wouldn't be the first time a government tried to use an enemy abroad to buy some unity at home," Wright said. "Not by a long shot."

Though every one of the fourteen Martian settlements was sovereign, the Central Martian Authority acted as a unified governing body. Whenever the CMA issued policy, its members all fell in line. At least, they always had so far.

"Same effect here, though," Coleman said. "If these were attacks, even if they were only directed against the Federation... I mean, shoot, even if they were only against the *United States*, it'd still risk giving us a reason to buddy up with all our local bad actors. Mars versus Earth shrinks the neighborhood an awful lot; maybe our differences with the Eastern Coalition don't seem quite so big anymore."

"Seems like we would've seen the buildup before now, too," Pence said.

"Maybe," Almeida said. "But if someone out there *did* want to go that route, throwing a little sand in our eyes is a pretty good way to get started, wouldn't you say? We're eight months out from Earth-Mars opposition, and our planets are going to be even closer together than the last time. Prime time to launch on us, if they're going to. The timeline makes sense."

"And the level of confusion all of this creates," Lincoln said. "If it *is* an attack, and we can't even tell... we spend our time trying to figure out what's going on, while they're busy executing the plan. Puts us way behind."

Almeida nodded.

"*If* it's an attack," he added.

"So what do you have for us?" Lincoln asked, anxious to get to the point. "What's our starting point?"

Davis stepped back from the podium and deferred to Almeida, who moved up and officially took over the briefing. He brought the image of Henry Sann back up and let it hang there in the air next to the scattered remains of LOCKSTEP; two phantoms at opposite ends of the loss-of-life spectrum, yet equal in significance.

"That's for you to tell us," said the colonel. "Our friends in the 23rd have a couple of threads for you to tug on, but no clear winners. Davis will transmit the full dump to you once you're in the ISOFAC. Sift through it, see what catches your interest. And keep in mind, this is a *quiet* operation, kids."

"When is it not, sir?" Mike asked from the back of the room.

"This one even more so than usual, Mike. It's already a political nightmare, and this is exactly the kind of thing that the hallway warriors at Higher will exploit to push an agenda regardless of whether it's appropriate or not. Everyone's going to spin this as proof of why we need to do whatever their pet project is. We're shortening the chain of reporting to keep as many hands off as possible. And that's just here at home. I'm sure I don't have to remind you about all the bad actors we've got watching us, sniffing around for any sign of weakness.

"Captain Suh," Almeida said, looking meaningfully at Lincoln. "I expect to have your team's CONOPS ready for my review by this time tomorrow." He put just enough emphasis on the *your* to make it clear without sounding forced. That wasn't a lot of time to put together a concept of operations, not on something this complex with so little data; there was no doubt who would be held responsible if they didn't hit the deadline. "Lord knows I'll be spending all the time between now and then arguing with Higher about why we haven't already done something. Questions?"

Lincoln glanced around the room, but the grim focus on the faces of his teammates told him everything he needed to know. This was exactly the kind of thing they were built for. This was a worthy one.

"No, sir," Lincoln said. "We're good to go."

"Then get to work."

With that command, Lincoln and his team stood and made their way out of the briefing room with a restrained sense of urgency. And as Lincoln followed his new teammates down the hall, all his anxiety about his decision, all the uncertainty about what he'd gotten himself into, melted away as the energy of purpose flooded him. And a strange suspicion began to grow in him then, that maybe the colonel knew him better than he thought. Jumping feet first into a chaotic situation and being expected to figure it out on the move... Lincoln could almost believe that this *was* exactly what he'd been made to do.

SEVEN

Piper's first impression upon waking was that she had fallen asleep in one of the station's service tunnels. Her second impression was that she must have gotten incredibly drunk the night before and *passed out* in one of the station's service tunnels. Then the flood of memories washed over her; the final moments of YN-773, the shockwave rushing towards her, and what she had assumed had been her death. Yet here she was, alive. As surprising as it was to discover that fact, her head and body warned her not rush to any conclusions. All she could really say for sure was that she wasn't dead *yet*.

Emotion threatened to overwhelm her, but some instinct told her to resist it. Now wasn't the time. No, it wasn't instinct. It was one emotion overriding the others, suppressing their intensity.

Fear.

Not terror, or panic, but a quiet, important warning, urging caution and stillness. And Piper knew then that she was in danger.

Piper couldn't identify the source, exactly, but the feeling was distinct, sharp around the edges. Another presence weighed on her; someone close. She had a sudden, childlike impression of hiding under a bed and seeing a pair of feet enter the room and stop next to her.

"She's waking up," a voice said. A man's voice, rough even in its whisper.

A moment later, the presence withdrew, and Piper heard a whirr and a click. She counted to fifty before she risked taking a look, and even then she only cracked one eye. There was no one in sight. The room was so still, in fact, that she started to wonder if she'd dreamed it.

She didn't recognize her surroundings. Gradually, her senses expanded outward, encompassing more than her immediate discomfort. Lighting was poor, but steady; a thin blue aura radiated meekly from fiberlights along the top and bottom of the wall, unobtrusive. It gave the room volume, but not much in the way of detail. The room was narrow, longer than it was wide, but not large. A regular rectangle, with walls that looked bare in the gloom. She certainly wasn't in the pod. A storeroom on a station, maybe, or a ship. When she raised her head, the dim room sloshed in a sloppy swirl, and it took a full minute of lying back before everything settled into place. Even lying still, her every joint seemed to be slightly out of alignment.

Piper closed her eyes, took a deep breath and exhaled. Decided to start again from the beginning, as if this was her first time waking up. Without opening her eyes, she made a mental list of the things she knew. She wasn't dead, and she wasn't in the pod. Obviously someone had rescued her. But a ship would have had to have been close to have rescued her so soon. Unless... how long had she been unconscious? Maybe she'd been out for a long time. Maybe her injuries had required they keep her in a medically induced coma. Maybe they'd already transported her to another hop, and she was being treated.

But no, the room hadn't appeared to have any medical equipment in it.

Maybe she *was* still aboard YN-773. Except it wasn't the station, it was just a piece of it; she was strapped down to a chunk of debris, hurtling through space. Her eyes popped open of their own volition, wide and wild. Her mind was still fuzzy, her thoughts, disjointed; with her eyes closed, her imaginings had a bizarre quality lent by the grey space between sleep and wakefulness. Better to keep them open, then.

Piper spent a few moments staring straight up at the ceiling, and then turned her head slowly to examine her surroundings. In this second look, Piper confirmed her initial assessment of her location. It really did seem like a storeroom. And if she were on a station, there would be no reason to put her in a storage room. A ship then. And why would anyone put her in a storeroom? It must have been something small, something that wasn't used to carrying a lot of people around. But then, if it was a ship, why hadn't they put her in the medical bay? Even the smallest runabouts were required by law to have some sort of medical station. And it was obvious enough to her just from the way her body felt that she needed some kind of aid.

But then, she caught sight of her right arm at rest by her side and saw that in fact someone had already given her medical aid. A thermoplast cast ran from the top of her knuckles almost up to her elbow, preventing her from rotating her hand and forearm. She wiggled her fingers, felt a burn radiate through the back of her hand. Piper recalled the initial shockwave passing through the pod, the sharp burst of pain. A broken wrist then, most likely.

She lifted the arm and brought it nearer to her face so she could examine the brace more closely in the weak light. Piper didn't have any medical training herself, but life on a hop had its risks; she'd broken enough small bones to have some idea of what a good cast should look like. And this one impressed her. Maybe she'd been expecting it to be a temporary fix, a makeshift, improvised solution slapped together by whoever had found her. But this looked clean and professional to her.

It was a custom print job, neatly executed. Whoever had applied it had been meticulous. A person concerned with precision. For some reason, it made her think of the military.

That might make some sense. Maybe the Central Martian Authority had happened to have a vessel in the area. If they'd been out on patrol, they could have been among the first to respond... but then, again, the room. And, she still hadn't shaken the sense of danger she'd first felt.

It only now occurred to her that maybe she'd only been afraid because she hadn't been fully awake yet. If she wanted to know what was going on, the easiest thing to do was to ask somebody.

Piper curled herself up to a sitting position with a good deal of effort and a fair amount of pain, and then swung her legs over the side of the... cot, she realized now, that she'd been lying on. She sat with her feet flat on the floor, waiting for the vertigo to subside. A wispy thought drifted through her fogged mind that dizziness was a common symptom of concussions. She started to sigh, but when she inhaled, an electric streak of pain made the breath catch in her throat. Even after the initial shock passed, a dull ache persisted on the left side of her ribcage. She wondered if she'd broken some ribs too. Careful of her newly discovered injury, Piper gently cleared her throat and raised her head towards the door.

"Hello?" she said. Her voice sounded strange; dry, and thin. She cleared her throat once more and tried again, "Hello? Is anyone there?"

She sat in silence for a few minutes, trapped between the idea of walking over to the door where she had a better chance of being heard and the impulse to lie down again and go back to sleep. Finally, the idea won out. She'd be able to rest better once she knew what had happened.

Just about the time she'd gathered the courage to test her strength, a voice sounded in the room.

"Lie down and face the wall," it said. Piper jumped at the sound, and earned another stab of pain.

"Hello?" she said, once she'd recovered. "Hello, can you hear me?"

"Lie down, and face the wall," the voice repeated. The voice came from overhead, somewhere in the top corner near the door. It had a compressed, processed quality, and not just from being transmitted through a speaker. Piper was fairly certain it was a man talking to her, but whoever he was, he apparently didn't want his voice to be recognizable.

Piper tried once more, "Please, can you tell me–"

"Lie. Down," the voice said again, cutting her off. "Face. The. Wall."

The man hadn't raised his voice at all, but the tone made it perfectly clear that he expected to be obeyed. As Piper eased herself back down onto the cot, she made a mental note not to push her luck until she had a better idea of what her situation was. At least she'd learned one thing from the man's interruption: he *could* hear her.

Piper situated herself on her back, and then gingerly rolled onto her side to face the wall. That put her on her left side and, though it was uncomfortable, it wasn't unbearable. Maybe her ribs were just bruised then, not broken. That'd be nice.

"Place your hands behind your back," the voice said.

Piper did as she was told, and slid her hands around behind her so whoever was watching her could see them. It made her shoulders burn.

"Good," said the voice. "Now be still. Do *not* turn around."

A few moments later, the door clicked and whirred. Piper had to clench her jaw and squeeze her eyes shut to resist the urge to look back over her shoulder. She drew in on herself, instinctively tried to make herself small. There was no way to know the man's intentions; for now she would do everything she could to seem compliant. That would make it easier to surprise him if he laid hands on her.

Someone entered the room, footsteps muted by the hum of machinery and the squeak of rubberized wheels on the floor. A cartbot bringing something into the room, no doubt. Piper waited a tense minute, listened carefully for any sounds that might warn her of aggression or bad intent. All she could make out, though, were noises typical of someone unloading a bot. Something large scraped dully across the floor as it slid into place across from Piper, in the rear corner of the room.

When it seemed clear that she wasn't in any immediate danger, Piper allowed herself to relax out of the protective ball she'd curled into. The person in the room with her went quiet at her movement, and a moment later the voice spoke.

"Keep your hands where I can see them," it said, but not threateningly. More like a police officer. Firm, but polite.

Piper nodded and pushed her hands a little farther out behind her back. The person in the room resumed his activities a few seconds later. Piper decided to risk it.

"Can you please tell me what's going on?" she said, keeping her voice low. "Please?"

The person in the room didn't even acknowledge that she'd spoken. Just kept busy with whatever he was doing.

Piper took a different approach. "My name is María Alejandra Reyes," she said, and then calmly offered a list of details. "I work for Veryn-Hakakuri. I'm a technical specialist. I was on Station YN-773. Something happened to the station. Something terrible."

The man in the room continued his work. Setting something up, maybe, or several things, from the sound of it.

"How did you find me?" Piper asked.

It sounded like the man was finishing up his work. The cartbot hummed and trundled its way out of the room. A plastic wrapper crackled as it was torn and crumpled. Then the footsteps started towards the door.

Piper tried one last time, asked the one question that she

needed the answer to more than any other.

"What are you going to do with me?"

The man paused, and Piper's heart pounded with sudden anticipation.

"You're safe," he answered, and to Piper's surprise it was a woman's voice. And with those two words, tears of relief sprang up and squeezed through Piper's still-closed eyes. But before she could respond, the woman added, "For now. It's up to you to stay that way."

A moment later the woman exited and the door whirred closed and clicked.

"You can sit up again now," the voice said from the ceiling.

Piper pulled her hands out from behind her back and rolled over. Her left hand tingled and prickled from having been in such an awkward position for so long. She opened and closed it repeatedly to work the feeling back in while she levered herself up on the cot. There were a few new additions to her room. Against the wall across from her, a flimsy table with folding legs had appeared, with a chair of similar design pushed up under it. A tall, clear plastic canister filled with what looked like water sat on the table next to a simple dish. Some kind of meal steamed on the dish; a slab of protein, pale vegetables, a disk of flat bread. There were no utensils. Directly across from the head of her cot was a blue box-shaped device that she recognized as a portable waste recycler, for a toilet.

Having taken all of that in, Piper covered her face with her hands and her tears of relief became something else. She wept then, quietly, with as much restraint as she could manage, but deeply.

Whatever the room had been before, Piper knew what it had now become.

Her prison cell.

EIGHT

Lincoln sat at one corner of the large, rectangular holoscreen table that dominated the middle of the isolation facility's planning room. Sergeant Coleman sat diagonally across from him, to his left, poring over some deep-level technical specs that radiated an aura of mathematically induced headache at least six feet wide. Sahil and Wright were in quiet conference at the far end. Behind Lincoln, Pence was lying on the floor with one arm draped over his eyes. They'd been at it a good fourteen hours. Fortunately, the planning room was stocked with water, food, and, most importantly, coffee. A fresh pot was brewing, and though Lincoln hadn't been out for fresh air in a while, he was pretty sure the aroma of the coffee was probably helping mask the funk of five people crammed in a planning room for over half a day.

Colonel Almeida had told them that the National Intelligence Directorate and the 23rd had a few threads for Lincoln and his team to pull on; good starting points. Images representing each were displayed on one wall of the room, a virtual murder-board to build and break connections as the team talked through it all. On it were several organizations, some government and many not, as well as a number of shady characters. A few of those represented were the usual actors: Eastern Coalition counterintelligence agencies, known radical groups with a history of violence, a handful of Mars-based government entities. Others were new to Lincoln. But Almeida had been right when he'd said none of them stood out as particularly stronger candidates than any of the others. The team had already gone around a few times arguing about where to begin, taking a few off the list only to put them back again an hour or two later. Somewhere around the six-hour mark they'd all agreed that it seemed like they could pick any one of them at random and get the same result.

At that point, Lincoln had flipped the process on its head.

"Forget the starting points," he'd told them. "Everybody pick a question that's bugging you, and go find an answer. Maybe one of them will lead us back to some of our friends here. Or at least away from some of them."

They'd split off then, each to dig into whatever caught their attention. For the moment, Lincoln had chosen to focus on Henry's death. An array of projected panels hung in the air above the holotable, where Lincoln had spread all of the information that Lieutenant Davis and her team had been able to collect on the event, and Henry's activities leading up to it. Field reports, clips of communications with his handlers and his contacts, surveillance video pulled from Elliston security, a deep background on Henry – it was all made directly available to Lincoln and his team.

Intelligence had always been a critical part of planning, but in his previous units Lincoln had only been given a focused, curated packet of information. Davis had provided a package of what they had considered the most relevant data, but she'd also opened up the entire archive for them to explore as they saw fit. Lincoln had never had this kind of access to intelligence before.

Davis had outlined several of the working theories under development by the 23rd, but she'd been hesitant to share any of the conclusions that she or any of her fellow analysts had reached. That, too, was different from how Lincoln was used to operating. In the past, he'd always been expected to take Intel Analysis as gospel, and to plan and act according to its every directive. This "tell me what *you* think" way of doing things added a tremendous amount of extra work to his plate, but after several hours of navigating his way through the data packets Davis had prepared, he found himself beginning to appreciate it.

He expanded one of the panels with a motion of his hand, dragged it over directly in front of him, and skimmed the report on the contact that Henry had been meeting with at the time of the attack. That man was one Rado Dekker, a midlevel lieutenant in a small-time organized crime syndicate operating in and around northern and central Martian settlements. Smugglers, mostly, moving goods on- and off-planet, with some regional distribution. Though they seemed to be largely concerned with narcotics and other illicit materials, the group had been involved in at least two transfers of weapons that the 23rd knew about. It was possible that Henry was developing Dekker as an agent, to gain access to the inner workings of the syndicate.

That wasn't unusual for Henry's line of work. By nature, his job required him to develop and maintain contact with all manner of people, most of whom were of the sort that could be convinced to betray the trust and confidence of someone close to them. Add to that the fact that Henry's specific focus seemed to be on radicalized groups and terrorist cells, and it was clear that he was swimming neck-deep in some of the murkiest, bloodiest waters there were to be explored.

But Dekker's particular gang had no known ties to any such operations. They mostly seemed like kids playing at being tough guys, not the genuinely bad people that might blow up a mall or murder a bunch of women and children downtown to get their point across.

And that was the tricky thing about NID's undeclared officers. Even without the NID's usual smokescreens and purposefully convoluted reporting structure, it was often difficult to determine whether or not undecs were working on official tasks or if they were off running their own operations on the side. If Henry had been using Dekker to make some extra money, he wouldn't have been the first.

Though Davis hadn't shared any of the conclusions that her team had reached, she'd included summaries of analysis from several of her team members in the packets she'd prepared. Lincoln had read through all of them and, as far as Henry's murder was concerned, the general consensus amongst the analysts of the 23rd seemed to fall along the lines of "wrong place, wrong time". There was no question that it had been a hit, well planned and well executed. But as far as the analysts could tell, there just weren't any signs that Henry had been targeted specifically, except perhaps as a tangential associate of Dekker. A target of opportunity, at best. If it hadn't been for LOCKSTEP, it was doubtful anyone would have blinked at the loss of Henry Sann.

Unfortunately, but unsurprisingly, there was no direct video feed from the surveillance cameras in and around the hotel where Henry was killed. The attacking party had disrupted the coverage of the area about twenty minutes on either side of the event, as best as the 23rd could figure. That they'd had that level of sophistication elevated the hitters above common street-level, but was still consistent with the capabilities of a rival organization. Though a few eyewitness recordings had emerged, none of them had captured any useful material.

The crime scene investigators did, however, have ample footage of the immediate aftermath, and Lincoln had spent a couple of hours scrubbing through the feed and slicing out still images of shots that caught his attention. He closed out the panel containing the report on Dekker and brought up the stack of images again. For many of the stills, Lincoln hadn't been consciously aware of what had given him pause.

At the time, it hadn't mattered. Any time he found himself scrubbing back and forward through a section more than once, he clipped it. Now, having given his eyes a rest by focusing on something else, he cycled through the images one at a time.

He'd seen enough of it up close and personal that the carnage didn't affect him on an emotional level. And in a strange way, there was something pure and simple about the process of analyzing the scene of an attack. Violence always told a story, if you knew how to read it. When you saw it firsthand, there was no way to hide its truth, no obscuring its intent. And firsthand experience made it easier to read the aftermath, to recognize the patterns. But Lincoln kept coming back to a close shot of Henry's body, curled on the ground with blood pooled by his head and a rivulet trailing away towards the eastern exit, as if it too sought to escape the brutality that had befallen the courtyard. He pulled that image off to one side and then flipped through the others until he found a similar image of Dekker's body. Lincoln didn't know why, but his gut told him the general consensus had it wrong. This hadn't just been some inter-gang takedown.

"Mike," Lincoln said.

"Yeah?" Pence answered from the floor, without taking his arm away from his eyes.

"The hitters. How would you rate them in terms of professionalism?"

"There's no question they're top-tier, sir," Mike said. "I'd say ex-military or high-level personal protection. Ex-law enforcement, maybe, but I think that's an outside chance."

"Why so sure?" Lincoln asked, even though he agreed.

Sergeant Pence rolled up off the floor and came over to stand behind Lincoln. He held up a hand next to Lincoln's stack of images.

"You mind?" he said.

"No, go ahead," Lincoln said.

Mike scrolled through the stack and slid one image out that Lincoln hadn't given much attention. It was of a man in the hotel, up on the fourth floor, if Lincoln recalled the details correctly. He'd been shot once, through the chest. The flexiglass window had a spiderwebbed hole about a half-inch in diameter punched out of it. A compact rifle sat on a table near the window, set up on a bipod but off to one side, out of view of the window. Lincoln recognized it as a takedown rifle, one that could be easily disassembled to fit in a small case. Easier to transport, easier to conceal.

Pence tapped the bullet hole in the window with his forefinger.

"Counter-sniper," he answered. "That's hard work, even if you know to look for it." He then tapped the rifle on the table, assembled but apparently otherwise untouched. "This guy up here on the fourth floor didn't have much of a chance to do anything, which says to me that he'd been detected before it all went down. So you're looking at an experienced crew here, not some gang-war spillover. And I don't mean just experienced hit squad."

Lincoln nodded.

"So we have primary shooter in the courtyard, with Henry, and then overwatch somewhere outside," Lincoln said. "Two, minimum."

"And a driver for exfil," Mike added. "Probably."

"Could have just used an on-demand," Coleman said from across the table. She was still intent on whatever she was reviewing, but somehow managed to follow along with their conversation at the same time. "Or preprogrammed one."

"Could have, sure," Mike said. "But I don't think so. I'm guessing a team that careful wouldn't leave it to chance. If things went bad, security could lock the whole area down. I get the impression our friends here were the four-levels-deep kind of planners."

"You think military then," Lincoln said.

Mike nodded. "What's your take?"

"The same," Lincoln said. "Looks sloppier than it actually was." He pulled up three images of the courtyard with an overlay indicating where rounds had impacted. "Mid-morning in the cafe, all these extra rounds fired, and yet no collateral damage. They only hit the people they intended to. And, if you've got someone good enough to do that," he pointed to the picture showing the sniper's work, "no need to have a shooter in the target zone."

"So we have conscientious killers," Mike said.

"Like you said," Lincoln said. "Top-tier professionals. So I think that pulls a couple of these folks off the list." He returned to the images of suspects displayed on the wall and adjusted the transparency on the panels for two terrorist groups and one organized crime cartel, leaving just their ghosts behind. "I'm saying it's not these guys. Anybody got problems with that?" Everyone took a moment to check out the changes, but no one offered any objections.

"Not yet, anyway," Wright said, returning to her work with Sahil.

Lincoln likewise went back to his own analysis, and found himself once again focused on the image of Henry's body. Something wasn't sitting right, but he couldn't put his finger on exactly what it was.

"Walk through this with me again," Lincoln said. He brought up an image from the Elliston medical examiner's report, all the violence reduced down to five man-shaped black outlines on a plain white background. Lincoln closed out the ones representing the security team for the moment. In the simplified depiction of Dekker, there were four markings indicating the locations of the entry points of the rounds. There were no exit wounds. Three of the shots were scattered around the torso: low right, near the appendix; center right side, through a lung; mid-center, an inch or so above the solar plexus. The fourth, and presumably final, shot was about a quarter-inch off center from being right between Dekker's eyes.

"The official version goes like this: the shooting starts, Dekker gets three rounds in the torso," Lincoln said, pointing to those markers, and then over to Henry's image. "And Henry gets hit by a stray, here, through the neck."

Henry's image also showed four wounds: the entry and exit wounds through the neck, and then two more entry wounds in the center of his chest. Well placed.

"Dekker then gets it in the head, so that makes him the primary target. Then Henry gets cornered, and they finish him off. Target of opportunity." Lincoln tapped the two indicators in Henry's chest.

"Two rounds, center of mass," he continued. "Those were the kill shots. This here," he pointed to Henry's neck wounds, "is a fairly clean pass-through. He maybe could have survived, if he'd gotten aid fast enough. So here's the kicker for me." Lincoln cleared out the panels with the coroner's report and brought up the background profile on Sann. He pointed at the relevant facts as he talked through them. "Henry's not your usual NID civilian officer. He'd been doing this sort of thing for a long time. Before NID, he was law enforcement. Worked gang units, organized crime, under cover. Moved to contracting for UAF, ran with high-risk details in Mumbai, Jakarta, all over the Philippines during the war. So he can obviously handle himself. He doesn't strike me as the kind of guy who would freeze up when shots start popping off. Nor does he seem like the type to lie down and let himself bleed out from a small-caliber wound."

Lincoln looked back at the actual image of Henry's body, collapsed on the ground, and focused in on the wound through Henry's neck. And now, having talked it out, saw what it was that had been bothering him. Sann's shirt had dark splotches from his chest injuries. But there was hardly any blood around the collar or shoulders. Not like it would have been if he'd been upright when he'd taken the wound. Mike saw it too.

"They shot him in the neck after he was already on the ground," Mike said.

"Yeah," Lincoln said. "And why would they do that? If they were trying to guarantee the kill, why not the head?"

"Because they're pros, trying to look like amateurs."

"And they don't want anyone to think he's the primary," Lincoln added.

Coleman was looking up at them now.

"Shouldn't the Elliston police have picked up on that? If that round went clean through his neck, there'd be a bullet impact somewhere underneath him."

"I don't think they did the most thorough job checking this one out," Lincoln said, shaking his head. "Once they ID'd Dekker, I'm guessing they wrote it off as some kind of bad-guy-on-bad-guy hit. Henry was the only victim they didn't already have a sheet on, and I'm sure NID did a good job making sure the locals didn't find anything worth investigating further."

"So Sann was the target. Dekker and his guards were the cover," she said.

Lincoln didn't like the implications of that, but when Coleman said it, he felt tension release, as if he'd just solved a particularly difficult crossword puzzle. It was the only way the pieces all fit together.

"That's how it looks to me," Lincoln said.

"Yeah," Mike said. "Yeah, I can see that. Don't much like it, though."

"Me neither," Coleman said. "Because I can't see my way around LOCKSTEP being anything other than a direct attack on our intelligence gathering abilities."

"What makes you say that?" Wright asked from the far end of the table.

"Because somebody got deep into their sensor systems to make sure they never saw it coming," Coleman answered. She ran light fingers over the holotable's controls and expanded the panel she'd been looking at for the past couple of hours, and sent it to the head of the table where everyone could get a good view. Lincoln couldn't make any sense of the stream of characters. "You want me to walk you through it, or you just want to take my word for it?"

Lincoln had gone through all the basic training on code like everybody else, but he'd never taken it any farther than absolutely required. Even so, as much as he wanted to take Coleman's word for it, he needed to understand her reasoning.

"Give me the executive summary," he said. And then added, "But the idiot's version."

"Oh, you mean the *officer's* summary, then," she said with a quick smile. "Easy day. You know how a sensor suite works on a hop…?"

"Remind me," Lincoln said.

"Yeah, OK," Coleman said, and she leaned back in her chair. "A refresher then. Space is big, it's got a lot of stuff floating around in it. If you're out there, mostly you don't want any of that other stuff floating into you."

"Maybe not the *complete* idiot's version, sergeant," Lincoln said.

She held up a hand. "I'm getting to it. On a hop, you're not usually moving all that fast. By galactic standards, you might as well be stationary. And space is big, like, really big, right? So you can't see everything all the time. So most stations don't even try. They just keep track of things that are close enough to matter."

"Which is relative," Lincoln said, to show he was following along.

"Which is relative, right," Coleman said with a nod. "Very good, sir." When she said that, Mike glanced over at Lincoln with an amused look and gave him a one-shoulder shrug that told him Coleman most likely didn't actually *mean* to be condescending.

"A rock a thousand klicks out and moving towards you fast enough," she continued, "matters a whole lot more than one that's just about in your hip pocket but not moving at all. So just because something's far away doesn't mean it doesn't matter. And in space, things can be really, *really* far away, and still matter.

"Sensor suites… they have to be a combination of active and passive. Active sensors shoot signals out, and measure whether or not anything comes back. But you can't rely solely on those, because what if you miss, right? So you complement them with passive sensors, which just soak up whatever's coming their way. And you can't rely solely on *those*, because not everything's emitting something for you to soak up, and also because there's so much other stuff out there spewing radiation at you that doesn't matter. You've got to filter out the vast majority of what you're picking up. So you use the active sensors to check up on whatever the passives are telling you about, and vice versa. A passive sensor's like 'Hey man, do we need to be worried about this?' and a couple of actives check it out and one says, 'Nah, don't sweat it,' and another one says, 'Looks OK to me', and a third one says, 'Man, I don't even see what you're looking at'. That sort of thing."

Lincoln was beginning to wish he'd just taken Coleman's word for it. She must have read it on his face, because she held up her pointer finger and nodded.

"I know," she said. "Hold on, you'll see how all this matters in just a minute. One more thing, and then I'll get to the good part, promise. To make things even more complicated, your long-range active sensors have to have a really tight beam to make sure the signal doesn't dissipate over distance to the point that it becomes useless. The problem is, space is really, *really* big, so at the distances we're talking, a thousandth of a degree of variation in your tight-beam sensor might be the difference between seeing a hundred meter-wide rock hurtling at you and missing it completely. Even the vibrations from normal operation can make a sensor beam hit an object one second and miss it the next. You can't count on sensors being able to consistently track the same object. So you have to sample it, take an aggregate, do all kinds of crazy math to figure out whether or not it's something you should be worried about.

"Just like ships, hops have overlapping sensor fields from tight-beam and wide-beam arrays, and all of that data from all of those sensors gets dumped into a central point where all the crazy math gets done." Here, finally, Coleman sat forward again and highlighted a large block of code on the panel she'd enlarged, sitting in the middle of an even larger block of code.

"Ignore all this nonsense, that's all pretty much standard solution," she said, indicating the portions of code that she hadn't highlighted. "This is the key part here. And it's subtle. But the executive summary, sir, is that this section here is designed to force YN-773's sensor suite to ignore a particular threat."

Lincoln couldn't follow the code, but he understood Coleman's explanation perfectly well. "So someone gave LOCKSTEP's sensors a blind spot."

"Not just a blind spot," Coleman corrected. "I'm saying, statistically speaking, they knew the *exact* rock they wanted the sensors to ignore. Composition, size, everything. For all intents and purposes, one, specific asteroid. The chances of there being another asteroid that fits the profile that also just happens to be anywhere near 773...?" She shook her head. "And this code is custom. I mean, really, *really* custom. These guys knew what they were doing. Even stylistically, it reads like everything else around it, even though it was inserted later."

"Inside job?" Lincoln said.

"Every cyberattack is an inside job, sir," Coleman said with a smile. "But if you mean, did they have a plant at Veryn-

Hakakuri, then yeah, that'd be my first guess. Current, or former employee. Or someone obsessed with VH's particular brand of internal software."

Mike chuckled at the last sentence, and Coleman looked at him. "I'm not kidding, Mikey. You'd be surprised how weird some people can be about code."

"Not *that* surprised," Mike said, and that made Sahil chuckle.

"Can you figure out when that code was inserted?" Lincoln asked.

"Maybe, if I can get access to LOCKSTEP's systems archive. I wouldn't count on it, though. Even if NID has access to it, I doubt that's the kind of thing they're going to share."

"Let's get a request in," Lincoln said. "Might as well ask."

"Yes sir."

"How'd they plant it?" Wright asked. "Operative on board?"

Coleman shrugged. "Probably, but not necessarily. I don't know. This isn't the sort of thing that's usually going to be accessible to your average corporate drone, even their top-tier techs. We're talking deep, deep level stuff here."

Lincoln said, "Deep enough that they'd need access to the hardware?"

Coleman looked back at the code and shook her head. "No, I can't say that for sure. I mean, with a hop, we're talking a massive system-of-systems here, so it's possible they attacked some other point in the architecture and the payload skipped to target. It's not quite down at the firmware level of things, but it's pretty close. In the actual control code. The thing is all these corporations have proprietary systems. Some of them are built on similar foundations, same concepts, like you see here," she waved her hand at the un-highlighted code on the panel, "but they don't share this stuff with anyone outside. Corporate security issues, you know. Only reason we're looking at it is because NID had access. It'd definitely help to have someone on the inside, but I can't say it's strictly necessary."

"Would it be somethin' you could do from a ship?" Sahil asked. He and Wright were still at the far end of the table from everyone else, but they were both now fully engaged in the discussion.

Coleman paused a few moments before responding.

"Yeah," she said. "Yeah, if you had the right access codes and the right people, I guess you could do it from about anywhere. What makes you ask?"

Sahil touched the holotable and sent the panel he had in front of him over to join the one Coleman had enlarged. On it were several images and specifications for a hauler called *Destiny's Undertow.*

"That fella right there," he said. "Showed up to 773 unannounced."

"That's weird," Coleman said. "I didn't catch that in the packet."

"Yeah," Sahil said. "It's sorta a footnote. Lost with all hands when the hop went down. I figure our folks checked it out a bit, coded it 'wrong place, wrong time'."

"Sounds familiar," Lincoln said, recalling his impression of the analysts' summaries of Henry's death. Both events had an element of the coincidental that nagged at him. It raised the ghost of a familiar feeling, strong enough to sense but too vague to be grasped. "They dig up anything interesting on it?"

"Not much. Hauler, registered out of Luna. Original plan had it travelin' out to the Belt, slingin' off Mars on the return trip. Everything about it seems legit."

"Except for it being way out by 773," Mike said.

"Roger that," answered Sahil. "Logs say 773 sent tugs out for it. Some kind of engine trouble. Musta been gettin' to dock right around the time the rock hit."

"Do we have access to any of the traffic between the ship and the station?" Coleman asked.

"I think so, yeah," Sahil said. "One sec." He worked a panel at his end of the table for a minute or so. While he worked,

Lincoln looked back at Coleman.

"Pros and cons, Sergeant Coleman. On an op like this, would you say it's definitely better to have someone on the inside?"

"Can you just call me Thumper, sir?" she said.

The comment caught him off guard. "I didn't think I'd earned it," he replied.

"Yeah, not really," she said, "but half the time I forget you're talking to me. Nobody else around here calls me that, so it just feels awkward."

"I think I could probably manage it," Lincoln said with a smile. "If you can give me the story behind the name."

"You *definitely* haven't earned that, sir," she answered.

"All right, fair enough. So, *Thumper*," he said, "between on-site and remote, what's the deciding factor for this sort of breach?"

"Mmm… comes down to a matter of intrusion detection I guess. Are you more likely to get caught with someone poking around on site, or when you connect to the system and start injecting code?"

"Here we go," Sahil said, and he sent a panel from his end of the table over to Thumper.

"Cool," she said. "Gimme a few."

While she was heads-down in the data Sahil had just sent her, Lincoln got up and grabbed a bottle of water and poured himself a cup of coffee. "Anybody else?" he asked, waving the pot around.

"No thanks," Sahil said. Wright glanced over, shook her head, and went back to studying whatever she was working on. Coleman didn't respond.

"Yeah, I'll take a hit," Mike said.

"Anything in it?"

"Nah," Mike answered. "I'm sweet enough already."

Lincoln poured a second cup of coffee, then balanced both cups in one hand, grabbed his water bottle with the other, and carried them all back to his seat at the table.

"Man of many talents," Mike said, as he took the offered cup of coffee. "You must've done time in a restaurant."

Lincoln shook his head. "No, this right here is all officer corps training. First two weeks is all coffee prep and delivery. Basically all I did as a lieutenant, too."

"OK," Coleman said. "So this is interesting."

She didn't look up, and she was quiet long enough that Lincoln started to think maybe she'd just been talking to herself.

"Thumper," Mike said. At the sound of her name, she looked up at them, but there was a distance in her eyes that said she wasn't entirely with them. After a moment she shook her head, and her eyes focused.

"Yeah, sorry. So here's something," she said, and she enlarged a panel and flipped it around so the others could see it. It was series of waveforms. It took a moment before Lincoln realized he was looking at the communications between the ship and the station. "You see this," Thumper said, pointing to a short but sharp peak at the head of several of the forms. "... it's a little hitch, each time the captain of *Destiny's Undertow* responds to 773's traffic controller."

"And that's significant?" Lincoln said.

"Well, yeah," she answered in a tone that implied that should have been obvious. She glanced around the room at her other teammates. Lincoln was relieved to see they all looked as perplexed as he felt. Thumper sighed and gave a little eye roll with a shake of her head. "Does anybody besides me pay attention to anything?" She fiddled with the holotable and a few seconds later another panel appeared, next to the first. It, too, was a series of waveforms.

"See anything familiar?" she asked. Lincoln scanned the forms and sure enough, at the head of each one was an identical triangular shape.

"What's this one we're looking at now?" he asked. "That's

me talking to Mom, from Phobos last time we were there," she said. She mentioned it casually, but Lincoln couldn't help but wonder what they'd been doing on the Martian moon.

"Uh…" Mike said. "Do you keep archives of all our communications?"

"Sure," said Thumper. "We pretty much have to."

"Yikes," Mike said.

"Anyway," Thumper said, pointing again to the recurring shape. "That blip is from a quantum relay. Same kind of stuff we use for deep-range commo."

"Military grade?" Mike asked.

"Not necessarily, no," she answered. "Can't tell that from this. But what it *does* tell us, is that the captain wasn't on his ship."

"What do you mean he wasn't on the ship?" Mike said.

"I mean whoever was talking to station control wasn't doing it from the bridge of that hauler. There's no reason for this otherwise. *Destiny's Undertow* was bouncing signals back and forth between 773 and wherever the captain really was. Which was probably somewhere really far away."

"Like Mars?" Sahil asked.

"Mars, Luna," Thumper said with a shrug. "Could've come from here. Or from Pluto."

"And NID didn't pick up on it?" Wright asked.

"I guess not," Thumper said. "But that's not that surprising, there's no reason to look for it. I wouldn't have gone hunting for it, if Sahil hadn't brought it up. And I only noticed it because I spend so much time staring at this stuff running commo for you guys."

"And *they* ain't our Thumper," Sahil said, with a smile. "You're the brains, Thump. Put it together for us. You got a ship on remote, a quantum relay, and a rock. How would *you* do it?"

Thumper sat back again, put her hands on top of her head and stared at the ceiling for half a minute. For as much as

Sergeant Coleman talked once she got started, Lincoln appreciated the fact that she always actually seemed to consider her words carefully before she began.

"Some of each, I guess," she said, finally. "Get someone on the inside to open it up. Do the rest remotely. Probably the usual kind of gig... exploit somebody inside who's maybe lonely, vulnerable somehow. Willing to do a favor or two without necessarily understanding what I'm really asking them to do. Then, I'd sneak the code in some routine procedure. A system update or something. Or... oh..."

She looked back down at the panels she had arrayed on the table in front of her, and disappeared back into her own head. Everyone gave her a little time. Sahil was the one to finally draw her back out.

"What is it, Thumper?" he said.

"Or in something like a handshake..." she said, blinking up at him. "Check this out. When a ship's coming into a station, their systems exchange some data. Helps the station keep track of the ship and vice versa, logs get updated automatically, that sort of thing. Theoretically, you might be able to hide a payload in that."

"Theoretically?" Lincoln said.

Thumper shrugged. "You'd have to be code god to pull it off. Typically those connection protocols are where you see the most robust security, because it's an obvious vulnerability. But if you knew the inner workings of a station well enough to convince its sensors to ignore a threat, you're probably the right person to give this a try. Or people. We're probably looking at a team, here."

She stopped and shook her head.

"Awful lot of trouble to go through to wipe out a hop full of civilians."

Her final comment triggered a strange connection in Lincoln's mind, gave him a new perspective. He could tell that somewhere in its hidden inner workings, his subconscious was busy constructing something it wasn't ready to offer up. But it didn't seem to mind tipping him off a little. Images of the courtyard restaurant where Henry had been killed played through his head. Stray rounds, no unintended casualties.

"What if you were genuinely concerned about mitigating collateral damage?"

"Then I probably wouldn't have put a rock through a space station in the first place," she said.

"But if you knew both Henry's identity and the true nature of LOCKSTEP?" Lincoln said. He was starting to catch on to what his subconscious was up to. Thumper looked at him blankly, not following.

"Then I could consider them both valid military targets," Wright said. Lincoln looked her way and pointed at her. She nodded, and in her sharp eyes he could see reflected her mind rapidly reframing the conversation. "I keep the moral high ground. Two relatively soft targets. And if I keep my name out of the papers, I can evaluate the results before I decide whether I want to claim any responsibility."

In that moment, he finally dredged up the memory that had been haunting the corners of his mind.

"Controlling the aftermath," Lincoln said, to himself.

"Say again?" Mike said. He was leaning on the edge of the holotable now, arms crossed. Lincoln shook his head.

"Sorry. This all just suddenly reminded me of something I learned back in the early days," he said. "It's kind of a story."

"Well, do tell," Mike replied.

Lincoln glanced around at the others, who were all looking at him expectantly. He leaned back in his chair, ran a hand over his chin. They'd been at it for hours; a little storytime probably wouldn't hurt anyone.

"Okay, so back when I was with 1st Group," he said, "we did some work around Ragon, out of Tumangang mostly. And the militia we were working with, it's basically what you'd expect. The big boss, can't tell if he's a gangster or a patriot.

Probably some of both. Pretty much ran Tumangang at that point, so he was loaded. He was married, loved his wife. Still had like five girlfriends, of course, but he absolutely doted on his wife. Anyway, he had this head bodyguard, he called him his chief of security, but you know, he's basically just some guy who worked out a lot and liked to carry guns.

"Well, we're there for about three days before it becomes obvious to us that the boss's chief of security is maybe a little too familiar with the daily business of the boss's wife. And that's none of our concern, except that apparently everyone else had figured it out, too, except the boss, and you know how that is. Erodes the boss's authority, gets tough to maintain discipline. I'm pretty green at that point, but I know I have to deal with it. And seeing as I'm an officer, you know that means I think I'm pretty clever, too.

"So I pull the boss aside one day and request that he assign the chief of security to us, as our direct liaison. Need someone to travel around with us, keep us out of trouble. Not going to be around the home front so much anymore. Well, the boss wasn't having any of it. Kept offering up all these other people, insists on keeping his chief of security close to home. So, finally, I give him some less than subtle hints about the goings-on with his wife."

"You didn't," Thumper said.

"Oh, I did," Lincoln said, nodding. He paused long enough to take a couple of swallows of water, and then continued.

"Two days later, the chief of security dies in an accident at a shipyard. Overseeing an incoming shipment, stack of containers tips over on him, or some such thing. Right in front of a whole crew of the boss's people. Everyone's shocked. *I* shouldn't have been, but I was. Obviously, I have to go have another talk with the boss. This isn't how we do things. And the boss looks at me like this…" Here Lincoln recreated the gesture, hands spread, apologetic shrug, "as if he has no idea what I'm talking about. So I explain how, you know, killing your own people is bad for morale. And he does the same thing, all sunshine and innocence. So finally I just come right and say, 'Look, you had your own chief of security murdered. I know you did. Your own people will turn on you for that sort of thing.'

"And now he just smiles at me, and nods, as if now he understands my concerns.

"'No, no, Mr Lincoln,' he says, 'it's OK. I take care of my people. I feed them, I give them clothes, nice things when they do well. They will not believe this about me.'

"And I tell him I'm not so sure about that. He says not to worry, he's sure. So I ask him how he knows for certain. And he looks at me with that same smile, easy as can be, and says, 'Because I gave them something else that they would rather believe.'

"Well, being an officer, of course I knew better, which I tried to patiently explain to him. He didn't seem to be too bothered about that. And you know what? Turns out he was right. There were some whispers the first couple of days, but pretty soon after that, the story took over. Terrible accident. Really sad. No more rumors about the chief of security and the boss's wife. Everyone just went about their business as if it was one of those random, unpredictable tragedies of life.

"A couple of weeks later, we're at his house and I'm trying to brief him on the latest developments. His wife comes in, sweet as can be, offers us tea, no hint whatsoever that her husband had her lover executed. When she's gone, the boss looks at me with that smile again and he says, 'You see Mr Lincoln, we cannot always control what happens, even in our own homes. But, when you control the aftermath, it is almost the same.'"

Lincoln glanced around at his team again, gave a little shrug. "That stuck with me." His teammates were silent for a moment, each thinking through what he'd just told them.

"Cool story," Sahil finally said. "But how you figure *that* into *this* again?"

"Giving people a lie that's easier to believe," Master Sergeant Wright said. "That they want to believe. Both attacks are plausibly deniable."

"Not just plausibly," said Coleman. "Anybody who doesn't *want* to see them as an attack doesn't have to. You can make a strong case here that these are both just things gone wrong, with no connection at all. A coincidence of coincidences."

"And while we argue about what it all means, the bad guys get some breathing room," Lincoln said.

"Well," Mike said. "I guess I can see that for ol' Henry, yeah? Undeclared officer gets whacked, NID probably doesn't want to admit he had anything to do with them. If they just pretend it's nothing, it's best for all parties."

"Except for Henry," Coleman said.

"But LOCKSTEP," Mike continued, ignoring the side comment, "you don't go to all that trouble unless you want someone to notice. It's too big to ignore, too expensive to pull off."

"It's actually a pretty low-rent solution," Wright said. "Biggest cost is time. And of course, the brains to make it all work. But the threat's been around forever. It's just never really been considered credible before."

"Why's that?" Mike asked. "If it's cheap, seems like that'd be the weapon of choice for all those oppressed off-worlders."

"Because most people don't want to *completely* destroy anything that's big enough to hit. Except those nutjobs a few years back," Wright answered. "You know the uh... ones who wanted to drop a kilometer-wide asteroid in the Atlantic, give the Earth a chance to start over without the human involvement."

"The Re-bEarth Movement," Lincoln said. Mike snorted and shook his head. Wright gave Lincoln a single nod.

"That's the ones," she said. "Other than *those* people. Rocks are good for killing moons and planets. Anything smaller, probably easier to just use a ship or something."

"Unless you want it to seem like an accident," said Thumper. "You can trace a ship. Pretty sure we haven't gotten around to tagging all the rocks in the Belt yet."

"Even so," Mike said, not entirely convinced. "How long you think it takes to prep an asteroid to move it? And the planning. No, forget the planning. Just think about the *math*. Trying to aim an asteroid at a hop in the middle of nothing? You can't even guarantee a station's path. That's not the kind of thing you're going to see a bunch of terrorists pull off, no matter how spunky they are."

"We don't know they haven't missed before," Wright said. "Maybe they've been trying for a while, finally got lucky."

"You could put guidance on it," Coleman added. "Couple of mining corps are working on that. Instead of sending ships out and back to haul chunks, they send a long-term crew out to rig them up. Basically build a drone around it, let it fly itself home. It's not like it has to be aerodynamic. Or even pretty, for that matter."

Mike shrugged. "Would you say that's common?"

"Nah, not yet," Thumper admitted. "But I think that's more of an insurance thing. Not too many people want to be on the hook for the bill if one of their long-term crews gets a little sloppy and a thruster falls off on the way home."

"And sends a rock through somebody's space station?" Mike said.

"Something like that, yeah," said Thumper. "You think LOCKSTEP was an accident, then?"

"No, no, I'm not saying that. But to me, there's no middle ground. It's either an accident, which I doubt, or it's an act of war. Nothing in between."

"And by act of war," Lincoln said, "you mean state-level."

"Yeah. Maybe not Central Martian Authority, but somebody with that kind of muscle. Could be closer to home."

"Eastern Coalition?" Lincoln asked. Mike shrugged again,

and Thumper shook her head.

"I'm not sure I buy that, Mike," she said. "If the Russians or Chinese cared about us looking at Mars, they've got a bunch of easier ways to get to us."

"Maybe they're about to do something down here we're not going to like, and they want us looking the wrong direction."

"Yeah maybe," said Thumper, "but–"

"All right people, look here," Wright said, cutting Thumper off. "Talking isn't planning. We're not here to figure out who did what and why. We're here to decide what *we're* going to do." She looked significantly at Lincoln. "Are we anywhere closer to that?"

"You're right, sergeant. Thank you," Lincoln said, nodding. He stood and walked to the head of the holotable, taking control of the room. "Here's what I think.

"Point one: Henry Sann and LOCKSTEP are connected, and both were intentionally targeted. I'm not sure which came first but I wouldn't be surprised if when the bad guys uncovered one, it gave them the other.

"Point two: there's not much we can do for Henry. I think it's clear he was the primary target of that attack, but we don't have much else to go on there. The hit was clean enough, I think it'd be a waste of our time to try and chase it down. Let NID handle the investigation; they can keep us informed. I think we follow the station, see where that leads. My guess is we'll get the folks behind Henry's death along the way.

"Point three: our bad guys are very good at deniable ops. That probably means using proxies whenever possible, but always keeping the tough work for themselves. Controlling the aftermath. That's their fingerprint. So we're looking for people who do things the way we do. Special people.

"I don't think these folks want to go *completely* unnoticed. I think they want to attract a very specific kind of attention. Thumper pointed out the way ahead a few minutes ago. Maybe we can't trace a rock but, as you said, sergeant, we can trace a ship. *Destiny's Undertow* is our thread. Let's all pull on it and see where it leads."

With that directive, the team returned to the intelligence dump that Lieutenant Davis had given them with renewed energy and fresh clarity of purpose. Walking backwards from *Destiny's Undertow*, and viewing everything through the lens of an intentional, coordinated attack, new connections emerged. Some were tenuous, but recognizable; the kind of connections Lincoln might have created himself, if he'd been running such an operation. Over the next three hours, they winnowed the list of possible entities involved down to a handful, and from a handful to just three. Finally, after nearly eighteen hours of intense analysis and debate, Lincoln stood in front of his team and tapped one image displayed on the wall.

"If I had to roll the dice," he said. "I'd put my money on these guys."

Apsis Solutions. A grey group based out of Shackleton, near the southern pole of Luna. They billed themselves as a full-spectrum security contracting corporation, and had ties to legitimate companies as well as tangential connections to darker organizations. They also had operational reach from Earth to Mars, and had been slapped on the wrist more than once for facilitating low-profile breaches of both technological and material embargoes. Somehow pleading ignorance had gotten them out of any serious trouble, which probably meant the group also had more than a little political protection.

"So," he said. "Who's up for a trip to the moon?"

Lincoln looked around the room at each of his team members in turn, and got nods of agreement from each of them.

"How's your Russian?" Mike asked.

"Rusty," Lincoln said. "Maybe we can practice on the way. Good work today, folks. I think all we've got left now is drawing up the official packet for the colonel. I can take care of that."

"I'll help you out," Wright said.

"I don't mind handling the tedious part, sergeant," he said.

"I think it'd be good to have an extra set of eyes on it," she answered. "Just to be sure."

It wasn't a direct challenge, but it was obvious to Lincoln that she didn't trust him to get it all right on his own.

"If you're up to it," he said, "then I'd appreciate the help."

She gave a single, sharp nod, and started organizing the panels on the holotable, grouping some together and clearing out the ones they no longer needed.

"As for you lucky folks," he said to the other three, "I recommend you try to rest up while you can. I'm guessing we're not going to have to wait around too long to hear back on this one."

"Roger that," Mike said. He, Sahil, and Thumper gathered up their personal effects and made their way out of the planning room. Lincoln returned to his seat at the holotable and brought up the standard template for a mission proposal. This had always been his least favorite part of the gig. He sat back in his chair for a moment, stretched his neck and shoulders, rubbed his face.

"Hey, cap'n," Mike called from the doorway. Lincoln turned to look at him and saw him standing in the hall with a wide grin. He tilted his head at something just out of Lincoln's view. "Your suit's here."

NINE

It wasn't often that Vector got to visit the high-class hops. And he'd never been on a five-star before. Even dressed as he was in a finely tailored suit, he was certain that the people around him could tell he didn't belong. There was something in the bearing of the super-rich; a softness in their eyes and hands that spoke of a life free of any true hardship, a superiority in their tone of voice that declared entitlement to such lavish surroundings while hinting that even this opulence was at least somewhat beneath them. No one said anything impolite to him, of course. They were all warm condescension and barely detectable disdain.

"And what was it you said you did again?" the man said.

It was a dangerous question to answer in these circles. Or, at least it would have been, if he'd cared about his social standing among these people. If your answer was too close to actual work, you risked being considered lowbrow new money. Too far removed, and you were simply living off the wealth generated by the *real* producers. For all their preening, these people did wield genuine power, and they were very concerned with making sure they only associated with others of equal stature.

"I'm a problem solver," Vector answered.

"Ha!" the man let out a single laugh, a little too abruptly, a little too loudly. "Don't we all! Don't we all! Solve problems. I like that."

The man's wife flicked her eyes down to Vector's shoes and walked her gaze back up until she met his, at which point she gave a beautifully charming smile that managed to clearly communicate her distaste for his attire. A shame. The suit was the second most expensive one he'd worn in his life, behind only the one he'd been issued for his previous job. The Woman had paid for this one; the United States taxpayers had paid for the other.

"I'm going to start using that," the man said. "'I'm a problem solver.' Brilliant. I do a bit of that myself, if I'm honest. Nothing to brag about, of course, not in this room, but I do have my hand in the occasional negotiation or two. Just managed the Coryn-Glenworth-Liao acquisition, for example. Touchy bit of work there."

Vector had no idea what the man was talking about, but he nodded and, by imagining how he might kill the man with the gold-flecked skewer holding the garnish of his drink, even managed a smile.

"I'm sorry," said a woman behind Vector, "but I'm afraid I need to deprive you of this fine man's company." She laid her hand on his forearm. He felt a thrill at her touch, but told himself it was only from concern for her safety.

"So soon?" the man said, "A shame, we were just discussing the Coryn-Glenworth-Liao acquisition. I don't mind mentioning that I was the principal negotiator–"

"I'll bring him back," the woman said. "I know he'll want to hear every detail of your involvement."

"Excuse me," Vector said, with a hint of a bow. He couldn't bring himself to look at her. Not yet.

As the woman led him away, he heard the man behind him say, "I'm sorry, I didn't catch your name…" Vector didn't turn back. Together, he and the woman navigated their way through the loose crowd, her hand still tucked in the crook of his arm.

"I don't know why you hate me so much," he said to

the woman. The Woman.

"Hate you?" she said. "I thought I was rescuing you."

"I wouldn't have needed it if you hadn't brought me here in the first place."

"This one's important to me," she said. "And I wanted you to get out a little more. Have a little dose of culture."

"If this is a *little* dose…" he said, shaking his head.

"Stop," she said. "Is it so awful to be here with me?" He risked a glance at her out of the corner of his eye, and caught her subtle pout. She was teasing him.

"It's an unnecessary risk," he answered.

They passed by a cluster of partygoers, and she dipped her head and smiled graciously at them before responding.

"A life without risk would not be worth living," she said. The Woman led him out of the main room to a balcony overlooking the vast atrium that was the hop's crowning glory. Below them, a sprawling botanical garden filled the lower level, traced throughout by delicate lines of meandering paths. Here and there, couples appeared and disappeared as they walked the trails. A lesser man might have been tempted to imagine himself down there, walking those paths with her. But not Vector. He was tempted, yes. But instead, he observed the romanticism of the setting, noted it, and remained detached from the sentiment. He was here on business, nothing more. Best if he kept that foremost in his mind.

The Woman took her hand from his arm and leaned forward on the rail of the balcony, inhaling deeply. The fragrance of the garden was strong even from several floors above it; vibrant, earthy. Healthy. They spent a minute or two in silence, she soaking in the beauty while he kept silent watch at her side. In moments like this, if it'd been possible, Vector would have been tempted to shut off the analytical side of his brain. The part that filtered out the beauty before him and dissected it into angles of approach, lines of sight, routes of escape. Nor could he prevent his mind from roughly calculating the expense for such extravagance. Other hops could barely afford to sustain staple crops for their crew. The gardens below almost seemed designed with wastefulness in mind; a display of the vast wealth that the people in the other room could throw away without feeling the effect.

"Is everything in place?" the Woman finally asked, without turning to look at him.

"Yes," he answered. She nodded and continued to scan the garden. And he saw it now, in the way she held her shoulders. Not hesitance, exactly. Never hesitance with her. But the tension of the moment, the weight of the action she'd committed herself to, had settled on her. The playfulness was her mask.

"I can see it through," he said. "You can go on home."

She gave an abrupt exhale through her nose, an almost silent chuckle. She shook her head.

"And the ship?" she asked.

"Let's discuss that later," Vector said. "When things are a little more private."

"Oh, Vector," she said, turning. "Always so serious. Always so concerned." She stepped close to him, draped her hands over his shoulders, clasped them behind his neck. Her touch was light, soft, but her eyes were intense with purpose. "Of all the people on this station, I assure you we are the least to be noticed. But here, now we can speak quietly and no one will suspect a thing."

He put his hands on her hips to complete the ruse, reminded himself that that's all it was. A performance. A cover. She looked into his eyes with her eyebrows raised. "My ship?"

"A couple of weeks to finish the work," he said. "Then travel time."

"Whose week?" she asked.

"Oh, sorry. Terran."

She nodded.

"Does that mean we're on schedule?" he asked.

"Close enough," she answered. "The timing doesn't need to be precise to the hour, or even the day. Just enough to keep momentum."

She stared into his eyes, searching them in silence for a span, lengthy enough for Vector to feel his emotional distance threatening to slip. Since she didn't appear to be intending to speak any time soon, he took the opportunity to rescue himself.

"While I've got you here," he said. "I'd like to ask you something, if I may."

"Anything," she said.

"I'd like you to answer the question, too."

"Ah, so demanding," she said. "In that case, no promises. But ask anyway."

"Why Vector?" he asked. Contrary to his expectations, the Woman had decided to keep his codename intact for the foreseeable future.

"It suits you."

"Obviously *you* think so. I'd like to know why."

"Because you are a man of magnitude," she said. "And you have purpose. Direction." She gave it a moment, and then gave him her easy smile, her dark eyes sparkling. "It's a math joke, see."

"Yeah, I get it," he said. "You sure it isn't from another definition of the word? Something to do with, say, I don't know, an agent responsible for the spread of a disease, maybe?"

She just smiled back at him. Without meaning to, he noticed her hair smelled of lilacs; the proximity made it impossible to miss.

"Yeah," he said. Back to business. "What do you want us to do about the girl?"

"She's secure on your ship?" she asked. Vector nodded.

"*Your* ship," he added.

"Is she troublesome?"

"Nah. But she's smart."

The Woman smiled at that. "Dangerous, then. Keep her as she is for now. I feel safer having her with you than anywhere else."

"Yes, ma'am."

"But," the Woman said pointedly, "if she becomes troublesome, I may need to reconsider."

"Understood."

After a moment her smile faded, her eyes hardened, and a grey stillness of iron resolve replaced the Woman's playfulness.

"I ask a lot of you," she said. "And you've been faithful in every way. It will only get harder from here."

"I know."

She nodded, unclasped her hands from behind his neck, drew herself away. Vector released her and tried to ignore the reluctance he didn't want to admit he felt.

"We should finish the business at hand."

"I really think you should let me handle it," he tried, one last time.

"No, dear," she said, in a way that was just soothing enough to make the condescension tolerable. And with that comment, the last trace of her impishness and any hint of softness melted away as she flipped the mental switch to go operational. Vector had seen it dozens of times, and even so it still unnerved him how different she became when it was time to work.

"Wrap up what you need to and prep the ship for departure," she said, and even her voice had changed. Sharper, deeper. "This one, I'll handle myself."

TEN

Lincoln stood still and looked directly into the reader, as he'd been told. Well, not quite exactly as he'd been told. Technically he was supposed to lean forward until his forehead and cheeks were in contact with the device, but given the number of people that came through Shackleton's infamous customs lines, there was no way he was touching any part of his face to that thing.

The device chirped, having confirmed his retina did in fact belong to him.

"Mr Kim," the customs agent said, motioning for Lincoln to step over to him. Lincoln glanced over at the agent at Booth 8, disappointed. He'd been trying to time it so that he'd be called over to the bored-looking older woman at Booth 6. Instead, two twenty-somethings had somehow missed the three thousand signs between the arrival gate and here, informing them that only one person was allowed to leave a line at a time. Security was still interviewing them at Lincoln's intended entry point, which was taking even longer than usual because of the two violators who were weeping like their lives were at stake.

The man at Booth 8 stared at Lincoln with cold expectancy. He was a big guy, intense. He'd been the one Lincoln had specifically been hoping to avoid. The agent at Booth 8 was former military, no doubt about it, and Lincoln knew the agent had already pegged him for the same. Something about service members; they could always spot each other from a mile away.

Lincoln nodded and walked over to the booth, doing his best impression of the weary traveler, which fortunately wasn't too tough since he'd been awake for at least thirty-two hours straight. He'd been stuck in a middle seat on the trip up between an overweight narcoleptic who snored and a skinny author who wanted to talk about his books the whole time. Lincoln would gladly have traded the author for the snoring man's twin brother.

"Morning," Lincoln said.

The customs agent acknowledged the greeting with half a nod.

"Been to Luna before?" the agent asked. His accent was English, marked by a few years in southern Luna.

"A few times," Lincoln answered.

"And the nature of your visit?"

"Here for work."

"And what do you do, Mr Kim?"

"I'm a filmmaker," Lincoln said.

"Yeah? What sorts of films?"

"Not the good kind. Corporate stuff mostly."

"And you're filming here, then?"

"Yes sir."

The agent waited for more, but Lincoln had learned a long time ago that the easiest way to spot a liar was to count the number of unnecessary details they included in their story.

"Not keen to share?" the agent finally asked.

Lincoln shrugged. "Usual propaganda-disguised-as-transparency gig. 'Hey, look at all these great things we're doing for the environment, see how happy everyone is to work here.' That sort of thing. I probably shouldn't name the client unless I'm required by law."

The agent shook his head. "Not required. Just curious."

"It's every bit as exciting as you're imagining, I assure you."

The agent cracked a smile then, and tapped something out on his console. Lincoln couldn't remember the last time he'd had a customs agent take such interest in him. Some part of his lizard brain started telling him something was up, something was wrong. NID had helped put the cover package together, but they hadn't had a lot of time to do it. Maybe the retinal scan picked something up it shouldn't have. He took a deep breath and exhaled, disguised it as a sigh. It'd be all right. He'd been in far tougher spots than this before. And at least in this case, if he *did* get caught, they probably wouldn't execute him where he stood.

He looked over at Booth 6, with what he hoped was a look of casual impatience. The two twenty-somethings had finally gotten cleared through customs and were off to one side, still crying. The bored woman at Booth 6 was practically waving people through. Lincoln sighed again, genuinely.

"And your crew?" the agent said.

"Just me and my camerawoman," Lincoln said. He scanned the crowd and caught sight of Thumper a few aisles over, waiting for him. Good, she'd made it through no problem. He pointed vaguely her direction.

"Duration of your stay?"

"Three weeks on the schedule," he said. "Less if I'm lucky."

The agent nodded again, tapped on his console some more.

"You serve in the military at all, Mr Kim?"

"Yep," Lincoln said. No point in denying it.

"I thought so," the agent said.

"How about you?"

"Eight years, Royal Marines."

"Nice," Lincoln said. "Miss it?"

"Only my mates," he said. Lincoln felt a hint of relief at that. Not an interrogation after all. Just a lonely Marine, glad to steal a little time with someone with shared experience.

A Royal Marine working customs probably had to grit his teeth a hundred times a day listening to the stories of security personnel around the port who liked the uniform and authority, but didn't have the steel to serve.

"Yeah. Hard to find good people out here with the regular folks sometimes," Lincoln said. The agent nodded. "When I was in, they used to say the only thing meaner than a US Marine was the Royal Marine that had to clean up after him."

The agent chuckled. "Hadn't heard that one. Is it meant to be a compliment or an insult?"

"Some of each, I think," Lincoln said. In fact, he'd just made it up on the spot. But it sounded like the kind of thing someone might say. The agent tapped a few more times on his console, and then turned back. Maybe Lincoln was imagining it, but the man's face seemed a little brighter.

"You have a good day now, Mr Kim."

"Cheers," Lincoln said.

Once he'd cleared Booth 8, he walked over to where Thumper was waiting for him and together the two of them headed towards the baggage holding area. Between them, they had a couple of hundred pounds of surveillance gear to pick up, all cleverly packed and disguised to look like standard film equipment. To Lincoln's great disappointment, they'd had to leave the recon suits back home for the Luna op. It was hard to stay inconspicuous doing street-level work while armored up. That hadn't stopped him from trying to find a way to work it into the plan, of course, but in the end he just couldn't make it work.

"What was that all about?" Thumper asked.

"Just a brother-in-arms looking for a chat," Lincoln said. And then he looked back over his shoulder, and quietly added, "I hope. Either that, or we're going to get picked up any second. Keep your eyes open."

"You got it."

Fortunately, apart from having to ask an attendant to track

down a missing bag for them, they didn't have any more trouble getting out of the port. Pence was supposed to be waiting for them outside somewhere. The team had all come in on commercial flights and staggered their arrival, with Sahil coming in last. He was scheduled to show up later that afternoon. Mike and Master Sergeant Wright had been first to land in order to lay some initial groundwork.

They found Mike waiting out front, in an old model car. Amazingly, even though car accidents were a rare occurrence, the one he'd picked up looked like it'd been in at least three. The front fender was crumpled; the side had a long trench gouged out from the front door almost all the way to the rear of the vehicle. There didn't appear to be a rear bumper. And that's just what Lincoln could see from the right side.

Mike hopped out and, after some struggle, opened the trunk for them.

"I was starting to worry I'd gotten the day wrong," he said as they approached. "Two days in and I still can't tell you what time it's supposed to be."

"Then how do you know it's been two days?" Thumper said.

"Missed you too, Thump," he said, grabbing one of the bags from her and loading it in the trunk. "What took you?"

"The boss here tried to pick up one of the customs agents," Thumper said.

"Yeah, any luck?"

Lincoln shook his head. "He was out of my league."

"Too pretty?" Mike said.

"Nah. A Brit."

Mike whistled. "Well good on ya for trying."

Once the gear was loaded up, they opened the doors to get in the vehicle. The interior emanated an almost tangible aura, thick with the scent of air fresheners, laced with subtle undertones of either curry or vomit. Possibly both. And the inside looked even worse than the outside. All the seats were forward facing, two in the front and a bench seat across the back, but the upholstery had been ripped out so that the rear seating was just bare metal.

"You can sit up front," Mike said. Lincoln was about to say thanks, until he saw the stains.

"Nuh uh, buddy," Thumper said, sliding onto the bench. Lincoln looked at the two of his teammates sitting in the back. He'd just spent twenty-two hours wedged between two unpleasant companions. There was no way he was sitting in the middle. He picked the front seat that seemed least likely to give him hepatitis. The doors closed, and the engine rattled online.

"Wow, Mike," he said, with a cough. "You going to have to drive this thing yourself?"

"It ain't that bad!" Mike replied, his voice rising in pitch with each word. His response was more defensive than Lincoln had expected. Thumper just laughed.

"Wright's been riding you about it, huh?" she asked.

"She won't let it go, man," Mike said, shaking his head. He seemed genuinely hurt.

"I know we're keeping a low profile," Lincoln said, "but uh…"

"You'll understand when you see the place," Mike said. He spoke to the vehicle, giving the address, and then sat back and waited. When nothing happened, he leaned forward over the front seat, pressed the module on the console more firmly into place, and tried once more. At this, the car lurched once, then pulled away from the curb and onto the thoroughfare. Thumper snorted.

"Next time *you* can handle acquisition, Thump," he said.

"I didn't say anything," she said.

It was about a forty-minute drive from the port out to the location, and the closer they got, the more Lincoln understood Mike's choice of transportation. The surroundings grew more industrial; everything out this direction was greyer, shabbier.

Still. It seemed like maybe Pence could have spent a *little* more on the car. Lincoln wasn't sure if it was the smell, the lack of sleep, or the after-effects of space travel, but as they drove, he felt increasingly queasy, almost like he'd developed a mild case of seasickness. He laid his head back on the seat and closed his eyes.

"Ugh," he said. "Probably shouldn't have eaten that fish on the trip up."

"*Probably*? Brother, it's just SOP to avoid seafood in space," Mike said.

"Standard op procedure or not," Thumper said, "I woulda thought it was just common sense."

"Yeah," Lincoln said.

"I'm feeling it, too," Thumper said from the back. "And I most definitely didn't eat the fish."

"Oh," Mike said. "Yeah. Gravity fields aren't super consistent out this way. I think they run between nine-eight and one-one, so that's probably causing some of it. You get to used it. Sort of."

Lincoln opened his eyes again when they came up on the first connector between sectors and watched the transition. Moving from one dome to the next wasn't that interesting, not much different than driving through a short mountain tunnel back home. But Lincoln had lived most of his life on Earth, had grown up with nothing between him and space but air. There was always something a little uncanny about the way the sky came bending down like a waterfall to kiss the ground at the edge of a sector.

The self-repairing nanocrystalline domes here on Luna were smaller than the ones that housed the Martian settlements. They were thicker, more resilient, and couldn't be sustained across as much open space. They were a few decades older, too, for one thing, especially down here in the southern pole where the first colonies had been established. Shackleton had been named for the nearby crater, though the city had expanded in leapfrog fashion well away from its original center. Supposedly the outer shells were impact rated up to something like five hundred kilotons, which was good enough to eat a twenty-meter rock without a breach. Fortunately, they'd never had a live event to test that limit. Like most people, Lincoln didn't want to think about what would happen if something ever did get through.

Once they'd passed into the next sector, the sky leapt heavenward again, and the industrialized scenery picked right back up where it had left off. A few minutes down the road, Lincoln realized these were the older shipyards, where many of the first generation ships had been constructed before sailing off into the Deep. Before the hops had become the primary facilities for ship manufacturing. Some were still hanging on, cranking out budget models or hoping to stretch out their legacy as being among the first, but it was obvious that the industry was drying up on Luna. With unfocused eyes, Lincoln watched it all flow past in a concrete blur.

"Apsis must've really doctored up their corporate materials," he said. All the public-facing material he'd seen while researching the group was clean, professional, very high-gloss. Nothing like the flat greys and rust browns that surrounded them now.

"Yeah, well we're not going to their main office, don't worry."

"You guys found an off-site already?" Lincoln asked.

"Wish I could say we worked that fast," Mike answered, "but NID gets the credit for this one. They'd already sniffed it out before we even landed."

"They've got people on the ground?" said Lincoln.

"Yeah. At least one. He might even be at the place when we get there. Seems like a good dude. Plays things kind of close to the chest, though."

"He's NID," Thumper said.

"Yeah. But I mean he's quiet even for one of them. Straight

shooter when he talks, but doesn't say any more than he has to."

"I'll take that over the other kind," Lincoln said.

"Yeah, roger that," Mike said. "One time, back in Indo, I had to work with NID Special Services and the officer I got assigned to…" He paused and shook his head. "We called him Best Guess. Not to his face, of course. But I swear that man must've had some kind of childhood trauma that made it impossible for him to say the words 'I don't know'. About the only thing you could guarantee with him was that however much you figured he'd underestimated enemy strength by, he'd underestimated it by at least twice as much. And if he said something was clear? Hoo boy."

They traveled on for a few more minutes. Lincoln was just about to comment on how glad he was that he didn't have to live in a dump like this when the vehicle slowed. It bumped up onto the curb before correcting itself and then parked along the side of the road, just in front of a narrow five-story building that Lincoln guessed was abandoned and condemned.

"I see what you mean about the car," Lincoln said.

"Thank you," Mike said. "Probably oughta leave most of the gear for now. We'll take it up in shifts after dark." The domes were scheduled to match the twenty four-hour day-night cycle of Earth using Greenwich Mean Time.

"You sure it'll be safe here?" Thumper asked.

"Nope," he answered, as he opened the door. "But it ain't worth blowing cover over. Just grab the essentials."

They unloaded a pair of packs, and Mike led them inside. When they entered, Lincoln was surprised to see an elderly man leaning against the door frame outside the first floor apartment by the stairs, smoking. He watched them with a mild hostility, as if they were walking across his front lawn.

"*Moy brat*," Mike said in Russian, jerking a thumb at Lincoln as they passed. *My brother.* The man didn't even blink.

After they'd climbed up the first set of stairs, Mike looked back over his shoulder and said, "Timur owns the place." A moment later he added, "Don't worry. I told him we had family coming in. He gave us the penthouse suite."

"Great," Thumper said, and her tone of voice implied the opposite. Thinking about having to hump all their gear up five flights of stairs, no doubt. There were elevators, but Lincoln figured using one of those was a good way to spend half a day trapped in a metal box.

When they reached the top floor, Mike went to the second door on the left. He knocked three times and waited five seconds before punching in the code on the lock. A series of bolts clicked on the other side of the door. Mike swung the door open, and Wright was standing there to greet them. She didn't have a weapon visible, but from her stance Lincoln knew she had one close at hand. When she saw it was them, she nodded a greeting.

"Welcome to it," Mike said. "Try not to make too much of a mess. I had to put down a security deposit."

It was pretty much what Lincoln had expected. The apartment was old and had a pervasive smell of dust, even though it looked like his teammates had cleaned the place up a bit. From the main entrance, there was an open common area, with a table and two chairs. Adjoining the main room was a small kitchen whose appliances looked like they predated the first lunar colony. Walking into the common area, Lincoln saw there were two bedrooms off the right side, with a single bathroom between. To the left, Wright and Pence had hung a large dark blanket up on the wall. None of their gear was visible from the door, except for two sleeping bags they'd laid out on the floor in the common area. When Lincoln poked his head into the front bedroom and saw the mattress on the bed, he understood the choice.

"Timur's charging us double," Mike said, from across the room, "for all the extra space." When Lincoln looked back

JAY POSEY   165

at him, Mike was standing by the wall with the blanket on it. He dramatically pulled the blanket to one side to reveal the adjoining apartment. Technically, the apartments *were* connected. But that was only because there was a hole in the wall big enough to walk through.

"Now that everyone's rolling in," Mike said, "We figure we'll keep this one for operations, and through the curtain here can be for downtime."

Lincoln set his pack down on the floor.

"Sounds good," he said. "What's the schedule been like so far?"

"I wouldn't call it a schedule yet," Mike answered. "I've been out running errands. Mas'sarnt's done all the real work. Not sure she's slept since we got here."

"You ready for a break, sergeant?" Lincoln asked Wright.

"Nah, I still got a good eight hours left of this stim," she said. "Maybe after."

"What'd you take?"

"Just a blue."

Lincoln nodded. "You got time to brief us?"

"Sure," she said. "Thumper, we saved you that room." Wright pointed to the front bedroom, as she walked over towards the one in the back. Lincoln followed. "Let me know what you need, I'll make One-time go get it."

"You saw the car he picked out, right?" Thumper asked.

"Don't," Mike said sharply. Thumper laughed as she disappeared into the front room to drop off her gear.

Wright took Lincoln into the rear bedroom, which they'd converted into their planning center. The bed frame had been broken down, and the mattress was leaning upright against one wall. In the middle of the room, they'd set up a couple of folding tables with chairs around it. Wright had stuck a thin-skin overlay on the longest wall so they could display whatever intel they needed to on it. A pair of terminals hummed quietly on the table. And, to Lincoln's surprise, a man was hunched over one of them, reading something on the holo.

"This is our NID minder," Wright said. The man stood slowly, apparently reluctant to take his eyes from the report he was reading. When he did finally look over at Lincoln, he extended his hand and smiled. He was in his early fifties, maybe; dark hair frosted grey at the temples and scruffy, dressed in rumpled clothes. His look gave the impression that he'd jumped out of bed in the middle of the night a couple of days prior and had been working ever since. And, given the nature of his job, there was a good chance that's what had actually happened.

"Captain Suh," he said. "Mr Self."

"Just Lincoln," Lincoln said, shaking the man's hand. "Mr Self, huh? Is that your real name?"

Mr Self's smile widened.

"Oh. All right then," Lincoln said. "I didn't know we were in spook country."

"I didn't know the 301st sent *technicians* out to handle this sort of thing," Mr Self said.

"Fair enough," Lincoln said. "No one told me you were going to be here personally."

"I didn't know it myself until recently," Mr Self said. "But the Directorate's trying to keep this one compartmentalized. Guess they figured I can keep a secret."

"Rumor is you've got a good history of that."

"Must not be *too* good if there are rumors," Mr Self said with a smile.

"Sergeant Wright was just about to get me up to speed."

Mr Self nodded and sat back down. "Still early, but I think we've got a good foothold to start from."

Wright woke the second terminal and tapped a few keystrokes on the interface it projected onto the table. A moment later, the lights in the room went out with a short, sharp buzz. Lincoln looked over at Wright who was bathed in the glow from the terminal interface. She glanced up at the ceiling and then shook her head.

"It happens," Wright said. "Don't sweat it."

She finished with the terminal, and the thin-skin on the wall lit up with a top-down view of a section of the city. Thumper came in just as Wright was beginning.

"What's with the lights?" Thumper said.

"Power distribution's not the best out this way," Wright answered. "Mainline will probably come back on in a few minutes. We're running everything on portable anyway. But you probably better plan on losing juice whenever you need it most."

"Roger that," said Thumper.

"All right. Apsis Solutions," Wright said. "When they say full-spectrum security, they're not kidding. Front page, they do all the usual stuff. Close protection, threat assessment, information security, nothing special there. But, come in through the side door, and you get a whole bunch of other services. In this case, for example, safehouses for people that don't want to be found."

"Or that *other* people don't want found," Mr Self added, without looking up from his terminal.

Wright walked over to the thin-skin and tapped it at a location near the bottom. At her touch, the image of the building turned blue.

"We're here," she said. Then, with her finger she circled a cluster of buildings a few hundred meters north. Within the circle she'd traced, labels popped up for several of the buildings and their surrounding streets. Street names were accurate, but the building labels were purely for convenience; for some reason, Wright had used the names of Shakespearean characters. "Safehouse is somewhere around here. We haven't been able to get a fix on it yet, but we've narrowed it down to this area for certain."

"And any idea who's in there?" Lincoln asked.

"Not yet. But they're taking a lot of measures to make sure we don't find out."

"You get any skeeters in?" Thumper asked.

"Nah. We tried, but they've got a net up. We've got a couple on station around the perimeter in case someone comes out. I didn't want to risk tipping anybody off, though. They're also masking the volume of traffic coming in and out of there, distributing it. Even so, it's still running pretty hot for the area. Thumper, once you get set up, you should take a look at it and see what you can pull out."

"Easy day," Thumper said.

"What's the assessment on security?" Lincoln asked.

"First look says about what you'd expect. Automated surveillance augmented with personnel. We've ID'd four return customers that fit the profile. I'm sure there are more we haven't sniffed out yet."

"Pop the sweeps up for me, would ya, Mir?" Thumper said. Wright walked back over to the terminal and keyed something in. A moment later, a series of multicolored arcs and circles appeared in the target zone.

"Blues for motion, greens for bioscan, reds for full capture," Wright said. "You can see the gaps in coverage, but I'd chalk that up to us not finding them all yet. These guys don't seem like the sloppy type."

"You got makes and models for these yet?" Thumper asked. Wright shook her head.

Lincoln scanned the top-down without looking for anything in particular, just soaking in the big picture. "I'd like to get up there and walk it as soon as possible. When's a good time?"

"I wouldn't recommend it, sir," Wright said. "Once Sahil gets in, we can handle the groundwork with good coverage. You just tell us what you need."

"You've been over, I assume."

"Sure, but Mom doesn't care if *I* get scuffed up."

"I'm pretty sure he doesn't expect me to sit around here and make you do all the work, sergeant."

"Actually, that's exactly what he expects. He told me explicitly to keep you out of harm's way on this one, sir."

"He's going to be disappointed."

"We'll see."

Lincoln scanned the image on the thin-skin, and took mild satisfaction in knowing that whoever was in that safehouse probably wasn't much more comfortable than they were.

"We'll wait for Sahil," Lincoln said. "And then I'm going to take a walk. You know. Just to clear my head."

Sahil arrived three hours late, which had him in after dark. Unfortunately, he wasn't on Lincoln's side of the argument. Like Wright, he wasn't a fan of the idea of Lincoln walking around the area at all, not to mention on his own. The other two weren't much help. Sahil had helped haul the rest of Thumper's gear up, and she was heads-down, bringing her AI-assisted surveillance system "Veronica" all online. Mike offered Lincoln some weak moral support, but seemed ambivalent at best about Lincoln doing anything other than running the op center. Lincoln got the impression that Pence was only on his side to get back at Wright for all the grief she'd given him over the car.

In the end, they'd compromised. The team agreed to let Lincoln out as long as Wright could escort him, with the assurance that she could pull the plug at any moment. Mike would be on standby in his getaway vehicle, in case there was trouble; Thumper rigged it up so Mike could have manual control if he needed it. Sahil would post up outside the zone but close enough to act as back up, and Thumper would man the temporary operations center, keeping watch over the whole team.

It all seemed excessive to Lincoln, but it was too early in the game for him to try pulling rank. Still, he did his best to make it clear he was letting them have their way this one time. He wasn't sure any of them bought it.

Now he and Wright were walking through the outer perimeter of the cluster of buildings she and Pence had identified. It was always a tricky business to introduce yourself into a new environment without attracting the wrong kind of attention. Fortunately, there was more foot traffic in the area than there was back at the temporary HQ. Even though it was just a few blocks over, this section of town showed signs of more normal life. It was still clearly low on the economic end of things, but at least there were a few restaurants, grocers, and other small businesses on each side of the street. Still, the target zone wasn't exactly the kind of place that seemed to attract a lot of tourists, and Lincoln knew any team serious about security wouldn't just have their own people watching. They'd have developed a network of regular people to help them out: bartenders, grocery clerks, baristas, anybody with a routine and consistent interaction with the local populace. Casual connections, but ones that might give early warning of anything new or unusual.

Early in his career, Lincoln had nearly blown his team's cover by buying a case of water after he'd told a clerk he was in town by himself for a couple of days. When internal security services had shown up later, he'd managed to persuade them that his religious beliefs required ritual washing eight times a day and that he didn't trust the purity of his lodging's water supply. It had taken a demonstration of said "ritual" and six bottles of water to convince them. That little caper had earned him a nickname from his team that, thankfully, hadn't followed him through the rest of his career.

It'd been a good lesson, though; well worth the grief it had caused him amongst his teammates. And it was one that he kept in mind while checking out the streets in and around the target buildings.

Wright had already pulled in a fair amount of data on the

area before they'd visited it, but it was a funny thing about surveillance technology: no matter how clear the images had gotten, or how good the audio, the eggheads still hadn't been able to come up with a device yet that could capture and communicate the *feeling* of a place. They could fly a drone array through and then simulate a city block with pixel-perfect precision. Lincoln had prepared for many operations using those simulations. Not one of them had ever compared to actually walking the route himself.

Lincoln really wanted to get down into the heart of the target area, but he'd had to promise to keep to the outer perimeter until Thumper got a better read on the surveillance and counter-surveillance measures that Apsis had in place. He was helping on that front, though, and not just with his own eyes and ears. Thumper had rigged him up with a detector.

It was a simple device: just a belt with small, vibrating elements arrayed around it. Interpreting the signals wasn't any more difficult than playing a game of hot-or-cold. The stronger the vibrations, the more signal was being detected. And depending on which elements were active, Lincoln could tell what direction he should head towards, or whether he was walking through the middle of a field. Thumper had fine-tuned the sensitivity to filter out the background levels of normal traffic. While they walked, directed by the whims of the strength-of-signal, the detector's sensors soaked up whatever electronic signals he and Wright passed through and transmitted any relevant information back to Veronica, Thumper's much-beloved surveillance system. Together, they were building a more complete picture of their area of operations.

They'd been at it for a little over an hour when they had their first hint of trouble.

"Captain," Thumper said over comms, "I think you picked up some interest. Veronica's tracking two men, one behind you, one across the street. Looks like they've been orbiting you for a few minutes."

"Roger that, Thumper," Lincoln said. "Mark 'em for us."

"Marking," she said, and then a moment later, "Marked."

Lincoln ran a thumb across the dermal pad in his wrist and activated his retinal heads-up display. Two pips appeared, one at six o'clock and one halfway between eight and nine o'clock. Both Lincoln and Wright maintained their pace, and kept their eyes forward.

"You get that?" Lincoln asked Wright.

"Yeah," she said. And then through the comm channel, "Thumper, can you get facial on them?"

"Negative," Thumper said. "Skeeters are too high, and I can't risk bringing them much lower."

"All right, copy," Wright said.

"Think we're pegged?" Lincoln asked.

"I don't see how you could be. But Veronica's running the loop now, and they've definitely been reacting to your movements for a couple of minutes. It isn't random. Take a right up ahead, let me watch what they do."

At the next cross street, Lincoln and Wright turned right and continued on their way. The pips in Lincoln's vision converged briefly, crossed over. One stayed fixed at six o'clock while the other worked its way gradually from six to eight.

"All right, yeah," Thumper said. "They're definitely trailing you. They just handed off. Guy in a black coat is on your tail now. Guy in a ballcap looks like he's moving up a block. Guessing he's going to rejoin you in a few."

"Roger," Lincoln said. "Designate Black Coat and Ballcap. Black Coat's on our six?"

"That's affirmative," Thumper answered. "Black Coat is trailing you."

"Could they pull a read on the detector?" Wright asked.

"Might be," Thumper said. "It's mostly passive, but it sends packets in bursts. If they knew what to look for, it's possible, I guess. Maybe you should kill it, just to be safe."

"Negative," Lincoln said. "If they're picking up some kind of signature off us, going dark will just be an admission of guilt. We'll figure something out."

"Ballcap's circling back your way," Thumper said. "He's picking up the pace."

"Give me range," Wright said. A few moments later, distance indicators appeared next to the pips in Lincoln's view. Black Coat was about fifteen meters behind them. Ballcap was farther, but closing.

"What else reads like a detector?" Lincoln asked.

"Not much," she said. "Uh..."

"Come on, Thump, give me some options."

"I don't know, sir," Thumper said. "Anything uh... anything that does burst transmission. Assuming they're just picking up signal and not actually intercepting packets."

"The idiot's version, sergeant," Lincoln said.

"Like... I don't know, some kind of low-profile recording device, a tracker, uh... maybe a high-end–"

"Pence," Wright said. "Come around, prep for a snatch. Thumper, find a spot, send us a marker. Somewhere close."

"Copy," Thumper answered. "Stand by."

"You need me?" Sahil asked.

"Negative, stay put," Wright responded.

A few moments later, another icon popped up in Lincoln's augmented reality display; a small triangle pointing down at a location just a couple of blocks away.

"Pushing it to you now," Thumper said.

"Roger, I see it. Pence, you got it?"

"Roger that," Mike answered. "Maybe three mikes out."

"Two's better," Wright said.

"I'll see what I can do. Who's the target?"

"I'll handle it, just be there."

Wright clearly had a plan and the team was executing it with smooth coordination. The fact that she hadn't consulted him or asked for permission should have bothered him, but

Lincoln knew in a moment like this, he had to swallow his pride and just let the team work. The best thing he could do was follow her lead.

"Ballcap's catching up," Thumper said. "And Veronica just picked up another possible threat heading your way."

"How possible?" Lincoln asked.

"About thirty percent," she answered. "He just changed direction, maybe to intercept. Maybe just because he forgot something."

"Understood. Mark him."

A third pip appeared, this one at about one o'clock. Black Coat and Ballcap were closing fast.

"Mir?" Sahil said over comms.

"Hold steady, Sahil," she said. "Mike, how close?"

"Forty seconds," Mike said.

"That's too long," Wright said, almost to herself. "He's not going to make it."

A moment later, Wright slowed her pace and stepped closer to the side of a building. Instinctively, Lincoln matched her, angled his body towards her to see what she was up to.

"Lean in and kiss me," she said.

"What?" Lincoln said. "Seriously?" The move was such a cliché, he'd never thought anyone actually used it.

"Just do it. Sir."

Lincoln hesitated for a moment, but Wright's eyes were intense, insistent. He leaned down, closed his eyes, brought his lips to hers.

They didn't meet.

Instead, a jarring impact on the right side of his jaw stumbled him. He brought his arms up reflexively to protect himself but before he could get oriented, a second blow caught him in the back of the knee and buckled him to the ground. An instant later, he was caught in a vicious chokehold from behind. His assailant was over him, crushing down. Black Coat couldn't have closed the gap that fast, they must have had a fourth guy. Fourth and fifth. Where was Wright?

Even as his mind was racing to process what was happening, Lincoln's training took over. His attacker's hold wasn't perfect, wasn't deep enough. Lincoln knifed his hands back and sought out those of his attacker. When he managed to grab hold of one, he snatched it down and forward over his shoulder, wrenched the wrist, forced the arm over his head and used it as a lever to break the hold. Free from the choke, he rolled sideways onto the attacker's ankle and shin, dropping his opponent hard to the concrete. Not knowing how many other attackers he had to deal with, Lincoln's first priority was to get off the ground. He twisted and whipped an elbow back behind him, felt it glance off the side of his assailant's head, and then wrested himself free and spun up to his feet.

He instinctively came up in a defensive posture, scanned the crowd around him for a second attacker, and for any sign of Wright. There, just behind the first row of people, stood a man in a black coat, staring right at him with a startled expression. Lincoln had just enough time and presence of mind to make one quick gesture before he realized that Wright was surging up off the ground in front of him, and someone behind him screamed. Pain exploded at the base of his neck. Blackness swallowed him.

ELEVEN

Piper laid with her face to the wall and her hands behind her back, hoping that the woman couldn't hear the sound of her heart pounding against the bed. It wasn't that she feared anything that might happen while the woman was in the room with her. She'd gotten used to the routine now of lying still until the door was closed again. It was what would happen after the woman left that had filled Piper with anxiety.

"I grabbed you an extra couple of pieces of bread," the woman said. Her voice was direct, purely informational, though the words themselves hinted at a sense of concern for Piper's wellbeing. "I know you like them."

"Thank you," Piper replied.

The woman finished up her work, and moved to the door. Paused there. Piper's heart leapt into her throat, and she had to shut her eyes and clench her jaw to keep herself still.

"If you need anything else, let me know," the woman said.

"I will," Piper said. "Thank you."

A few rapid heartbeats of silence passed, and then the woman left the room and the door slid shut. The lock clicked, as it always did, but there, if anyone had known to listen for it, was a second, quieter click just ahead of it. Piper made herself count to twenty before she came out of her position, and then to one hundred before she sat up on the bed. She was going to do it. Now that the moment had come, she knew she was going to. She had to try. Even so, it took all of her will to make herself stand to her feet.

Piper went to her little table and sat in the folding chair. The woman had left her a meal and, as promised, with it were three discs of the flat bread Piper had come to enjoy so much. She wasn't especially hungry at that exact moment, but she tore off some of the bread and nibbled at it, poked at the rest of her meal with its corners.

There was no way to know how long they'd been holding her. Her wrist seemed to have completely healed, and the woman had removed her cast. So that was probably at least a week of time, depending on what nanos they'd used to help heal the bone. But it had been a long stretch before Piper had even thought to try to keep track of time, and the only system she'd been able to come up with since then wasn't exactly reliable. She'd started counting the number of times she'd slept, which was now up to twenty-three. Unfortunately, she could never tell how long she'd slept at any given time, nor how much time had passed before she felt tired enough to go back to sleep, so she had no clear idea of how long she'd been a prisoner.

It must have been intentional on the part of her captors, as well. At first, Piper had assumed that her body was just out of kilter from the stress and trauma of her circumstances; that she needed more sleep than usual, or that sometimes she was ravenous when it was time to eat and other times she had no appetite at all. Over time, though, she came to suspect that the people holding her were purposefully avoiding establishing any sort of set routine for her. Maybe they would bring her two meals only a couple of hours apart, and then make her go a full day before the next one came. Piper had no way to measure it, of course, but once she started paying attention, it seemed very likely that they were manipulating her to keep her off balance.

That was OK, though. Because Piper had started

manipulating them right back. Carefully, cautiously, she'd begun to establish a routine of her own, to build a certain level of expectation and maybe even something like trust. She had no idea if she was under constant surveillance, but she'd decided to assume she was. After a couple of experiments, she'd located the camera they were using to keep an eye on her and, more importantly, the extent of its vision. It was high, near the door, and angled mainly to focus on the bed and table. Piper had managed to extract some concessions from the woman that brought her meals by mentioning several times how difficult she found it to use the bathroom knowing that anyone could be watching her. Eventually they'd brought a makeshift folding screen for her and set it up to give her a small corner of privacy.

Piper had also taken to doing yoga and some calisthenics to keep her strength up. For some of these, she made use of the wall by the door, just out of view of the camera. No one made any comment to her about it, undoubtedly to avoid acknowledging that there was a gap in their surveillance. But she was on good behavior anyway, and never gave them any reason to think she would do anything other than what they expected of her.

She'd made good use of her privacy screen. Over time, she'd managed to pull a few parts from the waste recycler; a spring here, some flexible tubing there, a small amount of some kind of thick pasty substance that clung to surfaces and never seemed to dry out or harden. A couple of components came from her table. And her work to establish rapport had gone far enough that they were even trusting her with an eating utensil now: a single instrument part fork, part spoon, with an edge that was enough to cut butter and not much else.

Over several sessions of sitting on the toilet behind her screen, she'd assembled a small device. Nothing special or fancy, by any means. Just a tiny, spring-loaded metal plate on a makeshift hinge crafted from flexible tubing. This device she'd stuck to the door frame during one of her stretching exercises. It was this device that had clicked, just before the lock had settled into place, preventing it from securing completely. And, with any luck, it was this device that would enable Piper to work the lock open. Studying the door and the lock had confirmed what she had begun to believe; the ship she was on hadn't been built with prisoners in mind, and her captors didn't consider her to pose any serious threat of escape. The lock was a simple catch, dialed in from the outside. Undoubtedly there were security measures preventing any sort of attempt to hack the control, but that was a common mistake. High-tech security often had the most embarrassingly low-tech vulnerabilities.

She poked at her meal a few minutes longer, with both bread and eating utensil. Then, after hopefully having given a good performance of not being especially hungry, she got up, sat on the edge of her bed for a span and let her nervous energy show. She bounced her legs, she fidgeted, she rolled her head around to stretch her neck. And she hoped no one noticed the utensil was no longer on the table.

She got up again and started going through a series of yoga poses. Her usual routine. If anyone was watching, they would know the whole series of movements, and how long it would take for her to get through them. After the first few minutes, she'd move over to the wall for a while. Twenty to thirty minutes or so, by her best estimation. How long would that give her before they came looking?

Piper completed the first part of her routine, and went calmly to the wall. There, she executed her first two stretches as usual. Partially to keep up the ruse, and partly because her hands were trembling with the enormity of what she was about to attempt. There was no telling what was on the other side of that door. She could very well open it and find her captors all sitting right on the other side. And what would she do if they caught her? Or, more likely, *when*.

She didn't know. But it didn't matter. She couldn't take being trapped in this room any longer. She had to get out, had to breathe other air, if even for a few minutes. At that very moment, the idea of a few minutes of freedom seemed worth giving her life for.

Piper steeled herself, and slid over to the door. She had to crouch down to examine the locking mechanism. Worried that she might show up on camera if she did so, she ended up standing with her back pressed against the wall, but bent over and twisted awkwardly so she could see what she was doing. Fortunately, all of the yoga she'd been doing had given her excellent balance and flexibility.

The moment of truth. Piper angled her view first this way, then that, trying to get a good view of the lock. With some disappointment, she discovered her device hadn't worked exactly as intended. Either she'd misjudged its location, or the pressure from the lock had shifted her catch. At first, it appeared that the lock had seated itself completely, and Piper felt a cascade of defeat, mingled with a wave of relief she didn't want to admit to. The idea had been sound, at least, if not the execution.

But then, on second look, she noticed her device was angled slightly inward, which suggested that perhaps it *had* caught part of the lock. She fished the eating utensil out from her pocket, and carefully inserted the handle just behind her device. It shifted again, and Piper's breath caught. Fortunately, the device didn't drop out to the floor. After that near heart-stopping moment, Piper began working the device and the lock once more with a surgeon's care. Sweat beaded on her forehead, her back and legs trembled from the strain of her unnatural position. But after a few minutes, there was a click, the device fell free, and the door slid open just enough to let light through from the other side.

Piper froze in place, listening for the sounds of any alarm, movement, or reaction from whatever was on the opposite side of the door. She waited in silence longer than was strictly necessary; she knew that once she slid the door open, everything would change. There was still time to close it back, to go back to bed, to remain safe in the meager comfort of her cell.

But no. She hadn't lived her life in fear, not since she'd left her home. Since she'd left the old Maria behind and embraced the new Piper, the talented technical specialist for Veryn-Hakakuri, who had emerged.

A deep breath. Stand tall.

Piper slid the door aside and crossed the threshold.

She stepped into a passageway, narrow but long. A few hatches lined the sides; some doors like the one she'd just opened, others larger, on heavy hinges. It was a ship, then, most certainly. And an industrial one, from the immediate look of it. Her first impression was that she was on a drilling rig, though she couldn't see anything that specifically identified it as such. Maybe it was a freighter. It didn't appear to be military in nature, at the very least.

Piper took soft, cautious steps down the passageway, her head cocked and listening for any sound of activity. At least this far, it was quiet, apart from the steady, deep, background hum of the ship. With each step further from her improvised cell, she felt the tether stretching, drawing her back, screaming a warning at the danger. She was free, yes, for the moment, but her freedom brought with it an exhilarating terror; the liberty of a sparrow in the open sky, with a hawk soaring high above it.

She crept about ten meters down the hall and came to a stop where a second passageway met the first in a T-intersection. There, she checked back over her shoulder, and noticed then the open door she'd left behind. She should have closed it. Anyone walking by would know she'd gotten out. But going back to slide it shut now seemed like a retreat, or a return to a cage. She couldn't bring herself to turn around. She'd just have to take her chances.

Piper peeked around the corner, first one way then the other. The second passageway stretched off in both directions, even longer than the one she'd first stepped into. Still no sight or sound of anyone else. She eased around the corner, turning right for no conscious reason, and continued her slow-motion escape.

As she made her way down the second, longer passageway, an uncanniness settled on her; the heavy, unnatural emptiness of such a large ship without its crew. It wasn't unusual for freighters or transports to run with just a handful of crewmembers, but this felt different to her. It felt wrong, somehow. Like a city block, abandoned in the middle of the day.

It occurred to Piper in that moment that she had no idea what she was doing. She'd been so focused on just getting *out* of the room, that she hadn't thought ahead to what she would do once she was free. So focused on executing the first plan, she hadn't even realized she needed a second. Adrenaline poured through her, icing her hands and making them tremble. She stopped again, panic threatening to paralyze her. Maybe she could find the communications room. Or a place to hide. Would hiding be any different than being held captive? Where was she going? What was she even looking for?

And some quiet, other part of her mind whispered an answer. A lifepod.

A lifepod, maybe. Though, they'd retrieved her from one before. It probably wouldn't be too much trouble for them to catch her again. How long would she have? Assuming they weren't already looking for her, activating a pod would most certainly alert them to trouble. But it would only take her a minute to prep the pod and launch. And what then? Once she was in open space she could at least get some idea of where she was. Maybe she could even use the communications array to call for help, if she could work fast enough. Or maybe, if she was truly lucky, maybe they'd decide she wasn't worth the trouble and wouldn't pursue her.

It wasn't much of a plan, but it was at least a goal. And a goal was enough to get her moving.

Piper moved down the passageway cautiously, but with a greater sense of purpose. The fear was still with her, but it was restrained now, tangled up with the urgency of the new plan. Her brain was busy scanning the surroundings for signs or directions to the nearest lifepod, it couldn't be bothered to focus solely on being afraid.

Further down, the passageway curved gently leftward, and Piper followed it around with one hand trailing along the bulkhead beside her. The ship had a strange shape, or at least one that was unfamiliar to her, judging from the layout. It occurred to her then that she might very well be in the middle of the ship, that she might need to go above or below or... outward, to find a pod. Another complication she'd forgotten to account for.

As she continued around the curve, the low rumble of someone speaking caught her by surprise. It made her freeze in place, a mouse in the open when the cat prowls in.

The person was too far away, speaking too quietly for her to make out the words. But as she stood there, listening for several seconds, it seemed to her that the voice was growing gradually louder. Underneath it, she could hear the edges of some other sound as well, something metallic. Though a woman had been bringing her food, Piper hadn't actually *seen* another person in who knew how long, and some deeply human need for connection overpowered her animal instinct to flee. She found herself creeping forward, curiosity drawing her. She moved to the inner curve of the bulkhead, pressed herself against it, slipped slowly around the bend. A second voice joined the first; lighter, tone more familiar. The woman, then.

Whatever the two were doing, they'd stopped moving. But they were working on something. She could hear the taps and clinks and occasional grunt of effort, sounds she'd been very familiar with on YN-773. It made her think of Gennady.

Piper continued her glacial advance until the empty passageway ahead of her was suddenly no longer empty.

The rounded, metallic edge of some device appeared in her view; something large, man-sized, maybe, though she could see only a small portion of it.

"Is that going to hold?" the woman said to the man, and Piper was shocked at how loud and clear the words were. It brought her back to herself, reminded her of how foolish she was being.

"Yeah, should be fine," the man answered. "Probably won't make much difference to him one way or the other, anyway."

Back the other way, then. Piper backpedaled a few steps, slowly, until she was sure she was out of view and not likely to be followed. When she turned around, she was nearly face to face with a man.

Piper jerked back reflexively and yelped. The man didn't react at all. And he didn't look happy.

"Doc, you all right?" the woman said from behind Piper, and the man raised his hand to silence her. He didn't take his eyes from Piper.

"I- I'm..." Piper sputtered. Her mouth started moving without any input from her brain. "I just... The door was unlocked, I thought..." she sputtered. The man shook his head. He was steel-eyed and sharp-jawed; not overly muscular, but rounded and thick at the shoulders in a way that spoke of long, enduring strength. A man used to work, and hardship. She fell silent under his gaze.

"I can appreciate you taking some initiative," he said. "And I can forgive it, once. *Once*. We all gotta try."

Piper couldn't look the man in the eyes. She dropped her gaze, nodded her head.

"You want to walk back to your room, or am I going to have to carry you?"

Piper shook her head.

"Well come on, then," he said.

Piper obediently returned to her room, with the man just behind her, and was amazed at how short a walk back it was. The strangeness of the silent ship and the fear had stretched everything, made it seem like she'd been out for hours, and had covered far more ground. In reality, judging from the thirty seconds or so it took to reach her room again, she'd probably only been out a few minutes.

When they reached the door, a small splotch of tan on the floor inside caught Piper's eye. She realized it was a bit of the paste she'd used to secure her device to the door frame, and she had the presence of mind to step on it as she entered the room. It was tricky in that split second to judge how much pressure she could apply without crushing it into the floor, but she didn't have any chance to ensure she'd gotten it right. The man continued into the room right behind her, and with his presence shepherded her towards her bed.

"Sit down," he said. Piper sat on the edge of her cot, kept her left foot firm against the floor. To her relief, she felt a bulge just behind her big toe. Thankfully, the device had stuck. "You sit there, keep your hands where I can see them, and don't move."

Piper nodded, kept her eyes on the floor, clasped her hands in front of her and rested her forearms on her knees. The man turned and crouched down by the door. He examined the lock, ran his thumb along the door frame and the edge of the door.

"It was just open," Piper said, quietly. She didn't raise her head, but she lifted her eyes towards him. "I don't even know why I checked, I just thought–"

The man glanced over his shoulder at her and silenced her with his look. Piper returned her gaze to her hands, but watched the man with her peripheral vision. He worked a few moments more, stood and checked the upper part of the door. The man's hands looked rough and heavy with strength, like a carpenter's, but his movement had an almost lyrical fluidity to it; like a pianist, or a surgeon.

And Piper realized, the woman had called him "Doc". Was he the one that had repaired her injured wrist?

He turned back around, caught her watching him.

"We've been trying to keep things as friendly as we can," he said. "I don't know what happened here, but do it again, and we're not going to be so nice anymore. Understood?"

Piper nodded. The man lingered in the room for a span, his heavy silence pressing home the point. It occurred to Piper then that none of them had laid hands on her except to tend to her injuries. But she understood from the way the man held himself that there was no guarantee such behavior would continue, if she made any more trouble.

He gave her a curt nod, his point thoroughly made, and then left the room. The door slid shut, the lock clicked, and Piper was prisoner once more. The door shifted back and forth a few times, the man – "Doc", she reminded herself – undoubtedly ensuring it was properly sealed. Piper flopped down on her bed, with tears of stress and exhaustion and defeat welling up and falling unheeded.

It'd been so stupid. So foolish to break out with no idea what to do next. She'd accomplished nothing other than angering her captors. And the precious few minutes of freedom, as haunted as they'd been, made her return to captivity seem all the more bitter. She lay on her bed weeping for herself, weeping for what she'd lost, and for the unknown future that lay ahead.

But even in the midst of her despair, Piper's mind was at work, of its own accord. Working on another plan. And after she'd cried her tears, and had settled enough to hear it, her mind whispered to her once again.

It seemed obvious to her then, lying once more in her cell. Of course she would try again. She had to. Because now, she knew what she had to do.

TWELVE

"Captain?" a voice said, calling Commodore Rianne Liao back to the real world. She looked up from her desk, where she'd been watching a short video loop of her husband and two sons at play.

"Yes," Liao said. She closed out the display and blinked away the memories, her mind already cleanly detaching itself from the family she'd left back on Mars and fixing itself on the one she commanded on her ship. "What is it?"

Commander Bismah Gohar, her executive officer, stepped through the door into her quarters, with a secure pad in hand.

"We just received this from Command, coded IMMEDIATE," Gohar said. He was tense, serious, as he handed the pad over.

Liao took the pad, synced with it, activated the graph. There was a lot of information attached, but the action items were clear and succinct.

"You're sure this is properly authorized?" she asked, looking back up at her XO.

"I confirmed it with Central," he answered. "We're not the only ones to receive it."

"Something going on back home that I missed?"

Gohar shook his head. "Not that I know of, captain. Nothing on the news, anyway."

"I'll have to make some calls," Liao said. She got to her

feet, straightened her uniform. "But before that, I guess we better hop to it."

"Aye, captain."

As Liao led the way back to the bridge of *CMAV Relentless*, her thoughts were divided. Half of them were occupied by a running checklist of all the necessary operations for changing course. The other half tried to untangle the mystery behind her new orders. What would be the motivation behind tightening the approach corridors around Mars?

There was already tension between her planet and Earth over the Central Martian Authority's management of the flow of trade and traffic. And though Liao was a staunch supporter of her own world, she understood the Terrans' concerns, however unfounded she herself thought they might be. And now, the CMA seemed to be taking the very action that the Earthlings had been so anxious about. Any further restriction of access to Mars would only exacerbate the issues. The fact that there had been no obvious emergent threat only made it all the more worrying.

But none of her uncertainty mattered when it came to her duty. As she stepped onto the bridge of *Relentless* and assumed command, she set aside her worries and directed her crew to their new course of action.

THIRTEEN

Lincoln's first thought was that he had thrown up in an artificial pine forest. When he opened his eyes and saw the shredded fabric of a car's roof interior, he realized that someone else had thrown up, long ago, and he was just lying over it. He intended to curse, but the only sound he made was a weak groan.

"Hey, there's our man," someone said from the front of the vehicle. A face appeared. Mike. "Hey buddy. Sorry about the headache. And, you know. The rest of you too. You got ornery. Had to use a stunner to settle you down."

Now that Mike mentioned it, Lincoln noticed that his arms and legs were heavy and aching, like he'd had an intense workout the day before. He thought about sitting up, but his abs didn't cooperate.

"Just relax, cap," Mike said. "Be home in a few."

Lincoln closed his eyes again, drew half of a deep breath and had to stop because the smell almost made him sick. He cleared his throat.

"We get jumped?" he asked.

"*You* did," Mike answered. "Not the most subtle extraction ever, but looks like it worked all right. I think you might've hurt mas'sarnt's feelings though."

Lincoln gave sitting up another shot and, with some effort,

managed to roll himself up on the bench seat. Mike and Wright were both up front.

"You just snatch-and-grabbed your ranking officer?" Lincoln asked.

"Yes sir, we did," Mike answered. "Pretty fun, actually."

"You could've given me a heads up."

"Had to make it look real," Wright said.

Lincoln touched his jaw, felt the puffy tenderness.

"I thought you were supposed to keep me *out* of harm's way," he said.

"I might've *hurt* you a little," Wright said. "But you weren't in any danger of actual *harm*." She glanced over her shoulder at him then and in the light coming in through the windshield, he saw the silhouette of a goose egg on her forehead, just above and in front of her right temple.

"That my work?" he said, pointing up at the injury. Wright touched it lightly with her fingertips, gave a little shrug.

"Next time I'll go deeper on that hold."

"Next time I won't fall for the ol' kiss-me trick."

"What?" Mike said, looking at Wright. "You did not!" he said, laughing.

"Are you going as fast as you can, sergeant?" she said, not amused. "We need to get back and see how much damage we just did."

"Nah, I let the car take over, to keep us inconspicuous-like. We got time. I want to hear more about this kiss-me trick."

"You think they'll buy the detector-as-a-tracking-device bit?" Lincoln said, ignoring Mike's comment. "I assume that's what you were after."

"Won't know until we see," Wright said. "But I think it's safe to say your little walk just burned three of us for any more live surveillance."

"Yeah, gosh, too bad we all had to go along instead of just me, on my own, huh?" Lincoln said, getting a dig of his own in. "Might not be a total loss, though." He activated his augmented reality holoscreen and accessed his image capture databank. The most recent one, taken more by reflex than by conscious thought, was the image he'd captured just before Mike had stunned him. A picture of Black Coat.

The man in the black coat's face was partially obscured by another bystander, but it looked like Lincoln had captured enough for Thumper to work with. "I got a closeup of one of our admirers."

Wright glanced at him sideways, with an eyebrow raised.

"Seriously?" Mike said. "When did you have time for that?"

"I had about two seconds between when Wright let me go and when you zapped me," Lincoln said.

Wright grunted and turned back forward. That was probably all of the reaction Lincoln could have hoped for from her. Almost as good as an actual pat on the back.

"Pretty quick thinking for someone busy getting his head kicked in," Mike said.

"I've had a lot of practice."

"With the thinking, or the head-kicking-in?"

"Both."

Back at their ramshackle HQ, Lincoln fed the image to Veronica, who through some combination of complicated algorithm and scary black magic would hopefully identify and start tracking the man in the black coat. Thumper had already linked her system in to Shackleton's local closed-circuit security system, so they had a wide net of coverage.

"So, that's my bad," Thumper said. They were all gathered in the planning room, looking at the top-down on the thin-skin. She pointed at a white circle on the map. "Right here's where they got you. Detector pinged home while you were in this sensor radius. Bad luck, really, but could have been avoided if I'd known they were that sophisticated."

"What kind of sensor is that?" Mike asked.

"Reads like a standard e-kit, which the detector's shielded

against. But it looks like someone's been making some modifications. It's a good bet they've tweaked other stuff too, so I'll have to be more careful in the future. Sorry about that guys, I should've known better."

"Even the screwups give us information, Thumper," Lincoln said. "Though I'm not sure how you could have known beforehand."

Thumper shrugged away the attempt to make her feel better. It wasn't *really* her fault, but she wasn't going to let anyone tell her that.

"How technical a job is it to do that kind of work?" Lincoln asked.

"It's definitely not something they teach you at community college," she answered. "Probably a good thing we didn't try with the skeeters."

"Does any of that give us a read on the safehouse location?" Wright asked.

Thumper shook her head. "Not yet. But Veronica's building up off the detector's data now. After she chews on it for a while, we might find some trails we didn't have before."

"Guess we'll be laying low for a couple of days, huh?" Mike said.

"I wouldn't count on it, Mike," Lincoln said. "Either we stirred them up, or we didn't. If we didn't, we operate as usual. If we did, I want to keep the pressure on, see how they react. Just enough to keep them up all night, not enough to make them pack up shop."

"You're not going back down there," Wright said.

"Me, no," Lincoln answered. "But I'm all right with you and Pence showing your faces around a little more. Nothing makes these people more anxious than the idea that someone else's operation might be overlapping their territory. You get enough secret squirrels running around out there, everyone starts getting concerned about the whereabouts of their nuts."

Mike chuckled.

"Thumper, are you in touch with Mr Self?" Lincoln asked.

"Yeah, I've got a direct line to him."

"Package up what you've got on our friend in the black coat and let him take a look. Maybe NID can save us some legwork."

Thumper nodded.

"What about the rest of us?" Mike said.

"Business as usual," Lincoln said. "Long days, little sleep, let's keep our eye on the ball."

For nine Terran days, they kept the buildings under constant surveillance, gradually narrowing the possibilities down. Veronica was able to pick up Black Coat's movements, and though it wasn't as simple as just following him back to home base, they were able to capture a substantial amount of data from him. Adding to that some well-executed go-look work by Mike, Wright, and Sahil, the team started piecing together at least a partial list of the man's associates. That in turn gave Veronica even more data to chew on, and eventually Thumper's analysis of the paths taken, the time spent in various locations, and about a hundred other data points gave them three high-probability targets to focus on. The buildings that Wright had named Othello, Juliet, and Puck.

It was just before the simulated sunrise of the tenth day that they finally got their break.

"Hey, Link," Thumper said. Lincoln opened his eyes. He'd racked out on the floor in the main room. "Come take a look at this."

He cleared his throat and rolled up to a sitting position on the sleeping bag, checked the time. Not bad. He'd slept almost half an hour. Wright was still at the main table, reviewing a packet NID had sent over. Lincoln got to his feet and went into the front bedroom. It took until he was crossing the threshold to realize she'd called him "Link"; the first time anyone on the team had called him by a nickname.

"Yeah, what's up, Thump?" he said.

Thumper expanded the projected screen and pointed to a still image of a man Lincoln hadn't seen before.

"This fella here just came out of Puck," she said.

"You recognize him?" Lincoln asked.

"Nope, and neither does Veronica here. I ran facial and came up empty. He might be coming out of the building here now, but he never went in. At least, not as long as we've had eyes on it."

"You get it over to Self yet?"

"Not yet. Wanted to see what you thought."

"Run it."

Thumper bumped the video feed back a few seconds, and then played it at normal speed. After a moment, the man came out cautiously, conspicuous in his attempts to be casual. He was a small man, slightly built, with long, wild hair, and a beard to match; Filipino, maybe, or Indonesian. Almost as soon as he appeared, two other men crossed the street to intercept him. They each looked like they outweighed the first man by a good hundred pounds or so. The three had a restrained but heated conversation, and then the smaller man went back inside.

"What do you think?" Thumper asked.

"I think that's our guy," Lincoln answered. "And I think maybe this safehouse wasn't exactly his idea."

"Yeah."

"Get it over to Mr Self, see if he can pull an ID," Lincoln said.

"Roger that. Might be a bit before we hear back. It's early."

"You want some coffee?"

Thumper nodded. Lincoln went to the kitchen attached to the main room and started the preparations. Wright was still sitting at the main table.

"Sergeant?" he said, holding up a mug. Wright looked over at him, gave him a shrug and a nod.

Mike and Sahil were both in the adjoining apartment, on the other side of the blanket covering the hole in the wall. They'd come back in an hour and a half or so ago, after doing a little more work Downtown, as the target area had come to be known. Under normal circumstances, he would have given them at least four hours of sleep. But if anything interesting came back from Mr Self, he was going to have to cut that short.

Lincoln set the brewer to maximum. Long years in rough places had taught him that no matter where you were, or what was going on around you, nothing soothed hurts and covered a multitude of sins like a freshly brewed cup of coffee. If he was going to have to wake Sahil up, he wanted to do it with a peace offering in hand.

He hung around the kitchen, leaning against the counter with his arms crossed and his eyes closed, stealing a few moments of light dozing. When the brewer chimed, Lincoln poured three mugs and fixed them up for himself and for his teammates. Cream and sugar for Thumper, way too much sugar for Wright. He delivered Wright's to her on his way back to the front room.

"Thanks," she said, without looking up.

"Yep," he said.

In the bedroom, he handed Thumper her mug, and then stood next to her, looking over Veronica's displays and sipping his own coffee.

"How long you think it'll be before we hear?" he asked.

Thumper shrugged. "Mr Self seems pretty on the hop, so I'm sure he'll get to it. But you never know with NID. Could take them hours to find something. Or, they might not find anything at all. Or, you know. They might find something that they don't want us to know, and then we'll hear back from them pretty fast that they couldn't find anything."

Lincoln chuckled.

"When was the last time you slept?" he asked.

"I got a couple hours," she answered vaguely.

"In the past forty-eight?"

"I don't know. Maybe. Hard to keep track around here."

"Why don't you knock off for a bit? Until we hear back? I'll run the station."

"Nah, that's all right, sir, I'm good." She waggled her coffee at him.

"If we get something to move on, I need you sharp," Lincoln said.

"I'm never anything but," she answered. "Sleep's for suckers, sir."

"Yeah, well," Lincoln said, and he took a seat in a folding chair by the wall. "You've got a pretty big sucker for a CO, then. I feel like I could sleep for a month."

They sat in silence for a few minutes, each sipping their coffee. But Lincoln felt sleep sneaking up on him in the quiet, and he didn't want to nod off.

"So, sergeant," he said. "What's your story? Where are you from?"

"I'm from Detroit, sir," she said.

"Oh, that makes sense. Grew up around this stuff then, huh?" Lincoln said, pointing over at Veronica.

"A bit, yeah. Lot of good schools. My folks were encouraging."

Lincoln nodded. And then a thought occurred to him.

"Wait... you're not... uh..." he said, suddenly unsure of how to ask, or even if he should. Thumper looked over at him and, after a moment of watching his struggles, smirked.

"Of *those* Colemans?" she said. "Yes, sir, I'm afraid I am. Vernor Coleman's my granddad, Tucker's my dad."

"Wow," Lincoln heard himself say. He tried to play it off. "Sorry... I just... That's cool."

"Yeah, I don't really like to float that around too much. Not that I'm ashamed of it or anything. But you can imagine the attention it brings."

Vernor Coleman was the visionary credited with nearly singlehandedly building Detroit into the second-largest spaceport on Earth, behind only the one in Bamoko. Which Coleman had also had a hand in creating. Lincoln didn't know how much of the story was true and how much was legend, but it was well known that Vernor Coleman had gone from the basement to the penthouse, and had taken a whole lot of people along with him to the top. There was no telling how many billions his family was worth.

"You mind if I ask how you ended up here?" Lincoln said.

"Stuck in a crappy apartment on the moon, you mean?" she said. "Pretty sure that's your fault."

She smiled and shook her head.

"You mean like, why am I sitting here as a sergeant instead of in some office back home telling everybody what to do?"

Lincoln raised a hand and shook his head. "I didn't mean to put you on the spot. If you don't want to go into it…"

"I always had a thing for the gear, I guess," she continued. "And I wanted to serve my country. It's been good to my family, seemed like someone oughta give a little back. And my folks were really supportive of the idea. At least until I enlisted. My dad was uh… a little irritated. I think he thought I was going to take advantage of the family connections, get a nice appointment, play air force for a while. You know, the safe stuff. That would have been good PR for the Coleman name. Tucker's little girl, off to serve the nation."

"Air force, huh?"

"Yeah," she said with a chuckle. "He flipped his lid when I told him I'd gone army. He's gotten used to it now, though."

"Does he know what you do?"

"Sure," Thumper answered, and then flashed a smile. "He knows I fix computers."

"And I'm guessing you're not here just for the hazard pay," Lincoln said.

"Not so much. I like the army. Growing up…" She paused,

looked down at her cup of coffee, took a sip. "You can probably imagine… a rich, black girl in tech. The neighborhood, the country club, the schools, the jobs… everywhere I went, somebody always had a reason why I didn't belong where I belonged, you know?" She shrugged. "Around here, nobody cares about anything except whether or not I can do my job."

"And nobody around here can do the job the way you do it, Thump," Lincoln said. He raised his mug in a salute. "I wouldn't trade you for the world."

"Yeah," she said. "But you haven't known me that long. You'll get tired of me once the shiny's worn off."

"Don't bet on it."

She smiled and sipped her coffee. "You know, sir. For an officer, you're almost tolerable."

"It's the coffee, isn't it?"

"It definitely helps," she said.

The conversation trailed off into a comfortable quiet for a few moments. Comfortable enough that Lincoln finally felt like he could ask a question he'd been hesitant to raise.

"Can I ask you something," Lincoln said. "About the Process?"

Thumper's posture changed, and the subtle shift in her expression made Lincoln wonder if, just by mentioning it, he'd already crossed a line.

"Yeah," she said. "But I gotta tell you it's not something we really like to talk about too much, sir."

"Sure. Sorry. I don't really know the etiquette…"

"Oh, it's not that. I don't think there are enough of us around for there to be any etiquette yet. It's just… it's like combat, right? No way to talk about it meaningfully with anyone who hasn't experienced it. And when you've both been through it, there's not much you need to say. But ask away."

"So you've uh…" Lincoln couldn't quite bring himself to form the words he'd started, and changed them midsentence.

"… been through it then?"

Thumper nodded. "Once, yeah."

"With the replica?"

"Oh," she said. "Oh, no, I've never had things go that wrong. Mine was just a training accident. Fluke kind of thing."

"I'm sorry," Lincoln said.

Thumper gave a little half shrug. "Hey, I'm still here, right?" And then a moment later, she added, "It does kind of freak me out if I think about it. So mostly, I don't."

"Has anybody had to use a replica yet?"

"That's… I think that's probably not my place to talk about, sir."

"Sure, yeah," Lincoln said. "I'm sorry, Thumper. It's still just… I'm having a hard time wrapping my head around the whole thing."

"Yeah, it's weird. But you know, the weirdest thing is how weird it *isn't*. How normal it feels… after. Seems like it oughta be a much bigger deal. And it is, in a way. Kind of the biggest of all deals. But… it also isn't." She took another sip of her coffee, then shrugged. "I'd say you'll see what I mean, but honestly sir, I hope to God you never have to."

Lincoln nodded. "No one's going to need it on my watch."

"I know you're an officer and all, sir," Thumper said. "But I'm pretty sure that's not a promise you can make." She gave him a little wink, but the weight of the comment remained. And of course, she was right.

Lincoln didn't have a response. But even if he had, there hardly would have been time to say it. Veronica chirped, and Thumper turned back to face her terminal. "Looks like Self got something."

"That was fast," Lincoln said. "Does that mean he's telling us he doesn't have anything?"

Thumper didn't respond at first, already lost in the report that NID was sending over.

"Oh, no way," Thumper said. And went quiet again.

"Yeah?" Lincoln prompted, after several seconds. He got up and walked over to stand behind her.

"I never would have guessed it," Thumper said. "That's Yayan Prakoso."

"Should I know him?"

"You don't?" she said. "Sorry, no... of course not, you probably don't follow that kind of news too much. But uh... remember how I was saying if you wanted to break in to 773's sensor suite through a handshake, you'd need a code god to do it?"

"Yeah."

"Well," she said, and she pointed at the image on her screen. The man on the display wasn't an exact match; he was beardless, with short, buzzed hair. But he had the same small frame, and the same sharp eyes. "He's kind of a celebrity in certain circles. Went dark a couple of years ago, had all kinds of rumors about him. I gotta be honest, sir. I'd kind of like to get his autograph."

"Well then," Lincoln said. "Let's go ask him for it."

The team assembled in their planning center, laid out plans on the thin-skin. Sahil and Mike both looked ragged, but the cups of coffee and the promise of action kept them from grumbling too much. Not that Lincoln could remember ever having heard Sahil grumble at all.

On the left side, the thin-skin showed images of a number of individuals, with Prakoso at the top. The others were all people the team had ID'd as Apsis personnel, or close associates of Apsis. The right side of the thin-skin displayed a top-down view of the three blocks surrounding the building labeled Puck, as well as a closer view of Puck itself.

Lincoln touched the thin-skin over the image of Puck, selected a wireframe view of the floorplan.

"This one ain't real complicated, sir," Sahil said. "Go in, get the guy, don't get shot."

"We could do it," Wright said, matter-of-fact. Apparently breaching a safehouse to pull a guy out was routine business as far as she was concerned. "But everybody would know about it. It doesn't help us if the bad guys know he's compromised. Or even if they believe it."

"Agreed," Lincoln said. "We'll have to cover it."

"How you plan on that?" Wright asked.

"Well, we can't do it perfectly," Lincoln said. "I'm guessing our bad guys aren't going to be happy about Prakoso being gone, no matter where he ends up. And I don't think we can pull off the old 'hey, we're Apsis employees moving him somewhere safer', though I'm sure you all love that one. Best thing I can think of is to make it look like he did it himself. I figure a criminal like Prakoso probably has more than enough reason to want to disappear."

"I don't think it's fair to call him a criminal, exactly, sir," Thumper interrupted. In response, Lincoln just held his hand out next to the image of Prakoso, where the long list of charges he was facing in a large number of different nations was displayed. "Well sure, yeah, he broke some laws, but I'd be willing to bet more than half the time he was working for some other country when he did it. If you picked up an Eastern Coalition report on any one of us, it'd probably say the same sort of thing."

"If anyone knew what we were actually up to, maybe," Mike said. "Which they don't."

"You hope," Thumper said.

"Fair enough, Thumper," Lincoln said. "But the point remains. Guy like this has motivation and skills. Given the tools at his disposal, how does he get out of there on his own?"

"Seems like he already would have done it, if he'd wanted to," Thumper said. "That's assuming he could."

"How would you do it? Put yourself in there."

She shook her head. "Too many guys, too many sensors, I don't see how I can do it and get more than about fifty feet before someone's on me. You saw how fast they reacted when he came out for a smoke."

Lincoln opened his mouth to encourage her, but Sahil stopped him with a look and a subtle shake of the head. A few moments later, Thumper continued. "I mean, I guess that's something. I guess maybe all those sensors and stuff."

Everyone gave her a few more moments, waiting to see if she'd continue on her own. But Thumper's eyes were unfocused, staring off at nothing in particular.

"Yeah, Thump?" Mike said at last. "What about them?"

Thumper shook her head. "I'm just saying, they've got all this gear rigged up, like they're worried someone's going to come looking for him, right? So, if I'm him, and I want to leave, and I mean, *really* leave, like never come back, maybe I make it look like someone *is* coming to look for me."

"Spoof the sensors?" Lincoln said. "Could you do that from here?"

"Something like that, yeah. Make everybody look one direction, while I head out the other, or something. I mean, I don't think I could get in there and make the network ignore you... we'd have to expect that they'd pick up on the intrusion. But if we went the other way with it, I might be able to do something. I'll have to get in there and see what we've got to work with. I don't know though, something like that, maybe they'll just lock him down. Or try to move him themselves. I don't see how any of that helps us."

"It's a start," Lincoln said. "Let's work through it."

"Talkin' about doing this quiet?" Sahil asked. "No shots fired?"

Lincoln nodded. "One hundred percent nonlethal. We make him vanish, with no one to blame but the guys he leaves behind."

"Tough ask, captain," Mike said. "This isn't a bunch of

boy scouts running around a campground waiting to get ambushed. And look at that cast of characters." He pointed to the images of the known security personnel. They were mostly male, mostly thick-necked. But every one of them looked like they'd seen action at some point or another, either in the field, or on the street. Mike shook his head.

"One time, in Juárez, me and a couple of teammates were in this bar and one of my guys, his name was Na, and Na was about five foot two and maybe a hundred and ten pounds. Little fella. Pocket-sized. And I guess some locals decided they didn't like us hanging around their spot, because they started giving us some noise. Maybe eight or ten of them, and just three of us. We didn't really mind it too much until one guy has to make it serious and pulls a knife. And he's waving it around at me and my buddy Ace, who's an even bigger ol' boy than me. Well, it just so happens Na is a world-class Thai boxer, and he, cool as can be, casually folds the guy in half with a roundhouse. The rest of the guys didn't seem to want to fight so much after that."

He let it hang in the air, as if the relevance were obvious.

"Point, Mike?" Thumper finally said.

"My point is, in any group of people, you never know who the Na is. Any one of those cats is likely to give us more trouble than we're counting on. And it's probably not the one we think it is."

"So let's not get in their way," Lincoln said. "Those are the parameters, folks. Let's work it out."

Three hours later, they were putting the final touches on the plan.

"You guys want to use Poke?" Thumper asked.

Wright thought about it for a second, then shook her head. "No, that's just another piece of gear to worry about. We'll do it old-fashioned."

"Poke?" Lincoln asked.

"Yeah, Pokey," Thumper said. "Our foldable." Foldables

were many-jointed self-reconfiguring drones, particularly useful for scouting out tight places, like buildings and ship interiors.

"You named it?" Lincoln said.

"Well, sure," Thumper answered, as if that was expected behavior.

"You're going to want another car," Mike said, looking at Lincoln with a trace of despair.

"I want another car," Lincoln answered. Mike's shoulders dropped. "You want to get started on it?"

"Guess I better," Mike said. "But I don't want to hear any lip about it when I get back, no matter what it looks like."

"Just make sure it can get from A to B real fast," Lincoln said.

"And it'd be nice if it could eat a bomb or two," Sahil added, as Mike was on his way out of the door.

"Thumper, let Mr Self know we're going to need to ship out, probably in a hurry. See if we can get NID to send a crew out to clean the place."

"How you want to work the jump off?" she asked.

"I want to mail him home," he answered.

"You got it," she said, and headed out to make the necessary arrangements.

"I'm gonna get the gear laid out," Sahil said, following her.

With the rest of the team out of the planning room, Wright made one final attempt at her case.

"You shouldn't be going in there," Wright said.

"Thumper's gotta run the rig, Mike's on overwatch. Sahil's out back in case Prakoso rabbits, or worse things happen. And you're not going in alone."

"It's your op," she said with a shrug. "But I want it clear that I don't like it."

"Duly noted," he said. "I appreciate the concern."

"It's not for you personally."

"I know. But I wouldn't be much of a team lead if I didn't

do my share of heavy lifting."

"Due respect, sir, but don't use a hit to try to make a point."

The words slapped Lincoln with unexpected force. He'd let this go far enough. "Sergeant, this is the plan," he said, sharply. "We're moving forward. Unless you have any concerns *relevant* to the plan, I suggest you get busy prepping."

Wright tipped her head back just slightly, and for a moment seemed like she might have something else to say.

In the end, she just said, "Sir."

She exited, leaving Lincoln alone with the plan they'd drawn up. He turned and stared at the thin-skin, inhaled deeply and then let out a long breath. Like all plans, the plan itself was probably mostly useless. The planning, however, was indispensable. Having been through the process so thoroughly, Lincoln felt confident that when the unexpected occurred, he and his team would be able to react accordingly.

But Wright's final words clung to him. Was he really leading the grab because it was the best option? Or was he just using this as an opportunity to try to prove to the others that he did truly belong here? It was an uncomfortable thought, but one he had to work out for certain. Wright was correct; this wasn't a time for ego. He ran through it all one more time, in brief.

By the end of it, he nodded to himself. Maybe not a great plan, but it was simple enough, and it was one they actually had. Best to get out there and get it done, instead of sitting around in a room waiting for the Good Idea Fairy to show up. About the only thing she ever contributed was a bunch of extra gear you weren't going to need anyway.

He joined the others in the main room.

"About time we got to break this stuff out," Sahil said, laying the final case on the table with some effort. "I was startin' to worry I'd lugged all this in and was gonna have to lug it back home without ever gettin' to use it."

The team started unloading the gear and laying out what

they'd need, each for the role they were expected to play in the hit. Mike, on overwatch, took a long rifle with a sleek optic mounted on top. Sahil, on standby as the heavy in case things went bad, loaded up with a full assault kit.

Lincoln and Wright, the grab team, each took two sidearms, both nearly silent in operation. One, subsonic and lethal, fired a nice hefty chunk of composite guaranteed to punch holes and ruin days. The other used a softer gel that held shape in flight and delivered a cocktail of nerve agent and fast-acting narcotic to knock targets cold before they even hit the ground. Lincoln knew if they left any bodies behind, it was a mission failure. But he wasn't so idealistic as to leave the lethal option at home.

"You sure you don't want to sit home and run it from here?" Thumper asked. She was standing in the doorway of her bedroom surveillance center, leaning against the frame with her arms crossed. Her eyes strayed over to one case that hadn't been opened yet.

"I'd hate to take you away from your first love," Lincoln said.

"Yeah, well," she answered. "I'd hate for there to be a fight and me not be in it."

"There won't be," he said. "This one's going to be super boring. Promise."

"I'll hold you to that," she said. He gave her a thumbs up.

The team spent the remainder of the day making the necessary arrangements, checking their gear, double-checking their gear, and trying their best to avoid tinkering with the plan. A little after midnight, they started heading out, one by one. Lincoln was the last to go, leaving Thumper to mind the shop.

"See you in a bit," Lincoln said.

"Knock 'em dead, sir," she said. And then added, "Except, don't."

FOURTEEN

At 0445, Earth-Luna sync time, the Outriders executed. Zero dark ugly. It was a magical slice of the night, when the nightshift guards were close enough to going home that they were counting down the minutes, and the dayshifters were still in deep sleep. No one in their right mind ever did anything at 0445.

"Thumper," Lincoln said. "Bump it. Five seconds."

"Roger, bumping," she replied. A moment later, the lights went out. Not just in the target building, but all around it. Street lights, store signs, the buildings adjacent, everything on the three or four blocks that shared the system. Lincoln counted, one-one-thousand, two-one-thousand. Just as he was getting to five-one-, the lights came back up. "And we're back up."

"Roger that," Lincoln said. "Sixty seconds, then bump it again."

"How long?" Thumper asked.

"Make it ten."

A minute passed, and right on schedule the power went out once more. Ten seconds later, it was back online.

"All right, everyone hold tight, let me know what you see," Lincoln said. He scanned the target building through a slender handheld optic, a multifunction device that he'd currently set to track thermal signatures. The first bump hadn't attracted too much attention, but the second one caused some mild stirring amongst the Apsis personnel inside. There were six signatures total in the building; two of them had been sitting in a small room on the ground floor, but now one was up, moving towards the front door.

"One man, moving to the front door," Lincoln said. He tapped a button on his optic, designated the man's signature for tracking.

"Roger, good track," Thumper answered over comms. Veronica locked on the signature, shared it out to the rest of the team.

"Two tangos, north side," Mike said. He was set up in an elevated position a couple of buildings away, watching the front of the target building. "Crossing towards Puck. Looks like… OK, yeah, they're meeting up with your guy now at the front door."

There were three ground level entrances to Puck; front, rear, and a basement entry on the right side. Sahil was stationed a few blocks over, waiting in the second car Mike had procured.

"Sahil, what's it like on your side?" Lincoln asked.

"Quiet," he said. "If anybody noticed the blip, don't seem to have bothered 'em much."

"Rear entrance is still clear outside," Lincoln said. "Thumper, bump it one more time, then give 'em a dose."

"How big?"

"Flood it."

"Roger that. Keep your heads down."

The power flickered, and the lights dimmed to half output for a few seconds before returning to full strength.

"You're probably going to be seeing some activity here in a second," Thumper said. "Maybe a lot."

Sure enough, personnel inside the building scrambled up, and moments later two pairs of previously undetected watchers on the outside rushed in, converging on Puck.

"Well that woke 'em up," Wright said.

"I'd guess so," Thumper replied. "I just fed their sensor network eighty-five contacts."

"Count 'em and mark 'em," Lincoln said. He scanned and targeted each of the responding individuals, keeping a tally of those he could find from his vantage. Inside, four people were moving with purpose, not counting the guy at the front door who was in a half crouch. That made five inside, and six outside. Eleven hostiles. One individual, however, was merely sitting up in bed. "And that's our man Prakoso," Lincoln said, designating the man in a corner room on the third floor.

"Roger that, I count eleven hostiles, one VIP," Mike said.

"I confirm eleven hostiles, one VIP," Thumper echoed. "Marked and tracked."

Lincoln lowered the optic and activated his augmented vision. Each of the eleven Apsis personnel now had bright red brackets highlighting them, while Prakoso was represented by a white circle.

"Confirm track," Lincoln said.

"Yep, got it," Mike said.

"Drop it off, Thumper," Mike said.

"Copy that," she answered. "Sensors should be showing clear now."

The activity inside and around the building slowed and separated, as each Apsis employee reacted to the sudden all-clear.

"Give them about thirty seconds," Lincoln said. "Then bump the power again."

Thumper did as requested, shutting the power off completely again thirty seconds later.

"Let 'em simmer for a bit on this one."

For the next half hour or so, Thumper continued the manipulation with a variety of patterns; sometimes power was completely down, sometimes it was back to normal, sometimes it was inbetween. And, at any given moment, their sensors might show anything from being completely clear to a full-out siege on Puck, or any one of the surrounding buildings. She was careful not to focus too much attention on Puck itself, but she also didn't ignore it completely.

The Apsis personnel spent some of that time geared up, checking doors, windows, and their principal. But after a while they relaxed, started forming little clusters. One of them eventually broke off and went back to bed.

"All right, that's our signal," Lincoln said. Other guards drifted off, including some of those that had been out on the perimeter.

"You've got an extra in there," Mike said. Lincoln did a quick count, and sure enough, not everyone who'd come in from the outside had left the safehouse. One stayed behind, bringing the total to six potential hostiles in the building. Three against one. Bad odds for anyone without close air support. Three of them returned to the sitting room on the ground floor while the rest headed back up to their bedrooms.

"That seems like a lot of guys to babysit one dude," Mike said.

Thumper cut in. "If Prakoso's working from home, he's probably sitting on a lot of choice gear. All that force might not be just for him."

"If you say so," Mike replied. "Still seems like a lot of guys, though."

"We'll just have to keep it nice and quiet," Lincoln said. "Gemini, ready to move." The codename was a convenience as well as a safety precaution; Gemini meant both Wright and himself, and there was less chance that one of them might slip a name while inside, where audio surveillance might be online. Thumper cut the power again, dousing the street in darkness.

"Copy that," Thumper said. "West approach is clear for you to move."

"Roger, Gemini moving to target."

"Gemini moving, copy."

Lincoln slipped out of his hiding place and moved to the corner of the building across the street from Puck, then dropped to a crouch. A few moments later, Wright stepped in behind him and put her hand on his shoulder. Lincoln counted to five, then patted Wright's hand, and together they crossed the open space to Puck. They tucked in close against the wall, just beneath a narrow window. This side of the building had no door, which made it likely that it was the least guarded entry point. The street outside Puck had a steep grade, and the window here was about eight feet above the ground.

Without speaking, Lincoln knelt down and braced himself against the building. Wright used his leg as a step stool, then stepped up on his shoulder, and affixed a slender device to the window frame. That done, she stepped back down and gave him an OK sign.

"Gemini ready to make entry," he whispered.

"Ready for entry, roger," Thumper said. "Thirty-second window, on your mark."

Lincoln looked up at Wright; her face had a slight shimmer caused by the light-intensifying protocols in Lincoln's augmented vision. She nodded once.

"Mark," he whispered.

"Thirty seconds starts... now," Thumper said. And on her final word, the streetlights came back up at half intensity. Immediately, Wright stepped forward and Lincoln boosted her to the window. He held her steady for a few moments, until a quick hiss like air escaping from a torn e-suit signaled that she'd breached the locking mechanism. She lifted herself off him and he looked up in time to see her feet disappearing through the window. Ten seconds later, she reappeared, stretching her arms down to him. The cylindrical bundle he was carrying on his back made the movement more awkward than it normally would have been, but together they got him through the window with hardly any noise.

"Ten seconds," Thumper said.

Lincoln drew into a corner of the corridor, pistol at the ready, aimed down the hall towards the three marked hostiles just two doors away. Wright slid the window shut, resecured the lock.

"Five seconds," Thumper said.

"We're in," Lincoln answered. After twenty seconds or so of waiting, the hostiles down the hall still hadn't made any move to investigate the window. Obviously Lincoln would have preferred to do the whole thing with the power out, but Thumper had insisted that flickering it on and off was the best way to keep her manipulation of the sensors undetected. Lincoln didn't have any way to see what she was doing to Apsis's sensor displays, but there was no question she'd done a good job of conditioning the bad guys to ignore their own alerts.

"From the first floor window, first door on your left, through the room, up the stairs at the back," Thumper directed, calmly directing them through the plan for clarity. They'd all memorized the layout, of course, but having the confirmation let Lincoln keep his mind focused on the immediate.

Wright slid in beside him. Confident that their entry had gone unnoticed, Lincoln came up in a high crouch, weapon ready, and moved down the hall with quick, light steps. The door was open at the first room on the left. Lincoln paused at the door frame, checked over his shoulder to make sure Wright had the hall covered. Of course she did.

Lincoln carefully peeked into the room, got as much of a view of it as he could without risking exposure. His augmented vision wasn't showing any marked hostiles in there, but that didn't guarantee anything. Could be they just hadn't found them yet. But what he could see of the room was clear. Without taking his eyes off the room or lowering his weapon, he reached back and tapped Wright's lower leg. She responded with a hand on his shoulder. When she squeezed, he pushed aggressively into the room with her right on his heels, each checking the corners and moving rapidly through to the stairwell at the back. The room was clear.

At the bottom of the staircase, Wright turned and covered the door while Lincoln edged around and verified there was no one on the stairs. Also clear. He patted Wright's shoulder, and started up. She sidestepped then backpedaled up the first few stairs, keeping her pistol trained on the door until they'd moved far enough upstairs.

"Continue up the stairs to the third floor," Thumper said. "The VIP is in the last room on the right."

Lincoln and Wright reached the top of the stairs, and paused. The stairwell led out right into the hallway, and two Apsis guards were stationed on this floor, one on each side of the hall. At the moment, they both appeared to be sleeping. The stairs to the second floor were beneath those to the third, so Lincoln and Wright moved into the hall, then doubled back to reach the base of the next staircase. Lincoln again led the way, while Wright covered their rear.

"Gemini, moving to third floor," Lincoln whispered, once he'd checked the stairs.

"Gemini moving to third, copy," Thumper repeated.

"Careful, Gemini," Mike said over comms. "Looks like you got a restless sleeper up there. Hostile's fidgety."

"VIP?" Lincoln asked.

"Hasn't moved. But it's weird. Kinda looks like he's sleeping sitting up."

Lincoln's view was only tracking the location of the other people in the building, so he didn't have a good view of the guard in question or of Prakoso. But Mike, with his powerful optic, was likely seeing the full heat signatures and had a better read on what was happening up on the top floor.

"Keep me posted," Lincoln said, as he ascended. Fortunately, the doors on both sides of the hall were closed.

"Last room on the right," Thumper reminded.

Lincoln moved silently down the hall, Wright shadowing his every step. At the last room, Wright swiveled and kept her weapon aimed at the door of the guard's room. Lincoln touched the door handle, slowly, slowly applied pressure. It was unlocked.

"Update on VIP?" Lincoln asked.

"Still hasn't moved," Mike said. "Make it quick, though, your friend down the hall just got out of bed."

"Gemini to target," Lincoln whispered. "Bump it, full black. Two minutes."

"Two minutes, copy," Thumper said. A moment later the power went completely out. Lincoln nudged Wright, and she pressed back against his shoulder. He squeezed the grip of his weapon, activating a low-intensity red light underneath. When he pushed the door open, Wright rolled smoothly in behind him. In a quick, precise motion, Lincoln checked left with his pistol and swept it to center, sweeping the room with the red light and looking for threats.

When it came to rest on the VIP, Lincoln was surprised to see the man sitting at the foot of the bed with his hands folded in his lap and his eyes wide open. He was even dressed. Wright closed the door behind Lincoln, and the man didn't move at all.

"Yayan Prakoso," Lincoln said quietly. The man didn't respond, he just sat there with his hands in his lap, paralyzed in the red light. "Yayan Prakoso?" Lincoln repeated. The man gave a short nod. "It's OK, we're friends."

"I have no friends," Prakoso answered.

"Well you do today, buddy," Lincoln answered. "We're getting you out of here."

Prakoso didn't respond. He was small framed, and his wild hair and beard made him look almost cartoonish in his proportions.

"Tango, tango," Mike said, his voice calm but with an obvious note of urgency. "Bad guy just left his room, headed your way."

Lincoln motioned sharply to Wright, directed her to the closet by the door. She understood and moved there immediately, out of sight of the door, and kept her pistol trained on Prakoso.

"Shhh," Lincoln said, as he slid over by the door. If the guard opened it partially, Lincoln could stay hidden behind it. If he opened it all the way, though... Lincoln tucked in on himself, kept his weapon pressed high against his chest with the muzzle down, ready to make a close-range snap shot if it became necessary. In his vision, the brackets marking the hostile floated down the hall towards him, paused outside the door.

Don't, Lincoln thought. *Don't do it, buddy. Keep on walking.*

He was disappointed. The handle of the door turned; a burst of white light spotlighted Prakoso on the bed.

"What're you doin'?" a gruff voice said with a hint of Russian accent.

Prakoso squinted his eyes against the light, but he kept them locked forward on the man at the door. Lincoln brought his weapon up, the muzzle nearly touching the door. The door itself seemed to be made of some cheap plastic composite, and Lincoln was counting on it being hollow rather than filled. The first gel round likely wouldn't have enough velocity to penetrate and still be effective, but a followup shot or two probably would. Probably.

The guard swept his flashlight around the room cursorily, obviously irritated, though he didn't seem to be looking for anything in particular. The room itself was sparse; the bed, a small table laden with Prakoso's equipment. A chair.

"Sixty seconds," Thumper said.

"You're not doin' anything stupid in here, are ya?" the guard said.

Prakoso didn't answer. The guard shone his light back on the small man on the bed, and in the movement opened the door a little wider, just enough to make bare contact with the muzzle of Lincoln's gun.

"Huh?"

"Meditating," Prakoso answered, quietly. The same tone of voice he'd used with Lincoln moments before.

"Meditating, huh?"

The guard just stood there for a span, and Lincoln wondered if that had been some kind of code between Prakoso and the guard that something was wrong. His finger tightened on the trigger.

"You should sleep," the guard said finally, then added, almost to himself, "Wish I could." He lingered a moment longer, and then the door receded from Lincoln and closed again.

Lincoln kept his pistol trained on the door until the brackets identifying the guard had descended to the floor below. He turned back to Prakoso and switched his light on again. The fact that Prakoso apparently hadn't tried to signal the guard in any way was a good sign.

"Thirty seconds," Thumper said.

"We're going to get you out of here," Lincoln repeated. "Is there anything you absolutely *must* take with you? If so, grab it, and let's go."

Prakoso didn't answer and didn't move. He didn't seem to be afraid at all, or anxious. He almost seemed bored.

"We've been trying to find you for a long time, Yayan," Lincoln said.

"Someone is always trying to find me."

The man remained in place, neither resisting nor complying. Lincoln was just about to lower his weapon when he heard a puff from his right. Prakoso's head jerked back with a wet slap and he flopped backwards onto the bed, limp like an empty pile of clothes. Lincoln looked sharply at Wright. She was already holstering her pistol.

"He had his chance," she said. "You cover, I'll carry." There wasn't time to argue. Lincoln turned back to the door and kept watch while Wright moved over and wrestled Prakoso up and across her shoulders in a fireman's carry. She came up close behind him, touched his shoulder. Lincoln switched off his light. The light intensification of his lenses was enough for him to see by, and Prakoso certainly didn't need to see where he was going now.

"Gemini has VIP secure," Lincoln said. "We're on the way out. Give us another ninety seconds on power."

"Roger that, reset to ninety seconds," she said. "Everyone's still busy downstairs, you should be good to exit to roof."

"Copy, Gemini moving to roof."

"Gemini moving to roof, copy," Thumper confirmed.

Lincoln eased the door open, scanned the hall before committing. Clear. He moved forward and turned right, led the way to the end of the hall and the door facing them there. It was narrower than the others, only about three-quarters the width of a normal entry. Lincoln tried the handle. Locked.

"Of course," he whispered. Wright turned and backed up to the wall next to him, drew her pistol and covered the hallway. Lincoln crouched and pulled a slender black device off his belt. With it, he scanned the locking mechanism. A moment later, the device pulsed twice in his hand, and the lock clicked. Good. An easy one. Lincoln returned the device to his belt, and eased the door open before coming out of his crouch.

"Sixty seconds," Thumper said.

The room inside was roughly the size of a closet. The walls were bare concrete, and the only feature was a ladder going straight up to a hatch in the ceiling. The hatch was square, and looked just big enough for Lincoln to get through without scraping his shoulders on either side. He glanced over at Wright, with Prakoso dangling across her shoulders.

"Great," he said.

"Problem?" Wright whispered.

He pointed into the room, up at the hatch. Wright leaned around the door frame to take a peek.

"Great," she said.

"Taking the roof might have been stupid," Lincoln said.

"If it works, it ain't stupid."

"*If.*"

Lincoln holstered his weapon and started up the ladder. The hatch was also locked.

"Thirty seconds," Thumper said.

Wright backed into the tiny room as far as she could but didn't have enough space to get around the door to close it behind her. Lincoln took the unlocker off his belt again, but held off on activating it.

"Ten seconds," Thumper said, and she counted down from there. As she reached zero, the power in the building buzzed back on to half strength. "You're good to exit."

Lincoln fired up the unlocker. Five seconds. Ten.

"Got a mover," Mike said. "Friend from earlier, looks like he changed his mind. He's headed back upstairs."

"Gemini, you're covered," Thumper said. "You can pop the hatch."

"Working on it," Lincoln answered.

Fifteen seconds. Whatever kind of lock they'd used for the hatch wasn't friendly. Wright shifted back, tried to work the door shut, but there just wasn't room enough.

"He's on the second floor now," Mike said. "Sahil, you might want to start the car."

Twenty-five seconds. The unlocker pulsed, the hatch unsealed. Lincoln pushed it open, scrambled through to the roof as quickly as he dared. A quick check to confirm no one else was up there, and then he was on his belly stretching his arms back down to Wright.

"He's on the stairs," Mike said.

Wright stepped up on the ladder, but there was no way she was going to get Prakoso through like that.

"Take him, take him," Wright whispered, and Lincoln tried to grab hold of the limp man on her back. He managed to get a grip on Prakoso's belt, and a tenuous hold of an arm. A moment later, Wright moved out from under, leaving

Prakoso dangling in midair, and Lincoln bearing the dead
weight that threatened to drag him headfirst back through
the hatch. She closed the door smoothly, holding the handle
so the mechanism didn't click shut.

"Tango's on your floor," Mike said.

Lincoln shut his eyes with the effort. Prakoso probably
only weighed about fifty to sixty kilos, but Lincoln was in
such an awkward position he couldn't do much more than
just try to hold on. Wright sure was taking her sweet time.

"He's in the hall," said Mike. "Not sure what he's doing.
He's kind of just standing there."

Lincoln opened his eyes. Wright was still at the door,
her hand still on the handle. He couldn't blame her for not
wanting to move, for fear of the latch making some noise that
might draw attention. But that wasn't going to be nearly as
noticeable as the sound it was going to make when he lost his
grip and dropped Prakoso on top of her. He crushed his grip
closed as tightly as he could.

"He's back in his room now," Mike said. "Door's still open
though."

A moment later, Prakoso magically lightened. Wright was
back underneath him again, taking some of the load. Lincoln
let go with his right hand to shake it out, letting Prakoso's
arm flop back down. When it fell, it made a thunking sound
and Wright exhaled sharply.

It took a minute or so for the two of them to work out getting
Prakoso's limp form up and onto the roof. Lincoln dragged the
man through and laid him beside the hatch. By the time he'd
gotten Prakoso situated and turned back, Wright was already up
and closing the hatch. After she'd secured it, she stayed next to
it, crouched on one knee. They were both a little out of breath,
probably as much from the close call as from the effort. When
she noticed he was watching her, she looked over at him.

"Coming up on the roof was probably stupid," she said.
Lincoln chuckled.

"Gemini's on the roof with the VIP," Lincoln said. "Moving to bridge."

"Copy, Gemini," Thumper said. "Watch your step."

Lincoln left Prakoso and moved over to the edge of the roof on the southern side, where the closest neighboring building stood. Its roof was maybe four meters away. Lincoln pulled the bundle off his back, and went to work setting it up.

"You sure no one's going to see this?" he asked.

"No," Thumper said. "Sky's still dark enough you shouldn't get silhouetted too bad, and the streetlights will make it hard for anyone to see you from the ground. But I wouldn't hang around up there for too long."

From the bundle, Lincoln drew out two small domes, each a little larger than his hand, connected by a nearly transparent polymer ribbon. These he placed next to each other on the lip that marked the roof edge, about two feet apart. When he activated them, four legs unfolded from both and clamped down on the synthetic concrete of the ledge. Lincoln pulled out two more similar devices and rigged them up to the first. Miniature drones with whisper-quiet operation.

"You set yet?" Wright asked from behind.

"Just about," he said. He glanced over his shoulder, and saw she already had Prakoso up on her shoulders again. "You want me to carry him across?"

"Nah. You just make sure there's nobody over there to greet us."

Lincoln activated the drones, and they flew in tight formation across the gap, spooling out a net of the flexible polymer behind them as they went. Once they'd reached the other rooftop, they settled down on the ledge and automatically locked their clamps on.

"Ladies first?" Lincoln said. Wright kicked him in the rump. Lincoln tapped one of the domes twice, and it clicked. A moment later, the drooping net tightened up and went rigid as steel. Lincoln tested it with his foot before he fully committed. As many times as he'd used these things, he'd never had one break. And yet still, every time, he had to convince his brain he wasn't stepping out on a thin layer of ice or glass. The surface held firm; Lincoln drew his weapon and quickly made his way across. Wright followed, not quite as quickly. He couldn't blame her for taking her time on that narrow bridge, especially with the awkward dead weight of Prakoso on her shoulders.

Once Wright reached him, Lincoln tapped one of the domes again, and the process reversed. The bridge went slack, the two drones on the opposite side spun up and flew over to him, retracting the netting as they came. He gathered the four up, and took them across to another edge.

Using the drone bridgelayers, Lincoln and Wright zigzagged their way across the rooftops until they'd put good distance between themselves and Puck. The buildings weren't quite clustered enough for them to make it all the way out of what they knew was Apsis-controlled territory, but it was close enough to the perimeter that they felt like they could risk extracting from there. As they reached the final building, Lincoln checked in with the rest of the team.

"Gemini's good for pickup at primary," he said, as he stashed the drones back in their pack.

"Primary looks clear, Gemini," Thumper answered.

"Copy that," Sahil answered. "On my way to primary."

"I'm gonna pack up too," Mike said. "Not sure how long it'll be before they notice their man's missing, but so far it looks good."

"Glad to hear to it," Lincoln said. "See you at home."

"Stash is in between two heat exchangers," Thumper said. "I'll mark it for you."

A pip appeared in Lincoln's vision, marking a location on the rooftop. He made his way to it, found a small duffel bag on the ground between two large heat exchange units. The gap was narrow, and he had to twist sideways to get his hand on it, but he managed to pull it free. Thumper had used a drone to drop the bag in earlier that night; in it were two sets of street clothes, loose enough to conceal the gear that he and Wright were hauling around. He took the duffel over to where Wright was waiting for him by the roof exit, and they quickly donned the clothes over their other outfits.

"I'm one mike out," Sahil said.

Getting down from the roof was a bit trickier than Lincoln had anticipated; he knew better than to *expect* that Prakoso would come quietly, and eagerly, but he realized now, from his level of disappointment, just how much he'd been hoping for it. They still had to get to the ground floor without attracting any attention, which was going to be tougher with Prakoso draped over Wright's shoulders like a trophy kill. The apartment building they'd chosen to exit through wasn't strictly Apsis-held, but there was no way to guarantee there weren't watchers in it.

In the end, they decided to play drunk. Lincoln draped one of Prakoso's arms over his shoulder and hauled on the little man's belt; Wright followed suit, her arm crossed over Lincoln's. Prakoso dangled between them like a dead man, his feet dragging and bumping the whole way down.

Thankfully the stairway ran from top to bottom in a switchback, so the only hallway they had to pass through was on the ground floor. Sahil was already waiting out front when they exited the building, and though there were a couple of people on the street, no one seemed to be paying any more than casual attention to the drunken trio trying to load their passed-out friend into the back of an old, beat-up car.

Back at the temporary HQ, the team got Prakoso moved upstairs and onto one of the beds through the hole in the wall. To be safe, they secured his wrists together with quick cuffs made of a hard plastic material. Thumper had already started tearing the gear down; the thin-skin in their planning room was packed up, as were a number of other terminals.

Veronica was still up and running, though, keeping track of the Apsis personnel and undoubtedly set to alert everyone if anything looked like trouble.

"Self's got a clean team on the way over," Thumper said. "Just pack up your personal gear, they'll handle the rest."

"What's our out?" Lincoln asked.

"United Cargo," she answered. "NID's prepping a box for us as we speak."

It was a relatively well-kept secret that certain units within the armed services maintained relationships with certain shipping corporations, in order to move personnel around into places that might otherwise be inaccessible. Lincoln had only used that method of transport a handful of times before, and while it wasn't necessarily a comfortable way to travel, it usually beat flying commercial. He'd never lost a bag that way, anyway.

"They can get us all out together?" he asked.

"Sounds like," Thumper said. "Short trip, though, just over to a hop, not all the way home. Best they could do on short notice."

"As long as they can get us out of here with the precious cargo, that's fine by me. How long until we leave?"

"About two hours. Be advised, though, Mr Self already made a couple of overtures about taking Prakoso into NID custody."

"Yeah? What'd you tell him?"

"I told him he'd have to talk to Mom about that."

"All right," Lincoln said. He swept his eyes around the main room. Most of his essentials were already gathered up, either on him, or by his pack on the floor. "I'm gonna wake our VIP up and explain the situation to him. We got any juice handy?"

"Yeah, here," Wright said, appearing from the back bedroom. She grabbed a jector from her pack and tossed it across the room to Lincoln. "You want a hand?"

"Nah, it's fine. Just make sure Mike gets all squared away when he gets in."

"Oh sure, give *me* the easy job," she said with heavy sarcasm and a shake of her head.

"Least I can do after all your hard work tonight," he said then added, "Hey. Seriously, though. Good work in there."

"It's what they pay me for," she said, shrugging as she returned to the planning room. Lincoln glanced over at Thumper, who was looking at him.

"Don't sweat it, captain," she said. "Run about eighty-seven more of those with her, and she'll warm up."

"Eighty-seven, huh?"

"Give or take," Thumper said with a smile. "I think that was her eighty-eighth grab if I remember right. Mike's coming up. We good to shut Veronica down?"

"Yeah, if we're all clear."

"I'll get to it then."

Lincoln nodded and headed through the blanket-covered hole in the wall. The room on the other side was lit in dusky orange, by the single functioning light fixture on the wall. Prakoso was on one of the beds still lying on his side, loosely curled with his hands held up near his face, just like they'd left him. Lincoln checked the cuffs one more time, just to be sure, then checked the welt on the man's forehead. Wright's shot had impacted maybe a quarter-inch to the left of being right between the eyes. The goose egg that it had left behind had a pale circle in the center, surrounded by a dark, angry ring of bruising. Prakoso was going to have a mother of a headache when Lincoln woke him up.

Prakoso was wearing a long-sleeve shirt with the cuffs unbuttoned. Lincoln pulled one sleeve back and placed the jector against the inside of Prakoso's skinny forearm. Judging from the sharpness of his wrist bones, Prakoso didn't seem malnourished, exactly, but definitely seemed like he could have used some fattening up. Lincoln couldn't help but wonder how long Apsis had been holding the man hostage.

He activated the jector, firing a jet of meds into Prakoso's bloodstream to counteract the effects of the gel round. Once he'd dosed Prakoso, Lincoln sat down on the other bed across from him and waited. A minute or so later, Prakoso stirred and a few seconds after that, his eyes cracked open. For a while he just lay there, eyes open but mostly unfocused, breathing steady. Then, without even looking up, he spoke.

"Where am I?"

"Safe," Lincoln said. Prakoso reached up and touched the knot on his forehead gingerly with his fingertips, then drew his hands away and looked at the cuffs on his wrists. His eyes slid over to meet Lincoln's. "Just a precaution," Lincoln said.

Prakoso inhaled deeply, closed his eyes for a few seconds. Then, he exhaled abruptly, and pushed himself slowly up to a seated position. He mirrored Lincoln; feet on the floor, hands resting in his lap.

"And now?" Prakoso asked.

"We're preparing to take you home, Mr Prakoso," Lincoln said.

Prakoso looked down at his hands in his lap, started rolling them back and forth over one another, slowly, methodically. Calming his nerves, most likely. Though he already seemed pretty calm.

"And where, sir, do you suppose home is for Mr Prakoso?" he asked with his head still down.

"That depends," Lincoln answered.

"On?"

"You."

"Naturally. You did not come to my rescue from only the goodness of your heart, sir."

"Not entirely."

"Yes, sir," Prakoso said, as if he'd been expecting it. As if this was the routine. He just sat there, rubbing the heels of his hands together rhythmically. There was something soothing about the motion, even to Lincoln.

"We know what you've been up to, Mr Prakoso," Lincoln said. "We know you've been involved in certain things. Bad things."

"You are no police, sir."

"No, no police, you're right. But we can help you," Lincoln replied. "Or, we can do the other thing. I'd rather help you."

Prakoso nodded. His hands stopped moving, and he held them in front of himself, palms together. He raised them towards his face and then stopped. Apparently having his wrists bound together prevented him from doing whatever he'd been about to do. After a moment, he used both hands to smooth his wild hair on the right side of his head, then repeated the movement on the left side of his head. He ducked his head further, and smoothed the hair on top of his head, and behind.

When he brought his hands back down towards his lap, he did it so fluidly, so casually, that Lincoln had no warning that anything unusual was happening until he heard a loud pop, and Prakoso's quick cuffs snapped off. In the next instant, Prakoso surged forward with both hands and snatched Lincoln's head, twisted it. Lincoln had just enough time to bring his forearm in front of his face, before Prakoso's knee rocketed up.

Lincoln's arm absorbed some of the blow, but the knee caught him on the cheekbone, just in front of the hinge of his jaw, and his vision sparked white with the impact. Stunned, Lincoln could only manage to drop forward into Prakoso's waist. He drove off his legs into an awkward tackle, but Prakoso melted back and away, and Lincoln ended up on one knee. Another stabbing strike caught him in the shoulder blade. He tried to regain his feet, but the room went sideways, and he ended up hard on his back, with Prakoso over him.

An instant later, another body flew into the room, a horizontal lightning strike that swept Prakoso away and into the wall. Lincoln scrambled backwards, too dizzy to follow exactly what was happening. A flurry of motion, someone called out, and then Prakoso was up again, raining vicious elbow strikes down on the person beneath him.

Sahil materialized and lunged for Prakoso, but Prakoso leapt to one side, up onto a bed and then sprang off again in a flying knee. Sahil rolled into the attack, caught Prakoso around the waist and threw the small man across the room. Prakoso impacted and flopped to the floor, then was somehow up again before Lincoln could even process what had just happened. It was like watching a monkey fight a tiger; Prakoso was everywhere. At one point, Sahil lunged, but Prakoso twisted and bent out of the way, and delivered a pair of strikes to the side of Sahil's head. Sahil took the shots and whipped around with a heavy fist that caught Prakoso square in the chest.

Without warning a slice of the night sky fell and draped itself over Prakoso, and then Thumper was there, with her arms locked around him. Shrouded, he writhed against her, but with her powerful arms she picked him up and launched him like a broken rocket back down to the floor. The impact made a dreadful crunching thud. Afterwards, Prakoso lay dead still, covered with, Lincoln now saw, the blanket they'd been using to block the hole in the wall.

For a moment, everyone sat in shocked silence. Then Sahil finally spoke.

"You all right, boss?"

Lincoln sat up, but kept both hands firmly on the floor. He nodded, and it made the room swim.

"Well, Mikey," Thumper said. "I think we found your Na."

Mike rolled up to sitting, with his back against the wall. Two rivulets of blood ran from a split above his eyebrow, leaving trails down the side of his face and threatening to drip into his eye. He wiped it with fingertips, then wiped his hands on his pants. He must've been the first one in, the streak that had tackled Prakoso.

"Told ya there's always one," he said. "Did you kill him?"

"Nah," Thumper said, and she nudged the form under the blanket with her toe. "Might've busted the floorboards a bit though."

"What'd you take his cuffs off for, cap'n?" Mike said.

"I didn't," Lincoln said. "He broke 'em off."

"I never seen anything like that before," Sahil said. He bent down and picked something up off the floor, and then held it up. A shard from the quick cuffs. "I gotta ask him how he did it."

"Next time *you* can wake him up," Lincoln said.

"Next time we'll have more people in the room," Wright said from the hole in the wall. Lincoln hadn't even noticed her standing there. She entered the room, and knelt down next to Prakoso, drew back the blanket. He was lying face down; his eyes were open and glassy. "Hey," she said, and she slapped his cheek a couple of times with the back of her hand. "Hey, Prakoso. You dead, kid?"

He blinked a few times, and then tried to lift his head. Apparently that was too much to ask for the moment, and he laid it back down again and groaned.

"You going to give us any more trouble?" she asked. He groaned again. "If so, I can arrange to have my friend here hit you with the planet again."

"No," Prakoso said, and he shook his head as best he could. "No trouble."

"Yeah, well, we're gonna have to secure those hands again, just to be sure," Wright said. She took hold of his hands and pulled them behind him. He didn't seem to resist at all.

"Sure a funny way of showing gratitude you got there, pal," Mike said, getting to his feet, with some help from Sahil. "We did just rescue you, you know."

"No, sir," Prakoso said, quietly. "No, sir. You just killed me."

FIFTEEN

"I'm glad one of us has good news," Colonel Almeida said on the viz, as Lincoln finished an impromptu debriefing of the team's lunar exploits. Thumper had rigged him up a secure line from the hop that was serving as their new temporary home, at least for the next few hours.

"Sir?"

"Central Martian Authority's got Higher all worked up," Almeida said. "Looks like the Martians are moving ships, tightening up their corridors. Official word is it's all part of routine exercises, joint maneuvers between all the satellite communities, planned months in advance."

"And we know it's not," Lincoln said.

"Opinions vary, as they usually do. But they put a war ship right out front, the *CMAV Relentless*. You don't move a vessel like that into a spotlight position unless you're sending a message. And piled on top of the recent unpleasantness, you can appreciate why it makes some people upstairs nervous."

"The important question to answer is whether or not the Martians even know about the recent unpleasantness."

"Fortunately, I've got some of my best people looking into that," Almeida said.

"Just some?"

"Jury's still out on the team lead."

Lincoln chuckled. "What's our response?"

"To the Martians? The usual chess match," Almeida said. "Everybody's doing one thing and saying they're doing another. State's holding a bunch of emergency meetings. We're contributing ships to a multinational force, deploying forward to monitor the exercises."

"Monitor, huh? Sending the usual suspects?"

"Not quite. All our friends and cousins of course, India, the Iranians, but even the Eastern Coalition's kicking in a few support-only vessels."

That caught Lincoln off guard. "And everybody's OK with that?"

"Yeah, funny how messing with trade routes on the far end can make all the spats at home seem less important."

"What about on the Martian side?"

"Apart from moving a bunch of ships around, it's business as usual, for the most part. Complaining about unnecessary aggression, that sort of thing. This is all high-level games of state sort of stuff right now. Average man on the street probably isn't paying too much attention to it yet. But as much as it's stirring up our folks, you've got to assume all *their* people who don't exist are working just as much overtime as *our* people who don't exist."

"Any idea what kicked it off?"

"Maybe nothing. Maybe something we don't know about. Maybe this is what they'd been planning to do all along," the colonel said. "Obviously, certain elements are taking it as proof that this is all part of a grand strategy to position for war."

"Sending a bunch of ships to 'monitor' exercises sounds like a pretty good way to guarantee something bad happens."

"Which is why it's all the more important that you get me something concrete to work with. Hard to trust people who say they don't want to start a war when everyone's acting like they do. We're way right of bang on this, captain. I'm counting on you to rewind the timeline."

"At least you temper your expectations."

"What's going on with your man Prakoso now?" Almeida asked.

"Wright's talking to him," Lincoln said. "Figured it was best for us to hold on to him for now, see what we could get out of him before we turn him over to NID."

"That's a good call," Almeida said. "Some of Mr Self's people have already been down here knocking on my door to assume custody."

"What'd you tell them?"

"I told them the next time you contacted me, I'd be sure to impress upon you the importance of turning him over at the earliest possible opportunity."

"I'll consider myself so warned."

"I said I'd do it next time you contacted me," the colonel said. "Unfortunately, you've been on mission and dark, and I have no idea when I might expect to hear from you again."

"Ah. Understood, sir."

"Do what you need to to keep your tempo up. I don't want a bunch of paperpushers getting in between you and the raw data."

"Roger that. Might be a while then, if we can convince him to help us. Maybe longer if we can't."

"Whatever you need. Just get it done," said Almeida, and he started to say one thing, but stopped himself to say another. "Oh, one other bit of news from the Secret World. One of the CMA's northern representatives was found dead in his room a few nights ago. On one of those luxury hops, further out towards the belt. He was one of the reps from the Martian People's Collective Republic."

The MPCR wasn't the largest settlement on Mars, but it was an economic powerhouse and an important player in the power dynamic. Technically the Central Martian Authority superseded any one colony's authority and kept things balanced on the red planet. Everyone knew the influence that the MPCR could wield, though, if it so chose.

"Turns out, of course, because nothing's ever easy, he wasn't just a diplomat," Almeida continued. "He was a courier for CMA intelligence, had a habit of moving sensitive info around using his credentials."

"Assassinated?"

"News says it was a heart attack. Personally, I think it probably had more to do with the sharp thing someone stuck through his brain stem."

"Any chance that was someone on our side trying to stir the pot and see what floated up?"

Almeida shook his head. "That someone would have gone way off into deep black territory to end up there. He wasn't on anyone's radar, really. Not a high profile concern. In fact, the only reason we know about the intelligence angle is because NID was developing him as an asset."

"Maybe CMA found out. Had someone kill him to keep him from talking with us."

"We don't think so. The Directorate hadn't made the approach yet, they just had an agent watching him. No one's quite figured out how to crack the Collective yet, at least not safely. But that's the thing, isn't it? We can't tell if he got it on our account, or if he earned it on his own. NID's getting paranoid. Even more so than usual, I mean. Couple of buddies of mine over there are starting to wonder if they've got a leaky pipe somewhere."

"But you think that's why Mars is moving their ships," Lincoln said. "Because their guy got whacked."

"Well, no, I'm not sure I'd say that exactly," Almeida answered.

"No, I'm saying that *is* what you think," Lincoln replied. "If talking about one thing reminded you of the other, then you think there's a connection, whether you realize it or not."

Almeida paused.

"Huh. Now that you mention it, it does sort of make you wonder, doesn't it? But something like that, by itself, probably isn't enough to warrant that kind of reaction. Typically, you wouldn't expect a political loss to lead so directly to a military response."

"Maybe they're in the same jam we are," Lincoln said. "Can't broadcast the loss if you aren't sure who the actors are. Better just to pretend everything's exactly what it seems. The thing that worries me is that these sort of events are like roaches. Once you see one, you can't help but wonder how many more there are running around that you haven't seen. Or haven't seen *yet*."

"You're saying the CMA's been hit more than once?"

Lincoln shrugged. "Just saying it's possible. We don't know what we don't know."

"You're starting to sound like NID."

"I'll pretend you didn't say that," Lincoln said. And then shook his head. "I don't know what we're going to find out here, but I don't think anybody's going to be happy about it when we do."

"What's next on the agenda?"

"I was thinking we'd come home, regroup. But if NID's getting grabby about Prakoso, we probably ought to find a reason to stay out a little longer."

"I thought you might say that," the colonel said, and he smiled.

"Uh oh."

"I've got you set to link up with the *USS Christopher T. Curry*. It's not a fancy ship, but I can get you on it for free, and people generally don't start asking questions until I start spending money. She's on her way out as a backing force in case things go pear-shaped on us."

"Might not be a bad idea to head Mars-ward," Lincoln said. "Probably going to end up there at some point anyway."

"Let's hope not," the colonel said. "I'll have Kennedy pass

on the details. Expect a runabout in a few hours."

"Roger that."

"Chase this thing down, captain," Almeida said. "Wherever it leads. That's what you're built for."

"Yes sir."

Lincoln shut down the connection and returned to the main room where the team was gathered. NID had found them a temporary hiding place on the hop; an unused office suite on the outer ring of the station. It was probably intended for maybe three people, or as an executive office for one. Lincoln had made his call home from the bathroom. Wright was working Prakoso in an attached meeting room, while the rest of the team sat around waiting for the news. Though, of course, the team had varying degrees of what "sitting around" actually entailed.

Mike was stretched out on the floor with his head on his pack and a hat over his face, grabbing a little sleep while he could. Thumper and Sahil were likewise on the floor, but for entirely different purposes; Sahil was feeding Thumper drills on her groundwork, giving her the opportunity to practice moving into a variety of takedowns and joint locks. Lincoln knew well how strong Sahil was, and how unlikely he was to let anything be too easy for anyone. Thumper's fluid transitions from one hold to another made him realize just how much he would not want to tangle with her.

Through the window of the meeting room, Wright saw Lincoln. He signaled to her, and she got up to join the group. She closed the door behind her, but stayed next to it, angled so she could keep an eye on Prakoso.

"Gonna be a little while until we get to breathe real air again, folks," Lincoln said. "We're hopping a ride out, so we can be closer to the action."

"Action?" Thumper said, releasing Sahil from an arm bar and rolling up to a seated position.

Lincoln nodded. "CMA's making moves on their approach

corridors. UAF and friends are sending vessels forward to monitor the situation. Mom's got us set up on the *USS Curry*."

"Aw man, the *Curry*?" Mike said from under his hat. "Isn't that like a laundry ship or something?"

"Nah," Thumper said, "It's a garbage barge."

"It's a Marine transport," said Wright.

"Yeah," Thumper replied. "That's what I said."

"And that's the last time you'll say it until we're well clear of any Marines," Wright said.

"Come on, Mir, it's all in good fun," Thumper said.

"The interservice rivalry thing is a great way to get remembered, Thump. The less anyone recalls about us or our time on board, the better. Understood?"

"Yeah, OK. Roger that," Thumper said, and then she looked over at Lincoln and made a we-never-get-to-have-any-fun face.

"What are we doing about our little buddy?" Wright asked.

"He's coming with," Lincoln answered.

"Not sure that's a good idea," Wright said. "Pretty sure the navy isn't going to like us bringing a potential threat on board."

"Yeah, I don't think we'll tell them that part."

"Trying to keep up with him *and* keep it quiet? It'd be easier to just let NID have him."

"Easier, sure. And that'd be the end of the trail for us. NID would lock him up somewhere, and we might as well go on home and wait for the next call," said Lincoln. "So he goes with us. At least until we know for sure we can't use him."

"You want to take a crack at him?" Wright asked.

"Nah, I'm sure you gave him a good run. We'll give him a break for a while, try again when we get on board the *Curry*. Runabout should be here in a couple of hours."

Wright nodded. "All right. I'll let him know."

She went back into the small office and closed the door behind her. Lincoln was fairly sure that Wright's version of keeping Prakoso informed also involved a few more rounds of questioning. After Wright had closed the door, Mike gave it a moment before he spoke from under his hat.

"Knock knock," he said. Lincoln glanced over at him, and then back at Thumper and Sahil. Sahil just shook his head. *Don't encourage him.*

"Come on guys," Mike said. "Knock knock."

"All right man," Lincoln said, more out of pity than out of any desire to hear the joke. Sahil made a face at him. "Who's there?"

"Master sergeant," Mike said.

"Master serge–"

"QUIT JOKING AROUND!" Mike bellowed. Thumper barked a laugh, and even Sahil cracked a smile.

"All right now," Lincoln said, chuckling and only feeling a little bad about it, since Wright wasn't in the room to defend herself. "You guys make sure you're all set to move when it's time. I don't want to keep that runabout hanging around any longer than it has to."

It was hard to avoid drawing attention on the *Curry*. Everyone the team interacted with was polite and professional, but there were plenty of stares and whispers. It almost certainly didn't help that Colonel Almeida had sent along a care package for them. Their suits. Even though Lincoln hadn't gotten a chance to run one live, after the pain of leaving them behind for the Luna trip, seeing those crates was like being reunited with a long-lost friend. Luna hadn't been the place for them. But now, not knowing what exactly lay ahead, it made sense to keep the suits nearby, just in case.

The specialized crates were kept locked safely in the *Curry*'s armory. Somehow, that made everything worse. The armor would have undoubtedly attracted some level of attention; but even just having a few mystery boxes on board sent the rumors pinging around the ship like a low-velocity round.

The team and their guest tried to keep to themselves as much as possible, but there wasn't a lot of privacy to be had on the vessel.

After three days of trying to keep a low profile without much success, Lincoln found himself accosted once more in the ship's mess by a couple of eager young sailors and decided to take a different approach.

"All right," he said, leaning close, and motioning to the two young men across from him to follow suit. "I'm not supposed to say anything, but you guys look like you can keep your mouth shut."

"Yeah, absolutely we can," one of them replied; a Petty Officer Third Class Trudeau by his uniform.

"Well... I don't want to say too much but... I do a lot of work with you know... *special* people." He gave them a meaningful nod.

"Oh man, I knew it," Trudeau said. He nudged his pal, who was still just staring at Lincoln. "You guys are SEALs aren't you?"

The navy's special operations force had a long and proud tradition, one that had begun all the way back when people were still stuck on one planet.

"No, but..." Lincoln checked over his shoulders before continuing. "You ever hear of *applied* intelligence?"

"No," Trudeau said, eyes wider. "What's that?"

"I mean I don't like to brag about it, obviously, but we do some pretty serious work." Lincoln shrugged a shoulder and picked at the food on his plate.

Trudeau pressed him. "So you're like, a secret ops kind of guy? Sneaking in places, getting intelligence, that sort of thing?"

"Well, I mean... I'm in the *information* division."

"Information?"

"Well," Lincoln said. "You know, information *support*, technically."

Trudeau's face changed. "Information support?"

"Yeah, I'm in the 301st Information Support Brigade. But don't tell anyone that, I don't want it to get around."

And now Trudeau's expression melted into something more like disappointment. "The 301st? What, do you like, fix computers or something?"

Lincoln played it up. "Well, I mean, yeah, but it's for super important stuff. Secret stuff, like you said."

"Aw man, are you kidding me?" Trudeau said, standing up. His silent friend followed suit. "I thought you were some cool guy, not just some egghead wannabe. Information *support...*"

"Hey, keep it down," Lincoln protested, but Trudeau just waved a hand at him and stomped off. It didn't take long after that episode for Trudeau's shipmates to lose most of their interest in their quiet guests.

And quiet they were. The team knew the drill, but even Prakoso seemed to understand the situation; either that, or the nature of the life he led had made him instinctively capable of blending into whatever environment he happened to find himself in. Whatever fire the small man had left in him had been quenched in the custody of the team. He was already a quiet man, gentle in his movements and tone of voice. Watching him, listening to him, it seemed impossible that he was at all capable of the violence he'd laid on Lincoln and his teammates. Undoubtedly being surrounded by a ship full of Marines had some effect on his desire to try his luck at another escape. But there was more to it than just that. Something seemed to have broken in him, since that last attempt; as if they'd witnessed the wild thrashing of a beast's final rage before its submission to the will of another.

Lincoln sat with Prakoso in one of two compartments the crew of the *Curry* had cleared for their use. Like everywhere else on the ship, space was tight, but Lincoln couldn't complain. He figured there were some junior officers somewhere on board who'd given up their quarters and were now probably sleeping eight men deep.

They'd given Prakoso a little time free of questioning, time to adjust and reflect on his situation. But the clock was ticking, and they couldn't afford to let things drag on for too long. Lincoln was back at it, with Thumper leaning against the bulkhead behind him, keeping casual guard. Lincoln sat in a chair across from Prakoso, but had angled it slightly to soften the sense of confrontation. Contrary to popular opinion, Lincoln had always thought of interrogation as a game of relationship, not a test of power.

"You're making this more difficult than it needs to be," Lincoln said. "But only on yourself. You understand that, yeah?"

Prakoso shrugged his slight shoulders. "Always, it's the same."

"I'm trying to help you here, Yayan. What do you think is going to happen if you don't cooperate with us?"

"What do you think will happen if I do?"

"We can protect you," Lincoln said. "Hide you. Give you a new life. Anything you want."

Prakoso just stared back at Lincoln. "Sir, all these things you say. Which of them do you believe I haven't heard ten thousand times before now? From men just like you."

"Surely it's better than the alternative."

"No, sir. For me, they are the same. All the same," Prakoso said. "Prison."

"Prison is what I'm trying to protect you from, Yayan. Hanging out with us, I know it's not your *first* choice, but trust me, this is an all-expenses paid vacation in paradise compared to what's going to happen if I have to release you to the people who *really* want you. I'm taking a lot of heat for you right now. I've got all kinds of threats coming my way on your account. I'm spending all my personal capital keeping you here, and I'm just about out. Pretty soon it's going to be out of my hands, and chances are someone's going to come take you away and they're going to stick you in a hole somewhere on a hop out in deep space. If that happens, *when* that happens, you're going to realize your old friend Lincoln here was telling you the truth, that he was the best chance you had, and it's going to be too late. Once you're gone, there's nothing else I can do for you. But if you help me now, I'll do everything in my power to make it right for you."

"I cannot help you," Prakoso said. And he looked down at his hands in his lap, and then added, "My part is done. They asked nothing of me more, not for days. Weeks." He shrugged.

It was such a small moment, Lincoln almost missed it. But he realized that it was the first time Prakoso had acknowledged in any way that he'd been working for someone. Lincoln knew he had to tread carefully now, to coax the information out without overplaying it, without giving any signal to Prakoso that he was slipping.

"Then why were they still holding you?" he said. "If your part was done?"

"Control," Prakoso said.

"And that was what you agreed to? Part of the deal?"

"It is never part of the deal," Prakoso said. "And yet, always." He smiled sadly then and took a deep breath. And his defenses came down. "This is not the life I wanted. Not what I meant to choose," he continued, and shook his head. "I just wanted to solve interesting problems."

And that's how it usually happened, how interrogations most often turned for Lincoln; not a sudden, explosive breaking of the will, but instead a quiet unfolding of the heart.

"That's what *we* do," Lincoln replied. "We're problem solvers. And that's all we're asking you to do for us. *With* us. Help us solve a problem. You didn't know what you were getting into, I get that."

"I knew enough," Prakoso said, shaking his head again. "I always know."

"Do you? Do you know enough about what they used your work for, Yayan?"

He shrugged.

"Do you want me to tell you the number of casualties?" Lincoln said.

Prakoso's eyes glinted, some combination of anger and fear. Whatever he thought he'd done for those people, he seemed genuinely shocked that it had caused any death at all, let alone thousands.

"It's a lot," Lincoln added. "And a lot more will follow if we don't do something soon. You can't undo it now. But you don't have to let it continue. You can help us stop it. *You* can stop it."

Prakoso looked over at Thumper, then back to Lincoln, then down at his own hands again. Lincoln leaned forward and put his hand on the man's shoulder.

"Help us stop it."

"I would like to go home," Prakoso said. "I would like only to go home. Whatever comes after, it would be worth it to see my home."

"Then help us," Lincoln said. "Help us, and we'll get you home."

"You will not," Prakoso said, looking up. There were tears in his eyes, but he did not heed them. "You *can* not. Your people would never allow it."

"I can't help it if you escape," Lincoln said. "And a man with your skill set... I bet once we lost track of you, we'd never be able to find you again."

"You found me once."

"We found Apsis," Lincoln said. "Their fault, not yours."

Lincoln could see the struggle in Prakoso's eyes.

"I'm going to make that happen," Lincoln said. "When you're done helping us, I'm going to get you home. I give you my word on that."

"I just wanted to solve interesting problems."

They were so close, Lincoln could feel it. But he was at a loss for which direction to go. What further promise he could make, or what appeal would resonate, and tip Prakoso over to the right side.

"Captain," Thumper said, from close behind him. "You mind if I talk with Yayan alone for a few?"

Lincoln looked at her over his shoulder. She was standing right behind him now, her fingertips resting lightly on the back of his chair. This wasn't part of the plan, but something in her look compelled him to let her take over. He nodded and stood.

"All right, sure." For a moment, he thought about adding a mild threat, making some comment about hoping she could get Prakoso to understand before NID came to take him away, but he caught himself, decided to take it a different direction. Lighten the mood, treat the moment as though Prakoso had already acquiesced. "And is there anything else you want me to do for you two?"

"You could get us some coffee," Thumper said, and then to Prakoso added, "His coffee's better than you'd think."

Lincoln didn't know what that was supposed to mean exactly, but he didn't want to press it.

"You drink coffee, Yayan?" he asked.

The man shrugged his shoulders.

"I'll see what I can scrounge up on this tub," he said, and left the compartment. Directly across the passageway was the other compartment they'd been given for their use, and the crew had been kind enough to leave behind a personal coffee brewer. Sahil and Wright were nowhere to be found, but Mike was racked out on one of the bunks. He raised his head when Lincoln entered.

"Hey, cap," he said. "Pop him yet?"

"Not sure," Lincoln answered, as he walked over to the coffee supplies. "Close, I think. Thumper's trying to close the deal right now."

"And you're doing what?"

Lincoln held up one of the disposable coffee cups.

"Sure, I'd love some," Mike said with a smile, and dropped his head back to his pillow.

Lincoln took his time, not sure exactly how long Thumper needed to do whatever it was she had in mind. Ten minutes, maybe. When he was done, he handed a cup off to Mike and crossed back over to the other compartment.

Upon entering the compartment, Lincoln knew immediately that something had changed. Outwardly the difference in Prakoso was slight; his shoulders slumped less, his eyes weren't as quick to avoid contact. But the atmosphere in the room had shifted, as if Lincoln had walked in and interrupted them sharing gossip about him. Thumper had moved her chair around even closer to Prakoso, at a ninety-degree angle to his; neither directly next to him, nor across from him. A position of mediation, or of counsel. She was leaning forward with her arms resting on her knees, but she sat back in her chair when Lincoln came in.

"You two aren't up to something in here, are you?" Lincoln asked.

Prakoso looked up at Lincoln with a neutral expression.

"Common interests," Thumper said with a shrug and a smile. Prakoso returned his eyes to his hands when she said it, but one corner of his mouth turned upward.

Lincoln handed Thumper her coffee, and then held the other cup out in front of Prakoso.

"So what'd I miss?"

"Just talking shop," Thumper said. "Nice to get a chance to chat with someone who speaks the language."

Prakoso took the coffee. "Thank you."

He took a sip, and after a moment his eyebrows went up, as if in surprise.

"Pretty good, isn't it?" Thumper said. Prakoso nodded.

"It's just coffee," Lincoln said. "It's not like I do anything special to it."

"It's probably the love that makes it good," Thumper replied. "'Koso here was just telling me a little bit about his recent work. It's pretty cool stuff."

"Yeah?" Lincoln said, trying not to react too strongly to the fact that she'd just called Prakoso by a nickname. "Care to share?"

Prakoso gave him the highlights, and Lincoln found himself gaining a new appreciation for Thumper's knack for explaining technical things, which previously he'd considered unnecessarily detailed; most of what Prakoso told him sounded just shy of gibberish, but Prakoso was so enthusiastic about it, Lincoln didn't dare interrupt.

"Which is all to say, the handshake protocol he developed… the one that interfaced with YN-773," Thumper interpreted. "It's mutable, self-modifying. Introduce it to a different codebase, and it can penetrate and inject new functionality, or override existing ones."

"That doesn't sound like something you'd use just once," Lincoln said.

"No, it doesn't," Thumper said.

"And I helped them secure their relay," Prakoso added. "A counter to prevent prediction attacks."

"That's impressive," Thumper said.

"I didn't develop the technique," Prakoso responded. "Only the implementation."

"*Only*," Thumper said. And she smiled at him like he was a teen pop star. He seemed genuinely embarrassed by the look.

"The relay," Lincoln said. "Is that something we can intercept?"

"There's nothing *to* intercept," Thumper explained. "It uses quantum simulation, same as our stuff."

Lincoln gave her what he hoped was his most patient face, waiting for her to actually answer the question.

"Buddy, you don't want me to get into that. But for all intents and purposes, you can basically pretend the thing here happens simultaneously as the thing over there, with nothing in between."

"Oh, so magic," Lincoln said. "You don't have to make it sound so fancy."

"It's *not* magic, it's math. And science," Thumper said, a little defensively. "Anyway, the point is, that's why we can talk across the solar system in real time. Once an encrypted system's set up, outside of a really well-executed prediction attack, which our man 'Koso here apparently secured them against, the only way to listen in is to have an ear on one of the actual boxes."

"Or to spoof one of your own," Prakoso said. "But to do that, you would need to have physical access first."

"If we got hold of one, could you crack it?" Lincoln asked. Prakoso shook his head.

"Really?" Thumper asked. "You didn't leave anything behind for yourself? A back door? Just in case?"

"No," Prakoso said.

"Are you sure? Because that seems like something I'd do. All that work, not knowing what it was going to be used for. It'd be easy. Why not?"

"Because I am not a fool," Prakoso said. "I work very hard not to be a loose end."

"We don't necessarily need to know what's in the message, though," Lincoln said. "We know there's a bad guy. We know he's got someone delivering his mail. We don't have to read the letters if we can just follow the mailman. Is that something we can do?"

Prakoso furrowed his brow in thought.

"The network has a unique ID obviously, but every box in it has a specific signature," Thumper said, and she went into that look that meant she was thinking out loud, not necessarily trying to communicate anything meaningful. "If we tap one, we still probably won't be able to do much with the messages getting sent around. We can maybe figure out what kind of traffic they're sending, from the pops and clicks. Commo, navigational data, that sort of thing. But you're right, depending on what we find, we might be able to track some of the return addresses. Figure out how many boxes are out there, maybe where they're stationed. If we get lucky and they're sloppy, we might even be able to pull something out of their access connections..."

"Theoretically, yes," Prakoso said, and his eyes brightened, as he picked up the thread and his mind went to work on the problem. He and Thumper were two peas in a pod.

"If we could just find one... Was there one back at the safehouse?" Thumper asked. "Where Apsis was holding you?"

"No," Prakoso answered. "But I know the seed for the one I secured."

"I thought you said you weren't a loose end.," Lincoln said.

"I said I try," Prakoso said. "I didn't memorize it on purpose. It's just the kind of the thing that sticks in my brain."

Thumper was looking at him with barely veiled wonder.

"That's like five hundred and twelve characters long, at least," she said.

"Yes," Prakoso said, a little sheepishly. "But only eight blocks of sixty-four. Anyone can do sixty-four."

"And how can we use that?" Lincoln asked.

"We might be able to localize its signature, the next time they use it," Prakoso said. "*Might.* It would be very complicated. And you would need some very special equipment. Very hard to get."

Lincoln nodded. "Make me a list."

Thumper and Prakoso went to work, and there was little Lincoln could do to help besides keeping them full of coffee and expensive gear. In the meantime, he spent a lot of time in the *Curry*'s weight room, and running drills in a hangar with the rest of the team. After a few days, Prakoso and Thumper emerged from their cave with exhausted smiles and some targeting data. Garlington Outpost 15-436. Flashtown.

"If we get access to this one," Thumper said, "it'll be a good starting point. Give us some idea of what we're dealing with."

Mike let out a low whistle and Sahil shook his head.

"I don't see there's any way to do that clean," Sahil said.

"So we do it the way we have to," Lincoln said. "And make sure someone else gets the credit."

"We're really gonna do this?" Mike said.

"Looks like," Lincoln said. "I think it's probably time for me to put that suit through its paces anyway."

SIXTEEN

Despite the fact that they'd been given the green light to deploy, Lincoln and his teammates had been standing around waiting for almost an hour and a half for their insertion vehicle to arrive. It happened every time, and it still surprised him, every time. Usually, the last thing Lincoln would want to do in these situations was review the plan again. There was such a thing as over-rehearsal. But in this case, the target site presented enough of a challenge that he felt like one more look wouldn't hurt anybody. In the down time, he had gathered his team around and activated the holo, projecting a 3D image that only they could see.

Garlington Outpost 15-436 was conveniently positioned about midway between Earth and Mars, and it wasn't exactly a sanctioned station. In fact, it could barely be considered a station at all. 15-436 had originally been intended as a staging area, more of a supply hold than anything else, for the now-defunct mining corporation. Looking at the scan data, Lincoln could still see hints of Garlington's design and infrastructure poking out here and there from under all the graftwork. Unfortunately, the company had been one of many to overextend itself in the early, mad rush to fill space and had gone bankrupt before 15-436 had been completed. Technically, Garlington was responsible for ensuring the property was sold off or destroyed. Instead, the outpost had been abandoned. At least by Garlington.

Lincoln didn't know the full history of the station, but at some point between the origin and now, a few enterprising individuals had claimed the half-completed structure and taken it upon themselves to make it operational. And they'd succeeded, after a fashion. Salvage rights weren't clear on the topic, and no one on either planet seemed to have all that much interest in enforcing any laws all the way out there anyway. These days, the outpost looked less like it had been constructed and more like it had accreted from man-made space debris.

The floating mass was more popularly known as Flashtown.

Flashtown was run by a woman who called herself Mayor Jon, and everything about the place had the feel of a gangster who wanted desperately to be seen as a legitimate businessperson. They were incorporated, after all; at least according to Mayor Jon's convoluted interpretation of interplanetary law. Predictably, Mayor Jon's outpost had attracted a particular demographic, and as a result 15-436 had earned a reputation; they didn't ask a lot of questions, but they did take security very seriously.

It wouldn't be fair to call it a pirates' haven. Flashtown was equally open and welcoming to any entrepreneurial criminal. Lincoln had never had cause to visit the station himself, and going over the schematics with the team one last time, he found himself wishing he could have kept that streak going.

"I don't think that's up to code," Mike said, pointing at the 3D image and at what appeared to be half of a transport's hull, welded into place to form a passageway.

"This is the best scan we've got?" Lincoln asked.

"It's fresh as of twelve hours ago," Thumper answered. "Whiskers went out and got as much as they could, filled in a bunch of holes."

Lincoln pointed at all the dark patches in the projection. "Missed a few."

"Yeah, well, the place is dense and doesn't exactly have the nicest floorplan," Thumper said. "Still think this is a good idea?"

"I never thought it was a good idea," Lincoln answered. "But if you're sure what we need is in there, there's no reason not to go get it."

He looked over at her.

"You are sure, right?"

"Sure," she said.

"Sled's up," Wright said, pointing further down the hangar. A gunship was finally being positioned for release. The team's low-signature delivery vehicle was tethered below.

"Two hours late," Mike said. "Right on time."

Lincoln shut the map down.

"This is going to be fun," he said. "I feel good about this."

"Are you being sarcastic right now?" Thumper said. "I can't tell with you."

"I can't either," Lincoln said with a smile. "Let's load it up."

For most of the trip out, Lincoln left his teammates to their own devices. Like any other team, everyone had their own way of preparing for a hit. Lincoln liked to do a slow check of all his equipment, which was completely unnecessary since he'd triple-checked everything already before they'd left the *Curry*. Still, there was something meditative about the process, something reassuring about the close contact with the tools of his trade. Wright seemed to have a similar ritual. Sahil was dead asleep.

Eventually the pilot's voice came over the ship's internal communication system.

"Rise and shine, kids," she said. "Sixty mikes out from separation."

The crew chief went to work and helped Lincoln and his teammates don their suits and run through the systems check on each. Once they'd confirmed all systems green, they transferred into the delivery vehicle attached to the gunship.

Technically, the delivery vehicle was called a Lamprey, but everyone in the teams had a different name for it: the Coffin. The vehicle was designed for medium-range insertion into non-permissive environments, which was milspeak for sneaking into places people weren't supposed to go. It was a complete ship on its own, with its own thrusters and guidance systems, but being in one felt less like flying a craft and more like being packed inside a missile and fired off towards some distant target. And there was some truth to that perception: apart from navigation, other systems were streamlined to keep the ship's signature as low as possible. That meant a bare minimum for essentials like life-support functions, and no weapon systems at all. Which was all fine, as long as no one saw them coming.

The Coffin's aspirations of virtual undetectability included its physical profile and the vessel was therefore necessarily slender by design. As a result, the interior was so narrow passengers had to sit facing each other down the length of the ship, typically with a knee in between the legs of the occupants across from them when the craft was full. Fortunately, it had capacity for eight; the team spread out as much as they could. The pilot's seat was up front, distinguished from the others only by its proximity to a console on its left side. Wright sat there to assume command of the ship, while Lincoln went to the rear. The others took up the seats in between.

Once they were loaded in and secure, the gunship pilot kept them informed with a countdown every few minutes until the critical moment.

"Reach 32, you are go for separation," she said.

"Roger that, Pagan 1," Wright replied. She looked down the line to Lincoln; he gave her an OK sign. "Reach 32 is go for separation."

"Here we go," the pilot answered. "Five, four, three, two, one, and... release. Reach 32 has full separation, trajectory looks good."

"Copy, Pagan 1," Wright said. "Reach 32 confirms good release and is systems green."

"Copy that, Reach 32. Pagan 1 is RTB. Good luck and Godspeed, friends. Pagan 1 out."

"Thanks for the ride, Pagan 1," said Wright. "Reach 32 out."

Once they'd cleared the gunship, the team switched communications over to their internal channel and did a quick commo check. Everyone sounded off, with Wright reporting in last.

"Wright, check check check," she said. "Good copy all around. And we are going cold." She tapped a few strokes on the console and set the Coffin to silent running, further reducing the vessel's heat signature.

Lincoln looked down the line at his teammates. Though their suits were identical, the individuals were identifiable by their size and shape, as well as by their kit. Each had a different arrangement of gear hanging on their suits, marking their roles and laid out to exacting personal preference. Mike had even customized his with a few nonregulation images and phrases, using the digital ink that only showed up through the suit's visor. On the shoulder facing Lincoln, he'd placed a tab that read "MEDIUM SPEED, SOME DRAG".

But even though Lincoln could tell who each figure was, and even though he was in one of the suits himself, there was something unearthly about the faceless, armored beings sitting patiently to his right. It didn't take much to imagine they were empty suits of armor, each animated by some dreadful avenging spirit. Knowing the people actually inside, he wasn't sure that was too far from the truth. And he was glad they were all on his side.

They covered the remaining distance to the target in silence. Lincoln tried not to think about how great that distance actually was, or how fast they were actually moving. For all the time he'd spent in space, he was a groundpounder at heart, and he'd never quite gotten used to the exponential change in scale. When they were on approach, Wright roused the team.

"Five mikes to target," Wright said. "Thumper, Mike, you're up."

Mike and Thumper stood up, folded their seats flat against the bulkhead. Mike had to hunch over to keep from hitting his head on the overhead.

"We headed out the top, or you gonna poop us out the back?" Mike asked.

"Back," Wright said.

"Seriously, Mike, you gotta stop calling it that," Thumper said, as they shuffled towards the rear of the craft.

"What? That's what it feels like."

Lincoln made room for them to get by and, as they squeezed past, wished he'd sat in the middle in the first place. The rear hatch leading to the airlock was three-quarters height. Watching Mike work his way through it, Lincoln understood Mike's description of the process.

"Can't you think of it like something nicer?" Thumper said as she followed Mike into the airlock.

"Like what, Thump?" Mike said.

"I don't know... like, I don't know, being born or something."

"Oh sure, that works too," Mike answered. "Forcible ejection through a canal filled with blood and water–"

"Ugh, nevermind," Thumper interrupted. "Just shut up and go."

Three minutes later, Wright had the Coffin in position. The first insertion point was on the lower decks, down where a lot of construction was never completed. The number of exposed beams, girders, and cables promised a significant navigation challenge to even a ship as slim and streamlined as the Lamprey. As a precaution, the team had decided to hold off a few hundred meters from the station; Mike and Thumper would freespace the remaining distance using the microthrusters on their suits.

"Downtown, you're good to go," she said, using the pair's mission codename.

"Copy that," Thumper said. "Stepping out now."

"Behold," Mike said a moment later, "the miracle of life!" and then he made a revolting sound with his mouth.

A minute or so later, Thumper reported back in.

"Downtown's on site," she said. "Prepping Poke for entry now. We'll hold for your call."

"Roger, Downtown," Wright answered. "We're moving topside. Stand by."

Wright moved the Coffin to the second insertion point a few hundred meters further up. Once there, she activated the protocol that had earned the vessel its designation as a Lamprey. Lincoln felt the ship roll and settle into position; a few moments later a low hum sounded through the hull as the craft attached itself to the exterior of the station. At least in this case, Flashtown's haphazard construction played to the team's favor. They'd identified several locations where the station was vulnerable to breach, and had selected one as an entry point. Now, the Lamprey was cutting through the external shell of the station's hull. As long as the ship's seal was secure, the station's internal atmosphere would go unchanged and thus the breach would go undetected. Once the team had entered, the Lamprey's mechanism would reverse the process before it detached, reforging the hull incision with integrity comparable to before the cut was made. And in Flashtown's particular case, Lincoln guessed it might even be improved.

"We're up," Wright said. Lincoln and Sahil joined her towards the front, where the upper airlock was located.

"I'll take point," Lincoln said.

"Negatory," Sahil said. "First in's my job."

"Whatever happened to chivalry?" Wright said.

"Bad guys always shoot high," Sahil said. "And ain't none of y'all can stay as low as me."

He didn't leave any room for argument and started up the ladder into the airlock before anyone could respond. Lincoln started forward after him, but Wright swatted his hand off the ladder and followed Sahil up. Lincoln was last in, and sealed the hatch behind him. The low-intensity red light of the airlock gave his teammates a hellish look, offset somewhat by their last names emblazoned in bright block letters across their backs. The names were visible only through the suit's visor, and remained easy-to-read white regardless of the actual environmental lighting conditions.

"Downtown, Highrise is ready to make first entry," Lincoln said, taking over comms as the team lead.

"Copy that, Highrise," Thumper answered. "Poke's still sniffing around for the exact location of the relay, but so far he's showing clear for us from here to there."

Thumper and Mike had a less glamorous entry point, through an arm of what appeared to be an uncompleted docking port, long ago abandoned.

"What's your route?" Lincoln asked.

"Through the port, service tunnel up to the holds," Thumper replied. "Then depends on what Poke finds. Hopefully we don't have to go too deep. It's pretty twisty in there."

"Roger that," Lincoln said. "We're headed in."

Lincoln signaled to Sahil, who nodded, drew his sidearm, and then activated the exterior hatch. On the other side waited a depthless emptiness, framed by the station's outer hull. Sahil climbed up and into the blackness, catlike in his movements, until all that was visible of him was the NAKARMI on his back. Wright waited for his call. Lincoln looked down at the short rifle slung tight across his chest, checked it one last time.

"Clear," Sahil said. At that, Wright moved up quickly, with Lincoln just behind. As Lincoln left the Coffin and entered the black space above, the suit's sensor suite dialed up the visibility, compositing an image from the various spectra it could detect.

There was no light for it to intensify or enhance here between the outer and inner hull of the station, but it interpreted all available radiation and translated it into a visual representation that Lincoln could understand. The result was a ghostly blue image of his teammates, amongst the station's interhull infrastructure. Beams and girders spanned open spaces that dropped below and curved away above. This particular section of Flashtown was old, but clearly hadn't been part of Garlington's original blueprint, judging from some of the strange angles and variety of construction materials used.

A virtual beacon designated their inner hull breach point a few dozen meters away, one that should take them to another out-of-the-way section of the station. It would've been more convenient if they could have found an entry point directly beneath their external breach, but the station's "design" didn't allow for that. And in any case, the only time anything was ever convenient on a hit was when it was a trap.

"Downtown, Highrise is in," Lincoln reported. "We're moving to the second breach point now."

"Roger, Highrise," Thumper said. "We're going to go ahead and move into the dock. It's dead down here."

"Downtown to dock, copy," Lincoln said.

The metalwork spread and overlapped like many hands with long fingers splayed; Sahil led the way as the trio navigated space that had never been intended for traversal. As Lincoln climbed over and around, ducked under, and stepped across, he was once again amazed at how natural the movement felt, at how closely the suit matched his body's expectations. If ever there was a place to catch a too-wide shoulder or clock a helmeted head, it was here, in between the hulls of a poorly constructed station. But there was none of that for Lincoln, nor for his teammates ahead of him, at least thus far.

After a few minutes of careful climbing, Sahil reached the entry point. He crouched and started assembling his necessary tools. Wright took a position next to him, and readied her weapon. Lincoln clambered in just behind Sahil, placed his hand on Sahil's shoulder. The three of them balanced on a three-foot-wide girder flush against the inner hull. Sahil attached a small device to the hull about waist height.

"How big a hole you want?" he asked in a whisper. There was no real need to keep voices low; Lincoln could have screamed and no one outside his suit would have heard it. But it was a hard habit to break. And Lincoln wasn't sure it was worth breaking anyway. Quiet voices reinforced quiet movement.

"Big enough to get through in a hurry if we have to," Lincoln answered.

Sahil produced a cylinder from somewhere on his hip, and used it to trace a silvery outline on the inner hull, roughly the size and shape of a normal ship hatch. When he'd completed the circuit, he tapped the bottom of it with his knuckle.

"Don't trip goin' in," Sahil said. He replaced the cylinder on the suit's belt, and then quickly went to work setting up two additional devices, one just above the top right corner of the outline, and one below it, at the bottom corner. Once he was certain they were secure, he activated the small device he'd first attached to the hull. As the device came on line, an electric border radiated outward from it, like lightning pooling against the hull, and wherever it spread, the hull appeared to become translucent. Outside the suit, nothing had changed, but from inside, Lincoln and his teammates had a good look at what was going on on the other side of the wall.

And what was going on, Lincoln was glad to see, was pretty much nothing.

"Downtown, Highrise is ready to make entry on the station," he said. "What's your status?"

"We're holding in the dock, by a service tunnel entrance," Thumper answered.

"You got eyes on that relay yet?"

"Not yet. Poke's reading strong signal, so he's close, but there's a lot of clutter. My guess is that they tucked it back in one of the secure storerooms and camouflaged it with a bunch of junk."

"You want us to wait?"

"Negative, we're ready to move. Poke should have it by the time we get there."

"Roger that. Stand by," Lincoln said. He switched his comms back to local. "Sahil, we set?"

"Set."

Lincoln pulled his short rifle up from his chest, shouldered it, kept the muzzle pointed low. "Burn it."

"Don't trip," Sahil said again. He pulled the small black box off the hull, and the image of the empty passageway on the other side dissolved. A moment later, Sahil touched off the silvery outline. There was no sound from it as it brightened into white, a white so intense that Lincoln's visor had to filter it to keep it from blinding him. It didn't take nearly as long as Lincoln expected. In just a few moments, the two devices at the top and bottom of the cut whined quietly, as they extended and then swiveled together to draw the cut section of the hull to one side. The instant there was enough of a gap, Sahil shot through it to the left. Wright moved in just behind him to the right, and Lincoln followed her through, mindful to step high over the lip at the bottom of the cut.

In the few seconds it had taken to get into the station, nothing in the passageway had changed. Still, the team held position, weapons ready, listening for any sounds of warning. Lincoln gave it thirty seconds to be sure.

"Downtown, Highrise is in," he said.

"Copy, Highrise," Thumper responded. "Downtown is moving into the tunnels now."

"Roger that," Lincoln answered. "Sahil, patch it up and let's go."

Sahil nodded, lowered his weapon and returned to the entry point. After a moment, Lincoln heard the mechanical arms on the other side of the hull reverse to slide the section back into place. There was a noticeable gap where the cut had been made, but the lighting in the passageway was poor, and this section of the station seemed to be fairly low traffic anyway. Lincoln wondered briefly how long it'd be before anyone noticed. Given the state of the station interior, though, it might not even seem that out of place.

Sahil brought his weapon back up and returned to his position ahead of Lincoln.

"Go camo," Lincoln said, "Move when ready."

Lincoln activated the reactive camouflage of his suit; the function surveyed the environment and adapted the suit's surfaces to blend in as much as possible from multiple viewpoints, using the sensor suite and threat matrix to prioritize the camo scheme. It didn't make anyone invisible, but in the right situations, it could be pretty close. Ahead of Lincoln, the pattern on Sahil's suit shifted like thin trails of mist and shadow stretching to meet.

"Camo's up," Sahil said. "Mir, you set?"

"Roll," she answered from behind Lincoln.

Sahil moved forward with quiet steps and careful aggression; a delicate dance of speed without haste, masterfully executed. Lincoln matched pace, with Wright following close and providing security to the rear. The route they took was cleanly plotted and clearly marked through the augmented display, but within the first few minutes, Lincoln knew there could be trouble ahead. Though they didn't have to redirect at any point, there were places along the way, passages blocked that should have been clear or doors where walls should have been, that warned of bad mapping data. The deeper they got into the station, the worse it seemed to get.

There was nothing to do about it now. The suit was capturing all the new data, correcting as they went, so at very least they'd know what to expect when they came back through on the way out.

"Thumper wasn't wrong about twisty," Wright said.

The three pressed on in silence the rest of the way to their target; a high-security hold on Flashtown's upper decks. Under normal circumstances, this was the kind of operation Lincoln would have carried out in the dead of night; an oh-dark-ugly kind of hit. But Flashtown was special. There was no dead-of-night on the station. Officially, it ran on a thirty two-hour clock, though Lincoln didn't know what the point of that was. Mayor Jon's way of keeping some sort of nonconformist order, maybe. Whatever the case, people were up and about at all times, which made everything that much more difficult. Lincoln and his team weren't here to cause indiscriminate murder and mayhem. But given the kinds of folks who generally populated Flashtown and the chances of bumping into someone unexpectedly, there was a very real and present risk of doing just that.

Fortunately, after some careful navigation and thanks to Sahil's good instincts, Lincoln's element reached the deck without alerting any of the station's citizens. Green Deck was dedicated to loading, unloading, and storing cargo from Flashtown's various clientele. Unlike most stations with their contraband and safety regulations, anyone could store just about anything at Flashtown, as long as they paid. And the more they paid, the better the security got. From the look of things, Lincoln guessed he and his team were in the cheap seats. Several holds were little more than open hangars, sectioned off by haphazard fencing. Security personnel patrolled in and around the aisles between these areas.

And calling them security personnel seemed generous. Mostly they were skinny kids with rifles too big, with a few mean-looking roughnecks mixed in here and there. Lincoln had seen the same composition in any number of irregular military forces back on-planet; exploiting young would-be warriors was a common recruitment tactic favored by warlords, cartels, and paramilitary groups. No matter how far from home they got, people didn't really change.

Across from one of the bargain-rate hangars, separated by a thoroughfare wide enough to drive a couple of trucks down, sat the target area, and it was clearly a different story. It too appeared to have been a hangar at some point, but had since been substantially reinforced. A pair of guards lounged near the front entrance, which was a large, thick steel door that Lincoln guessed had maybe once belonged to some sort of vault. The guards themselves weren't exactly professional, but they both had a veteran look; mercenaries who'd seen some action, or maybe a couple of former pirates who'd managed to survive to retirement. Or, Lincoln thought, maybe not former at all; pirates who were taking a couple of weeks off to earn some pay.

Lincoln decided to set up shop in the hangar across from the target. With some well-timed maneuvering and a quick lock circumvention, Lincoln and his two teammates gained access to one of the holds and took up concealed, elevated positions among the stacks of crates and containers. From his perch atop a double stack of large shipping containers, Lincoln had a good view of several of the patrolling guards below as well as the two men posted at the entrance of the target area. He tagged those he could see, and his visor marked each with a thin bracket. Those tags were in turn automatically distributed to his teammates' suits. From that point, as long as at least one of them had visual on the guards, the tags would update in real time.

"Downtown, Highrise," Lincoln said.

"Stand by, Highrise," Thumper answered. Lincoln waited, keeping careful watch on his surroundings. About twenty seconds later, Thumper spoke again. "OK, go ahead, Link."

"We're set up across from the target, and about ready to make some noise."

"Copy that," Thumper said. "We're almost to the relay. Poke's got it ID'd."

"How long you going to need, you think?"

"Couple more minutes to get there at least. Ten to do the work, maybe. Lot of activity down here though, it's slow going."

"We'll see if we can pull some attention up our way. You OK for us to get started?"

"As long as you don't hassle me when I'm on the box."

"No promises," Lincoln said. "I'll let you know before we get loud."

"Roger."

Lincoln held a quick conference with Sahil and Wright to form a plan of attack. Two minutes later, Wright crept off and made her way to a second hold, deeper in the hangar. Sahil kept watch over her while Lincoln kept his eyes on the guards across the thoroughfare. He was doing more than watching, though. He'd boosted the magnification on his visor and zeroed in on the hold door's locking mechanism. The suit executed a scan and fired up a process. In a few seconds, it had run through the army's extensive library of known locks and methods of defeat, and had fed the information back to Lincoln. It was an older digital model, expensive but not as secure as its manufacturer or its price made it appear. Before Wright had finished setting up her end of the plan, Lincoln accessed the lock remotely, spoofed the necessary credentials, and loaded them up for later use.

"Wright's in place," Wright said over comms. "Say when."

Lincoln checked over his shoulder. Sahil was already holding up an OK sign.

"We're set," Lincoln said to Wright, before switching channels. "Downtown, Highrise is about to make some noise."

"Copy, Highrise," Thumper answered. "Make it pretty."

Lincoln switched back to local. "Wright. Execute."

"Executing," she said.

A few seconds later, a sharp bang rattled the hangar, followed by a series of pops and the deep rumble of crates overturning. To Lincoln's trained ears, the pops were easily identifiable as a multistage flash grenade. But he understood why the security personnel might mistake them for gunshots.

The commotion caused a variety of reactions, all of which revealed the experience levels of the guards. Several of the younger ones scattered to the nearest cover, clutching their rifles. One of them stood frozen in the open, eyes fixed in the direction of the sound, apparently unable to process what he should do next. The two guards at the target entrance, predictably, had the most casual reaction of any of them. They perked up, exchanged a few words, and crossed about halfway to the hangar.

"Yo!" one of them called. "Yo, what's that in there?"

"Somebody's shooting!" one of the young ones called back.

"You see 'em shooting, or you think they're shooting?"

"I don't see anything, man!"

"Sahil," Lincoln said. "Time to move."

"Yep," Sahil answered.

"Wright, we're climbing down," said Lincoln. "You got eyes on?"

"Yeah, I got you," she answered.

Lincoln carefully climbed down from his hide and met Sahil at the gate of their hold. He couldn't see Wright directly from where they were, but the visor displayed a ghost image of her position, up high in yet another hold closer to the hangar entrance.

"You're clear to move to the hangar entrance," Wright said.

"Moving," Lincoln replied, and in the next moment he and Sahil were out and on their way towards the thoroughfare. The Flashtown security guys were still yelling back and forth, trying to figure out who was where and what had happened. The two brackets representing the guards from the target advanced on the hangar.

"Keep going," Wright said. "If you go quickly you can make it across."

"Copy," Lincoln said. From his view, it looked like he was

going to step out into the open before the guards entered the hangar, but he trusted the master sergeant's judgment. He kept the same pace and sure enough, just as he stepped out of cover, the guards passed into an aisle and remained out of view. Lincoln didn't look back. Sahil was right behind him, and the two swiftly covered the ground to the target. Before they reached the door to the hold, Lincoln activated the spoofed credentials and heard the locking mechanism respond. He reached the vault door and pulled it smoothly open. There wasn't time to do a careful peek before they entered, so Lincoln relied on speed and training to carry him through. He rolled straight in, and Sahil followed without missing a beat.

Fortunately, there was no one directly on the other side of the door, and he was able to close it behind them without drawing notice.

"We're in the hold," Lincoln said.

"Still clear," Wright answered.

"Keep us posted," Lincoln replied.

He and Sahil worked quickly, moving amongst the long aisles, using their suits' sensor suite to scan the various cargo containers and identify the contents. The vast majority of goods were undoubtedly stolen, smuggled, or otherwise black market material. Damaging any of it was likely to cause someone some heartache, but as long as they were here, Lincoln figured they might as well try to do a little good. He wanted something with impact. It took a couple of minutes to find anything that could definitively be said to be a target of opportunity, but eventually he found one. In a container in the middle of the hold, there were pallets of what appeared to be medical supplies packed in an outer layer. But beneath and behind that were several stacks of long crates with high metallic and chemical content. Weapons. Lincoln didn't have access to the shipping manifest, so he couldn't say for sure where they had come from or where they were headed, but it was a safe bet that they weren't going to the good guys.

"Here," Lincoln said to Sahil. The sergeant appeared a few moments later from around a corner.

"What ya got?"

"Weapons cache."

"How you want to handle it?"

"Melt it down, then blow it up?"

"Sounds good," Sahil said, and he started pulling charges off his harness. "Two minutes."

"Get a move on," Wright said over comms. "They're getting it sorted out over here."

"Two mikes," Lincoln said.

"Sooner's better," Wright responded.

Lincoln provided security while Sahil crouched to prep and arrange the charges on the container. A minute and a half later, Sahil was back on his feet, ready to move.

"We're ready to come back out," Lincoln reported to Wright.

"Group's breaking up, but they're still in the hangar," Wright said. "You're good, if you hurry."

"On the way," Lincoln said. And then, when they'd reached the door. "At the door now. Clear?"

"You're clear, go," she answered. Lincoln swung the vault door, did a quick double check. Clear. But a moment later, Wright called.

"Wait, wait!"

Too late. Lincoln was three steps into the open when a young guard came out of the hangar across the thoroughfare, no more than twenty meters away. Unmarked, none of the team had picked him up before. He was maybe sixteen years old. Younger than the rifle he was carrying.

If the guard had been any older, Lincoln wouldn't have hesitated. As it was, the barrel of the boy's rifle was nearly on target before Lincoln squeezed his own trigger. His rifle puffed once, then again, putting two rounds center of mass.

The boy staggered with the impact and in a spasm, fired a single round from his own, unsuppressed rifle. Whatever the effectiveness of Wright's distraction, the unmistakable clap of the gunshot drew all attention back towards Lincoln.

The reaction was quick, and vicious.

"Back, back, back!" Lincoln shouted at Sahil as he backpedaled into the hold. The first guards were just emerging from the other hangar as he crossed the threshold, and they didn't waste any time unloading in his direction. Rounds popped and pinged off the wall and the still open vault door. Sahil dropped low and returned fire, a steady *tap-tap, tap-tap* of calmly paired shots, sent with deadly accuracy.

Lincoln took cover on the other side of the hatch from Sahil and added his own fire to Sahil's.

"Downtown, Highrise is in contact," he said, "Repeat, we're in contact!"

They hadn't planned on kicking off the hostilities while they were still in the hold. That was going to complicate matters.

"Roger, Highrise," Thumper answered. "We're at the relay now. Keep 'em busy for me."

"Not a problem!" Lincoln replied. The volume of fire had dropped off as the security guards scrambled for cover; the initial torrent was reduced to sporadic bursts, poorly aimed. Some of the guards weren't aiming at all, in fact, they were just holding their rifles over their heads or around corners and firing blindly. But the situation was still deadly, and Lincoln knew every second they spent pinned in the hold was tipping the balance in favor of the bad guys. Reinforcements were surely on their way.

Lincoln looked over at Sahil, still crouched on the opposite side of the doorframe. On Sahil's back, high along his right shoulder blade, were four canisters attached to his suit. Two smoke grenades, two flash. Lincoln had his own set of options on his belt, but the ones on Sahil's back were there precisely for team use. Better to keep his own handy for later. He checked across the thoroughfare, fired twice at an exposed guard, and then crossed the gap to Sahil.

"I'm gonna pop smoke," he said. "I'll follow you out."

"Yep," Sahil said.

"Wright, smoke coming!" Lincoln called through the comm channel.

"Copy that, pop it!" Wright said.

Lincoln pulled the top two canisters off Sahil's back, primed them, and then tossed them out into the thoroughfare, one to the left and one to the right. Three seconds later, the grenades hissed with violence, billowing storm clouds from both ends.

As the thoroughfare filled with the dense, grey smoke, Lincoln's suit filtered out the visual noise, reduced it. In that view mode, he could still tell where the smoke clouds were heaviest, where their edges were, how much concealment they'd provide, but he could also see clearly across the thoroughfare.

"Smoke's good," Lincoln said. "We're coming out!"

"Roger," Wright said. "Covering!"

A few of the guards, emboldened by the smokescreen, popped out of their hiding places and sprayed rounds. Sahil squeezed off a quick series of shots, then ducked back into cover.

"Reloading," Sahil said. And then two seconds later, "Up. Moving."

"Move!" Lincoln answered. Sahil came up out of his crouch and burst through the door, headed right. Lincoln followed, staying low and not bothering to engage the enemy. Cover first. Shoot later.

Sahil found a position in the next hangar over, and the two of them took cover behind a pair of large metal containers.

"We're in place," Lincoln said over comms. "Wright, bound back."

"Roger, moving," she answered. And in his visor, Lincoln saw Wright's outline drop as she leapt from her perch twenty feet up, straight to the floor. The suit absorbed most of the energy from the fall; she barely registered the impact before she broke into a sprint out of the hangar, barreled towards them. Behind her, the guards were emerging from the hangar; some advancing on the hold, others fanning out. And further down the thoroughfare beyond them, other fighters were starting to trickle in.

Wright rounded Lincoln's container at the opposite end, slammed her back against it.

"Primary's back the other way," Lincoln said. "Assault through?"

Wright shook her head. "Hostiles are all coming from that direction. Scrub it."

"Downtown, Highrise," Lincoln said. "We're not going to make primary. Cut the Coffin loose, we'll pick it up at alternate."

"Uh, OK, roger Highrise," Thumper answered. "I'm sending the Coffin to alternate extraction."

The alternate extraction point was the opposite direction from their primary, but down on the same deck. Lincoln did a quick scan, found the nearest access to lower deck, marked it for his teammates.

"Wright, you're one, I'm two, Sahil is three," Lincoln said. "Peel back to that beacon, on my go."

"Roger," Wright said.

"Got it," said Sahil.

They all topped off their weapons with fresh ammo. Lincoln checked down the thoroughfare. A quick estimate of the bracketed guards they'd marked before plus the new ones he could see through the smoke put the bad guys at fifteen or so. A cluster of them were closing in on the entrance to the secure hold, weapons raised. The guards had clearly lost them for the moment, but some had emerged from the smoke cloud, and there was no way Lincoln and his teammates would cross the thoroughfare unnoticed.

"Sahil, how long for the charge on that cache to burn through?" Lincoln asked.

"Six seconds to burn, six more to boom," Sahil answered.

"Get ready to touch it off."

"It's set," Sahil said. "Say when."

"Wright, go on the boom."

"Go on boom, roger," she answered.

Lincoln judged the distance between the men and the entrance to the hold. A few more steps. A few more seconds.

"Hit it."

"Detonating," Sahil said.

Lincoln counted the seconds. Three. Four. The men continued to advance on the hold. Three others cautiously patrolled in Lincoln's direction. Ten. Eleven. Twelve.

Thirteen. Fourteen.

"You sure you hit it?" Lincoln asked.

"I'm sure," Sahil answered.

Seventeen. Eighteen.

The three guards reached ten meters away.

"You sure you used–" Lincoln said, but he was cut off by the muffled thunderclap of a contained explosion. The men near the hold entrance threw themselves in every direction, and the guards closest to Lincoln's position whipped around back towards the sound. Wright didn't miss the moment.

"One, firing!" she called, and she opened up with long bursts on the guards.

"Two, moving!" Lincoln responded, and he rolled out five meters into the open, then dropped low and added his suppressive fire to hers. "Two, firing!"

"Three moving!" Sahil called, and he dashed out of cover, passing behind Wright and then Lincoln. Seconds later, he said "Three, firing!"

Wright answered an instant later, "One, moving!", and she bounded past Lincoln, past Sahil, took up her position. "One, firing!"

Repeating the maneuver, the three bounded back to the point Lincoln had marked. He was the first to reach the access, a narrow stairwell. The stairs were clear going up, but below three more guards were on their way up from the lower decks. Lincoln drove them back with a few well-placed rounds, but couldn't get an angle to do any real damage. Sahil rolled in behind him.

"Up, we gotta go up," Lincoln said. Sahil shifted gears immediately, started up the steps, scanning for targets. Wright swung into the stairwell, and fell in right behind Sahil. Lincoln fired off a few more shots at the guards below, and then joined his teammates on the upper staircase. As he cleared the landing, he pulled a small thermal grenade off his belt and dropped it at the entrance. A few seconds later, white-hot sparks erupted from it, promising a searing shower of pain to anyone unlucky enough to get too close for the next minute or so. Assuming it didn't just melt its way through the landing.

That would buy them a little time and space from their immediate pursuers, but there was no telling from how many different directions they were going to have incoming. Trying to make their way back down to the alternate extraction point seemed like a great way to ensure they ran into more trouble.

"Downtown, Highrise," he called. "Alternate's blown. Thumper, pull the Coffin to you. Once you're out, you come get us."

"Roger that," she said, perfectly steady and calm. "Where are we picking you up?"

"Contingency," he answered. "Unless I tell you otherwise."

"Copy."

"How long you got left on that box?"

"Five minutes. Less if you quit asking."

"Sahil, we're going to contingency!" Lincoln called.

"Yeah, I heard," he called back, and for the first time, there was a hint of urgency in his voice. Lincoln set a new destination; his suit mapped a route.

The three emerged two decks up, Deck 47, where they intended to extract from a service dock. There were already people waiting for them. A brief but intense exchange of gunfire broke them free and left their would-be ambushers dead or dying, but there was no doubt now that fully breaking contact was impossible. The plan had been to cause a stir, and then escape in the confusion. What they'd lost in surprise, they'd have to make up for with speed and violence of action.

"Think we made a bigger racket than we meant to," Wright said.

"A bit," Lincoln answered.

Deck 47 was a residential area, a rat's nest of narrow corridors and patched-together apartments. A shantytown that spread like a fungus into any available space, without rhyme or reason. Sahil led them aggressively towards their goal, with shouts and sounds of pursuit trailing close behind. And, Lincoln now realized, running parallel. There were too many people on them, coming on too fast, to just be Flashtown's official security response. The citizens were getting involved.

As the team pushed down the corridors, doors started opening, heads peeked out of windows and then quickly disappeared. Some reemerged with weapons, others just seemed to be watching for fun. Lincoln's suit went hyper, scanning for weapons and trying to help Lincoln prioritize threats. But it was getting overloaded. Each new person was a threat to be evaluated, and there were just too many popping up and vanishing to be able to process them all meaningfully. Lincoln shut off the threat assessment assist, trusted in his instincts.

A round snapped past Lincoln's head, fired from behind. He turned just in time to see an old woman ducking back inside her door. Lincoln backpedaled, keeping his weapon fixed on the woman's door until it was out of sight, but she didn't reappear. Just an opportunist with no interest in leaving her home.

Lincoln swiveled back around, caught back up the extra few paces he'd lost on Wright, and then ran smack into her when she stopped abruptly in front of him. She pushed off him and dropped to a crouch, instinctively providing security down one corridor. Lincoln followed suit, bringing his weapon around to cover the direction they'd just come.

"What's the problem?" he called.

"Door's a wall," Sahil said.

"What?" Lincoln said, and he glanced over his shoulder.

"I mean there ain't a door here," Sahil answered. "Ain't nothin' but a wall."

Sure enough, the route on his visor was leading them right through a sheet of solid steel. With the new data, the suit's navigation system tried to reroute, but after a few seconds flashed a warning. NO ROUTE. Either there was no way to get there from here, or the suit realized it didn't have enough data to plot a new route. The result was the same either way. Lincoln's element was stuck in the middle of Flashtown with no idea how to get out.

Wright fired off two quick shots, and someone cried out in answer.

"What are we doing, captain?" she called.

From back the way they'd come, a pair of thugs came around the corner, one with a pistol and the other armed with what looked like a machete. Lincoln fired a burst, dropping the man with the gun, and sending the machete wielder scampering back to cover. The mob was on its way. If Lincoln and his teammates got hemmed in, there was no way they'd be able to shoot their way out. Lincoln's mind raced through the possibilities, threatened to overwhelm him. They were too exposed here. There wasn't time to cut through the wall, and even if they did, there was no telling what they'd find on the other side, no guarantee they could reach a known exit.

And every second he spent thinking through it was a second lost.

The machete-wielding man risked another peek, and Lincoln fired, punched a hole through the man's right biceps. The machete clattered to the ground.

Out. What was the best way out?

But then his training kicked in, words from a mentor sounded clear above the confusion.

Relax. Look around. Make a call.

He took a breath, steadied himself. *Best way out* was the wrong goal. *Any* way out was best.

Lincoln had an idea. Good enough to act on, and he didn't dare think beyond that.

"Sahil, how much boom do you have left?" he asked.

"Couple charges," Sahil answered.

"Follow me!" Lincoln replied, and he set a new destination that he knew his system could route to: the nearest location adjacent to the station's hull. His team fell in behind him without hesitation, and they pushed through a dangerous tangle of irregular passageways. Even the urban combat Lincoln had seen didn't match the complexity of the environment he was moving through now. The only thing they could count on with Deck 47 was its blind corners and sudden intersections; they always popped up at the worst possible time and place. He took to firing suppressive rounds in the direction of anyone who emerged, bystander or otherwise, directly engaging only the few who appeared with guns in hand. Behind him, Wright and Sahil fired sporadically, using whatever protocol they'd developed for themselves in the chaos.

"Highrise, this is Downtown," Thumper said. "We've got good tap on the relay, we're on our way out. Looks pretty clear, whatever you did must be working–"

"Contingency's blown," Lincoln said over top of her. "Say again, contingency's blown. We're scrambling."

"What do you need?" Thumper said, his intensity creeping into her own voice.

"Get the Coffin, get clear, watch for my beacon."

"Roger, Downtown's moving!"

After a mindnumbing number of twists and turns, and low on ammo, Lincoln arrived at the destination. A small apartment at the outer edge of the deck. The thin, metal door was shut. Lincoln didn't even slow.

He kicked the door right below the handle; it blasted open, slammed back into the wall with a crack as he rocketed into the front room. A man and woman sat on the floor by a low table, both with eyes wide in shock and fear, hands up in defensive positions. The man had a knife, Lincoln brought his weapon on target–And held fire. Plates on the table, food, drinks. The man wasn't threatening, he was in the middle of eating. In a blink, Lincoln flicked on the suit's external speaker.

"Down, get down, get down on the floor!" he shouted, pointing his weapon at them. "Down!"

The man screamed and both he and the woman flopped face down on the floor, covering their heads with their hands. Wright continued straight through the room, stepped up on the table and leapt off, sending the meal flying in every direction as she moved violently to clear the back room. Sahil slammed the front door shut, and with one hand grabbed the nearest piece of large furniture, a short empty bookshelf, dragged it over.

"Clear!" Wright called from the back.

Lincoln dropped to a knee beside the woman, placed a hand on her back. The man was too hysterical to reach, but the woman seemed to be keeping it together for the moment. Sahil grabbed the table they'd been eating on, threw it into place to wedge the front door.

"We're not here to hurt you, stay calm, stay flat. Nod if you understand," he said. A moment later, the woman nodded.

"Good. Is this room pressure sealed?"

The woman nodded again. Sahil continued to stack whatever he could find against the door.

"Good," he said. "My friends and I are going to go through to the back room, as far back as we can get. We'll seal the doors behind us. Stay down, stay flat, do not follow us. Do not let anyone follow us. Nod if you understand." She nodded. Lincoln motioned to Sahil to move through to the back. Outside, the shouts and sounds of pursuit grew louder, closer. Sahil pushed through to the back, waited at the door.

"I'm going to say it again, so it's clear," Lincoln said to the woman. "Do not follow us, and do *not* let anyone open the door."

The woman nodded vigorously. A sharp bang rattled the front door of the apartment, angry voices shouted for them to open up.

"Good," Lincoln said. "I'm sorry about the mess."

And then he was up, and into the back where Wright was waiting for them. Sahil closed the door behind him, locked it.

"If the map's right, this should put us closest to the exterior," Lincoln said.

"Yeah, if," Wright said.

"Which room's smallest?" he asked. Wright pointed, and Lincoln went to it. "Sahil, set up here, back wall."

Sahil nodded and went to work.

"Punching through?" he asked.

"Yeah," Lincoln said.

"How far?"

"All the way."

Sahil turned back to look at him over his shoulder. The faceless metal plate somehow still managed to express skepticism.

"All the way," Sahil said, "like to the outer?"

"No, all the way like *through* the outer. All. The. Way."

Sahil hesitated only for a moment, then shook his head,

and said, "All right. Gonna take me a couple to shape. And we don't wanna be in here when it goes."

"We'll hold the corridor," Lincoln said. And then, "Downtown, what's your status?"

"Downtown's in the Coffin," Thumper answered. "Pulling free now. Where are you?"

"Deck 47, outer rim. Watch for my beacon!"

"Copy that, we're on our way up. What lock are you using?"

"Just watch for my beacon!"

Lincoln raced back to the door leading to the front room, Wright following right on his heels. He unlocked the door and cracked it open, saw the man and woman still on the floor, face down, just as they'd been directed. The roar from outside the apartment told of dozens, struggling to break in. The front door shuddered under heavy blows. Someone fired a burst, punching holes through it and spraying splinters off the furniture Sahil had stacked as a barricade. Wright dropped to a crouch, angled around so she could get a shot on the door without getting in Lincoln's way.

A few seconds later, the front door rocked and bulged near the cluster of holes. A second blow followed; this time the heavy head of a maul punctured the door.

"Sahil," Lincoln said, "time?"

"Two minutes!" Sahil answered.

"We don't have two minutes!" Wright called.

"Make it!" Sahil replied.

The head of the maul worked back and forth until it was free, leaving a rent. Another blow struck, tearing the hole wider.

This time, when the maul withdrew, Lincoln sighted in on the gap and fired a burst. A scream rose above the clamor, but there was no way to tell if it was from pain or rage. Whether Lincoln had hit anyone or not, the maul didn't strike again.

For a few seconds, the door remained unattacked.

Then, a gun barrel poked through and went spiraling around, spewing rounds into the interior. Lincoln ducked back behind the wall. The low-velocity rounds of the enemy's weapon didn't penetrate the wall, thankfully. That likely meant it wouldn't penetrate Lincoln's armor either, but given what they were about to do, he didn't want to take any chances. He waited until the gun clicked empty, and then leaned around and fired two more rounds through the gap in the door.

The front door shuddered again and this time drove inward, ramming hard against the makeshift barricade. The table fell out of place, tumbled to the floor. The front door opened three inches, enough for Lincoln to see faces on the other side. The man and woman scrambled up, crawled on all fours to the far side of the room.

Wright fired a burst, then another, driving back the swarm from the door for a few moments. But it was hopeless now. Whether expecting reward from Mayor Jon, seeking vengeance of their own, or just looking for a fight, the crowd was frenzied. They were coming through that door, no matter the cost.

"Sahil!" Lincoln called.

"Almost!"

More gun barrels appeared in the gap of the front door, these aimed in a much more deadly direction, and erupted. Lincoln pulled back, but too late. A hard impact punched his left shoulder, spun him, sent him stumbling. Wright stepped up into the doorway and fired back.

"Hit, Lincoln's hit!" she called.

Lincoln recovered his footing, glanced at his shoulder. The plating was scored on top from the round, but there didn't appear to be any penetration. The suit's readouts were all green.

"I'm good, I'm good, I'm good!" he answered. And he rejoined Wright at the doorway, opening up on the front door, now open six inches or more.

The guns had all been withdrawn, and the people outside had mostly backed out of harm's way. A few moments later, Lincoln saw why. A small black sphere bounced heavily into the room.

Wright shoved Lincoln to the side, and he flew off his feet, back down the corridor towards Sahil. She threw herself back against the wall, flung the door closed and braced it with her legs.

The concussion from the blast clouded the corridor with dust and warped the door. Smoke filtered in around it. There was no way they'd be able to seal it now.

"Wright, you good?" he called.

"I'm good!" she answered, as she was struggling up to her hands and knees. Lincoln rolled up to his feet, grabbed her arm, dragged her up.

"We're primed," Sahil called. "Cover up, keep your arms and legs tucked in!"

Lincoln looked down the hall to see Sahil emerging from the small back room.

"Ready?" Sahil called. Lincoln could hear the crowd flooding into the front of the apartment. They were all about to have a really bad time.

"Hit it!"

"Detonate, detonate, detonate!" Sahil said. And a moment later, the back wall of the room evaporated. Lincoln's suit capped the volume of the explosion and absorbed some of the concussion, but there was no way to miss the vibration that passed through him. In the next instant, he was hurtling towards the ragged three-meter-wide hole in the side of the station. He tucked his arms and legs as best he could as the evacuated atmosphere ejected him and rocketed him out into open space.

It was twenty seconds before he had his tumble under control enough to be able to get his bearings. He located

Sahil and Wright, both floating a few dozen meters away. With practiced fluidity, Lincoln kicked around and used his microjets to stabilize and then propel himself in the direction of his teammates. As far as he could tell, they were the only ones floating outside the station, which was a minor miracle. Maybe that inner door had held after all. Or at least, was holding for the moment.

"Highrise, sound off," he said.

"Wright, OK," Wright responded.

"Nakarmi, OK," Sahil said.

"Suh, good to go," Lincoln said. He activated his beacon. "Downtown, Highrise is floating. Got a second to pick us up?"

"We're en route, captain," Thumper said.

Lincoln joined up with Wright and Sahil, and waited the few minutes it took for Thumper to bring the Coffin around. Lincoln hated open space. It felt unnatural, the yawning nothingness in every direction. Lincoln had no fear of heights, but the fact that there was absolutely nothing below him filled him with a subtle anxiety. And the fact that there wasn't even technically a *down* just complicated matters.

Fortunately, the wait wasn't too long. Once they had visual, the three teammates freespaced towards the ship, and loaded in through the upper airlock. It wasn't until everyone was secure on board and well on their way towards the linkup with their transport that the tension finally broke. Sahil was the first, and he broke the post-op silence with a rumbling chuckle that grew into a full-throated laugh.

Nobody had to say anything at all. They all joined in. Even Wright.

Mike pulled his helmet off.

"I can't believe that actually happened," he said. "You know nobody's gonna believe that actually happened."

"It didn't just *happen*," Sahil said, and then he pointed at Lincoln. "He did it on purpose."

"I think Mayor Jon's gonna be irritated about what you did

to her station, brother," Mike said to Lincoln.

"No man, that wasn't me," Lincoln said. "I'm not the breacher." And then to Thumper. "You get what you needed in there?"

"And then some," she said. "As long as nobody goes poking around the relay too closely, next time they use it, we ought to be able to see what lights up."

"Let's hope they use it soon," Lincoln said. "That wasn't quite the quiet exfil I'd been planning on."

"Gutsy, I'll give you that," Wright said, and she flopped down two seats away. "Next time we split team, though, think I'll opt to be on the *other* one."

"I'll trade with you," Mike said. "I could use a little excitement for a change."

"No way," Wright said. "The two of you yahoos together, probably none of us would make it home."

Mike sat down across from him.

"I reckon that was one for the history books, cap," he said. "Too bad no one will ever know about it."

"Let's hope," Lincoln answered.

There were a few more exchanges, a combination of informal debriefing and teammates swapping stories. But with the mission more or less accomplished, and everyone on their way home safe and sound, the last traces of Lincoln's adrenaline burned off. It left his body feeling simultaneously empty and impossibly heavy. The rest of the team seemed to be feeling it, too. Conversation gradually died down again. They had a few hours of travel ahead, and then who knew how many more of waiting after that to see if anything they'd just been through would pay off. Lincoln laid his head back, and let out a long, deep breath. There wasn't much more they could do now but sit and wait.

Lincoln had never been very good at either one.

SEVENTEEN

"When you say 'lost him'," Vector said, "what exactly does that mean?"

"Just what it sounds like," the Woman answered. The intensity was there, all business. "Gone. Cannot be located anywhere on Luna or the vicinity of."

"How long?"

"At least seventy-two hours," she said. "I'd guess longer. I suspect Apsis was not immediately... forthcoming about the disappearance."

Vector did the quick mental math; travel time, logistics. Even if there was a vulnerability, it didn't seem likely there was any connection. Not in that timeframe.

Still.

"Flashtown?" he asked.

"No evidence of a connection," she said. "The trouble was contained to the upper decks, far from the relay. It sounds like rival gangs violating Mayor Jon's cardinal rule and paying the price."

"So coincidence, huh?" he said. "Just so happens?"

"It would seem."

"Sounds a little familiar."

"Too," she said. "How badly can Prakoso hurt us?"

"He's compartmentalized," Vector said. "But... he's

Prakoso. His work's done, and he never knew exactly what its purpose was, never had direct connections to any of our first-tier people. If he really wanted to come after us, I'm sure he could find a way, but he's not stupid. Seems more likely he'd just disappear."

"I agree. But I'm moving the timetable up, to be safe. How close are you?"

"Not long now. Ship's rigged up, we're just taking care of some the internals. Few more days at most."

"And if the next strike goes forward immediately?"

"Shouldn't interfere if it comes a couple days early," he said. "That's all friends-of-friends kind of work. No impact on us, assuming it goes through."

"Very well. I'll have them execute. Get your ship underway, nearer to position, but somewhere out of the way, off scopes. I may need you to to move more quickly than anticipated. I don't want you having to burn in and make a lot of noise."

"Understood. What about you?" Vector asked, trying to keep the tone professional, operational. "You at home now?"

"Yes. To stay, I should think," the Woman answered. "Too close now for me to be stepping out for fun. I don't expect you to run into any trouble, but I trust you will take precautions nonetheless."

"We will. And we are."

"Let me know the instant you're ready to move."

"Yes, ma'am."

"Good. Signing out now. I expect to hear from you soon."

"Sure thing. Stay safe."

"Safe?" she said, and she arched an eyebrow in cold amusement. "No, my dear. I plan to stay very, *very* dangerous."

EIGHTEEN

As it turned out, the wait wasn't nearly as long as Lincoln had feared it would be. But that wasn't necessarily good news. They'd been back on board the *Curry* for less than twenty-four hours, and he'd been asleep for less than two, when Thumper woke him up.

"Captain, we got a hit," she said, before he was fully awake.

"Yeah, OK," he said, but he couldn't quite remember what she meant by it. He sat up, rubbed one eye with the palm of his hand. "OK... so, what now?"

"The relay," she said. "Caught a lucky break on it."

It all snapped back into place.

"Show me," he said.

Thumper took him to the compartment across the passageway, where she and Prakoso had set up their makeshift tracking station. To Lincoln, it looked like a cross between a middle-school science fair project and some high-tech startup in a garage. Prakoso was chewing his left thumbnail while tabbing through some stream of data on a display.

"What are we seeing?" he asked.

Thumper flopped into a chair, tapped out a few commands on her console, and transferred the image from her display onto the thin-skin mounted on the wall.

"That's just a visualization," she said, "not an actual map, but those nodes are the network of relays. Basically any time you use one, you're using them all, so we know they've got at least twelve. They may have more they're keeping offline for the moment, but they definitely have these twelve."

"Can you pull a location off these?"

"Sure," Thumper said. "Veronica's working on it now, but that might not mean anything. Like Flashtown. These could just be in storage somewhere, that won't necessarily help us. But what *can* help, is this." A second layer appeared over the visualization, thin colored lines streaming between multiple points. "These are access requests to the relays. Different colors for different requesters, brighter means more activity on the same access. Important takeaway is that these guys are talking to each other. A lot. We don't have a baseline established yet on what normal usage looks like, but my gut says this is elevated chatter.

"Now, if you're the paranoid sort, the right way to do this is, you set up your system to drop and reacquire access every so often. But that's a pain, slows you down, you have to build in the recycle time to your schedule, communication gets blacked out for a few minutes, maybe an hour at a time depending on your gear. So if you're lazy, or you're in a hurry, you just send traffic on the same relay access. That's what you're seeing in those bright lines there. Same folks, using the same access, sending a lot of traffic."

"And that's something you can track?" Lincoln said.

"If you've got the gear and the knowhow," Thumper said. "Which we do." She smiled and reached over, punched Prakoso in the shoulder.

Lincoln looked at the flow on the thin-skin, filtered out the relevant bits, and interpreted what he guessed Thumper was implying in her own technical way.

"They're going to hit us again," he said.

"They're going to hit us again," Thumper confirmed. "But we've got target information now. And an operational window."

"I thought you said we couldn't pull messages out of the relay," Lincoln said.

"We can't," Thumper said. "But we didn't have to. 23rd's already got taps on these guys," she pointed to one of the streams on the thin-skin. "Veronica pulled them out for us already, processed it, found the pieces we needed. And NID's watching these guys," she pointed to another line. "We just had to put them together."

"So you've already talked to Mr Self then."

Thumper shook her head. "We haven't talked to anybody yet."

"Then how'd you get access to Directorate feeds?"

Thumper looked at Prakoso. Prakoso looked at Thumper, then at Lincoln with a do-you-really-want-me-to-tell-you expression.

"Nevermind," Lincoln said.

Thumper said, "There wasn't time to ask–"

"I said *nevermind*," Lincoln repeated more firmly. "We get an ID on where it's all coming from? Who's giving the orders?"

Thumper shook her head again. "We haven't been able to find the other end yet. I doubt we will any time soon. These are the foot-soldier types down here, and I'm guessing we've got layers to peel back before we ever even see the puppet-strings, let alone who's pulling them."

"All right. Get everything together, get a packet over to the colonel, a-sap. Everything you've got."

"What about NID? Or the 23rd?"

"You really want to tell NID what you've been up to?"

"It's another NID target. One of their front companies, looks like. On Mars."

Lincoln thought about it for a bare few seconds before he answered.

"Whatever gets this to the right people the fastest," Lincoln said. "If that means NID, then do it. I'll take the heat if it comes."

"Roger that," Thumper said.

"Good work, you two," Lincoln said. "Great work." He pounded Thumper on the shoulder, reached over her and clapped Prakoso on the arm. "You did a good thing here, Yayan. Except maybe the NID thing. But I won't mention it if you don't."

Prakoso nodded with a mild smile, as if he was secretly pleased but didn't want to admit it to anyone, especially himself.

"And I meant what I said," Lincoln added. "About getting you home. You're saving lives today."

Prakoso nodded again.

"I'm gonna ping the colonel, give him a heads up," Lincoln said again. "Great work, guys."

Lincoln left the compartment and went to fire up a session with Almeida. He had no idea what time it was back on Earth, but it didn't really matter. There were lives on the line, and for the first time since he'd joined the Outriders, he was ahead of the curve. Admittedly, some part of him was eager to share the win, to earn the approval of the legendary colonel and show that the man's trust in him hadn't been misplaced. But the urgency of the moment didn't go unmarked; if they didn't act quickly enough, this little victory could easily vanish into catastrophe.

NINETEEN

Vector watched the two of them on the display, Kid standing in the room, and the girl sitting on her cot. Kid was leaning against the wall, arms crossed, in obvious conversation. Vector could have turned the audio on, but he felt uncomfortable spying on his own people, even though Kid knew he could be listening in.

"I still don't know why we didn't just leave her floating," Kev said.

"Someone else would have found her," Vector replied.

"Yeah, but so what? One survivor from the whole station. I doubt she even knows what happened, let alone what *happened*, you know what I'm saying?"

"Maybe."

"Could've just popped the pod for that matter."

"Look, Kev. There are a lot of things we could've done that wouldn't involve that girl being on board. But the only one I know of that guarantees she's controlled, is the one we did. She's on the ship, we know where we she is, we know she can't hurt us. Maybe if we'd dumped her out an airlock, there's only a millionth of a percent of a chance that anyone would have found her and wondered how she got where she did. But there was no reason to take even that chance. And that's one less thing to worry about."

"Except now we've got to deal with her."

"*You* haven't had to," Vector said.

"Yeah, but, you know. Takes energy, anyway. And Kid's been down there a lot. Maybe too much."

Vector didn't like hearing the implication. Kid was his closest partner, the one he'd worked with the longest. He loved her like a sister. But at the same time, Kev's suggestion echoed something he'd been trying to ignore himself. Kid *had* been spending a lot of time with the girl. Seemed like a good bit more lately.

"Seems like it'd be easier just to go ahead and plug her," Kev said.

"We're not murderers, Kev."

Kev chuckled darkly at that. "Yeah? I got a lot of folks in my head that might disagree."

"War's a different thing," Vector replied. "Every target we've hit has been a valid military one. You know better."

"To be honest, I'm not so sure I do, these days."

"You want to walk down there and do it? Kill that girl in cold blood? If so, then you're not the man I thought you were. And you're not the man you used to be."

"Ain't none of us the men we used to be, Doc."

Vector glanced over at Kev, but Kev was busy watching the display. He shook his head.

"What are they doing now?"

Vector looked back at the viewscreen to see the girl getting up off the cot. She embraced Kid. It looked almost like she was crying.

"Come on, Kid," Vector said. "What are you doing?"

"Think maybe you oughta have a talk with her about that," Kev said.

"Yeah," said Vector, getting up out of his chair. "Yeah, I think you're right."

But before he could do anything more, the girl made a sudden motion and Kid's legs buckled. An instant later, Kid was down on the floor on her hands and knees, and the girl was gone.

Vector bolted for the door.

Piper sprinted down the hall. Left turn, second left, up the ladder. Second right. That should get her to the exterior section of the ship. Talking with the woman who had become her caretaker, she'd learned enough details about the ship to piece together a rough layout. The adrenaline was coursing now, her heart hammering. She hoped she hadn't hit the woman too hard. She'd hated doing that. A terrible betrayal. Even though the woman was technically her captor.

How much time did she have? A minute? Maybe less. She raced down the hall, found the ladder. The adrenaline made it hard to grip the rungs. At the top, she missed a step and stumbled coming out of the hatch, fell hard in the passageway. Piper scrambled up, but stopped, panting. The passageway stretched off in both directions. Which way? The second right, but the second right from which facing? She spent too long thinking about it; she had to move.

She went left without knowing why. Ran down the passageway to the second right, took the turn, and slowed to a jog, scanning for directions. After ten seconds, she still hadn't found what she was looking for. She should've seen something by now. Should she have gone the other way? Was she still in the exterior of the ship, or was she running back towards the middle? What if she'd gotten the directions wrong?

There, a few meters further down the passageway. A small, square sign directing her to the nearest lifepod, reminding her to remain calm. Piper took off again at full speed, following the path laid out by the evac signs. They led her to take a turn and then further down, another; she realized she'd still been too deep in the ship. Her rough layout had been an educated guess, but a guess just the same.

The turn she took led her to a short, connector passage and almost into the bulkhead; she skidded out at a T-intersection, and had to catch herself to keep from colliding face first. She looked up and down the passageway for the next sign, realized her left hand was covering it. Right, ten meters. Piper turned that direction just as a man came dashing out at the far end. A man she hadn't seen before.

For a moment, they just stood there, each shocked to see the other. The pod entry was between them; Piper was closer.

She ran for it.

As soon as she moved, the man launched forward. He was fast. Faster than Piper could have guessed.

She wasn't going to make it.

He was maybe five meters away when she hit the latch to pop the pod door; almost arm's length by the time it was open. He was going to grab her. Already, his hands were outstretched.

Without thinking, Piper dropped to a knee, ducked her head. The man crashed into her, knocked her over, and went sprawling to the deck, hard. Piper scrambled up to her hands and knees, threw herself into the airlock. Lurched up to her feet, through the pod hatch.

The man appeared at the airlock entrance as she was hitting the emergency latch to shut herself in. The door sealed just as the man reached it; so close, he had to snatch his hand back to avoid losing his fingers.

Piper took a few disbelieving steps back from the door. She'd done it. She'd made it. She was safe, for the moment.

And with that realization, she collapsed to her knees by the door, shaking, panting, crying from the terror and the relief. Displays glowed to life and the pod hummed as its systems came up. One of the screens showed a view of the airlock, where a second man had now joined the first. There was no audio, but Piper didn't need it. The image alone was enough to communicate the fury.

Piper threw the metal-handled switch by the door, a double safety that locked the hatch mechanically and made it impossible to unlock from the outside without specialized equipment. If they wanted to come get her, they'd have to cut her out. Retrieval arms typically had a built-in interface that could do the job, but that was only a possibility if she launched and they recovered the pod. And she didn't plan on doing that.

She gave herself a few moments to recover from the emotional toll of the adrenaline dump, and then forced herself back to her feet. There was no telling how long it would take them to find a way to get her out, but there was no question that her captors were smart. The only safe thing to do was to assume she didn't have much time.

The pod had a ring of seats positioned to cram as many people in as possible. One, however, was ostensibly the command chair, closest to the essential controls. Piper sat there and went to work.

"How long until she launches?" Vector asked as he ran through the arming protocols. While the rig didn't have much in the way of weaponry, the point defense cannons were enough to get the job done, as long as he could manually target the lifepod. He'd at least make an attempt at recovering the pod before it got too far, but he wasn't taking any chances. If it looked like it was getting out of range, he'd just have to explain to the Woman that the girl had become *troublesome*.

"Could've done it by now, if she was gonna," Kev said.

"What do you think she's waiting for?"

"No idea. Maybe she doesn't know how to launch it."

"Did she get out?" Kid said from the door. Vector looked over his shoulder at her. She held up her hand before he could say anything. "It was stupid, I know, you don't need to say it."

Vector looked at his long-time friend, saw the hard look in

her eyes. There wasn't anything he could say that she hadn't already said to herself; and she probably hadn't been nearly as kind about it as he would have been.

"You all right?" he asked.

"Yeah, fine," she answered. "Did she get out?"

"Nah, she's holed up in a pod," Vector said, returning to his console. "Not sure what she's up to yet."

"Maybe she just got scared, didn't really think it through…"

"No, I almost caught her," Kev said. "She could've run the other way, but she ran towards me instead, raced me to the pod. That was where she was headed, no doubt."

Vector finished bringing the retrieval arm and the cannons online.

"Kid, go grab Royce and see if he has any ideas about overriding that hatch," he said. "Maybe some of his guys know a trick or two."

"You got it," Kid said, and she left the control room.

"There it goes," Kev said. "She's trying to bring up the commo."

"Can she do that?" Vector asked.

"Sure. Pod's got a great array on it. It's still slaved to the main ship, but smart girl like her, I bet she can figure a way around it."

"Anything we can do from here?"

"Depends on what she does in there, I reckon."

Vector eyed the console. He could force-launch the pod and try to recover it, but he knew that the girl would blast a distress signal out as soon as the pod was free. That was attention he didn't want to deal with, not unless it was the only option.

"Let's wait and see, then," he said.

Piper was deep in the lifepod's system configuration, modifying settings and permissions. By default, the communications array was inactive unless the pod had been launched, preventing any sort of accidental interference with the main ship or erroneous distress signals from going out. But there were protocols hidden to the normal user that had to be accessible to the technicians who ran diagnostics and safety checks on the equipment.

She remembered well sitting in the lifepod connected to YN-773's bubble, with Gennady leaning over her shoulder, walking her through the process. Remembered the quiet smile on his face at her excitement when she realized just how much of a secret world lay behind the surface of all the technology she interacted with. He'd been so generous to share his vast knowledge with her, so patient with her constant questions and curiosity. And now what Gennady had taught her out of the goodness of his nature was quite possibly the thing that would save her. Save her *again*. Piper's eyes welled while she made the final changes.

The communications array bleeped when it woke, its display spooling out diagnostic data as it stepped through its startup routine. A distress signal would have been the best way to get some attention; they were designed to radiate signal in a specific pattern, in all directions. But even if she could have overridden the protocols that prevented it, she knew her captors could easily explain it away as a malfunction to whoever came looking. Unlike the distress signal, the communications array was tight-beam, designed for targeted transmission. If she wasn't smart about how she used it, she'd literally just be screaming into the void. Not that she had much choice. Without launching, the array was limited by the pod's housing in the ship.

Piper coded up a simple message; she'd been kidnapped and needed help. That was about all she knew anyway, and it was enough to get noticed. In minutes, she had a basic macro set up to cycle through the array's effective range, blasting out thousands of messages a second to whoever might be out there. It was shamelessly brute force, with no guarantees. She had no way to know where in space she was, or what direction the nearest hop might be, but if she could let the cycle run long enough, there was a reasonable hope that her message would land somewhere. At least she told herself it was reasonable. Reasonable or not, it was the only hope she had.

The array ran her routine for about three and a half minutes before it abruptly quit. It only took Piper half that time to figure out why. Someone on the ship had counteracted her override and locked the comm array down, killing her message and Piper's hope along with it. All of that struggle, and planning, and effort. Three and a half minutes.

Piper covered her face with her hands.

"That ought to hold her just fine," Kev said.

"Permanently?" Vector asked.

"Yeah, I shunted all her diagnostics off to the mainline, so we're back in control again, and she's locked out. She's pretty clever, but she's no wizard."

"Hey, Kid," Vector said over his communications.

"Yeah?" she responded.

"What's Royce got to say?"

"He still thinks you ought to force launch and kill it."

"We've got her contained now," Vector said. "She can't hurt us as long as she's on the tether."

"That's fine, but his crew's still got work to do. You want him wasting time on her?"

"Only if it's an easy fix."

"It's not an easy fix."

"Then no. They can get back to it."

"I'll let him know."

"Might actually be better for us anyway," Kev said. "I kind of wish we'd just stuffed her in one of those in the first place. She's got food, water, everything she needs in there for a couple of weeks at least. And we don't have to deal with her."

"Unless she tries to come back out and run for another," Vector said.

"Now that I know what she was up to, I can set up an override on the rest of the pods so we don't have to worry about it," Kev replied. "And maybe later I'll go down there and rig a motion sensor on the hatch just to be safe."

Vector tapped his fingers on the edge of the console, irritated that he was even having to think about this right now. But maybe Kev was right. If she really was contained, then the girl could stay in there all the way to Mars as far as he was concerned. He just couldn't quite bring himself to believe she'd given up yet.

Piper lay curled on her side, her arms folded around herself, on one of the crash couches. Crying seemed like it might be an appropriate response given everything she'd been through, but she found it impossible to do so. She was too drained, too spent, to feel much of anything anymore. For a time, she lay there letting her mind run its wild course unheeded. Maybe it wouldn't be so bad. She was still captive, yes, but the pod felt safer. She didn't have to worry about people coming in and out without warning, at least. There were plenty of supplies, so she knew she wouldn't starve to death. She'd be fine, as long as she could cope with the fact that she was all alone, lost somewhere in the middle of deep space.

And then she realized that, too, was a problem she could do something about – the being lost part, anyway.

She got up and went back to the command center, brought up the navigation interface. The display locked out course plotting, since the pod was still tethered to the main ship, but if nothing else, she could at least get some sense of where she was. Even though she couldn't do anything else about it, just having some idea of where they'd taken her felt something like stealing back a little power for herself.

After a few minutes of scanning through the star maps

and other positional data, she saw that they'd taken her out further from YN-773 in the direction of Mars, trailing the planet's orbit. And though she wasn't particularly well trained or practiced at reading astronomical maps, from her best guess, it didn't seem likely that her three-and-a-half-minute burst of calls for help found anyone. She scrolled the map around, zoomed in and out, changed the angle. There just wasn't anyone out there. Piper knew space was vast and mostly empty, but even when she found Earth and scanned around, there weren't nearly as many hops on the display as she had expected. It finally occurred to her that the navdata in the pod was out of date. From the look of it, it might have even still had the default data from however many decades ago the pod had been installed.

Sloppy maintenance work in her opinion. Sure, there wasn't much need for navigational data in a pod until it'd been launched, but it never hurt to be proactive. Piper had always kept the bubble's pod on YN-773 updated with the latest from Veryn-Hakakuri's central maps. Those maps used data regularly collected from all the company's numerous hops and were available to any employee with access to the system. It was a simple process. She shook her head at other people's laziness.

And then a thought jolted her.

The navigational computer.

She sat up straighter, her energy renewed.

Vector had told himself not to worry about the girl anymore. He had enough to keep him busy, and Kev had reassured him that there was nothing she could do to hurt them from in there. But he couldn't help it. His gut wouldn't let him leave it alone. And he couldn't remember a time that he'd ever been glad he'd ignored his gut.

He stopped back by the ship's command station, just to check. Kev's feed was still monitoring activity in the lifepod where the girl was, and as far as Vector could tell, everything was still fine. She was just fiddling around with the nav map. Bored, probably. And he couldn't blame her, really. It had to be hard on her, not knowing where she was or what was happening. He turned to leave again, but stopped at the door. Went back to the display. It never hurt to double-check.

"Hey Kev," he said over comms.

"Yeah?"

"You got a sec?"

"Not really. What's up?"

"The girl's doing something with nav in the pod."

"OK. And?"

"Nothing to be worried about?"

"What's the feed say?"

"Looks like she's trying to update the data on it, but it keeps failing."

There was a pause before he responded.

"I'll be there in a second."

It was a couple of minutes before Kev arrived, and he had grease on his hands, even though he'd obviously tried to wipe them before he sat down to look.

"Well, that's weird," he said after he'd scrolled back through the log of activity. "You're right, she's trying to pull new maps in, but wherever she's trying to connect is kicking her back out."

"Are we blocking it?"

Kev shook his head. "Not on purpose. I think it's something *she's* doing."

He tapped out a few commands on the console, opened new windows on the display that meant nothing to Vector.

"I'm just gonna track this back, see where she's grabbing the data…" He trailed off, and then a few moments later cursed to himself.

"What?" Vector asked.

"She's hitting Veryn-Hakakuri's plot data," Kev said, and

the urgency in his voice made it sound worse than the words. "And failing the security check. Over and over again."

"What does that mean?"

"I don't know exactly, but you can bet VH isn't going to ignore that forever."

"Could they track the source?"

"Eventually they might," Kev said. And then his face changed. "She's piggybacking off our relay."

"Shut it down," Vector said.

"I can't," Kev said. "The pod's nav system is totally independent, it's not hooked into the mainline at all–"

"No, shut it all down. The pod. Cut the power."

Kev looked up at him. "If I do that, everything goes."

"I know."

"She'll die."

"Or she'll come out. Her choice."

Kev hesitated only for a moment, and then nodded.

It didn't take long before the cold took over. And Piper knew that was the thing that would kill her. At first, the complete darkness had thrown her, and after that she'd started worrying about oxygen levels. But once she'd thought it through, she realized that she had plenty of air in the pod to breathe comfortably for hours. More than enough time to freeze to death.

She hadn't really thought about it before. In her mind, the pods were all dormant until someone opened the hatch on one. But of course that wasn't true. Of course they had to run on minimal power, to keep the temperature up and the oxygen fresh. None of that was happening now. And it was taking its toll.

In the darkness, she'd managed to feel her way to a supply crate and rummaging through had produced a small light. With that, she'd located a pack of thermal blankets. But it hadn't taken long for her to realize that even those were no match against the heat-draining power of deep space. And then she'd set her light down somewhere and lost it.

She'd been shivering so badly that she could hardly keep the blankets pulled tight around her, but oddly in the past few minutes, the shivering had stopped. Piper wondered if maybe that meant they'd turned the power back on. Or at least the temperature regulator. But it was still dark. Was that normal? She couldn't remember when she'd gone to sleep, but then remembered she wasn't asleep, she was in a room and it was dark. No, not a room. A pod.

It was so hard to think. Maybe she just needed to sleep. That seemed right. If she slept, when she woke up, it would be easier to think, and then maybe she could remember what she was supposed to do. The blankets were too tight, they made it hard to move and she couldn't get comfortable. Piper unwrapped herself. She'd sleep first, and then she'd remember.

But even as she was lying on the crash couch, some tiny part of her brain screamed not to sleep, that there was something else she had to do first, and no matter how hard she tried to ignore it, she found she couldn't. There was something about the door, it told her. Something she was supposed to do with the door before she went to sleep.

It was so hard to stand. It took so much energy to stand. And the door was somewhere over there, somewhere in the darkness. Was there even a door in space? But she wasn't in space. She was in a room, and she had to open the door before she went to sleep.

With leaden steps and dead hands, Piper forced herself around the outer edge of the pod, feeling for whatever it was she was supposed to find. Several times she stopped, thinking she might sit down for a few minutes before she continued the search, but always that part of her mind refused. *After*, it told her, *after*.

And then, at last, *there*, it told her. There. Some kind of bar or ladder, maybe. Was she supposed to climb it? She couldn't climb, not without her hands, and her hands were somewhere else, she couldn't find them or remember where they were.

But that screaming part of her brain wouldn't relent, and she fumbled with the thing in front of her. She hooked her forearms over it and under it, pulled at it, pushed at it, but nothing happened. She wasn't even sure what was supposed to happen. And she was tired, and dizzy, and she knew if she could just sleep for a few minutes, she would be able to remember what to do.

And as she sank down to her knees, the bar shifted one direction, and there was a loud clank in the distance.

Piper, having accomplished whatever it was she was supposed to have accomplished, let herself slip off towards her well-deserved rest. But something snatched at her. Rough hands. And though she couldn't understand what was happening now, her main thought was that whoever those hands belonged to wasn't happy.

TWENTY

"Affirmative, *Merciful Justice*," answered Paul, the dock's controller. "Credentials are good, you are clear to approach. Proceed to bay Oh Three Seven, and observe station protocol while in proximity. Repeat, bay Oh Three Seven is your lock."

Paul sat back, casually keyed in the clearance information for the approaching hauler, and checked his contact list. It'd been a busy couple of hours, but traffic seemed to be getting settled.

"Big plans for the weekend?" asked Joaquim, the other controller on shift.

"Oh yeah, huge," Paul said sarcastically. "Lisa and I are supposed to go out to Deimos on Sunday. With her parents."

Joaquim grunted, some combination of a chuckle and his condolences.

"One of those fly-by moon cruise things, you know. You ever done one of those?"

"Nah," Joaquim answered. "Only time I been off-planet is twice for work, and that was two trips too many for me."

"Lisa found some deal, I guess," Paul shrugged. It seemed like a lot of hassle just to spend a couple of hours flying around a big rock you could see just fine from the ground. "I don't know though. We might have to postpone it until the CMA settles down."

301

He tried to sound disappointed, even though in reality he was glad to have a legitimate excuse to cancel the outing.

"I don't think they're putting too much trouble on outgoing," Joaquim said. "Just a hassle for incoming."

"Yeah, well, we gotta come back too, don't we?" Paul replied. He was already working on the bullet points to make the same case to Lisa later.

"Hey, what bay did you send that last tub to?" Joaquim asked.

"Oh Three Seven," Paul said.

"Pilot seems a little janky," said Joaquim, and he pointed at the display showing *Merciful Justice*'s approach vector. The ship was still on course, but it was riding right up against the safety zone. Paul tapped the console, brought up correction numbers.

"*Merciful Justice*," Paul said. "Correct course to one-nine, nine-seven zulu."

It wasn't that unusual for pilots coming out of orbit to take a couple of minutes to get used to atmospheric flight again.

"How about you?" Paul asked.

"I'm pulling a double shift Saturday," Joaquim said. "Probably just sleep all day Sunday."

"Lucky."

"I'll trade Saturday with you if you want."

Paul chuckled. "It's Sunday I need, buddy."

The pilot of *Merciful Justice* hadn't responded to the message yet, and the ship still hadn't corrected course. Maybe the pilot thought he knew better than the controllers.

"*Merciful Justice*, we need you to correct course. Your current line is going to take you over bay Oh One Seven. Please correct to one-nine, nine-seven zulu, and confirm."

Paul waited fifteen seconds for the confirmation to come in. It didn't.

"Say again, *Merciful Justice*, correct your course to one-nine, nine-seven zulu, and confirm."

The ship's position and its projected path were both off the mark, and getting worse by the second.

"*Merciful Justice*, do you copy? You are in violation of station protocol and at risk on approach. Correct your course as directed, and verbally confirm!"

"Are they accelerating?" Joaquim asked.

"Maybe they're in trouble," Paul said. "Call down and tell Marni we might need a crash team on standby."

Joaquim wheeled his chair over to another console, while Paul tried one last time to reach the crew of the ship.

"*Merciful Justice*, abort approach, abort approach! You're too hot!"

He flipped over to the emergency channel, called down to the dock chief.

"Tanya, clear the decks, we got a burner coming in! And get a net up!"

Through the window overlooking the floor thirty meters below, Paul saw the lights flare to red as emergency procedures kicked in. Workers scrambled to clear the deck. He glanced at the display showing *Merciful Justice*'s vector, then back down at the people in the docks. Some of them weren't going to make it. A lot of them.

"*Merciful Justice*," Paul cried into the comms, "Abort, abort, abort!" He knew it was useless. But it was the only thing he could do.

The roar of the craft shook the control tower. And then he saw it, hurtling towards them, through the massive gateway to the docks. Paul had just enough time to think how uncanny it was to see something that big moving that fast before the impact, and the fireball, and the blastwave threw him into darkness.

TWENTY-ONE

"What do you mean they didn't stop it?" Lincoln said. Mike's face was grim; seething anger tinged with grief and disgust.

"Docks got hit, just like we said. Might as well not have told anybody anything."

Lincoln felt a cold shock pour down on him, as if the worst strain of the flu had decided to hit him all at once.

"What happened?"

"I don't know," Mike said. "Somebody somewhere dropped the ball. Warning didn't get to them in time, or they didn't get the right info on what they were looking for."

"We gave them everything they needed! That was a lock!"

"I don't know what to tell you, man. Damage is done."

Lincoln looked down at the display blinking in front of him, waiting for him to put the final few slides together on his report on the Flashtown hit. He'd just spent the past three hours writing up why the mission had been a success, with actionable intelligence coming as a direct result.

"Casualties?" he asked.

"Deaths in the twenties," Mike said. "Maybe as many as a hundred wounded. They're still digging out, though. Numbers are gonna get worse."

"What's the news say?"

"Freak accident. Hauler came in too fast, they think the

crew blacked out on the way in."

Lincoln shook his head and got to his feet, leaving the debrief incomplete and, for the moment, forgotten.

"Where's Thumper?" he said, "I need a line to NID."

"Mess, probably," Mike said. "Last I saw, she and Prakoso were headed to get chow."

Lincoln nodded and exited the compartment, headed towards the mess deck. He was just about to climb up the steep stairs to the deck above when Thumper came hurtling down, sliding along the rails on her hands like a true sailor. He caught her arms when she hit the bottom to keep her from crashing into him. Her eyes were intense, like she'd just been in a fight that wasn't over yet.

Someone from a nearby compartment shouted, "Shipmate! This ain't a playground!" but neither Lincoln nor Thumper paid any heed.

"They took Prakoso."

"What?" Lincoln said. "Who?"

"Self and a couple of his spooks. Marines have him under guard."

"Self is here?"

She nodded. "Don't know how long he's been on board, or how much longer he'll be here. Asked me to find you, though."

"Good," Lincoln said, trying to keep his emotions in check. "I have questions."

Mr Self was waiting for them in a small briefing room up on the command deck. He was leaning against the table in the front row when Lincoln entered, but as soon as he saw them, he stood and held up his hands, placating.

"Before you say anything, you have to know I wasn't even supposed to come along for this," Self said. "I felt like the least I could do was give you a familiar face to punch."

The admission of the situation didn't soothe any of Lincoln's anger, but it was at least enough to keep him from choking the man out on sight.

"If you two don't mind, could you give us a minute?" Self said, waving a finger vaguely at Mike and Thumper. "I need to talk to your CO alone."

Mike and Thumper held their ground, but grudgingly retreated at a nod from Lincoln.

"We'll be right outside," Thumper said.

Lincoln watched over his shoulder until they were out and the door was closed, then turned back to face Self.

"You've got ten seconds to explain before I invite Sergeant Coleman back in and turn her loose on you," Lincoln said.

"I'll take five," said Self. "NID's got enough to move on, we're taking the lead."

"Yeah, sure, that makes sense," Lincoln said, spitting the syllables. "Especially with that real bang-up job you did stopping the attack we warned you about."

"You did your part, captain," Self replied. His quiet composure made Lincoln even angrier. "You should feel no sense of guilt or responsibility."

"We gave you everything!"

"You did, absolutely," Self said. He gave it a moment before he gently added, "Except… for the faction responsible."

"You didn't need it to save those lives!"

"That's true, you're right. We didn't. But ultimately, without that knowledge, the folks upstairs at NID decided it was best not to act on the intelligence you provided."

Lincoln was stunned by the revelation, shocked to the point of being unable to respond. Genuinely at a loss for words. He'd assumed there'd been some kind of screwup, some miscommunication, or too much bureaucracy. It hadn't occurred to him that it might have been a conscious decision to let the attack through.

"If they know we've got a line on them, they'll change tactics and we'll lose the precious few threads we have. This isn't a new concept, captain. You've studied military history. This shouldn't come as a surprise. A shock, perhaps. Certainly. It's difficult for all of us. But, grim as it is, these are the mathematics of war."

Lincoln leaned against the table, then turned and sat on it, hanging his head as the emotions and thoughts hurricaned together. He was too clouded, too overwhelmed to have any answer.

"If it's any consolation, it wasn't a total loss," Self said. "We were able to pull out our key personnel, under cover of a shift change."

A humorless laugh escaped Lincoln's mouth.

"*Key* personnel?" he said. He couldn't bring himself to raise his head and look at Self yet. "And how many people did that leave behind?"

"We couldn't evacuate, captain, not without tipping our hand. But thanks to you and your team, we didn't lose anything essential." Self seemed to realize what he had just said, cleared his throat. "I don't mean to be callous about it. Of course it's a tragedy. Every loss of life is. But on a strategic level, at the scale of full-blown war, this is a blow we can absorb. Take what solace you can in that."

"We're not *at* war, Self," Lincoln said.

"Not yet, perhaps," Self answered. "But it's coming. I'm sure you're familiar with the old saying: twice a coincidence, three times, enemy action? This makes three. NID's been targeted, and now we're going to turn things around."

"So that's it?" said Lincoln, finally looking up at the other man. "You're just going to take our work, and use it for whatever ends you see fit?"

"Look, I'm doing what I can. I've requested that the 519th remain attached to my group at NID, so I can keep you part of the process. I don't mean to diminish any of what you've done. And you're a smart man, captain. I'm certain you don't *really* believe you're the only ones that have been working overtime on this. You've given us some additional tools, and we're grateful. But please show us the same courtesy in remembering that you haven't done everything."

"You can't have Prakoso," Lincoln said. "He's in our custody, and he'll remain that way."

Self smiled thinly, a cracked mask showing his patience was waning.

"No, he's in *our* custody now, as he should have been from the beginning."

"I gave him my word."

"And what value is that?" Self asked, and now his anger was seeping out. "You're a soldier, Captain Suh. That's it. A soldier. You don't make policy, you don't make deals. If you thought you had any sort of authority in this matter, then you were either sadly misinformed or gravely mistaken. Now, my team and I are going to leave and get back to work. And you and your team will stand down."

"Those aren't my orders," Lincoln said. He stood up, drew his shoulders back, dropped his chin to reinforce the point.

"They will be, shortly," Self responded, undaunted. "Don't take it so hard, Suh. Nothing about this is personal. You and your team have done excellent work. But it's time to hand off now. I'm sure there's going to be plenty more for you to do in the coming weeks. Now, if you'll excuse me, I've got another long flight ahead of me."

"You're not going anywhere with Prakoso."

"You'll have to talk with the Marines about that, captain. And there are a lot more of them than there are of you."

Self brushed past him to the door, but before he opened it, he paused. His head went down, his shoulders dropped. Wrestling with himself over something. When he spoke, he didn't turn to look at Lincoln.

"My sister-in-law was stationed at that facility," he said. He paused, took a breath, glanced back over his shoulder. "We all have sacrifices to make, captain. Burdens to bear. Secrets to keep, terrible as they are. But these are the jobs we signed up for. Do yours. Trust me to do mine."

He opened the door then, slid out between Thumper and Mike, and disappeared down the passageway. Lincoln felt a pang of sympathy for the man. And then immediately wondered if there was any truth to the bit about the sister-in-law. People like Self, you never really could tell.

Thumper leaned around the entrance to the briefing room.

"So?" Thumper said. "What's going on?"

Lincoln didn't know how to tell her. Or even what to tell her, for that matter. "I need to call Mom."

"I just got the word myself," Almeida said. His face was still red from the tirade he had undoubtedly unleashed, and Lincoln couldn't help but feel sorry for whoever had had to deliver the news to the old man.

"So it's true?" Lincoln asked. "We're standing down?"

"NID doesn't tell us what to do, as much as they like to think they can," the colonel said. "Best they can do is pressure my boss. And I'm getting some heat from Higher, but I can handle it for the time being."

"Self made it sound like it's a done deal. Like we're going to war."

"Things are moving that direction. You have to understand, plenty of people down here think war with Mars is inevitable. Nobody knows what that's going to be like, the first time two planets get after it. No one's done it before. I get the impression that some of our top brass seem to think we might as well kick it off and see what lessons we can learn, while we've still got the upper hand. So yeah, we're on that road, unless you dig up something convincing that sends us somewhere else."

"No pressure," Lincoln said.

"I told you the stakes were high before you signed up. Don't blame me."

"Yeah, I'm not sure you made that all especially clear at the time. What about Prakoso?"

"Hands are tied on that, I'm afraid. I'm sorry, Lincoln. There's only so much even an old goat like me can do."

"So what are we supposed to do from here?"

"Like I told you earlier, chase it down, wherever it leads. Keep doing what you're doing. Just don't count on NID for support. Worse comes to worst, I'll tell everyone you're on a training mission. Oh, and try to keep your gear requisitions to a minimum, huh? You about broke my budget for the whole year with whatever you put together out there."

Almeida was trying to lighten the mood, but it fell flat. Lincoln sighed, and shook his head. He felt empty, lost. More off course than he'd ever felt in his life. He thought back to that stupid document he'd been working on, the one where he'd almost declared the whole series of operations since Luna a success.

"You know, colonel... I was almost starting to believe I was getting the hang of this crazy world you threw me into," Lincoln said. "But now... now I don't think I even know what a win looks like anymore."

The colonel's expression softened, and he nodded with a weight that spoke volumes of understanding. In that moment, he was no longer a commanding officer; he was a mentor, and a friend.

"So, I hope it's obvious I wasn't born looking like this," Almeida said, waving a hand around his face. He paused a moment, looked down, scratched the side of his face. "That ambush hit us right outside the wire, in an area that all our operations guys had designated as safe. Friendly locals, no attacks in months, you know the drill. Afterwards, they must have spent... well, I don't even want to guess how much time or money went into the aftermath. But they had dozens of boys and girls out there, picking up debris, taking pictures, analyzing the attack pattern. Somebody wrote a big report and kicked it up the chain. New procedures came back out. Everybody patted themselves on the back for having figured out what went wrong. When I was in recovery, a general came by and sat down next to me, and you know what he told me?"

Lincoln shook his head.

"He said, 'Mat, I want you to know, what you went through, and what you're going through… it's not for nothing. We've learned from it, and we're making sure it'll never happen to anyone else ever again.' And you know what I said to him?"

Lincoln shook his head again.

Almeida smiled. "I said, 'Yes sir. Thank you, sir.' He was a three-star, after all. But after he left, I had a good chuckle at the idea that people thought they could figure out how to keep soldiers from getting hurt while trying to kill each other.

"You can spend the rest of your life trying to figure out who should have done what, when; what you should have known that you didn't. And that's fine, that's part of the ritual. But even if you find the answers to all that, it's just a story you tell yourself. A story to help you believe you've got some measure of control over everything. It's a good story, I like it. But it's still just a story. Truth is, in our world, sometimes things just blow up."

The old man paused, let his words sink in.

"But people like you and me?" he said a few moments later. "We don't let that stop us from doing the good we can. Whatever it is, wherever we can find it… Just do the good you can, son."

It was torture to watch, but Lincoln didn't feel he had the right to avoid it; he stood on the observation deck overlooking one of the *Curry*'s hangars, where Self and his contingent were marching a bound and hooded Prakoso to the ship that would take them back Earthward. There was no reason for them to treat Prakoso like a hostile. After all he'd done for them, they should have been treating him with honor.

Thumper stood next to him, tears in her eyes. On the other

side of her stood Wright, impassive. Lincoln had noticed that with her, the more intensely she was feeling something, the less she seemed to express it. Judging from the neutral look on her face, she was probably the most upset he'd ever seen her. Not for Prakoso, he suspected. Likely she was more angry about the Directorate's power grab.

"That man's an artist. His work oughta be in a museum," Thumper said. "And they're gonna take him and throw him in a hole somewhere."

"Let's not forget why we had to track him down in the first place," Wright said coolly.

"Don't do that," Thumper shot back. "Not now."

"At least on *that*, NID's within their authorit–"

"I said not now, Amira!"

Wright drew a breath to respond, but clamped her mouth shut instead. Her clenched jaw told Lincoln everything he needed to know about what she'd been about to say.

"Let's not eat our own here, huh?" Lincoln said. "This is on me."

Even though he meant it, part of Lincoln's ego was quietly hoping that one of his teammates would come to his defense, would remind him how much of this was beyond his control, how he'd done the right thing every step of the way. But no one spoke up on his behalf. In the hangar bay below, everyone was loaded up, and the ship was running through its final preflight checks.

"So what now, captain?" Wright asked. "Just packing up, heading home?"

"No, sergeant. Not until the colonel himself brings us in."

"I don't know what more we can do," Thumper said. "NID just stole our only lead."

"We've still got the relay to work with," said Lincoln.

"There's not much I can do with it now," Thumper replied. "I was just helping. Without Prakoso… I… I can't do this stuff without him, Lincoln."

He'd never heard her sound so dejected, so unsure of herself before. This wasn't like other times, when the team had coaxed her into working out a solution to something she thought was impossible. Then, her doubts had always been external, her uncertainty based on whether or not a problem was fundamentally solvable. Now, she seemed to have lost confidence in herself, faith that if there was an answer to be had, she could find it. A thought struck Lincoln then that maybe Prakoso was the first person she'd ever met in her life who could do something she didn't understand.

"Of course you can," Wright interjected before Lincoln could answer.

Thumper looked over at her.

"You were doing magic long before he showed up, Thump," Wright continued, her eyes still on the ship down below. "I'm not going to let you slack off just because your boyfriend's gone."

"This is different," Thumper said. "It's a whole different world from what I'm used to–"

"That's enough, sergeant!" Wright barked, snapping her head around to look directly at Thumper. "You were selected for this team, chosen precisely for your expertise and skill set, with the expectation that you would aggressively attack any problem set to the utmost of your ability and beyond. I will not have you questioning the capability of *any* of my teammates, is that clear?"

Thumper actually leaned back at the power of Wright's voice, and fell into a stunned silence. Down below, the ship carrying Mr Self and Prakoso drifted up from its moorings, flared its engines, and launched from the bay out into open space.

"Is that *clear*, sergeant?" Wright repeated.

"Yes, ma'am," Thumper answered.

"Now," Wright continued. "Prakoso's gone. We lost a resource. That doesn't change the mission, or your responsibility to it. Deal with it. And get back to work."

Thumper stood there looking at Wright for a few moments, then blinked at Lincoln. At a loss for words; probably another first for her. Lincoln's instinct was to say something to lighten the mood, or to soften the edge, but he checked himself. Wright's intensity wasn't the way he would have handled the situation, but he certainly wasn't going to undermine it now. He just waited, kept his face as impassive as possible.

"I guess uh..." Thumper said. She looked back off at the hangar, through the open bay, at the engines of the ship that carried her friend Yayan Prakoso, rapidly shrinking away. "Well. I guess... I'm gonna go scrub through the archive. See if there's anything we missed."

She didn't make eye contact with either of them as she left, but she stood a little straighter, walked with a little more purpose. Lincoln waited until she was gone before he said anything more.

"So. Maybe not the approach I was going to take, but uh... Well done, sergeant."

Wright nodded once. "Well. I appreciate you not stepping in, sir. It's a rare officer that knows when to shut up."

Lincoln cracked a smile. "Careful, sergeant, I'm almost tempted to take that as a compliment."

"Do, or don't. I don't really care, sir." She said it deadpan, but after a moment the corner of her mouth turned down in a suppressed smile.

"Ready to get back to it?" he asked.

"Yeah," she said, turning and heading towards the door. "I'm gonna go find Mikey. Lord knows he'll use any excuse to take a nap."

"Roger that. Anything you need from me?"

"Last I checked," she said as she was on her way out, "that coffee pot was empty."

•••

Later that day, with nothing more immediately pressing to do, Lincoln, Wright, and Mike were sitting in their compartment, playing cards.

"So," Mike said, out of the blue. "One time, in Hereford, me and a couple of buddies were out on the range—"

Lincoln chuckled at a sudden realization.

Mike stopped and looked at him. "What's so funny about that?"

"No, nothing," Lincoln said shaking his head. "It's uh... I just realized how you got your nickname."

"What? One-time?"

Lincoln nodded.

"Yeah, it's because I'm a sniper," Mike said, deadpan. Lincoln couldn't tell if he was joking or not, so he just waited, without responding.

"You know," Mike continued. "A sniper. So I only have to shoot the guy one time."

Lincoln glanced over at Wright, who was covering her mouth with one hand and looking intently at her cards, trying not to laugh. Mike looked at her, then back at Lincoln.

"What?" Mike said. "That's what it's for."

"OK, buddy," Lincoln said. "Sorry. Please continue."

"Nah, forget it," Mike said, and he flopped his cards down with a trace of bitterness. "Ten high flush."

Lincoln looked at his own hand of cards. He had the same flush, with a king high.

"Beats me," Lincoln lied, and he threw his cards into the pile face down. Mild penance for hurting Mike's feelings.

"Hey Link," Thumper said from the door of the compartment. They all looked at her, leaning her head through the doorway. "I think I found something. I don't know if it's anything, really. But it's not nothing."

"Yeah? Whatcha got?" Lincoln asked.

"Come see what you think," she answered, jerking her head back towards the compartment across the passageway.

Lincoln got up and followed her over.

"OK, what're we looking at?" he said, steeling himself for another one of Thumper's enthusiastic lessons.

"I didn't really pay much attention to it before because it looks like a glitch. I thought it was bad data. Remember what I said about the relay access? Using the same one?"

"Yeah," Lincoln said.

"Well, this here, this thin line, it wasn't open for all that long, but it sent a bunch of traffic. It looks like nav data, except it's all one way. That's why I thought it was a glitch, because it's an almost constant stream of open-close. I can tell that just from the pattern of the access, and I can't see what's going on in the relay exactly *but* nav data requests all go through the ICC to start with–"

"You know what, Thump," Lincoln said, holding up a hand. "I don't need to know how you got it. I trust you. Just tell me what it means."

"Oh," she said. She seemed a little disappointed. "Well. OK. This is a request for access to Veryn-Hakakuri's plot data. The reason why it's only one-way is because it fails the security check every time. The login ID belongs to a VH employee named Maria Reyes. UAF citizen. Lincoln, according to her last personnel assignment, she was stationed on YN-773. She was on LOCKSTEP. So either someone's trying to use her creds and being really stupid about it…"

"Or," Lincoln said, completing the thought, "that's a cry for help."

"Access request is on this relay here. And see, this is where it was when we started tracking it, and here's where it is now. It's moving."

"It's on a ship."

Thumper nodded. "Headed towards Mars."

Lincoln looked at the thin-skin, weighed the new information. Thumper was right. It wasn't much, but it wasn't nothing, either.

"All right," he said. "Let's pull the team together."

Lincoln brought the others in, gave them a quick briefing on what Thumper had found and his thoughts on it.

"So maybe we have one girl," Wright said. "Stranded on a ship somewhere. Not sure how that helps us."

And here Lincoln was again with a high-stakes decision to make, and barely any information to go on. This was probably the last chance they'd get to run an op before they were recalled. If they chased the ship down and it turned out to be nothing, that'd be the end of it. If they stayed around, kept poking at it, maybe a stronger lead would turn up. And maybe not.

It was a thin thread at best. But Lincoln couldn't shake the feeling that that fragile strand was the only lifeline that girl had left.

"No guarantee this is going to be the break we're looking for," Lincoln said. "But we know for a fact that relay's connected to the bad guys. And we know there's a UAF citizen on board that ship."

"Or *was*," Wright said.

"If she's alive, I'm guessing we're the only chance she's got of getting home," Lincoln said. "If not... least we can do is grab hold of the line she threw us and make the most out of wherever it leads."

Lincoln looked at each of his teammates in turn, gauging their reactions.

"Well," Sahil said. "Why are we standin' around just talkin' about it then?"

Lincoln looked at Wright. She held his gaze for a moment, then dipped her head.

"OK," Lincoln said. "Let's go get her."

TWENTY-TWO

"That's affirmative, *Relentless*," Vector said. "We've received your coordinates and are adjusting course to the new approach corridor as directed now. Sorry for the mix-up."

"Thank you for your cooperation, *Yoo Ling 4*. Safe travels."

"And to you. *Yoo Ling 4* out."

Vector sat back and glanced over at Kev, who gave him a thumbs up.

"We clear?" Vector asked.

"Looks like," Kev said. "Handshake went through just fine, no flags. Probably oughta give it a few minutes before we pop the champagne open just to be sure, but yeah. I think we did it. How long you wanna wait to kick it off?"

"Not up to me," Vector said. "I'll hand it off to the Woman, let her decide. I think it'll mean a lot to her to push the button herself."

"It's not really a button–"

"Metaphorically, man. Talking in metaphors here."

Kev chuckled and leaned back in his chair.

"You know Doc, we been at this so long, I'm not even sure what I'm gonna do with myself when it's over."

"Sleep for a week, probably."

"Yeah, but after that, I mean."

"I'm sure we'll have plenty to do, bud. It'll be nice to get a little downtime, though. Assuming nobody comes looking for us."

Kev shook his head. "If they haven't come looking by now, I don't think they will."

"Never hurts to keep your head on a swivel."

"Not great for the neck," Kev said. He sniffed, rubbed his nose with the back of his hand. "The Woman, though. She's a sharp lady. It's been a rough ride at times, but not nearly as rough as it coulda been."

"Yeah," Vector said.

"You, uh," Kev said. "You thinkin' about... you know, after?"

"No."

Kev nodded and shrugged. "Gotta be tough."

"Ping *Relentless* again in ten minutes," Vector said, standing and changing the subject. "Just to confirm we're following orders."

"You got it," Kev said, taking the hint.

"I'm going to go let *her* know what we're up to."

He turned to leave the bridge, but Kev called to him before he left.

"Hey, Doc."

"Yeah?"

"The girl. What're we gonna do with her when we leave?"

Vector had been thinking about that since her most recent adventure in freedom. Apparently she hadn't done any damage after all, but he was still wary of what she *could* do. He didn't want to just kill her in cold blood. That wasn't his way. That wasn't any of his team's way. But the girl was a risk, no doubt.

"I doubt anyone will find her, and even if they do, by then it won't matter," Vector said. He hadn't realized he'd decided anything about her until he heard it come out of his mouth. "She stays."

•••

Piper had given up trying to eat halfway through the bowl. Not because she wasn't hungry; she felt like she'd barely eaten in the past… well, however many days it had been. But they'd cuffed her wrists together and bound them on a short chain to her ankles, so short she couldn't stand without hunching over. They'd taken almost everything from her compartment; bed, table, chair. The bed had been replaced with a blanket; the toilet, a bucket. They didn't even trust her with utensils anymore, requiring her to eat with her hands. Given the meal of thin… she wasn't quite sure what it was. Too thick to drink, but barely enough to consider a food. Something like watery oatmeal or rice. Whatever it was, it had very little flavor, and was next to impossible to scoop with her fingers in anything more than about half a mouthful at a time. She'd taken to holding the bowl tipped towards her mouth, scraping the meal towards her, but the reward wasn't worth the effort. There was no doubt it was nutrient rich; there was just hardly any flavor. And once she had the thought, Piper couldn't get the idea out of her head that she was eating wet paper.

Now, the bowl sat at her feet, while she sat curled against the wall. To her surprise, her captors hadn't been needlessly cruel to her. Certainly they'd done nothing to make her comfortable, but there had been no savage beating, no threats. They'd nursed her to relative health. But apart from the meals and occasional emptying of her bucket, they had left her alone. And that had been the hardest part. The isolation.

The woman hadn't been back since Piper's last escape attempt. Kid. That was the name she'd said Piper could call her. Kid had been the kindest of them all, the one that seemed most genuinely to have cared for Piper. And Piper had betrayed her. In her desperation to escape, she hadn't really thought about the repercussions, the consequences Kid might have to face. Having not seen her since the attempt, Piper couldn't help but wonder if something had happened to her.

So it was all the more surprising when the door opened and the woman entered, with a cartbot behind her. She made eye contact briefly with Piper, but the look was more utilitarian than anything; making sure Piper wasn't going to try anything before she committed to entering the compartment fully. When she came in, she posted up by the door, and kept her eyes forward, intently ignoring Piper. A stubby weapon hung on her back. That was the first time Piper had ever seen her armed. Though, now that she thought about it, the men who had been bringing her her meals previously had all been carrying them too. Since her second attempt.

The woman remained by the door while the bot trundled in and took care of emptying the contents of the bucket, sanitized it, replaced it. When the bot was done, it wheeled out into the passageway, whirring quietly as it went. The woman looked over at Piper then, down at the bowl in front of her, back up at Piper again.

"I couldn't eat any more," Piper said.

Kid lingered by the door for a few moments, her face impassive. But then something shifted in her expression, and she walked over and picked up the bowl.

"I'm sorry," Piper said. The woman didn't respond, didn't make eye contact. She just took the bowl and started back towards the door.

"I mean, I'm sorry for what I did to you," Piper continued. And the woman stopped. "I'm sorry for betraying your trust that way."

Kid stood there in silence for several seconds, long enough that Piper thought maybe she was just waiting to see if Piper had anything else to say. But finally she spoke, without turning.

"I really wish you hadn't done that," she said.

"I know," Piper answered. "It wasn't right. You've been kind to me, kinder than anyone else."

The woman shook her head.

A man poked his head through the door, someone Piper hadn't seen before.

"Not too chatty, ladies," he said, gruffly. The way he said it, Piper couldn't tell if it was supposed to be directed more at her, or at the woman. He withdrew again, but from the way he'd leaned around the door frame, Piper knew he was standing guard outside. That wasn't like them at all, at least as far as she knew. Maybe they'd always had a second person out in the passageway whenever someone came into her compartment, but she'd never seen or heard anyone else.

Kid turned back around and returned to Piper, crouched down in front of her.

"I understand," she said. "I understand why you did what you did. It was a smart play. Well executed."

"It wasn't *all* a play," Piper said, looking into Kid's eyes, hoping the woman saw her sincerity.

"I'm not angry with you," Kid replied. "I'm angry *for* you. It's just..."

She stopped, glanced back at the door, then looked back at Piper and lowered her voice.

"You complicated things, María," she said. "For us. For yourself."

Her eyes softened then; melancholy shadowed the anger.

"There's not much I can do for you now," Kid said. "But I'll come back and cut you free at least. Before we leave. I promise I won't leave you chained up like some animal."

"Before you leave?" Piper said. "What do you mean? Where are you going?"

Kid stood up and looked down at Piper.

"You're not going to just leave me on the ship are you?" Piper asked, panic rising. "You're going to take me with you, right?"

The woman touched the top of Piper's head with light fingers; a silent blessing, or an unspoken farewell.

"Kid, please!" Piper said. "Please, you can't just leave me here! Don't leave me by myself!"

"I won't leave you chained," she said. "I promise."

"Kid!" Piper said. But Kid had turned her back, was on her way out. And dread cascaded cold over Piper, as if she'd been left behind in an open grave. Words flooded her mind, promises, bargains, pleas, but all of them caught in her throat.

Then something hissed in the passageway and the man outside made a funny sound. It was followed by a heavy thump, as if he'd collapsed. Piper froze, and so did Kid. After a moment, Kid moved very slowly to place the bowl she had in one hand on the deck, while her other hand reached with equal care for her weapon.

And then Piper went blind.

Plunged into darkness, disoriented, she lost even the sensation of the deck beneath her, the bulkhead behind her. Floated in nothingness. She called out, kicked her feet, flailed as much as her bonds would allow, bumped off something hard and cold from an unexpected angle.

A strange, soft sound, *pat pat pat*. Kid shouted something; she sounded farther away, her words cut short.

All in a few heartbeats.

And then all was still. A yawning quiet swallowed her, heavy with presence. And in that silence, she lost her sense of time, space, belonging. Piper wanted to call out, but was too frightened of what might answer.

She *felt* like she was still awake, conscious. But when she stretched out her hands, she could feel nothing around her. Had she passed out? Was she dreaming all of this?

Then, the lights came up, and Piper felt her weight again, fell hard against the deck. She pushed herself up to her elbows, bewildered to discover she was now three feet closer to the door, and facing a different direction than she'd expected.

And at the door stood a figure. One she'd never seen before. Like a man, but with no face at all; the marbled texture of his body swirled and shifted, distorted, as if he were made of smoke. Terrifying.

Piper scrambled backwards, back into the compartment, into the corner.

The figure stepped in, following.

"Maria Reyes?" it said. Its voice was thin, processed; simulated. Piper just stared, unable to respond. It entered the room fully, strode to her, crouched in front of her with fluid grace. When it was level with her, a thin vertical line appeared through the center of its faceless shell. The faceplate was separating, retracting. She leaned her head back, into the bulkhead, afraid of what might come out.

But behind the plate was a visor, and behind the visor, a face.

"María Reyes?" it said again. Not it. He. Piper nodded her head slowly. "María, can you tell me the name of your father?"

A strange question, asked with gentleness. "My... my father?"

"Yes," the man said. "Your father's name?"

His face looked Korean, but his accent had the edge distinct to the United States.

"Basilio," Piper answered. "Why?"

The face behind the visor smiled.

"Just making sure we've got the right girl," he said. "It's OK, you're safe now, María. We're here to take you home."

"Precious cargo is secure," Lincoln reported. "Sahil, how we looking?"

"All clear," Sahil answered over local comms. "These two ain't gonna bother nobody now."

"You good to check the VIP?"

"Yeah."

Sahil appeared in the door, secured his own weapon, and placed two others on the deck inside the compartment.

"María," Lincoln said to the girl, in front of him. He kept his voice low, his words calm, measured. "My friend here is a medic. He's just going to give you a quick onceover, and then we'll get you out of here, OK?"

The girl nodded. She still had a wild-eyed look; a caged animal wary of its liberators. Undoubtedly she was disoriented by the sudden change in her circumstances, and the method by which her freedom was secured. It would take some time before she'd trust them. But hopefully she wasn't going to be the type to give them trouble.

Sahil knelt next to her, opened his faceplate, smiled at her.

"Ms Reyes," he said, holding out his hands, open towards her. "Can we get those cuffs off ya?"

He was close enough to take her arms, but instead he waited for her to make the first move, to present her wrists to him. She did so, cautiously. Sahil cut the bonds with a surgeon's care.

"How ya feelin', Ms Reyes?" Sahil asked. "Sustain any injuries while you been here?"

The girl blinked at him, dazed.

"Any persistent pain?" he asked. She slowly shook her head.

"I'm gonna keep an eye on the passageway and check in," Lincoln said to him, over internal comms. "You good here?"

"Yeah."

Lincoln stood and went back over to the door, while Sahil walked María through a series of questions, probing for any health concerns before they got her up and moving. He double-checked the passageway, saw that Sahil had already moved the bodies of the two hostiles. If they hadn't been armed, they might still be alive. Lincoln hated that part of the job, necessary as it was. Seemed like Sahil might have had similar feelings. He had laid the two with care along the right side of the passageway, positioned them with an obvious respect for the dead. No longer the enemy. Without their weapons, they were just people again.

"Alpha, clear," Lincoln said on the team channel, then waited. If the others were still busy working, he didn't want to do any more than notify them of his team's status for the moment.

A few moments later, Thumper replied, "Bravo, clear."

"Roger that, Bravo," Lincoln said. "Precious cargo is secure. We've got two hostiles, KIA, no friendly casualties. Status?"

"Power and G restored," Thumper said. The adrenaline was still apparent in her voice and breathing, even though her words were calm and steady. "Obviously. Bay is secure. Control room is secure. We have five enemy, KIA; one enemy capture, wounded. With your two, all hostiles accounted for. No friendly casualties."

"Alpha copies all. Sahil's checking the VIP over. We'll move her topside when he's done, link up with you in control."

"Yeah, roger that. See you in a few."

Sahil completed his evaluation of the girl, gave the OK to move her. They escorted her out of the room, into the passageway, and she followed along without any resistance. But when she passed by the second hostile, the woman, she stopped abruptly.

"Why did you do that?" she said. Her voice trembled. "Oh, why did you do *that*?"

Lincoln looked back over his shoulder to see her standing with her hands pressed to her mouth, tears already forming in her eyes. She was staring down at the body of the woman.

"No... no, why would you do that?" she said.

Sahil gently took her arm and led her on, past the bodies in the passageway. The girl allowed him to pull her away, but she kept her body angled so she could keep her eyes on the two unmoving figures left behind, until they took her up through the hatch and out of view. Once they'd reached the upper deck, María went quiet and nearly limp. When they reached the control room, Sahil took her off to a quiet corner to talk with her and keep her under his watchful eye. Though Lincoln had only been involved in a handful of hostage rescues in his day, he knew that an acute stress reaction could have unpredictable and sometimes dangerous consequences. Sahil's concern for the girl's health was undoubtedly genuine, but his first priority was his team. If María took a bad turn, Sahil was on hand to control it.

Wright met Lincoln near the entrance and gave him a quick rundown of the events that had unfolded since the team split; the short, violent encounter with the two men in the bay, the more prolonged assault on the control room. There was a gouge in her suit, near where the left shoulder component merged with the neck.

"That giving you any trouble?" he asked, pointing to the damage.

"Nah, round deflected, probably won't be more than a bruise."

"Probably?"

"I'm fine," she said, and then jerked a thumb back towards the front of the control room. "But these guys wouldn't let it go easy."

Near the front, a man was seated on the deck with his back against the bulkhead, Mike standing guard over him. Wright handed Lincoln a weapon; a short personal defense weapon. It was high grade and well maintained, well used, and familiar to him. Disturbingly familiar.

"This is UAF issue?" he asked, looking up at Wright. She still had her faceplate closed, so he couldn't read her expression, but she shrugged one shoulder. He looked at the weapon again. Whether it was issued or stolen, there was no doubt it was authentic to the UAF Navy. The model was favored amongst UAF Special Naval Warfare units, especially boarding teams. A combination of on-weapon sensors combined with smart munition capabilities to enable engagement of soft and armored targets, without fear of errant shots accidentally penetrating the hull. Not that those teams typically had many errant shots.

Lincoln's own team was running similar weapon platforms.

"You talk to him yet?" Lincoln asked.

"Some, but not much. Figured you'd want to handle it."

"Yeah, all right." He handed the weapon back, and then walked over to the man. As he got closer, he saw the man had multiple wounds; treatment had been hasty, improvised. Mike stepped forward to meet Lincoln.

"He's hit pretty good," Mike said, his voice lowered. "Won't let us plug him up though."

Lincoln nodded. He secured his weapon and then crouched in front of the sole survivor. For a long moment, they just looked at each other. Enemies. Brothers.

"I've got a trained medic over there," Lincoln said. "Will you allow us to provide you with aid?"

The man shook his head. "Not much he can do for me," he said, his voice calm, steady, though Lincoln could hear the effort it took to keep it that way. His breathing was already shallow.

"Fight's over," Lincoln said. "You don't have to die here."

"I'm a corpsman," the man said. "I know what's going on with me. And I'm telling you, there's not much your man can do for me now."

"You got a name, Doc?"

The man smiled grimly at that. "You can call me Vector."

"Well, Vector. You feel up to explaining why you were holding that girl hostage?"

Vector's smile gradually faded to a neutral expression.

"We know what you've been up to," Lincoln said. "We know everything. And we're shutting it all down. All of it. You lost."

The wounded man gave a languid blink, unimpressed, unmoved.

"We know the whole story," Lincoln lied. "I'm just curious

as to why a UAF Naval Special Warfare corpsman would let himself get tangled up in all of it."

"I'm not that," Vector said. "Not anymore."

"Yeah? You got a story about how you lost your way?"

"Wasn't me that lost it."

Lincoln waited, kept his eyes locked on the other man's. Dying men usually had a habit of telling their secrets. But not this one. He seemed content to sit there and bleed.

"I'm not going to force medical on you," Lincoln said. "But the instant you pass out, my man's going to patch you up. We're going to take you in, and a lot of people are going to ask you questions, for a long time. That's going to happen either way. Might as well let us get you patched now."

Vector remained impassive.

"All right," Lincoln said. There was a lot more work to be done, and there'd be time later to deal with the man. "I'll talk with you later then."

Lincoln stood and turned around.

"My people… any of the others make it?" the man asked quietly. And though the man's voice was steady, Lincoln could hear the weight in the question, the burden. It had been his team, then. He was the man in charge.

Lincoln turned back, looked Vector in the eye, shook his head. Vector dropped his gaze to his bound hands. Lincoln lingered, waiting to see if there was any more to be said. He remembered that turmoil all too well; the guilt for having put his people in harm's way, and for having survived. Vector didn't appear to have anything further to say, though. Lincoln started to move away.

"You're not gonna stop her," Vector said.

Maybe this was the moment after all. Lincoln looked at him casually, trying to seem as if he didn't really care what Vector had to say. "Yeah? Who's that?"

"The woman," Vector said, with curious emphasis on the words. He didn't look up at Lincoln when he spoke. "Just letting you know. No matter how backed up and cornered you think you got her, she'll find a way."

"We'll see."

Lincoln went to join Thumper by one of the control consoles, and Mike returned to stand guard over their wounded adversary.

"What's the word?" he asked, through internal comms. No reason to let the other guy hear what they had to say. She had her faceplate open, her weapon secured, and was already at work on the console.

"We must have caught them on the tail end of things," she said. "I'm guessing they were about to clear out."

"What makes you think that?"

She pointed to a section of the navigational display.

"Headed towards Mars," she said. "Under AI. And they had a runabout prepped in the bay when we came through."

"Can you get us stopped?"

"Looking into it, but I'm not feeling optimistic. It's not your typical autopilot. There's some kind of weird bypass in here. Like, a physical one. Something they put on the ship."

Lincoln looked at the navigational display. If the ship held course, it was going to take them right into Martian territory. About six hours of travel time. And Lincoln assumed whatever it was going to do when it got there probably wasn't nice.

"And there's other weirdness in here too. Multiple manifests, looks like. It was the *Yoo Ling 4* when we were inbound, cargo hauler. I didn't see a lot of cargo coming in, though. And checking it now, it's broadcasting as *Pride of Europa*. Civilian cruiser, fifty-seven passengers."

"I don't recall meeting any of them on the way in, either."

"No, sir. There may be more. Manifests, I mean. But there's a lot of encryption going on here."

"All right," he said. "I'm going to go take a look around, see what else I can find. Keep working this end of it, grab everything you can. If you get any hits that might tell us what they've been doing out here, let me know immediately."

"Roger that," Thumper said.

"Wright," Lincoln said, turning back towards the entrance. "I'm trading you Sahil for Mike."

"All right," she answered.

"Mike, you're with me. Let's go see what else they've done to this tub."

"You got it," Mike said. Wright took charge of their captive, and Mike followed Lincoln out.

According to all the reconnaissance they had done, every person aboard the ship was accounted for. That didn't keep them from having their weapons out and ready while they moved down the passageways, checking each deck. It had never hurt Lincoln to expect surprises. They focused their first efforts on the middle decks. Lincoln and Sahil had inserted on the underside of the ship, and, with the exception of the trip up to drop the girl off in the control room, had confined themselves to the lower decks. Those decks had been very utilitarian; no frills, main focus on function. The middle decks were a step up, almost to something like a mid-tier pleasure cruiser. A long-distance passenger transport, maybe not for the rich, but at least for the aspirational. The compartments were largely the same in layout; small staterooms, with room for a comfortable two, or a very cozy four. Apart from the furnishings, though, they were all empty.

"Doesn't look particularly lived in," Mike said.

"Yeah."

They continued down the passageway, giving each compartment a cursory check, before heading to the deck below. And that was a different story.

The passageway was wider, the staterooms gone. And here and there along the sides were a number of large, sleek containers; wider than tall, and rounded, like cylinders that had been compressed.

"You guys come through this way before?" Lincoln asked.

"Negative," Mike said. "We came through the top, down the centerline. This is all new to me."

"I don't think I like the look of this too much."

"Yeah, not so much."

Lincoln flipped through his suit's sensor filters, scanning for the usual signs of threats. The canisters didn't appear to be giving off any sinister signatures. Even so, there was something unsettling about the arrangement; a bizarre puzzle that clearly had meaning, but the meaning escaped any simple analysis.

"All right," Mike said. "Hang back. I'm gonna check it out."

"Hold up," Lincoln said.

"Nah, you got the good brains," Mike said. "Better keep 'em at a safe distance, just in case."

Lincoln was about to protest, but Mike was already advancing down the passageway with careful steps and weapon raised. Lincoln kept him covered, even though he wasn't sure what he was trying to keep him covered from.

Mike approached the first canister, eight meters down the passageway, and cautiously knelt by it. He went still for a minute or so. Running deep, close-range scans with his suit's sensor array, no doubt, trying to determine the contents of the container without having to open it up. And then, finally, he spoke.

"Good God," he said.

And he turned and looked at Lincoln.

"Lincoln. There are people in here."

TWENTY-THREE

"Havoc Lead copies Whiplash," Lieutenant Colonel Will Barton said. "Send your traffic."

"Havoc Lead, we've just received orders to withdraw immediately," the communications officer responded. "We are to return to station at Point Artemis."

The order came as a surprise to Will, lead pilot for Whiplash's escort element. His wing had been assigned to provide protection to the Corsair-class ship, far forward of the main UAF-led fleet. Whiplash was a deep reconnaissance vessel, pulling double duty in this case thanks to its low signature as a launch craft for a special operations delivery vehicle. The Lamprey had gone out a few hours before, and as far as Will knew, it hadn't come back yet.

"Say again, Whiplash," Will said. "Did you say you've got orders to pull out?"

"That's affirmative, Havoc Lead. We're withdrawing to Point Artemis, effective immediately."

Point Artemis was an arbitrary point in space; a rally point for one component of the Terran fleet that had been moved into position to monitor CMA Naval maneuvers. Whiplash and its escort weren't in Martian territory yet, but they were far enough forward of the rest of the fleet that it'd be hard to convince any CMA vessels that they weren't up to something. Will was all for heading back in before anybody noticed they were out this far.

"Roger that, Whiplash," he said. "I didn't see Lamprey come back in, I must have missed it."

"Uh... that's a negative Havoc Lead," the comms officer said. "We have not linked up with the Lamprey."

"Then why are we withdrawing?"

"That's... that's under discussion at the moment. But apparently the mission was unauthorized."

"What do you mean *unauthorized*?" Will asked. "We wouldn't have launched if it hadn't been authorized."

The comms officer apparently wasn't in the mood. His professionalism slipped.

"Well," he said, "then it's been de-authorized. I don't know man, we're just following orders here. We're prepping to change course and return to Point Artemis as directed."

"What about the team you just inserted? You talk to them yet?"

"Negative, they're on radio silence."

"So... how are they going to know who to call when they're clear, then?"

"I'm sure they've got another solution worked out. Another ship or whatever. Different approach vector, probably."

"You're sure because Command told you that?"

"No, Havoc Lead, I'm sure because we wouldn't just leave our people stranded," the officer answered. "Look, I've got other lines to work here. We'll be pulling out in five mikes, stand by and be prepared to maintain relative position off starboard on the return trip. Whiplash, out."

"Five mikes, copy that, Whiplash," Will answered. He switched over to wing communications. "Havoc Two, you copy all that?"

"Roger, Havoc Lead," his wingman answered. "Five mikes, we'll hold off starboard on the return."

"Negative, Havoc Two. I want you to hold position until further notice."

"Uh…" the other pilot said. "OK, copy, Havoc Lead, we'll hold for your call."

Will closed the external channel, leaving open only the internal one to his weapons officer, seated behind him. Major Noah Barton, who also happened to be his little brother.

"Hey, Bear," he said. "Any of that sound right to you?"

"No, buddy, it does not."

Will checked the tactical scanner display, but nothing concerning showed up. No imminent threats that he could see.

"You got anything on the scopes back there?" he asked.

"Negative," Noah answered.

Will shifted in his seat, rolled his head around to loosen up his neck. It was possible that another ship had been assigned to take over for Whiplash, but it seemed unlikely that UAF would risk having *two* ships this far out, especially since that meant putting additional escorts in harm's way as well. Maybe CMA had intercepted the Lamprey. That seemed like the kind of thing that Whiplash would have communicated though. Something just wasn't sitting right.

"Do me a favor and get a line open back to Command, would you?"

"Sure thing," Noah said.

A breach of protocol, and poor etiquette. Whiplash was technically running the show; as escort, Havoc element was subordinate. But, Will decided, the crew would get over it. And even if they didn't, it was worth the friction to double-check that there wasn't a ball being dropped somewhere along the line. Will didn't know who'd gone out on that Lamprey, but he knew whoever they were, they were brothers and sisters-in-arms. He didn't have any intention of leaving until he was absolutely certain they had a way to get back home.

"Signature reads as a *Mako*-class cruiser, captain," the tactical officer reported. "At current velocity and bearing, it will cross into protected space in two hours, ninety minutes."

Commodore Liao let the words sink in for a moment before she responded. What was that vessel up to out there? Tensions were already high, with the Terran fleet holding off just out of striking distance. Was this an initial probing attack? Or did they just think they could slip a vessel by, while everyone's attention was focused on the main body? Were they trying to provoke a response, looking for an excuse to bring their fleet in? Or was this a taunt?

"Captain?"

Liao didn't want to start a war. But she wasn't going to stand by and let the UAF dictate the course of events, either.

"Helmsman," she said. "Plot an intercept course. Coordinate with tactical to follow trajectory, and correct as necessary."

"Plot to intercept, aye, captain," the lieutenant answered.

"Communications," Liao continued, "inform Higher Command that *Relentless* is moving position as response to possible contact."

"Aye, captain."

The *Mako* didn't appear to be doing anything to mask its approach. That likely meant they were either doing something completely benign, or that there was some deep treachery underway. There didn't seem to be any middle ground.

"Course laid in, captain."

"Very good, helm. Take us on."

"Aye, captain."

Whatever the cruiser was up to, *Relentless* would be the first ship it met. And, depending on how the next few hours unfolded, possibly the last.

Lincoln had joined Mike next to one of the canisters, bewildered by the discovery. They hadn't checked all of the containers in the passageway, but the handful that they'd scanned all showed the same. Each one held at least one person; in some cases, two. An adult with a child.

"You think they're in stasis?" Mike asked. He'd opened his

faceplate once they'd confirmed the passageway was clear, and his expression showed he was as unsettled as Lincoln was about their finding.

"Hard to say," Lincoln answered. "Stasis, or maybe already dead and on ice. Either way, this is all real creepy."

"I'm gonna see if I can get one open," Mike said. "Be a lot easier to tell once we can take a look inside."

"I don't know, Mike. This seems one of those things better left to the experts."

"Well, sure. All right, tell you what. I'll work on it for now, and then when they get here, I'll let them take over, how about that?"

Lincoln looked at the canister, and the simple panel on the front. He didn't like it, but Mike's point was well taken. If there was anything to discover here, they were the only ones to do it.

"All right, Mike. But be careful. You see anything you don't like, leave it alone."

"Roger that," Mike said. He knelt down in front of the canister's panel and started to work. Lincoln stood by, watching for a few moments until Mike said, "I know I'm pretty, captain, but you don't have to stare."

Lincoln chuckled and took the hint.

"I'm going to walk to the far end of the passageway, get a count," he said. "Let me know when you get it."

"Yep."

Lincoln moved further down the passage, stopping briefly beside each canister to let the suit run its scan. By the time he'd counted seventeen individuals, Thumper's earlier mention of multiple manifests sprang back to mind.

"Hey Mike," he said over direct comms. "Want to make a guess about how many people we've got down here?"

"Closest buys the beer when we get home?" Mike said.

Lincoln chuckled. He wasn't sure Mike had been paying attention to anything Thumper had said earlier.

"OK, sure."

"All right, I'll say forty," Mike said. "No, forty-five. I'll say forty-five. What's your guess?"

"Fifty-seven," Lincoln said.

"Pretty specific."

"I like to be precise."

"Hope you like to buy beer, too."

"Uh, Lincoln?" Thumper said, cutting in over the team channel. Lincoln switched to team comms.

"Yeah, go ahead, Thumper," he answered.

"I cracked the communications log," she said. "Want to guess who they talked to last?"

"Just tell me."

"It was a CMA vessel. The *Relentless*."

Lincoln's mind leapt forward from those words. Were these people all CMA military? A special unit like Lincoln's, working some black operation? If so, this could be the definitive proof they'd been looking for. Confirmation that CMA was waging a shadow war, laying the groundwork for future conflict.

"Can you pull the feed?" he asked.

"Yeah I did, it's all just chatter, but that's not the important part. They exchanged ship credentials, authorization information," she said. Lincoln didn't respond immediately, still thinking through the implications of CMA involvement. Maybe Mr Self had been right after all. After a moment, Thumper spelled it out for him. "The handshake, Lincoln. Prakoso's code."

And now Lincoln's thoughts wrenched the other direction. They hadn't been working *with* the CMA vessel. They'd just infected it with Prakoso's injection attack.

"We're coming back up," he said. He turned around and headed back towards Mike. Whatever was going on with the canisters could wait. "Hey Mike, we need to head back up to the bridge."

"All right, yeah, one sec," Mike said. "I've almost got–"

He was cut off by a loud pop, and he toppled over backwards from the container.

"Whoa, Mike, you all right?" Lincoln said. Mike didn't answer. He didn't even stir. And Lincoln felt a coldness hollow him out. "Mike!" he called, and he ran to his teammate.

"Sahil, I need you, now!" Lincoln called through comms. "Mike's hit!"

"What?" Sahil said. "Hit by what?"

"Now, now, now!" Lincoln repeated. There wasn't time to explain. He dropped to his knees next to Mike. The front of Mike's armor was pockmarked around the neck and shoulders with divots that looked like someone had pressed fingertips into clay. But there was a hole through his visor, low and near the left side. Mike's eyes were wide, his mouth, open. His jaw, working like he was trying to say something, was spattered on one side with blood.

"Hang on, Mike," Lincoln said. "Hang on, we got you."

Lincoln scrambled around, trying to get a view of a wound, but there was nothing he could find. All the damage was on the front as far as he could tell, and it didn't seem like the suit had been penetrated.

A loud and heavy thump signaled Sahil's arrival on deck; he'd leapt down through the hatch, and was now sprinting towards his fallen teammate, trauma kit already in hand.

"What happened, what's he got?" Sahil asked, sliding to his knees next to Mike.

"I don't know, some kind of countermeasure on that thing," Lincoln said, pointing at the canister. "It popped, he fell. Suit's intact, but it breached his visor."

"Hang on, Mikey," Sahil said, doing a rapid assessment of his own. And then, to Lincoln. "We're gonna have to get this helmet off." They worked together quickly to override the security protocol and unseal Mike's helmet from its attachment point.

As soon as they did, blood poured out onto the deck behind Mike's head.

Sahil pulled the helmet off and tossed it aside, and Lincoln's first thought was that there wasn't going to be anything they could do. Blood pumped from a hole on the left side of Mike's neck, just next to his Adam's apple. A ragged exit wound tore through the back side, on the right. He'd taken damage to his jaw as well.

Sahil went to work anyway, plugging what he could.

"Hold his head, hold his head," Sahil said. Lincoln moved around and put his hands on either side of Mike's head to keep him from turning it.

"Hang on, Mikey," he said, keeping eye contact. Already, Mike's eyes were weak, losing focus.

Mike reached a clumsy hand up and grabbed Sahil's shoulder. Squeezed it.

"I got you, brother," Sahil said, working feverishly to staunch the bleeding. "I got you."

Lincoln hadn't seen Sahil's medical skills in action, but they were impressive. Fluid, expert, patient in the middle of the chaos. Just like he was in combat. The nanoagents on the bandages worked quickly to seal off the blood flow, to numb the damaged nerves. In maybe sixty seconds, Sahil had the bleeding under control.

But even that wasn't enough.

Mike's hand relaxed, slipped off Sahil's shoulder. He closed his eyes, and a moment later his face went slack.

"Mike," Sahil said. "Mike, buddy, come on now. Don't do that."

Sahil continued to work, kept a steady stream of encouragement coming, even though he seemed to know he was talking to a dead man. After a minute or so, Lincoln touched Sahil's forearm.

"I know," Sahil said. "But I ain't gonna just leave him lookin' all tore up."

They finished in silence. Once the bleeding had fully stopped, Sahil wrapped fresh bandages neatly around Mike's neck, and placed a patch over the wound on his jaw.

"Whatever that was," Sahil said, "came in through the visor. Looks like it deflected off the jawbone, went through the neck, and then where?" Lincoln couldn't tell from his tone whether he was looking for an answer, or just talking to himself.

"Didn't come back out the suit," he continued. "So..." Here, he looked up at Lincoln. "It just ping-ponged around inside till it stopped."

And now Lincoln understood why Mike had slipped away so quickly, despite Sahil's efforts. The two men sat next to their fallen brother for a minute or two, neither one seeming to know what should come next. Nothing seemed right, or appropriate.

But Lincoln was the team lead. His burden to be the first to set the shock and the grief aside, to get the team back on focus.

"Let's get him up topside," Lincoln said. Sahil nodded, packed up his trauma kit, got to his feet. He rolled Mike... or rather, Mike's body, onto its side, positioned him to lift in a fireman's carry.

"Let me help you," Lincoln said, moving to assist.

"I got him," Sahil said.

"Be easier if we both carry–"

"I said I got him," Sahil said, sharply. Lincoln held up a hand, acquiescing. It wasn't an easy process to get a man up off the ground on your own, but Sahil didn't struggle at all.

"Lincoln," Wright said over comms. "What's your status? What's going on with Mike?"

"We're bringing him up now," Lincoln said.

"How is he? Is he all right?" As controlled as it was, there was more emotion in her voice than Lincoln had ever heard before.

"Amira," Lincoln said. "He's gone."

•••

"Understood, Hawkeye," Will said to the officer in charge of command and control for his current operation. "I'm just trying to verify that nobody's getting left behind here."

"I appreciate the concern, Havoc Lead," the officer replied. "And the initiative. It's all being handled."

"Roger that, you've got another element inbound to receive the Lamprey then?"

A pause.

"It's being handled, Havoc Lead."

"Hawkeye, be advised, we're zero on scopes, and not seeing anything projected our way. Is there a reason we shouldn't remain on station until that team gets back?"

"Colonel," the officer said, and the tone of his voice suggested he had Will outranked. That too was unusual. "The situation's hot enough as it is. If anybody runs across you out there, I don't expect they'll take time to ask any questions. And if they shoot, then we have to shoot. And that's going to get real ugly, real fast. It's been decided that it's best to recall you now."

"… and what about the team we inserted?"

There was a long pause before the response came in.

"Those assets are deniable, colonel," the officer said, his words clipped. "You are not. So, execute the mission you've been given, continue your escort, and return to Point Artemis. End of discussion."

That settled it, then.

"Havoc Lead copies all, Hawkeye," Will responded. "Thanks for the time."

"Hawkeye, out."

On the viewscreen, Whiplash's maneuvering thrusters flared, preparing to bring the ship about.

"Havoc Lead, this is Whiplash. We're preparing to come about. Adjust course to follow station."

He'd done his due diligence. Whatever was going on was way above his paygrade. He eased the throttle, nudged the stick to maintain his relative position to the sleek *Corsair*-class vessel that was his charge.

"Roger that, Whiplash," Will answered. "Havoc Two, bring it around."

Lincoln led the way into the control room, dark herald of the darkest news.

Thumper and Wright both turned to the door when he entered, but nobody said anything. Sahil followed, with Mike over his shoulders, then laid him gently on the deck.

Wright approached and knelt next to Mike, placed one hand on his forehead and the other on his chest. Thumper's hands went up to her visor and then stopped, as if she'd been about to wipe tears away and then remembered she couldn't.

"Why'd you have your plate open, you big idiot," Wright said quietly. "I don't know how many times I've told him to stay buttoned up."

And that was the moment that Lincoln felt the most coldly nauseated. The memory flashed back in perfect detail, Mike crouching down to work on the canister, Lincoln too distracted to remind him to close his faceplate, just in case. It was such a simple thing, a detail Lincoln should have noticed, should have commented on, and that should have saved his man. And that made it all the worse. If he hadn't felt so sick, he would have been furious at how such a mundane detail overlooked could extract such a terrible cost.

Lincoln gave them some time, himself included, to come to terms with the reality of the situation, but he couldn't let it linger. They'd have to pack the loss away for the moment, and get back to work. There'd be plenty of time to grieve when they were done. And now, a man down, that meant more work for everyone.

"Sahil, take him on, get him loaded up in the Co–" Lincoln caught himself. The nickname didn't seem that funny anymore. "Get him loaded up in the Lamprey."

"Maybe oughta get the girl out of here too," Sahil said, nodding at María.

Lincoln nodded. "Good call. Wright, why don't you help Sahil out, get everyone situated."

"Then what?" Wright asked, getting up to her feet. She was already flipping the switch, getting back on point.

"I'll let you know as soon as I have it figured out," Lincoln said.

"And him?" Wright asked, dipping her head towards Vector.

"I'll keep an eye on him for now."

Wright nodded. She helped Sahil get Mike up across his shoulders again, and then went to talk with María.

"Piper," Lincoln heard the girl say. "You can just call me Piper." And her voice sounded stronger, steadier. She seemed to be breathing more easily. Starting to believe she really had been rescued, maybe.

As Wright led her out, Lincoln turned back to address Thumper, only to discover that she was already back at the ship's console.

"Hurts, doesn't it?" Vector said.

Lincoln looked over at him.

"Losing a man," he said. Lincoln's first thought was to walk over and stomp the man's face in, but then he realized it hadn't been meant as a taunt. He seemed sincere. Still, Lincoln couldn't restrain his tongue.

"I wouldn't think a man willing to kill fifty-seven men, women, and children would have much room for sentiment."

Vector blinked slowly; his face was ashen, his breathing, strained.

"All those below decks were already dead," Vector said. "We're not monsters."

"Oh? Just grave robbers then?"

"Gathered up from the gutter… We're giving them more dignity, than they ever got at home… And purpose."

"Tell yourself whatever you want, bud. There's no way to justify what you've done."

Vector grunted a weak and brittle chuckle.

"Spoken... like a man... who's never seen behind the veil," he said. He gave a ragged, wet cough, and winced. "Ain't none of us... can justify... what we've done."

He closed his eyes.

"Not a one," he said.

After that, he said nothing more.

Lincoln stood in the center of the control room for a long moment, looking at the man slumped over against the bulkhead. There was a story there, to be sure. They'd served the same nation once, maybe even at the same time. Lincoln couldn't help but wonder how their paths had diverged, and why. Another mystery to solve later. Or, most likely, that would never be solved.

"Link?" Thumper said.

"Yeah," he answered.

"This ship is definitely being run remotely," Thumper said. "And I mean *remotely*, not just on AI. I'm locked out of commo right now, but look. Someone's broadcasting on our channel, probably hopping off that relay I'd guess."

"Making it look like there's a crew on board?"

"That'd be my guess."

"You been able to figure out what they're saying?"

"No, I haven't, captain," she said, with obvious irritation. "There kinda hasn't been time with you wanting me to shut the ship down *and* crack all these logs *and* dump all the system data–"

"Yeah, all right, Thump, I got it. First priority is getting the ship under control. The more space we can keep between us and the Martians, the better. We'll figure the rest of it out after that."

"Well, I don't think that's going to be a problem," Thumper said.

"You got that figured out already?"

"No," Thumper said, and she flicked a hand at the display. "We're stopping."

"There's no way we reached Martian territory already..." Lincoln said, checking the nav chart. He was right, they were still outside Martian-controlled space. They didn't have all that far to go, astronomically speaking, but there was no doubt that the ship was still in open space, and would be even if they had a nice, leisurely deceleration. "For some reason, this doesn't make me feel any better."

"No, sir."

The ship's purpose wasn't a mystery; it was a puzzle. All of it had to make some sort of sense, if he had the right information, but his mind was too off balance, too stirred up to be able to put the pieces together. And it didn't seem likely that he had much time left to figure it out.

Commodore Liao kept her eyes on the scans, but her attention was on the exchange taking place between her communications officer and the one aboard the UAF *Mako*-class cruiser that had just entered Martian space.

"You have entered territory under control of the Central Martian Authority," her communications officer said, "in violation of interplanetary law and the Planetary Sovereignty Treaty. Change course as directed, or we will have no option but to assume hostile intent and to respond accordingly."

"Negative, *Relentless*," came the response, "we are in universally acknowledged open space. We will hold course."

"They're slowing," Liao's tactical officer reported. "Should I initiate calculation of a firing solution, captain?"

"No, lieutenant commander," Liao answered. Once she initiated weapons systems lock-on, the other ship's defensive system would warn its crew. They would have no choice but to respond in kind. And then, any hope Liao had of de-escalating the situation would vanish. But there was another way to probe for hostile intent, without becoming the aggressor.

"Helm, maintain course. We'll consider ourselves in a blocking position," she said. "Tactical. Go to half ECM, monitor for signs of disruption attempts."

There wasn't much place to hide in space, and with the weapon systems the navies had on board, it was trivial to hit just about anything you could see. Electronic countermeasure, or ECM, capabilities were where the real battle took place. Typically, the first ship to defeat the other's ECM was the guaranteed victor, unless the other ship managed to get its own firing solution worked out before impact. In those rare cases, everyone lost. Of course, calling them ECM was almost as archaic a term as port and starboard, but the navy was nothing if not traditional.

"Half ECM, aye," the lieutenant answered.

Half ECM would be enough to draw the desired attention, without revealing *Relentless's* full capabilities.

"Let's see how they respond."

Will and his wing had been underway for only a few minutes before the nagging feeling finally got the better of him. Something about those *deniable assets* out there. Sounded too much like leaving someone behind.

"Hey, Bear," Will said. "What'd you make of Hawkeye's little speech?"

"Oh, I don't know," Noah said. "Kind of sounded to me like he was saying the guys out there are on their own."

"Yeah," Will said. "That's kind of what I thought. Any thoughts on what we should do about it?"

Noah was quiet for a few seconds. "Well. What do you think Dad would have done?"

"What do I think *he* would have done, or what do I think he would tell *us* to do?" Will said. Noah chuckled. And then Will added. "You know what Dad would have done."

"Then why are we talking about it?"

"You sure?"

"A thousand percent," said Noah.

"Well, all right, roger that," Will said. "Hope you've got a retirement plan."

"It's fine," Noah answered. "Being a major isn't as cool as I'd been led to believe, anyway."

Will switched over to the wing communications channel.

"Havoc Two, Havoc Lead," he said. "You guys see that ping at our six?"

"Negative Havoc Lead, we're zero on scopes."

"Uh, roger that," Will said. "It was just a blip. There and then gone. You didn't catch it?"

Havoc Two didn't respond immediately, and when she came back, she sounded a little concerned, like she'd overlooked something she definitely should have seen.

"Negative Havoc Lead, uh... no we didn't see anything."

"Copy," Will said. He gave it a few seconds, long enough to imply he'd had another conversation in between responses. "All right Havoc Two, maintain escort with Whiplash. We're gonna drop back and check it out, just to be safe."

"You want us to hold position?"

"That's a big negative, Havoc Two. Whiplash made it clear they're expected at Point Artemis. Maintain speed and heading. We'll call if we run into trouble."

"Uh... all right," Havoc Two replied. "Hope you know what you're doing, Will."

"Always do, Lena," he said. "Havoc Lead, dropping formation, and out."

"Copy that, Havoc Lead. Be smart."

Will throttled back and let some distance stretch between the main ship and Havoc Two before he brought his gunship around and headed back the direction exactly opposite from his orders.

•••

It was while he was laying Vector's body down and composing it that Lincoln's mind unexpectedly gave him a solution. *A* solution, but one he hoped wasn't *the* solution. The pieces fell into place too neatly, though, and brought with them that strange sense of satisfaction that came with solving a difficult puzzle, even when there's no way to verify the answer was correct.

"Thumper," Lincoln said. "Those multiple manifests. Is that the sort of thing you could spoof to make a ship look like a different ship?"

"On scopes you mean?" she asked.

"Yeah."

She thought about for a moment. "Well. Not like just *any* ship. But, if you had something of a similar enough shape and size, yeah you might be able to pass yourself off as something else. Sensor profile would just have to line up enough. You mean like, between a hauler and transport?"

"No, I mean more like a civilian vessel and a military one," he said, walking over to the navigation display.

"Oh," Thumper said. And then, again, with more gravity. "Oh."

"Yeah."

"I don't know what good that would do though," Thumper said. "If it's only one-sided, I mean. *Relentless* might think this ship is part of the Terran fleet or something, but UAF knows it's not. Not like they're going to take it as an attack on the fleet."

"But what if our side thinks it's a Terran civilian vessel, with fifty-seven innocent souls aboard?"

And now Thumper saw where he was going.

"If Prakoso's code could hide a rock from a sensor array," Lincoln continued, "is there anything keeping it from being able to fudge the location of a ship, by, say, a few thousand kilometers?"

"None at all."

"And would that force a ship's weapons systems to miscalculate?"

"Not necessarily," Thumper said, "I guess... yeah, you could maybe wedge an interface in there, between the sensors and the output. Tactical designates a signature, not a location in space. So, you know, on scopes maybe it looks like the thing is in one place, but all your weapon systems see it accurately where it really is. Doesn't matter if you think it's in one place or another, firing system's going to do all the math and hit what you tell it to hit. You think that's what they're going to do?"

"I think we better get off this ship," Lincoln said. "Dump what you can of the data. The rest of us will do a quick pass, see what physical we can scoop up. And get a line to Whiplash, let 'em know we need to pull out."

"They've stopped responding," Liao's communications officer reported.

"Captain," said the tactical officer, "*Mako*-class vessel is showing weapons hot. I must advise that we initiate a firing solution immediately."

They hadn't picked up any activity from the ECM scatter, and there were no warnings of impending target lock. But Liao understood the urgency in her officer's voice. The longer the situation went unresolved, the more likely it became that the final resolution would be combat.

"Communications," she continued, "what's the closest allied vessel to our position?"

"That would be..." the officer responded, pausing to check the system. "*CMAV Ardent*, captain."

"Open a channel to *Ardent*, and request verification of our target data."

"Aye, captain."

Communications coordinated with tactical to share data across to *Ardent*. A few minutes later, the communications officer shared the results.

"*Ardent* confirms, one *Mako*-class vessel, at four thousand kilometers inside Martian sovereign space, showing weapons hot. They've asked if we need support."

"Very well. Thank *Ardent*, but decline the offer of support, they should remain on mission," Liao answered. "Tactical, proceed with target acquisition, maintain a firing solution. But do not arm until my order."

"Captain, with all due respect," the tactical officer responded, "if they fire first, it'll be too late for us to do anything but pull the trigger before we die."

"Then undoubtedly we will be remembered as heroes, lieutenant commander. But as long as I am in command of *Relentless*, she will *not* be remembered as the ship that started the war."

"Can't reach them, meaning what?" Lincoln said over comms. He and Sahil were loading a few pieces of gear into the Lamprey, gear they'd stripped out of the runabout in the ship's main bay.

"I mean like radio silence," Thumper replied. "Dead channel. I don't think anybody's listening."

"That doesn't make any sense," Lincoln said. "Were they supposed to do a handoff?"

"If they were, no one mentioned it to us."

"All right," Lincoln said. "Well, keep trying to raise them, while we finish up. Maybe they had to go dark to skirt some CMA vessels. If we can't get a response, we'll load up anyway, catch up with them on the way out. What's your status?"

"Almost done with the data dump," Thumper answered. "Still working the commo channel to see if I can pry it free."

"Roger, keep me posted."

There wasn't all that much physical evidence to gather. A few weapons, some terminals, a couple of larger devices that neither Lincoln nor Sahil had seen before. Hopefully the techs back home would know what to do with them. Other than that, for the most part the ship was pretty clean, not counting the fifty-seven perfectly preserved bodies in canisters down below. Lincoln didn't have any interest in trying to load any of those up.

After a few minutes, Thumper called back in.

"Link, got good news and bad news."

"I need the good first," Lincoln said.

"Okay, I've got a parallel line open now."

"Okay, what's that mean?"

"I sort of have commo capability now. We could at least send messages out from here."

"And the bad?"

"I broke something with navigation. I locked out the remote access, but I didn't get local control back. I think the ship's dead in the water."

"Oh," Lincoln said. "Well that's not so bad."

"And... uh...""And what, Thumper?"

"And *Relentless* has target lock on our ship."

That was the bad news. If they had a firing solution already worked out on the ship, the thunder could already be on its way. Lincoln's first instinct was to get everyone in the Lamprey and off the ship. But if they didn't prevent *Relentless* from destroying the vessel, then nothing they had done on board would matter.

"You say we can send messages out?" Lincoln asked.

"Yeah," Thumper answered.

"Open a channel, I'll be right there."

"Coming in from where?" Liao asked.

"It's reading like it's coming from the *Mako*-class vessel, captain," the communications officer said. "But it's on a different beam protocol than before."

"ECM attack?"

"No, captain, it's clean. Legitimate communications

channel, but using civilian protocols."

"It could be a ploy, captain," the tactical officer said. "Trying to buy time while they line up a shot."

"I'm perfectly aware of what it *could* be, Tactical," Liao said. "Thank you for your counsel. Communications, accept the message, patch through directly to me."

"Aye, captain, patching through to your station."

When the channel opened, Liao spoke in her most commanding voice. "This is Commodore Rianne Liao, captain of *CMAV Relentless*. Identify yourself."

"Captain, your ship sensors have been compromised," the man on the other end of the channel said. "The ship you are targeting is a civilian vessel outside of CMA's sovereign territory, do not fire. I say again, your ship's sensors have been compromised."

"Identify yourself, or we will have no choice but to assume hostile intent."

"Even if we had hostile intent, the only weapon systems on board are point-defense cannons. The vessel you are targeting is an unarmed civilian craft."

"And how do you know which vessel *Relentless* is currently targeting?"

"Because I'm standing on its bridge," the man said. His lecture didn't sound prepared, his voice didn't carry the strained notes or false confidence of someone seeking to deceive. That alone kept Liao from ordering her crew to make ready to fire. But she didn't mind testing. She muted the channel.

"Tactical, arm weapons, prepare to fire. Hold for my command."

"Arming weapons, aye, captain," the tactical officer answered. There was a little more pleasure in his voice than Liao cared for.

She reopened the channel to her mysterious caller. "The ship we are targeting is a *Mako*-class cruiser, four thousand kilometers inside Martian-controlled space," Liao said flatly. "This has been verified. If you are in fact on the bridge as you say, then you will no doubt have noticed our weapons are now armed and ready to fire."

"I do in fact see that, yes," the man said, "A few hours ago, you made contact with *Yoo Ling 4*. At that time, it was under the control of elements hostile to both... to both CMA and the Terran fleet. At that time, control code was injected into your sensor system, code designed specifically to misrepresent the position and nature of this vessel. This is the same ship, the one you saw as *Yoo Ling 4*, and is now appearing to you as... well, I guess as a *Mako*-class cruiser. Only, it's not where you think it is."

Liao muted the channel momentarily. "Tactical, give me a run-back on *Yoo Ling 4*. Project forward to the cruiser's current location."

"Aye, captain," the tactical officer answered.

Liao reopened the channel. "I had both position and signature verified by a second ship, which had no contact with *Yoo Ling 4*."

"If you use standard protocols, then *Relentless* will propagate that same code to any ship she communicates with. It's in the handshake routine, during credential exchange. Any ship you've communicated with is at risk of spreading the same."

"That sounds like you're asking me not to fire on your ship, and not to communicate with any of my allies."

"Uh," the man said. "Yeah, that does sound like an accurate representation of what I'm saying, yes, captain."

"You can perhaps appreciate how this might be difficult for me to accept."

"If I were lying, I'd be telling a better story," the man said.

"Captain," tactical reported. "*Yoo Ling 4* couldn't have reached the same position as the cruiser. There hasn't been enough time."

Liao nodded thanks to her tactical officer. But before

she could mention it to the man on the other channel, he continued.

"Captain," he said, "if I told you who I really was, you wouldn't believe me. If I told you how I ended up here, you wouldn't believe that either. And if I told you what I found when I got here, well... I'm not sure that even I quite believe it myself. I can't think of a single thing I could say that I'd expect you to believe."

"Then why are we talking?"

"Because I'm hoping that you're just as desperate to avoid starting a war between our planets as I am."

The words had the ring of truth to them, and gave Liao at least a hint of who she was talking with. He *was* from the other side. But not in the way she'd expected. The moment seemed suddenly absurd, that she as captain of a CMA warship should be confronted with such a bizarre situation, with the stakes as high as they could possibly be. There was no training for this, no amount of mentoring or study could have prepared her for the ridiculousness she was now facing. On paper, the choice was easy. Ignore the nonsense, engage the ship. Perhaps the cruiser's ECM systems had failed, and this was the captain's desperate attempt to buy time.

But Liao's gut wouldn't allow her to make that call. There was a way to test whether anything the man had said was true or not. The time it would take might very well be the doom of her ship and her crew if she was wrong. But if he was telling the truth, the consequences of firing would cost many more ships, and many more lives.

"Very well," she said. "You've bought yourself a reprieve for the moment. Understand this, very clearly. If your ship moves, you will be destroyed. If any additional ships approach, you will be destroyed, and then they will be destroyed. If we detect the slightest hint that anything you have told us is a lie, you will be destroyed."

"Understood, captain. Thank you. You may very well have

just averted a war."

"Or guaranteed the death of my crew," Liao said. She closed the channel. "Tactical, maintain firing solution. Scramble whiskers to verify target position."

"Scramble whiskers, aye," the officer replied. A minute later, the tactical officer reported. "Whiskers away."

The crew sat in tense silence, undoubtedly wondering whether the whiskers' intelligence would reach them before enemy fire did.

"All right, we've done everything we can," Lincoln said, last to climb into the Lamprey. "Let's get out of here."

"We've got a problem with that," Wright said from the pilot's seat. "We still can't raise Whiplash."

"We better launch anyway," Lincoln replied. "Get us pointed the right direction, we'll figure it out on the way."

"Captain, you're talking about putting us out into open space in a practically impossible-to-detect speck of a craft. If we can't reach Whiplash, we'll be floating to a slow and cold death."

"What other option do we have, sergeant? If we stay, they're going to either capture us, or just kill us outright. And there's nothing tying any of this to UAF, except for us. It's going to be mighty hard to convince anybody this wasn't a botched UAF operation if they find us on board."

"We don't know what they're going to do," Wright countered. "I'd rather take my chances with the CMA Navy than open space."

The Lamprey's sensor array bleeped once, indicating new contacts.

"What's that?" Lincoln asked.

"Looks like we've got whiskers inbound," Wright said. "Combat capable."

There wasn't going to be a perfect solution. There was no point in looking for it.

"We're going to shove off," Lincoln said. "If it goes bad, we'll pop distress, and whoever comes to get us first can have us."

"Wait a sec," Thumper said. "I've got a signal here... It's not Whiplash, but it's got the right credentials."

"Incoming?" Lincoln asked.

"Yeah."

"Take it."

"Go ahead," Thumper said, trying to sound as neutral as possible. "We read you."

"This is uh... this is Havoc Lead, wingleader for Whiplash's escort element."

Thumper exhaled with relief. "We copy, Havoc Lead, good to hear from you. We've been trying to raise Whiplash. Is their commo down?"

"Not exactly. Could you, uh, identify?"

"Oh yeah, this is Growler," Thumper said, and she flashed the team's credentials across to Havoc's array. "We're in a Lamprey delivery vehicle, looking for a ride home."

"All right Growler, good copy. So here's the situation. Whiplash got recalled. Some kind of confusion about mission authorization, I don't know. Point is, your piggyback ride is gone. Do you have another ship inbound to pick you up?"

"Negative Havoc," Thumper answered. "We were counting on Whiplash for that."

"That's what I was afraid of," Havoc Lead said. "I'm in a gunship, closing on your position at full burn. If you got grapples, I should be able to tow you in. Won't be as comfortable as riding with Whiplash, but it's probably better than getting left behind. Are you clear?"

"Negative, Havoc, we've got whiskers inbound."

"Understood, we've got 'em on scopes."

"Havoc Lead, this Growler Lead," Lincoln said, taking over. "If we launch, can we meet you halfway?"

"Uh... that's going to be risky, sir. I don't think I can read you on scans. If you launch, I'd say there's a better than ninety percent chance I'd miss you. But I can read that ship you're on just fine."

"You sound like you've got an idea."

"It's not a great idea, but it is an idea."

"Shoot."

"All right. I need you to move your craft as far aft on the ship as you can get without detaching," Havoc Lead said. "As absolutely far aft as you can get, and dead along the centerline. And then I want you to deploy grapples."

"How many?"

"All of them," Havoc Lead answered. "Everything you've got. As fast as you can, and let me know as soon as you're in place."

"Roger, Havoc. Stand by," Lincoln said. He closed the channel, and looked at Wright. "You want to take us out, or you want me to do it?"

"Sit down, and strap in," Wright said, and she fired up the thrusters.

"Whiskers will be in range in four minutes," Noah said.

Will checked the scopes, checked the gunship's velocity.

"We're not going make it," he said. "Not in and back out again."

"Six whiskers," Noah said. "If we get the jump on it, we might be able to hit a couple of them on the way, and then bug out."

"*Might*," Will said. "But I'm pretty sure getting noticed is the thing we *don't* want to have happen. If those whiskers get a read on us, we're going to blow open the whole op, and who knows what that would bring down."

"I don't see how we have much choice," Noah answered. "Either we go in and they see us, or we don't, and we've got to tell Growler down there we're not coming after all."

Neither option was acceptable, but those did seem to be the

only two choices. Will checked every setting he could think of one last time, but that only confirmed that he already had the ship on full blast; they just couldn't close the gap fast enough.

"Well," Noah said. "Unless we go in cold."

"How's that?"

"Whiskers primarily track heat and transmissions," Noah answered. "If we go to full shutdown at the right time, we might be able to coast through, make the grab on the way by. If we're quiet enough about it, we might be stay under the detection threshold."

Full shutdown meant *full*. No communications, no weapons, no life support. No maneuvering thrusters. They'd have to rely on their flight suits to keep them breathing and warm for however long it took to make the grab and get clear. And if they had any hope of making the grab at all, that meant Will would have to line it up perfectly before they shut down. After that, they'd be drifting at high velocity with no chance to change course.

"You think you can make that shot?" Noah asked.

"Do you?" Will replied.

"I know you can," Noah answered.

"Sounds like there's going to be some math involved, though. Figuring out when to shut down, how fast we can go, all that."

"I'm working it out right now," Noah said. "Better let Growler know it's going to be a bumpy pickup."

Will nodded and opened a channel back up to the Growler team, gave them a quick overview of the plan. The team leader didn't sound enthusiastic about it, but he didn't try too hard to talk them out of it either.

"Roger, Havoc," the boarding team's leader said. "We've got the Lamprey moved to position, aft and along the centerline."

"Roger that, Growler. We're going to be coming in pretty hot, so make sure you and your teammates are strapped in real good."

"Understood Havoc, we'll be ready."

"Once those whiskers get in, we're going to have to go dark on communications until we're safely out of range. Might be a while before you hear from us again."

"Do what you have to do, Havoc. We're good."

"All right, Growler. Stand by. I'll let you know when we're going dark."

"Standing by."

Will adjusted course, positioned his gunship to approach the target ship on a vertical axis.

"How fast can we take her in, and what angle should I hit?" he asked his brother.

"Pushing numbers to your console now," Noah said.

The relevant data appeared on Will's display, and he started making the necessary adjustments to his flight path.

"You're sure the grapples can handle this?" he asked.

"How much do you trust my math?" Noah said.

"As much as you trust my flying."

"Then we'll be good," Noah said. "But, you know. Don't miss. And let's not tell Mom."

"Deal," Will said. "All right, Bear…" He nudged the stick, rolled the ship a few more degrees. The AI-assist produced its own approach solution, but it was counting on having full thruster functionality. Nothing in the system was built to do what they were about to try. Will flicked off the AI-assist, and then muted the warnings blaring that AI-assist was now offline. "On my mark, shut her down."

"Hey. Bubba," Noah said.

"Yeah?"

"Love you."

"Love you too, buddy."

Lincoln looked around at his teammates, each strapped in, faceplates closed, and braced for whatever came next. Wright was still in the pilot's position, Thumper sat in the middle.

Sahil was at the far end, with the girl seated next to him. She was quiet and still, but her fear was obvious. Lincoln couldn't blame her. He was scared himself. She'd thanked him for coming to get her. He'd told her to save her thanks until they'd gotten home.

It'd been almost twenty minutes since Havoc had gone dark, and it had seemed like hours. The temptation to make contact was almost unbearable. Despite the risk it posed, Lincoln felt a gnawing desire to confirm one last time that Havoc was still out there, still on the way. That Lincoln and his team hadn't been left behind after all.

Lincoln drew a deep breath to steady himself. And when he exhaled, a heavy impact shuddered the Lamprey. An instant later, Lincoln was thrown hard at an odd angle, his harness strained against sudden acceleration. Though the Lamprey's internal grav was active, he felt wild vertigo, a sign that the craft was tumbling. An alarm sounded from the main console, warning of the out-of-control spin, as though there was anything any of them could do about it now.

It was impossible to tell whether they'd just experienced a high-velocity pickup, or if *Relentless* had decided to open fire after all. Or, worse. That Havoc had miscalculated the approach and had slammed into the hull of the main ship. It was entirely possible that they were still attached to the aft section of *Yoo Ling 4*, and that it was spiraling out into space after the ship's destruction.

The tumbling continued for a long span, longer than Lincoln had ever imagined possible. Long enough to confirm his fears.

And then, the comm channel came to life.

"Growler, this is Havoc," the pilot said. "You read us?"

Lincoln was so surprised to hear the call that at first, he forgot to respond.

"Growler, you alive back there?" the pilot repeated.

"That appears to be affirmative Havoc," Lincoln finally

answered. "How we looking?"

"Light, bright, and aaalll right," Havoc Lead said. "We just cleared detection range, and we're getting systems back up and online. We'll get this tumble under control and get pointed the right direction, and then we'll be underway as soon as I can feel my fingers again."

"Roger that, Havoc, that's great news. And some seriously impressive flying."

"Well, to be honest, there wasn't much flying between going dark and now. A whole lot of praying, but not a lot of flying."

"Then that was some seriously impressive praying, Havoc."

The pilot chuckled. "Can't take much credit for that, either, Growler. Sit back and relax. We'll get you all home soon enough."

Lincoln felt a flood of relief, followed by a wave of exhaustion. All the emotion that he'd kept in check and bottled up on mission erupted. He and his teammates shared a few moments of raw celebration, a collective release of built-up tension and fear unrealized. But it was all tinged with heaviness, and for Lincoln, at least, there was one thought that rose above all else, that dominated his mind and demanded account.

Havoc Lead had said he'd get them *all* home. But Lincoln knew that wasn't quite true. Not for Mike. And there, once the team had shared their moment, finally safe, Lincoln muted his comm channel and allowed himself to weep.

"I know it's an unusual request, Deshi," Liao said over her personal communications channel. "There's some concern that our sensor system might be off calibration, and I'd rather that not be a matter of official record, if it's something we can take care of ourselves."

"Sure, Rianne, I understand. You just want us to verify your whiskers?"

"That's all."

"OK," Deshi said. "Shouldn't take but just a minute."

Deshi was a rear admiral in the United American Federation Navy, running one of their prize carriers in the group that'd been sent as a show of force. And an old friend. A couple of minutes elapsed, and then he returned to her line.

"We're showing them in open space, at 2,593 kilometers outside Martian control, shadowing a civilian cruiser," he said. "Is that what you expected?"

On Liao's display, *Relentless's* whiskers were arrayed around the *Mako*-class cruiser, 3,966 kilometers *inside* Martian control.

"Sounds about right," Liao lied, with a smile. "A little bit off, but nothing we can't correct. Thanks, Deshi."

"Of course," he said. "Buy me dinner next time we're both on the same planet?"

"A drink, maybe," she answered. "I need to go yell at some engineers now."

"Don't hurt anyone."

"No promises," she said. She closed out the personal channel, and then addressed her crew, "Communications, contact *Ardent* and direct them to cease communications with all other vessels immediately, pending a tech review of their sensor system. Tactical, what's the feed from the whiskers?"

"*Mako*-class cruiser status is unchanged, but they're picking up no signs of life aboard."

His mood had changed; quieter, chastised. Not quite so eager to pull the trigger. A valuable lesson for him, perhaps.

And no signs of life aboard. Whoever her mysterious caller had been had vanished as surprisingly as he had first appeared. Liao had the feeling that was one mystery she would have to live with.

"Commander Gohar," Liao said.

"Yes, captain?" her XO responded.

"Who's the best tech on board?"

"I, uh… I'll find out, captain."

"Do, and then have them report to me in my ready room."

"Aye, captain."

Commodore Liao handed command of the bridge over to the next ranking officer and retired to her ready room. There, she poured herself a drink, and sat down to consider how close they had just come to tipping over the brink of war.

A full crash team was on standby when the gunship dragged Lincoln and his team into the hangar, but fortunately they weren't needed. Even towing the sled in behind on tangled grapples, Havoc maneuvered them safely and expertly into the bay, which, given the previous demonstration of skill, surprised no one. Once they touched down, a medical team took charge of Piper, and started to lead her off for treatment and evaluation. She resisted, pulled away to approach Lincoln.

"Sir," she said. "I... I don't have the words..."

Lincoln nodded. "None necessary, ma'am."

"But..." She struggled for a moment to find something to say, looked over at the Lamprey, where only three of Lincoln's four teammates were gathered. "The cost..."

"Is one we're willing to pay. Every one of us."

"I can never repay it."

"Ma'am, if you hadn't done all you did to call for help, we would never have found you. And if we hadn't found you, there's a very good chance Earth and Mars would be shooting at each other right now."

She continued to stare at the Lamprey.

"Hey, María," he said. "Piper. Listen." He put a hand on her shoulder, gently turned her away from the ship. "Your actions saved far more lives than they cost. If my whole team had gone down pulling you out, it still would have been worth it. And I mean that, truly. You go on, live your life, guilt-free. Do the good you can. That'll be thanks enough."

She watched him for a moment, tears in her eyes. Then leaned forward and wrapped her arms around his neck.

Lincoln eased an arm around her, patted her back a few times, and then motioned for the medical team. This time when they stepped up and drew her away, she didn't resist.

After that encounter, Lincoln made it his first priority to find the pilot that had brought them in, to meet him face to face, shake his hand, and express his overwhelming gratitude. He managed to find him and his weapons officer just as they were climbing down out of the cockpit of the gunship.

"Hey Havoc," Lincoln said, extending his hand. "Lincoln Suh. Growler Lead. I don't even know how to begin to thank you."

"Hey Lincoln. Letter of recommendation might be nice," the pilot said. "Will Barton. This is my brother Noah."

"Brothers, huh?" Lincoln said, shaking Noah's hand. "I didn't know they let family serve together."

"Normally they don't," Noah answered. "But our ratings have been so high together, they had a hard time refusing the request."

"That might have been our last run anyway, though," Will said. "I don't think Command was too thrilled with our little detour there."

"Hey, if there's anything I can do for you, you let me know," Lincoln said. "If I have to fight somebody for you, I will. Guns, knives, whatever."

"Well, I don't know what kind of pull you have," Will said, "but I we could probably use some help from on high when our CO gets hold of us."

"*I'm* not anything special," Lincoln said. "But I know a few people who are. I'll make some calls."

"I'd appreciate that," Will said. "We better get going. CO's hot enough as it is, probably shouldn't keep him waiting."

"Thank you again for coming to get us."

"Hey, no sweat," Will answered. "It's a team job."

They shook hands again, and this time, Lincoln slipped something into Will's palm. Will looked down at it.

"Sorry I've only got the one on me," Lincoln said to Noah. "I'll make sure to send you one."

"519th Applied Intelligence Group, huh?" he said, looking at the challenge coin in his hand. "Don't think I've heard of you guys."

"You sure?" Lincoln said. "We've got patches and everything."

Will chuckled, and they said their final goodbyes. Though all his thanks felt inadequate, there wasn't time for more. They parted ways, the Barton brothers off to face their superior officer, and Lincoln to face his team's loss. Whatever good they'd done getting the girl back and preventing those shots from being fired, all of it seemed grey and distant now, under the light and weight of having lost a man. He knew he'd have to report to Almeida as soon as possible. There was so much to tell.

But first things first. Lincoln returned to the Lamprey and set about the heavy task of unloading his fallen friend.

TWENTY-FOUR

"That was quite a take you pulled in from *Yoo Ling 4* or *Pride of Europa* or whatever that ship actually was," Almeida said via viz. "I overheard someone from 23rd saying it was the richest pull he'd ever seen. They're having a field day going through it all. If I'm honest, I think they're having more fun just knowing that they're getting to see it before NID does."

"I assume you're sharing," Lincoln replied.

"Of course. But you know how it is. Normally we're at the mercy of the Directorate's decision trees about who gets to see what and when. Some of our folks might be taking a little extra pleasure in releasing it a little bit at a time, instead of all at once."

"So what's the outcome? Did we do anything worthwhile out there?"

"It's not a magic bullet, captain, if that's what you're asking. Tensions are still high, fleets are still nose to nose out there. But the material you've brought in is bringing a lot of pieces together. A lot of solid intel. It's making it hard to sell the idea that CMA had direct involvement or knowledge of the attack on LOCKSTEP, or on the Martian facility. And NID seems to have shifted focus, walking back a lot of their earlier analysis. They're not saying they were *wrong*, of course, but their reports are expressing lower confidence than they were previously.

"The most interesting thing to come out of all this though is the Martian ship that secured *Yoo Ling 4*... that was, uh, what..." Almeida checked his notes. "*CMAV Relentless*. The captain... a Commodore Liao, apparently took the unusual step of requesting UAF support to assist with evaluation and investigation of the vessel."

"UAF specifically?"

Almeida nodded. "Odd that she'd reach out across the lines like that, but I have to take it as a good sign. Gives both sides something to talk about besides blowing each other up. With enough time, cooler heads may prevail."

Something in his tone of voice was different, more relaxed than usual. Or, more resigned.

"Colonel," Lincoln said. "The way you're talking about all this... it's giving me a funny feeling that you think things are winding down."

"Well, Lincoln. As I said, it's no magic bullet. Nothing ever is. But we take our wins where we can find them. You stopped the immediate threat. You brought that girl home. You changed the conversation. By all counts, that's a mission accomplished."

"Not all counts," Lincoln said. "That team was working for *someone*, colonel. We still don't know who."

"Your work took some names off the board," Almeida said. "Important ones. Sometimes that's all you get, knowing who wasn't involved. You know how this works. We don't always get the bad guy."

"We've got to finish this thing, sir."

Almeida took in a long, slow breath.

"NID's still running the show, Lincoln. I let out your leash as far as I could, but there *is* a chain of command, and even *I* have orders to follow. As far as they're concerned, we've done enough."

"Chase it down, no matter where it leads," Lincoln said. "Your words."

"You don't have to come home, captain," Almeida said. "If you think there's something out there that needs doing, I'm not going to sit here and tell you not to get after it. But I don't have the support, and I don't have the budget to send you out anywhere. If you tell me you need a couple more days to wrap up, I can maybe buy you that time. But after that, your job on this is done."

"I need a couple more days to wrap up."

"Send me a postcard."

"Oh, I need you to do me a favor. The boys that picked us up, couple of brothers. The Barton boys. They're going to catch a whole lot of friction for what they did–"

Almeida waved a hand. "I'm already on it, Lincoln. Kennedy's handling the workup for commendations for them both. And the officer that ordered your transport to withdraw is about to have a very thorough and very unpleasant review of his decision and command process."

"Roger that," Lincoln said. "I guess I'll sign off. I've got a lot to do in the next couple of days."

"Before you go," Almeida said. "Got somebody here for you."

He made an adjustment on his end of the line, the view plane expanded, and Lincoln saw another man flopping into a seat next to the colonel. The man smiled, gave a casual wave. Lincoln's mind twisted with the shock.

It was Mike.

"Hey, captain," Mike said. "Just wanted to let you know I'm real sorry I'm missing out on whatever you're up to. Med won't let me fly for at least a week."

Lincoln's brain couldn't process, couldn't accept he was seeing. Mike was dead. Mike was gone. And Mike was sitting there, next to the colonel, talking to him like nothing had happened, like he hadn't died with his head in Lincoln's hands.

"You all right, Link?" Mike said.

They'd called the Process death-proofing. Lincoln knew that. In his mind, he knew it. But this was the first time he'd seen what it meant, what it really, actually meant. And more than that, they'd loaded Mike's body up for transport only a couple of hours before; there was no way he could have made it back to Earth already.

"Mike?" Lincoln said.

Mike smiled and chuckled. "If I were a less clever man, I might make a joke about you seeing a ghost."

"It's... it's good to see you, Mikey," Lincoln said. "Real good."

He meant the words, felt them truly, but they didn't come out that way. Mike nodded, seeming to understand.

"Medical said the other one was too torn up to be worth it," he said. "Had to pull one out of the freezer."

Lincoln nodded, swallowed. Tried to give a smile. He knew he should be elated. And he was, in a distant way. The joy just hadn't made its way through the shock yet.

"Well..." he said. "You look good."

"Of course I do," Mike said, flashing his smile. "I *am* the pretty one, after all."

Lincoln chuckled, and for some reason that moment of mild humor broke the dam. His chuckle turned into a laugh, and the laughing brought a flood of relief and acceptance. It really was Mike.

"Hey, that wasn't supposed to be a joke," Mike said.

"Yeah," Lincoln said. "It wasn't funny anyway. I'm just glad you came through all right."

"I don't know about that," said Mike. "I woke up about six pounds heavier, and my deadlift max is down by fifteen."

"It's not unusual for a replica to lag behind by a few days," Almeida said. "Small price to pay to get you back."

"For *you*, yeah," Mike said to the colonel. "I'm the one's gotta work to get back in shape." Then he looked back at Lincoln, and the lightness in his eyes melted away. "How'd it uh… how'd it happen, anyway?" he asked.

"How'd you get…" Lincoln said. He didn't know what the proper way to talk about it was.

"How'd I die, yeah," Mike said.

"You don't remember?"

"Uh, no, no way. I definitely don't remember. They don't let you. Who would want to?"

"Back in the early days," Almeida said, "they used to keep everything intact right up until the moment of death. Thinking was, when you came back, you could analyze everything, learn from your mistakes. Turns out being able to recall your own death had a less than positive psychological impact. So now they spin you back a few minutes, before you get any serious trauma."

"Oh," Lincoln said. He gave Mike a quick account of what happened, without going into too great of detail.

Mike shook his head. "Why'd I have my faceplate open? I gotta stop doing that. Mas'sarnt was mad, huh?"

Lincoln nodded. "I'm sure she's got a few choice words for you."

"They'll have to wait," the colonel said. "You can have a proper reunion when you get back. Forty-eight hours, captain, then I'm bringing you in. Use your time wisely."

"Yeah, understood."

"Take care, Lincoln," Mike said. "I won't be there to watch over you this time."

"Roger that," Lincoln said. "Enjoy the vacation."

"I'd rather be on mission."

"We'll keep it boring. Lincoln out."

The whole team shared Lincoln's relief when he told them Mike was already up and about, though, also like Lincoln, each of his teammates seemed to be holding on to some measure of grief as well. It was strange how much the loss still clung to them, even knowing their friend was back on base, safe. There'd be more to process later, some mix of emotions to sort through when they all got home. For now, though, they each compartmentalized the incident in their own way. There was still work to be done, and not a lot of time left to do it.

The answer Lincoln was hunting for came, as it always seemed to, through Thumper. She'd gathered them all together around her hacked-together workstation.

"You remember that thing you told me not to tell you about?" she said. "The work Prakoso was doing... the NID stuff?"

"Yeah," Lincoln said.

"Well, turns out what I asked him to do wasn't all he was doing."

She pulled up a file on the display for them all to see. An old NID packet, from some deep archive. It was titled OPERATION HUNTER JANES. It'd been heavily redacted, but there were some parts that the censors had missed, or had left open because there was nothing deemed sensitive or identifiable. And though the gaps were substantial for any outsider, Lincoln had spent enough time in special operations to recognize a few key hallmarks. He couldn't tell exactly what had happened, but he had enough of a framework to understand.

And among those unredacted sections were references to codenames. References, for example, to a Mr Self.

"Why do you think Prakoso was digging around in this?" Lincoln asked.

"Because it ties directly back to whoever was running these hits on NID," Thumper answered. "I think he knew a lot more than he let on. And I think he wanted to know why."

"You sound pretty sure," Wright said.

"That's because I am. The Directorate archive had some footage, some old voice data locked away. I fed it to Veronica, and compared it to the logs we pulled off *Yoo Ling 4*. There was a match."

Thumper pulled up a series of images, taken from

surveillance footage, mostly. At first, Lincoln thought it was several individuals, but on closer inspection he realized they were all of one person. The same woman. Vector's words flashed through his mind. *The woman.*

"Get me a line to Mr Self."

"Captain," Mr Self said. He looked tired, even more so than usual. "I don't suppose you're calling to wish me a happy birthday by chance?"

Lincoln didn't waste any time.

"Tell me about Operation Hunter Janes."

The blink told Lincoln everything he needed to know, before Self's mask fell into place.

"I'm uh…" Self said. "I can't say I'm familiar with that particular topic, I'm afraid."

"Really? Huh. That surprises me. Seems like you'd remember something that had your name all over it."

"I'm not sure what you think you've found–"

"Let's not play this game, Self. We're both professionals. It's beneath us."

Self looked down at his hands, tugged on the cuffs of his shirt sleeves. He scratched his nose.

"I don't know why you think any of this matters, captain," he said finally. "But Operation Hunter Janes was what held the United American Federation together in its darkest, most vulnerable days."

"Saving the world, huh?"

"Something like. You're probably too young to remember the early years, after the Americas united. You almost certainly don't know what those years were really like."

The mention of those days brought memories of Royal Warden to mind. The Honduran Defense Force. The Sino-Russian Confederacy.

"I'm far more familiar with it than you might expect," Lincoln said.

"Oh? Then maybe you understand that for much of that time, UAF was on the verge of fracturing and turning back on itself. The Eastern Coalition… they were just the Confederacy back then. And they were in their glory days, penetrating agencies left and right, winning the propaganda war. Canada, the United States, Brazil, Peru… from the North Pole to the South we were supposed to be united. We had a common enemy, but no one wanted to admit it. No one could see it. So we helped focus their attention. Provided a more immediate threat."

"You *created* an armed radical group on American soil, and turned them loose. And then built a false trail leading straight back to the Confederacy."

"No," Self said. "No, captain. The trail was already there. We merely highlighted it for others to see."

Lincoln couldn't chase the memories of Royal Warden from his mind. There was no proof of any connection, no reason to believe that that terrible mission had been at all related to anything under Operation Hunter Janes. But he couldn't shake the idea that his path had crossed Mr Self's before, the thought that this was not the first time their work had overlapped.

"You can't build unity on a foundation of lies," Lincoln said.

"And yet, the UAF exists," Self answered. "Stronger now than it's ever been. I don't want to get into a philosophical debate with you, captain. And I certainly don't feel the need to justify myself. I find it difficult to believe that you've operated as long as you have and are still capable of thinking about the world in such terms of black and white."

"Well, I find it hard to accept that you feel no responsibility for Henry's death, or LOCKSTEP's destruction, or any of the rest of the trail of carnage that leads right back to your door."

"That's a bit of a stretch."

"I wouldn't say so. Not when the woman directing all those

attacks was NID trained."

Mr Self blinked again, the same almost-flinch he'd given when Lincoln had first mentioned Operation Hunter Janes.

"Amanda Flood. Or should I call her Joana Cardoso? Nakia Taleb?"

"I assure you that's impossible, captain. That woman is dead, and has been for a long time."

"You sound certain."

"I oversaw the strike myself. I'm sure I could find the footage for you to review yourself, if it hasn't been completely destroyed."

"Then, would you like to offer an explanation for how she ended up in the Martian People's Collective Republic?"

Mr Self rubbed an eye with his fingertip, seemed lost in reflection for a few moments. Then he smiled to himself.

"Amanda wasn't NID trained," Self said. "She was just a quick study. Had a natural talent for the work. I never knew her personally, of course. Few of us did. But we did have a hand in getting her connected to the right groups, nudged her towards radicalization. We'd identified her early, helped her get picked up. She was our mole, without her knowledge or consent. Turns out we'd won the lottery with her. She advanced quickly, and ended up becoming a highly effective operative for the group. The fact that the Directorate had her under observation from the very beginning made it that much easier on us when it came to shut it down."

"I lost a man on this," Lincoln said. "Chasing down your mess." After he said it, he remembered that first team briefing, when Thumper had made the comment about betting this was another "NID bag".

"And I distinctly remember telling you to stand down, captain," Self said. "Besides, you didn't lose anybody. I thought that was the whole point of you guys."

He said it almost dismissively. As if their deaths didn't count, somehow, weren't part of the equation. And the way he said it made a connection in Lincoln's mind, one that he hadn't even realized his subconscious had been working on. Why had Whiplash been recalled? And who had been in charge, calling the shots, making those decisions?

"You left us out there to die."

"That would have been an easy way to get you back home, wouldn't it?" As far as Self was concerned, the only thing they would have lost was whatever hard evidence there was on that ship. "The thing you don't seem to be able to grasp, captain, is that it doesn't matter, at this stage. Too many things are in motion. Whether CMA was involved with LOCKSTEP or not, all of the actions they've taken since then have revealed their intentions anyway. You've seen for yourself how they've responded. Hostility at every turn. Whatever you found on that ship, or whatever you think you have left to find, would just muddy the waters. Ultimately no one cares. Read your Aeschylus," he said, obliquely referencing, Lincoln guessed, the famous quote about truth being the first casualty of war. "I don't know why you keep acting like you or I have any power in this. I didn't make the decision to leave you out there. No one did, really. The situation did. The machine did. There's not some big conspiracy against you, captain. No shadowy cabal that knows everything and is pulling the strings of the world."

"We're going to finish this," Lincoln said. "Whether you have the courage to do it or not."

"Go, or don't. I don't know what you think you'll find. Or why you would think it would matter. It would be an aside, a footnote, an entry in your diary. Nothing more. I don't know why you believe it'd be worth risking the lives of your fellow soldiers for that."

Lincoln didn't know what more to say.

"I'm not evil, captain," Self said. "Just experienced. I'll do you the courtesy of pretending I have no idea what you're planning to do. But I strongly urge you to make certain that whatever it is, doesn't end up kicking off the very war you're trying so desperately to prevent."

Mr Self closed the connection then, leaving Lincoln to wrestle alone with his thoughts. What was he after, really? Truth? Justice? Some sort of redemption? Or was it just his need to see a job through to the end?

In the end, he came to the conclusion that it didn't really matter what his motivation was. Maybe Self was right, and the machine was too big to control. But as long as Lincoln was alive, he would do his part to serve the nation he'd sworn to protect. An enemy was out there, an enemy he had the knowledge of and means to confront. And confront her, he would.

TWENTY-FIVE

"Because it's right in the middle of the Martian People's Collective Republic," Wright said. "I thought we were trying to *prevent* war with the Martians. I can't think of a better way to guarantee one than to go invading the Collective."

"We can't just leave her there," Lincoln said. "You've read the file. She's a planner. There's no way this would be the end for her. She lost her ship, lost a team, sure. Who knows what else she has going on."

"I'm with the cap'n on this," Sahil said. "Sorry, mas'sarnt."

"I'm in too," Thumper said. "I wouldn't be able to sleep at night, knowing we had a chance at her and we let it get away. Gotta do the good we can, right?"

"The thing I don't know about," Lincoln said. "Is how we're going to get there, and out again."

"If you jokers are dead set on it," Wright said. "Then we can do it."

"You gonna fly us in yourself, Mir?" Sahil asked.

"No," she said. "But I know a guy."

The hop where they met wasn't in quite as bad a shape as Flashtown, but it wasn't exactly the most well-kept station Lincoln had ever seen. The passageways all had a strange yellow tint that seemed to be less decorative and more a sign that the air recyclers were in dire need of maintenance. It was just an outpost, intended for not much more than a refueling point or place for quick repairs. For some reason, though, it appeared that it'd become something of a party town, or a place where extralegal activities were, if not invited, at least unremarked upon.

"Wright," Lincoln said. "Please tell me these guys aren't pirates."

"I definitely wouldn't say that to *them*," Wright answered. "They work in salvage. I wouldn't ask too many questions about that, though."

Wright had made Sahil and Thumper wait in dock, still aboard the shuttle that brought them in. It wasn't clear if it was because she didn't want too many people talking business, or because she wanted to make sure they could get out fast if they needed to. Both, maybe.

"And how do you know these people again?"

"I don't think the history of my romantic life is any of your concern, captain," she said, answering the question without answering it. "Here we go." She pointed to a bar. Even the front door was greasy. "They'll probably offer you a chair, but I recommend you stand. And do *not* drink anything in here."

They stepped inside, and the thick haze made Lincoln want to immediately step right back out. Wright marched with purpose, though, and Lincoln didn't dare let her get too far away. The place was packed, music was loud, and nobody seemed to pay any attention to them passing through. Not even enough to avoid bumping into them, which several patrons did, repeatedly.

There were three people sitting at a corner table near the back, about as far away from the music as they could get, without straying too far from the bar. One man and two women. The man and one of the women stood up when they saw Wright approaching, both with welcoming smiles. The other woman, small and leathery faced, kept her seat and stared at them hard, with eyes like a rodent's.

"Hey hey hey," the man said. "Little Meer-meer. How you livin', girly?" He held out his arms as if he was expecting Wright to give him a greeting hug. He was disappointed.

"Same as ever, Uncle H," she answered. "Good livin', every day."

"That's what I like to hear! Who's the pretty boy?"

"Just some guy," Wright said.

"Oh… all right then. Well, welcome, some guy. Grab a seat, get comfortable."

"I'll stand," Lincoln said. "Thanks."

"Oh. All right," Uncle H replied, and he sat back down. "Drinks?"

"We're good," Wright said. And then she turned to Lincoln and pointed to each person in turn. "This is Uncle H, Baby Vegas, and this here," she said, pointing at the little woman, "is Mad Ethel."

Baby Vegas was taller than Uncle H, and she stretched a long arm across the table and shook Lincoln's hand. Mad Ethel just sat there.

"When H said you'd called," Baby Vegas said to Wright, "I thought he was kidding around. I didn't know you still knew where to find us."

"Yeah, I know it's been a while," Wright said. "I've been uh… been pretty busy."

"Always are," Baby Vegas said, and she smiled, but there seemed to be some sadness there.

"YEHH!" the little woman screamed, without warning or obvious provocation. Uncle H punched her in the shoulder.

"Settle down, Ethel!" he yelled. "Sorry, don't mind Ethel. She just does that to people she likes. Well, cut to the chase, Mir. I assume you ain't just here for chats."

"I need a ride, H," she said. "Probably a bumpy one."

"Huh. Business or pleasure?"

"Business. But unofficial."

"Huh. How unofficial?"

"I'm talking to you, Uncle H."

"Ahhh, yeah. Got it. Where we headed?"

Wright looked at Lincoln. He gave her a nod.

"Rocknest."

"Rocknest?" Uncle H said. "The Collective?"

Wright nodded. His expression changed, and he flashed a look at Baby Vegas. Baby Vegas held up a hand, waggled it back and forth.

"Definitely bumpy," Baby Vegas said. "What's the cargo?"

"Passengers, mostly," Wright answered. "Four on the way in. Between four and five on the way out, depending on how it goes."

"Better be four *or* five," Baby Vegas replied. "With people, I don't do halfsies."

"Gear?" Uncle H said.

"We packed light," Wright said. "But what we packed is heavy."

"You're not gonna get my ship shot up, are you Mir?" he asked.

"*I'm* not, H. I'm hoping you won't either."

"Yeah, well. You caught us at a good time. Been thinking about cruising the Martian scene a bit anyway. I don't think we can do it for free, though."

"I wouldn't ask you to," Wright said. "What's your price?"

Uncle H made a show of thinking about it, then flashed a toothy grin. "Couple of dates with me?"

"Too steep," Wright said.

"I'll run the numbers," Baby Vegas said. "And get back to you. But I'll give you the friend discount."

"But you'll do it?"

"You don't want to know the cost first?"

"It's gotta be done," Wright answered.

"We'll do it, Mir," Uncle H said. "But we got a business to run. Out and back, nothing funny in the middle."

"That's all we need, H."

"How soon did you want to get underway?" Baby Vegas asked.

"You busy now?" said Wright.

Uncle H chuckled, and looked at Baby Vegas.

"Hangar 17," Baby Vegas said. "We can be out in three hours."

Two and a half hours later, they were loading the last of their gear onto Uncle H's ship, *The Lightfinger*.

"A bit on the nose there, don't you think?" Lincoln said to Wright, pointing at the name. She nudged him with her elbow, as Uncle H was only a few feet away.

"Hey, you hear about Flashtown?" Uncle H said.

"No," Wright answered. "What now?"

"Got raided by some feds."

Wright snorted. "*Whose* feds?"

"Don't know. Some think Eastern Coalition, some UAF, some CMA. Doesn't really matter. Couple hundred dudes showed up, made a big mess, confiscated some gear. Mayor Jon's in a bad way."

"Sounds like Mayor Jon decided to clean house and blame it on outsiders."

"Yeah, that's what I thought too," Uncle H said with a shrug. "Still though. Probably gonna steer clear of there for a bit."

"That's probably good practice no matter what, H."

"Yeah, but... the place has style, you know? And there's this one noodle bar on deck 34 that's worth shooting your way to."

"What about on the way back out?" Lincoln asked.

Uncle H looked at him and smiled. "If you didn't make it back out, it'd still be worth it."

"We're cleared to go," Baby Vegas called from the front. "Get yourselves comfortable, and if anybody stops us to ask questions, keep your mouths shut!"

•••

The team spent the entire trip in jump seats back in one of the cargo holds. It wasn't luxurious, but actually wasn't that much more uncomfortable than most of the military transports Lincoln had been on. Not quite comfortable enough to sleep, but he was at least able to doze.

They'd already been over the schematics, laid out the plan as best they could. It was amazing how much information they had access to, once they knew what questions to ask. Between Thumper's work and ample support from 23rd, they'd tracked Amanda Flood, or whoever she was now, down to a compound in Rocknest. From there, it was just a matter of pointing a few satellites in the right direction, and they had enough to work with to plan the assault.

But now, on the way in, he couldn't stop thinking about Mike. Mike was fine. Alive and well. Just back home, instead of on mission with his teammates. But somehow, that didn't matter. Not as much as it should have, or as much as Lincoln wanted it to. The fact remained that Mike had been killed in action, under Lincoln's command. As strange as it may have seemed, as hard as it would have been to explain to anyone else, the fact remained that Lincoln now faced an entirely new burden of leadership. It was bad enough to lose one of his people. But now, he faced the very real possibility of losing his people more than once. And that thought nearly crushed him. How many times would he see Mike die? How many memories would he accumulate of his friends, killed in action, over and over again?

Undoubtedly the four-stars back home had thought this was a tremendous breakthrough, an unmitigated triumph over death and loss of warfighting capability. To Lincoln, as a team leader, it seemed something much closer to hell.

"Sure could use Mikey on this," Sahil said, from across the bay.

"You'll do just fine," Wright said.

"Yeah, I know. But I always feel better when he's on the long gun."

Apparently Lincoln wasn't the only one thinking about their missing teammate. And he was missed, sorely. Lincoln hadn't really noticed how much the team needed Mike's easy nature to round them out. And, now that he thought about it, he hadn't really noticed when he'd started considering himself such a part of the team, either.

Baby Vegas came in over internal comms.

"We're coming up on a CMA check," she said. "Then we'll be headed down-planet. We'll let you know when we're on approach."

"Thanks, BV," Wright answered.

"Almost go time," Lincoln said.

"Sure could use Mikey on this," Sahil said again.

"Two hostiles," Sahil said. "North side, three hundred meters."

"Copy that, I see them," Lincoln answered. "Thumper, you good?"

"Got a smoker," she replied. "Trying to wait until he goes back inside."

"How much time do you need at the box?"

"Depends on what I find when I get there," Thumper said. "Thirty seconds at least. Couple minutes at most."

"Sahil, you have a good line to her?"

"Yeah."

"Wright and I are moving up."

"Roger," Thumper said.

Lincoln led the way on the approach, with Wright close behind, just off his left shoulder. The compound was isolated, built on an outcropping thrust out in an artificial lake, and surrounded by a wall, three meters high. The main gate didn't have any guards posted outside, but their early reconnaissance had mapped out several vantage points from the central house that had clear lines of sight to the entrance. There was too much courtyard to cross between the gate and the nearest building. They'd decided the infiltration team would go over the wall; that meant Lincoln and Wright.

"All right," Thumper said. "Smoker just left. Sahil, am I good to move?"

"You're good," Sahil answered.

"Thumper, moving up."

Lincoln reached the wall of the compound and dropped to a crouch. Wright slid in behind him, covering the opposite direction. The darkness of the Martian night and the limited lighting around the wall probably made their reactive camo unnecessary, but they were both running it anyway. Judging from what they'd seen earlier, their suits gave them an overwhelming advantage, but when it came to this kind of work, Lincoln never wanted to go into a fair fight. He'd take any and every advantage he could get.

"On the box now," Thumper reported.

"We're at the wall," Lincoln answered. "Holding for you."

"Sixty seconds," she said.

"Prepping ascenders," Wright said. She released a pair of palm-sized drones, which lofted silently upward, each spooling out a thin cable as they went.

While the ascenders attached themselves at the top, Lincoln pulled a device off his harness and affixed it to the wall next to him. A guard house was on the opposite side. The device was a penetrating scanner, and once it had identified human signatures, it would track them and continuously update the team's threat matrix without requiring anyone on the team to maintain visual contact. When it came online, the scanner showed five figures manning the guard station. That was two more than they'd seen throughout the day. Five was a lot to deal with.

The guard house posed the first big risk; that was where the most immediate response would come from. Thumper was working on the automated security system, but there were redundancies built in. For Lincoln and Wright to breach the guard house undetected, Thumper had to bring the system down from an external source. But once she took it offline, Lincoln and Wright only had a few seconds to get in and disable the system from the inside, to prevent the whole thing from going off.

And with five hostiles inside, that was going to be tricky work.

"Thirty seconds," Thumper said.

Lincoln and Wright hooked in to the ascenders, activated the retractors, and climbed the wall. They held just below the top.

"Sahil, are we good to top the wall?" Lincoln asked.

"Negative, stay put," he answered. "Fella on the balcony, main house."

They held position, feet against the wall, waiting for the all-clear. Even though he knew the chances that anyone could see them were remote, Lincoln still felt exposed and mostly helpless, suspended there.

"Ten seconds," Thumper said.

"Lincoln, you're clear to top," Sahil said. "Thump, you got two hostiles headed around your way."

"We're going over," Lincoln said. He switched to direct channel with Wright, and counted it off. "One, two, three."

On three, they simultaneously completed the ascent, clambered over the wall, and reset on the opposite side. From there, Wright descended just far enough to where she could kick off the wall and reach the balcony on the second floor of the guard house. Lincoln continued all the way to the ground level.

"Box is tapped," Thumper said. "I'm pulling back."

Lincoln unhooked from the ascender, drew in close against the back wall of the guard house. Above him, Wright slid silently over the balcony rail and into position.

"Wright, in position."

"Lincoln, in position."

"Thumper, good to go."

"Sahil," Lincoln said. "I'm gonna need your help downstairs."

"Roger, Link, I got you. Two hostiles front room. One in the back."

Lincoln pulled his short-barreled rifle in tight, slid up next to the rear door, let his suit scan the lock and spoof the credentials.

"Wright, you have good marks?"

"Roger, good marks," she said.

Lincoln activated the lock on the rear door, grasped the handle and turned it, keeping his weapon shouldered with one hand.

"Go on Thumper's count. Thumper... on you."

"Stand by..." Thumper said. And then, "All right, security shut down in five, four, three, two, one. Go, execute, execute, execute."

Before she'd finished saying her first "execute", Lincoln was already in motion. The rear door swung smoothly open, and before the man inside could even turn at the sound, Lincoln had felled him with three quick shots. One of the men in the front room cried out in surprise, but in the next moment, Lincoln was there, dispatching him before he could sound any alarm. The second man in the front room was already down, taken by Sahil's long range shot.

"First floor, clear," Lincoln said.

"Top floor, clear," Wright responded.

He let his weapon dangle on its sling, and went to work on the console, quickly overriding the failsafe. The whole team held still for fifteen seconds, waiting for any sign that they'd been discovered. But there was no hostile response, no alarm, no shouted warning.

"Looks clear," Sahil said.

Wright rejoined Lincoln on the first floor, and they exited through the rear entrance, and took up position at one corner. Inside the compound was much more well lit, and there wasn't a covered approach from anywhere by the outer wall to the main house. There wasn't much hope of reaching the target building without alerting someone to trouble, so the team had decided to go ahead and alert them themselves.

"Thumper, what's the word on power?"

"Almost there, Link," she said. "Charge is set, but I'm blocked. Got two hostiles between me and approach."

"Sahil?" Lincoln said.

"I see 'em," he answered. "You want the tall one, or the fat one?"

"I'll take the tall one," Thumper said. "Be harder for you to miss the fat one."

"Sure do wish Mikey was here," Sahil said, and then a moment later. "All right, I'm dialed in. Say when."

"Three, two, one," said Thumper, then, "fire, fire, fire."

Lincoln couldn't hear the shots, but a few seconds later, Thumper reported.

"Good hits. Two hostiles down. I'm moving to position."

Wright recalled the ascenders, and then redeployed one towards the main house. She, again, would take the top floor, and work her way down. Under normal circumstances, Lincoln would never have sent anyone off on their own, armor or no, but they had too much ground to cover too quickly to be able to stick together. He just had to hope for the best.

"Thumper, in position."

"Everyone set?" Lincoln asked.

"Sahil, set."

"Wright, set."

"I already said I was good," Thumper said.

"All right. Thumper, hit it."

"Detonating."

A muffled thump sounded from the opposite side of the main house, and an instant later, the lights sparked out with a dull buzz. Lincoln launched from the corner of the guard house in a dead sprint for the front door. Wright, behind him, veered off headed towards her ascension point. And through his visor, Lincoln saw Thumper's tracking indicator closing in on the rear entrance.

"Hostile, top floor, east side," Sahil reported. And then a second later. "Nevermind."

Lincoln reached the front entrance and didn't slow for the door. He barreled through it, his strength coupled with the weight of the suit destroying the locking mechanism as the door exploded open. Two armed men were in the front corridor, but neither one of them had time to raise their weapons before Lincoln's rounds found his targets. He was already past them before they'd even finished falling. Lincoln's visor automatically amplified the light, and though it was nearly pitch black for everyone else in the house, he saw everything in perfect clarity.

The first two rooms he checked were empty, but the centermost room had its door wide open. He moved through it with quick, but quiet, steps and there, standing by a window, he found what he'd come for.

She was facing away from the door, as if unconcerned by the darkness and the noises she had undoubtedly heard. But she had a pistol in her hand. Lincoln stood in the center of the room, silent, his weapon trained on her. A few moments later, thirty-five seconds after they'd shut off the main power and just as Thumper had predicted, the emergency power kicked in. The lights came back up, dimmer, and the woman turned. When she did, she flinched, but she didn't seem all that surprised to see Lincoln standing there.

"Well," she said. "I don't believe I've seen *your* kind before. Seems I've attracted some very important attention."

She looked younger than he'd expected, healthier. In her mid-forties, perhaps, and fit. Capable. Dangerous.

"It's over, Amanda," Lincoln said. "Put the weapon down, lie on the floor, and place your hands behind your back."

She smiled.

"Amanda," she said, and she gave a single, clear note of a laugh. "No one has called me that in a long time. A long time."

Her voice was steady, with a pleasing tone.

"Get on the floor," Lincoln repeated.

"Why?"

"Whatever you had hoped to accomplish, you've failed," Lincoln said. "And I'm here to take you back to face the justice you deserve."

"Oh, are you?" Amanda said. "It looks to me like you've come to deliver that justice yourself. Or, what you believe is justice."

She was completely calm, completely at ease. And seeing how she held herself, so poised, so confident, Vector's words came back to Lincoln then. About how no matter how cornered he thought he had her, she'd find a way out. Lincoln had thought it was just the nonsense of a fanatic at the time. But now, given her demeanor, he couldn't help but think he was overlooking something.

"And what would justice be?" she asked. "What crime have I committed?"

"The murder of hundreds of innocents is a pretty good start," Lincoln said. Wright and Thumper both checked in, reporting all clear, but Lincoln barely heard them.

"You fight for a nation that has killed a thousand times more," the woman said. "A million times. What is it that makes my actions so much more detestable?"

"I'm not going to argue philosophy with you," Lincoln answered. "You almost started a war."

"War is man's disease," she said. "And now, it is our gift to the stars."

"Not yet," Lincoln said. "I said *almost*. Yours failed. We stopped it before it could even start."

She smiled. "You dear boy," she said, "war is not an *event*.

It is a process. And once that process begins, it is very difficult to stop, until it has run its full course. No, no, you may have delayed it a bit. A week, a month. A year. But you haven't *stopped* anything."

Lincoln had every intention of shutting her up, of cuffing her hands, putting a hood over her head, and marching her out. But for some reason, he wasn't doing any of that. There was something about her, something almost mesmerizing, that kept him from taking any action.

"This used to be a game of state, you know. War was the province of nations, and we, the people, were at their mercy. But not anymore. All this I built with my own hands, and with a handful of trusted friends. Capture me, kill me. Let me go free. It will make no difference. My work is done. The board is set, and I've chosen the pieces. And the United American Federation will finally reap the war they planted and never got to harvest."

Whatever her intent, her words struck Lincoln with unexpected force. Maybe it was the echo of Mr Self's lecture, or maybe she was simply powerfully persuasive. But for a moment, she shook Lincoln's confidence, made him question his own intentions. What *was* he expecting? Was she right? Would anything he did here matter? Did his decision matter?

But no. Of course it did. Lincoln couldn't control the future. He couldn't control the UAF, or the CMA. He couldn't control anything, outside of where he was right then, at that moment. But that moment was his, and he would see justice done.

But before he could order her one last time to surrender, Amanda spoke.

"Here," she said. "I'll save you the burden of choice."

She raised the pistol, pointed it at him. But it was a small caliber affair. It wouldn't penetrate his armor, and thus posed no threat to him. If she'd been trying to force his hand and get him to pull his trigger, she'd failed.

But in a fluid, almost casual motion, she bent her arm and placed the muzzle against the side of her own head. Lincoln was astonished to see her smile, as if she'd pulled some great trick or had outsmarted him, just before she pulled the trigger.

The Lightfinger was already warmed up and ready to go when they reached it. The cargo ramp was down, and Baby Vegas was waiting for them at the top of it.

"Just four?" she said.

"Just four," Wright answered.

"Well," Baby Vegas said. "All right."

Lincoln boarded, last of the team to do so. Still in a daze over what had just happened.

"You OK?" Baby Vegas asked as she activated the ramp to close.

"Yes ma'am," Lincoln said.

"Anything I can do for you?"

Lincoln nodded.

"Take us on home."

TWENTY-SIX

The team was in the middle of enjoying a mini-reunion in the gym of their facility back on base. Back on Earth. They'd shared a meal together, and more than a couple of beers. Now, Lincoln stood over by the door, watching his team as they blew off some steam and celebrated being home again. *His* team.

His head was still spinning with everything he'd come through. There was no telling how long it was going to take him to process it all. And Amanda's bizarre final moments. The others had all shared their theories; that she couldn't face capture, or that seeing all her plans come to nothing had been too much for her to bear. But none of those sat well with Lincoln. Another mystery. Another question that might never be answered.

None of that seemed to be bothering any of the others, though. Sahil and Thumper were going at it hammer and tongs on the mat, with Wright and Mike standing to one side, acting as commentators. Actually, Lincoln noticed, only Mike was doing any commentating. But he was talking enough for both of them, using two different voices as he called out the various moves on display, and added color commentary with whatever embarrassing stories he could come up with on the spot. Wright glanced over and saw Lincoln watching them, dipped her head and gave him a smile and a little shrug, as if she didn't know what they were going to do with Mikey.

And as right as it seemed that Mike should be there, there was a strange melancholy hanging over Lincoln for it. As if something in their relationship had changed, even though nothing really had. Mike was still Mike; same jokes, same stories, same easy smile. But there was a distance there, too, that Lincoln couldn't quite explain. But then, there was a lot he couldn't explain these days.

"Did you get what you were after?" Almeida asked from behind him. Lincoln turned to see the old colonel standing in the hall, just outside. He waved him in, and Almeida crept in and stood beside Lincoln.

"Not exactly," Lincoln said, looking back at the others.

"I hate to tell you I told you so," the colonel said. "But... get used to it, son."

"I don't know how I did on my first time out, colonel," Lincoln said. "But right now, I'm just glad to be home."

"Getting home is a win," Almeida said. "Maybe the *only* win. The rest of it..." He shrugged.

"I'm putting the team on standby for two weeks," he continued. "I think we can get you some time to get squared away on base, make sure we get Mike back up to full speed. All that travel's hard on the body, it'd be good for you all to get a little down time."

"Actually, sir, I'd like authorization for a training exercise."

"Training exercise?"

"Yes sir. Team's not gelled as much as I'd like, I've got a scenario I'd like to tackle with them."

"Huh," Almeida said, and he looked at Lincoln with more than a little suspicion. "You have a location in mind, captain?"

"Yes sir, I do."

"Care to share?"

"No sir, I do not."

Almeida chuckled. "Captain Suh," he said. "I hate to admit

it to your face, but I think you might be getting the hang of this job already."

"I'll try not to let it go to my head, sir."

"See that you don't. Let me know what you need for your *exercise*," said Almeida, turning to leave. "And how long you expect it to take."

"We won't be gone long, sir."

The colonel nodded. Lincoln saluted. Almeida returned it, and left.

Lincoln turned back and watched his team. Mike had joined the others on the mat, and was trying to pin Sahil's arms behind his back while Thumper continued the assault from the front. *His* team.

"All right, Outriders!" Lincoln called. The others reacted immediately and stopped dead, looking at him, surprised at his booming voice.

"I think you've all had enough fun for a week," he said. "And I have a promise to keep. Time to get back to work."

EPILOGUE

"I don't know," the NID security officer said. "Some kind of glitch in the detector, I guess."

"You checked it, though?" his partner asked.

"Yeah, three times. But look, it's showing like fifty contacts right now, and I don't remember a single day where I've ever seen fifty people on the whole station."

"Well, what do you want to do about him?" asked the partner, flicking his head towards their charge. The small man was seated on a bench by the wall, his hands bound at the wrist with quick-cuffs. He was rolling his wrists back and forth; slowly, rhythmically, back and forth.

"He's not going anywhere," said the security officer. "Why's he doing that with his hands, though?"

"I don't know. Nervous, I guess."

"See, there it goes," the officer said, tapping the display. "Now it's all clear again. I'm telling you man, one of those techs must've goofed something up."

The words were barely out of his mouth when the power went out with a pop.

And the small man on the bench, Yayan Prakoso, smiled to himself.

ACKNOWLEDGMENTS

Even though my name is on the front of this book, there are many people responsible for its existence. My most sincere thanks to:

… Jesus, for courageously leading a twelve-man team on the greatest hostage rescue mission in all of history, and for making the ultimate sacrifice.

… my wife and children, for your faithful love and unwavering support, and for being my greatest reward and treasure.

… Marc Gascoigne, Phil Jourdan, Mike Underwood, Caroline Lambe, Penny Reeve, and everyone else at Angry Robot for all their patience, encouragement, and their assurances that I'll be spared when the robot uprising begins.

… Lee Harris, for giving this book a chance to be.

… Richard Dansky, for your mentoring, and for being the best uncle ever.

… the denizens of the Dark Tower, particularly the Lorde who dwells therein, for providing a place for me during many cold morning hours.

… Jocko Willink, for challenging me with the 0445 Club.

… all the fans who've taken the time to reach out and let me know they like my books. Your kind words have kept me going through the "why did I ever think this was a good idea?" moments.

ABOUT THE AUTHOR

Jay Posey is a narrative designer, author, and screenwriter by trade. He started working in the video game industry in 1998, and has been writing professionally for over a decade. Currently employed as Senior Narrative Designer at Red Storm Entertainment, he's spent around eight years writing and designing for Tom Clancy's award-winning *Ghost Recon* and *Rainbow Six* franchises.

A contributing author to the book *Professional Techniques for Video Game Writing*, Jay has lectured at conferences, colleges, and universities, on topics ranging from basic creative writing skills to advanced material specific to the video game industry. His acclaimed Legends of the Duskwalker series is also published by Angry Robot.

jayposey.com • twitter.com/HiJayPosey

PREVIOUSLY...

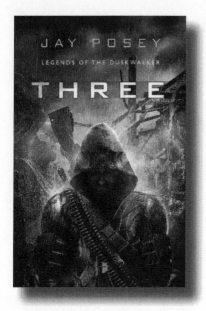

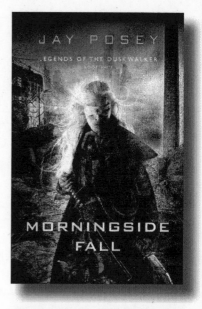

"GRITTY ACTION-
PACKED DRAMA SO
HI-RES AND REAL
YOU'LL BELIEVE YOU
GOT SOMETHING IN
YOUR EYE."

MATT FORBECK,
AUTHOR OF AMORTALS

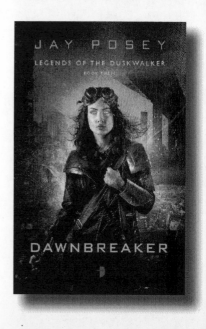